Of Outlaws,
   Con Men,
   Whores,
   Politicians,
   and
   Other Artists

Also by Larry L. King

Nonfiction

. . . And Other Dirty Stories
Confessions of a White Racist
The Old Man and Lesser Mortals
Wheeling and Dealing (with Bobby Baker)

Novels

The One-Eyed Man

Plays

The Best Little Whorehouse in Texas (with Peter
    Masterson and Carol Hall)
The Kingfish (with Ben Z. Grant)

Of Outlaws, Con Men, Whores, Politicians, *and* Other Artists

☆

Larry L. King

The Viking Press   New York

79-2216

Library of Congress Cataloging in Publication Data
King, Larry L.
    Of outlaws, con men, whores, politicians,
    and other artists.
    I. Title.
PS3561.I48O34   814'.5'408   79-21645
ISBN 0-670-50227-8

Printed in the United States of America
Set in CRT Gael

Acknowledgment

New Directions Publishing Corp.:
From *The Poems of Dylan Thomas*.
Copyright 1952 by Dylan Thomas.
Reprinted by permission of New Directions.

This collection is for
a collection finer still:
Cheryl, Kerri, and Bradley

The grateful
author wishes
to thank the
following publications for permitting
materials first appearing in their
pages to be republished—in slightly
different form—in this book: *Texas Monthly,*
Playboy, New Times, the *Atlantic Monthly,*
Esquire, Sport, Classic, the
Washington *Post,* the
Washington *Star,* and
American Heritage.
Ya'll real good
folks, ya
hear?

☆

Contents

☆

Introduction

Hello.

This is the third time I've stuffed yesterday's manuscripts between hard covers and offered them as a literary sandwich. Such fare fails to constitute a full feast if only because little that is garden-fresh appears on the menu. Yet such is the chef's personal vanity that he believes this slumgullion may contain a pleasing morsel or so.

Let me assure the fastidious that the worst leftovers from my typewriter's prior cookings have been tossed into the garbage pail as ingredients so perishable or bland as not to deserve reheating in this mix. Good riddance: When a working writer boils enough murky broths to extract from it his bread, wine, rent, and taxes, then he's certain to leave some smelly residues in the bottom of the pot.

Writers concoct collections of their short work because they cannot bear to see so much of the product of their sweat live for only a week or a month in a magazine before dying little mourned. They also do it because (1) they feel overdue to be in hard covers again, even though not yet prepared to issue some weightier work-in-progress or (2) they have another book or play, currently being offered in the marketplace, which they hope will help hype their newest collection. For all the above reasons I here offer this book. May modest money and good utterances be made of it.

A writer and friend by the name of Buck Ramsey once observed that I have been selling my autobiography, a chapter at a time, for almost fifteen years. Damned perceptive feller, Ol' Buck. Let an editor assign almost any subject, and I'll find a way to mine my past so that conclusions are drawn from it and comparisons made against it. Sometimes I fret that this may be a weakness. And yet I believe that my better stuff is derived from my roots: from where I've been and what I saw or heard or felt there. Never have been worth a hoot when it comes to the abstract, the philosophical, the analytical, or the intellectual. I just tell stories, and it seems that a lot of them turn out to involve myownself.

So be warned. The first section of this three-tiered monument to literature runs almost exclusively toward the autobiographical. Them what can't face it may find a modicum of relief in the second section; by the time they reach the third they may be wondering what became of me, relatively speaking.

There is not much said, anywhere in this collection, of learned academicians, high-minded statesmen, or pious saints. I've always seemed to gravitate toward rascals, clowns, and pirates simply because they provide more entertaining shows. If it strikes the reader that there are numerous reports here of drinking, doping, and loose-ladying, he or she is to be congratulated. Much of this material was researched or written when such pursuits tended to coincide with my professional interests, me being between marriages and all. Because I now fear damage from my old liver, and my new lady, I here attest that lately I've cleaned up my trashy act. Hereafter, as part of my ongoing rehabilitation, I plan to hang out with fewer outlaws, ward heels, and whores. I expect, instead, to consort with solemn bank clerks, saintly parsons, and proper iron virgins. I'll write you about it when I do.

Part I ☆
Myself
of rednecks, hard times,
ambitions, and foolish fantasies

1 ☆
The American Redneck

I

The maddest I remember being at my late wife (a Yankee lady, of Greek extraction and mercurial moods) was when she shouted, during a quarrel the origins of which are long lost, that I was "a dumb Redneck." My heart dangerously palpitated; my eyes bugged; I ran in tight circles and howled inarticulate general profanities until, yes . . . my neck turned red. Literally. I felt the betraying hot flush as real as a cornfield tan. My wife collapsed in a mirthful heap, little knowing how truly close I felt to righteous killing.

Being called dumb wasn't what had excited me. No, for I judged myself ignorant only to the extent that mankind is and knew I was no special klutz. But being called a Redneck, now, especially when you know in your genes and in the dirty back roads of your mind that you *are* one—despite having spent years trying not to be—well, when that happens, all fair has gone out of the fight. I do not cherish Rednecks, which means I dislike certain persistent old parts of myself.

Of late the Redneck has been wildly romanticized; somehow he threatens to become a cultural hero. Perhaps this is because heroes are in short supply—we seem to burn them up faster nowadays—or maybe it's a manifestation of our urge to return to simpler times: to be free of computers, pollution, the urban tangle, shortages of energy or materials or elbowroom. Even George Wallace is "respectable" now, having been semimartyred by gunfire and defanged by defeat. Since 'Necks have long been identified with overt racism, we may be embracing them because we long ago tired of bad niggers who spooked and threatened us; perhaps the revival is a backlash against hairy hippies, peaceniks, weirdos of all stripes. Or the recent worship of Redneckism may be no more than the clever manipulations of music and movie czars, ever on the lookout for profitable new crazes. Anyway, a lot of foolishness disguised as noble folklore is going down as the 'Neck is praised in song and story.

There are "good" people, yes, who might properly answer to the appellation "Redneck": people who operate mom-and-pop stores or their lathes, dutifully pay their taxes, lend a helping hand to neighbors, love their country and their God and their dogs. But even among a high percentage of these salts-of-the-earth lives a terrible reluctance toward even modest passes at social justice, a suspicious regard of the mind as an instrument of worth, a view of the world extending little farther than the ends of their noses, and only vague notions that they are small quills writing a large, if indifferent, history.

Not that these are always mindless. Some value "common sense" or "horse sense" and in the basics may be less foolish than certain determined rote sophisticates and any number of pompous academicians. Some few may read Plato or Camus or otherwise astonish; it does not necessarily follow that he who is poor knows nothing or cares little. On the other hand, you can make boatloads of money and still be a Redneck in your bones, values, and attitudes. But largely, I think—even at the risk of being accused of elitism or class prejudice—the worse components of 'Neckery are found among the unlettered poor.

Attempts to deify the Redneck, to represent his life-style as close to that of the noble savage are, at best, unreal and naïve. For all their native wit—and sometimes they have keen senses of the absurd as applied to their daily lives—Rednecks generally comprise a sad lot. They flounder in perilous financial waters and are mired in the sociopolitical shallows. Their lives are hard: long on work and short on money; full of vile bossmen, hounding creditors, debilitating quarrels, routine disappointments, confrontations, ignorance, a treadmill hopelessness. It may sound good on a country-western record when Tom T. Hall and Waylon Jennings lift their voices, baby, but it neither sounds nor feels good when life is real and the alarm clock's jarring jangle soon must be followed by the time clock's tuneless bells.

Now, the Rednecks I'm talking about are not those counterfeit numbers who hang around Austin digging the Cosmic Cowboy scene, sucking up to Jerry Jeff Walker and Willie Nelson, wearing bleached color-patched overalls, and rolling their own dope, saying how they hanker to go live off the land and then winging off to stay six weeks in a Taos commune before flying back on daddy's credit card. May such toy Rednecks choke on their own romantic pretensions.

No, and I'm not talking about Good Ol' Boys. Do not, please, confuse the two; so many have. A Good Ol' Boy is a Redneck who has acquired a smidgen or much more of polish; I could call him a "former Redneck" except that there ain't no such when you bore bone-deep. One born a 'Neck of the true plastic-Jesus-on-the-dashboard and pink-rubber-haircurlers-in-the-supermarket variety can no more shuck his condition than may the Baptist who, once saved, becomes doctrinarily incapable of talking his way into hell.

The Good Ol' Boy may or may not have been refurbished by college. But bet your ass he's a climber, an achiever, a con man looking for the edge and the hedge. He'll lay a lot of semi-smarmy charm on you, and bullshit grading from middling to high. He acts dumber than he is when he knows something and smarter than he is when he doesn't. He would be dangerous game to hunt. Such parts of his Redneck heritage as may be judged eccentric or humorous enough to be useful will be retained in his mildly self-deprecating stories and may come in handy while he's working up to relieving you of your billfold or your panties. Such Redneck parts as no longer serve him, he attempts to bury in the mute and dead past. And he becomes maniacal when, say, a domestic quarrel causes him to blow his cool enough that those old red bones briefly rise from their interment so that others may glimpse them.

A Good Ol' Boy turns his radio down at red lights so that other drivers won't observe him enjoying Kitty Wells singing through her nose. He carefully says "Negro," though it slips to "Nigra" with a shade much scotch, or even—under stress, or for purposes of humor among close associates—slides all the way down to "nigger." He does not dip snuff or chaw tobacco, preferring cigarettes or cigars or perhaps an occasional sly hip toke of pot. He has forgotten, or tells himself he has forgotten, the daily fear of being truly ragged and dirt poor—and, perhaps, how to ride a horse, or the cruel tug of the cotton sack, or the strength of the laborer's sun. He may belong to a civic club, play golf, travel, own his own shop, or run somebody else's. For a long time he's been running uphill; sometimes he doesn't know when he's reached level ground and keeps on struggling. Having fought and sweated for his toehold, he'll likely be quick to kick those who attempt to climb along behind him.

While all Good Ol' Boys have been at least fringe Rednecks, not nearly all Rednecks rise to be Good Ol' Boys. No. Their gizzards don't harbor enough of something—grit, ambition, good fortune, con, education, flint, self-propellants, saddle burrs, chickenshit, opportunity, whatever—and so they continue to breed and largely perpetuate themselves in place, de-fanged Snopeses never to attain, accumulate, bite the proper-tied gentry, or smite their tormentors. These are no radicals; though the resentful juices of revolution may ache their blood-streams, they remain—with rare, crazed exceptions—amaz-ingly docile. They simply can't find the handles of things and drop more than they can pick up.

Though broad generalities deserve their dangerous reputa-tion, one hazards the judgment that always such unrecon-structed Rednecks shall vote to the last in number for the George Wallaces or Lester Maddoxes or other dark ogres of their time; will fear God at least in the abstract and Authority and Change even more; will become shade-tree mechanics, factory robots, salesmen of small parts, peacetime soldiers or sailors; random serfs. (Yes, good neighbors, do you know what it is to envy the man who no longer carries the dinner bucket, and hope someday you'll reach his plateau: maybe shill for All-state?) The women of such men are beauticians and waitresses and laundry workers and notions-counter clerks and generally pregnant. Their children may be hauled in joustabout pickup trucks or an old Ford dangling baby booties, giant furry dice, toy lions, nodding doggies and plastered with downhome bumper stickers: "Honk If You Love Jesus," maybe, or "Goat Ropers Need Love Too." Almost certainly it's got a steady mort-gage against it, and at least one impatient lien.

We are talking, good buddies, about America's white niggers: the left behind, the luckless, the doomed. It is these we explore: my clay, native roots, mutha culture. . . .

I didn't know I was a Redneck as a kid. The Housenwrights were Rednecks, I knew—even though I was ignorant of the term; couldn't have defined it had I heard it—and so were the Spagles and certain branches of the Halls, the Peoples, the Conines, the many broods of Hawks. These were the raggedest

of the ragged in a time when even FDR judged one-third of a
nation to be out-at-elbows. There was a hopelessness about
them, a feckless wildness possible only in the truly surrendered,
a community sense that their daddies didn't try as hard as some
or, simply, had been born to such ill luck, silly judgments, whiskey thirsts, or general rowdiness as to preclude twitches of
upward mobility. Such families were less likely than others to
seek church; their breadwinners idled more; their children
came barefoot to the rural school even in winter. They were
more likely to produce domestic violence, blood feuds, boys
who fought their teachers. They no longer cared and, not car-
ing, might cheerfully flatten you or stab you in a playground
fight or at one of the Saturday-night country dances held in
rude plank homes along the creek banks. Shiftless badasses.
Poor tacky peckerwoods who did us the favor of providing
somebody to look down on. For this service we children of the
"better" homes rewarded them with rock fights or other tor-
ments: "Dessie Hall, Dessie Hall/Haw Haw Haw/Your Daddy
Never Bathes/But He's Cleaner Than Your Maw."

Ours was a reluctant civilization. Eastland County, Texas, had
its share of certified illiterates in the 1930s and later, people
who could no more read a Clabber Girl Baking Powder bill-
board than they could translate from the French. I recall witnessing old nesters who made their laborious "marks" should
documents require signatures. A neighboring farmer in middle
age boasted that his sons had taught him simple long division;
on Saturdays he presided from the wooden veranda of Morgan
Brothers General Store in Scranton, demonstrating on a brown
paper sack exactly how many times 13 went into 39, while
whiskered old farmers gathered for their small commerce
looked on as if he might be revealing the internal rules of
heaven.

We lived in one of the more remote nooks of Eastland
County, in cotton and goober and scrub-oak country. There

were no paved roads and precious few tractors among that settlement of marginal farms populated by snuff dippers, their sunbonneted women, and broods of jittery shy kids who might regard unexpected visitors from concealment. We were broken-plow farmers, holding it all together with baling wire, habit, curses, and prayers. Most families were on FDR's relief agency rolls; county agriculture agents taught our parents to card their cotton by hand so they might stuff homemade mattresses. They had less success in teaching crop rotation, farmers feeling that the plot where daddy and granddaddy had grown cotton remained a logical place for cotton still. There were many who literally believed in a flat earth and the haunting presence of ghosts; if the community contained any individual who failed to believe that eternal damnation was a fair reward for the sinner, he never came forward to declare it.

Churches grew in wild profusion. Proud backwoodsmen, their best doctrines disputed by fellow parishioners, were quick to establish their rival rump churches under brush arbors or tabernacles or in plank cracker boxes. One need have no formal training to preach; the Call was enough, a personal conviction that God had beckoned one from a hot cornfield or cattle pen to spread the Word; this was easy enough for God to do, He being everywhere and so little inclined toward snobbery that He frequently visited the lowliest Eastland County dirt farmer for consultations. Converts were baptized in muddy creeks or stock tanks, some flocks—in the words of the late Governor Earl Long of Louisiana—"chunking snakes and catching fevers."

It was not uncommon, when my father was a young man, for righteous vigilantes to pay nocturnal calls on erring wife beaters or general ne'er-do-wells, flogging them with whips and Scriptures while demanding their immediate improvement. Such godly posses did not seek to punish those who lived outside the law, however, should commerce be involved; when times were hard, so were the people. Bootleggers flourished in those woods in my youth, and it was not our responsibility to reveal them. Even cattle thieves were ignored so long as they traveled safe distances to improve their small herds.

My father's house was poor but proud: law-abiding, church-ridden, hardworking, pin-neat; innocent, it seems in retrospect, of conscious evil, and innocent, even, of the modern world. Certainly we had good opinions of ourselves and a worthy community standing. And yet even in that "good" family of work-worn, self-starting, self-designated country aristocrats there were tragedies and explosions as raw as the land we inhabited: My paternal grandfather was shot to death by a neighbor; an uncle went to the pen for carnal knowledge of an underaged girl; my father's fists variously laid out a farmer who had the temerity to cut in front of his wagon in the cotton-gin line, a ranch hand who'd reneged on a promise to pay out of his next wages for having his horse shod, a kinsman who threatened to embarrass the clan by running unsuccessfully for county commissioner a ninth straight time. My father was the family enforcer, handing out summary judgments and corporal punishments to any in the bloodline whose follies he judged trashy or a source of community scorn or ridicule. It was most tribal: Walking Bear has disgraced the Sioux; very well, off with Walking Bear's head.

So while we may have had no more money than others, no more of education or raw opportunity, I came to believe that the Kings were somehow special and that my mother's people, the proud and clannish Clarks, were more special still. A certain deference was paid my parents in their rural domain; they gave advice, helped shape community affairs, were arbiters and unofficial judges. I became a "leader" at the country school and in Bethel Methodist Church, where we took pride in worships free of snake handling or foot washings—although it was proper to occasionally talk in tongues or grovel at the mourners' bench.

I strutted when my older brother, Weldon, returned in his

secondhand Model A Ford to visit from Midland, a huge metropolis of 9,000 noblemen in oil, cowboy, and rattlesnake country more than 200 miles to the west. I imagined him a leading citizen there; he had found Success as manager of the lunch counter and fountain at Piggly Wiggly's and announced cowpoke melodies part time over the facilities of radio station KCRS. More, he was a hot-fielding second baseman with the semiprofessional Midland Cowboys baseball team. Any day I expected the New York Yankees to call him up and wondered when they did not.

Weldon epitomized sophistication in my young mind; he wore smart two-toned shoes with air holes allowing his feet to breathe, oceans of Red Rose hair oil, and a thin go-to-hell mustache. In the jargon of the time and the place he was "a jellybean." Where rustics rolled their own from nickel bags of Duke's Mixture or Country Gentlemen, my brother puffed luxurious "ready rolls." When he walked among local stay-at-homes on his rare visits, he turned the heads of milkmaids and drew the dark envied stares of male contemporaries who labored on their fathers' farms or, if especially enterprising, had found jobs at the broom factory in Cisco. He was walking proof of the family's industry and ambition, and he reinforced my own dreams of escape to bigger things.

Imagine my shocked surprise, then, when—in my early teens —I accompanied my family in its move to Midland City, there to discover that *I* was the Redneck: the bumpkin, the new boy with feedlot dung on his shoes and the funny homemade haircuts. Nobody in Midland had heard of the Kings or even of the Clarks; nobody rushed to embrace us. Where in the rural consolidated school I had boasted a grade average in the high nineties, in Midland the mysteries of algebra, geometry, and biology kept me clinging by my nails to scholastic survival. Where I had captained teams, I now stood uninvited on the fringes of playground games. My clothes, as good as most and better than some in Eastland County, now betrayed me as a poor clod.

I withdrew to the company of other misfits who lived in clapboard shacks or tents on the jerry-built South Side, wore tattered time-faded jeans and stained teeth, cursed, fought, swigged beer, and skipped school to hang around South Main Street pool halls or domino parlors. These were East Texans, Okies, and Arkies whose parents—like mine—had starved off their native acres and had followed the war boom west. Our drawls and twangs and marginal grammar had more of the dirt farmer or drifting fruit picker in them than of the cattleman or small merchant; our homes utilized large lard buckets as stools or chairs and such paltry art as adorned the wall likely showed Jesus on the cross suffering pain and a Woolworth's framing job; at least one member of almost every family boasted its musician: guitar or banjo or mandolin pickers who cried the old songs while their instruments whined or wailed of griefs and losses in places dimly remembered.

We hated the Townies who catcalled us as shitkickers . . . plowboys . . . Luke Plukes. We were a sneering lot, victims of cultural shock, defensive and dangerous as only the cornered can be. If you were a Townie, you very much wished not to encounter us unless you had the strength of numbers; we would whip your ass and take your money, pledging worse punishments should the authorities be notified. We hated niggers and meskins almost as much as we hated the white Townies, though it would be years before I knew how desperately we hated ourselves.

In time, deposits of ambition, snobbery, and pride caused me to work exceedingly hard at rising above common Redneckery. Not being able to beat the Townies, I opted to join them through pathways opened by athletics, debating, drama productions. It was simply better to be in than out, even if one must desert his own kind. I had discovered, simply, that nothing much on the bottom was worth having.

I began avoiding my Redneck companions at school and dodging their invitations to hillbilly jam sessions, pool hall recreations, forays into the scabbier honky-tonks. The truth is, the Rednecks had come to depress me. Knowing they were losers, they acted as such. No matter their tough exteriors when tormenting Townies, they privately whined and sniveled and raged. The deeper their alienations, the smaller they seemed to become physically; excepting an occasional natural jug-butted Ol' Boy, Rednecks appeared somehow to be stringier, knottier, more shriveled than others. They hacked the coughs of old men and moved about in old men's motions somehow furtive and fugitive. I did not want to be like them.

Nor did I want to imitate their older brothers or fathers, with whom I worked in the oil fields during summers and on weekends. They lived nomadic lives, following booms and rumors and their restless, unguided hearts. It puzzled me that they failed to seek better and more far-flung adventures, break with the old ways and start anew; I was very young then and understood less than all the realities. Their abodes were tin-topped old hotels in McCamey, gasping-hot tents perched on the desert floor near Crane, a crummy tourist court outside Sundown, any number of peeled fading houses decorating Wink, Odessa, Monahans. Such places smelled of sweat, fried foods, dirty socks, the bottoms of the barrel, too much sorry history.

By day we dug sump pits, pissanted heavy lengths of pipe, mixed cement and pushed it in iron wheelbarrows ("wheelbars"), chemically blistered our skins while hot-doping new pipeline, swabbed oil storage tanks, grubbed mesquite or other prickly desert growths to make way for new pump stations. We worked ten hours; the pay ranged from seventy to ninety-four cents for each of them, and we strangely disbelieved in labor unions.

There was a certain camaraderie, yes, a brotherhood of the lower rungs; kidding could be rough, raw, personal. Often, however, the day's sun combined with the evening's beer or liquor to produce a special craziness. Then fights erupted, on the job or in beer joints or among roommates in their quarters. Few rules burdened such fights, and the gentle or unwary could suffer real damage. Such people frightened me. They frighten me now, when I encounter them on visits to West Texas beer joints or lolling about a truckstop café. If you permit them to know it, however, your life will become a special long-running hell: *Grady, let's me and you whup that booger's ass for him agin.* Often, in the oil patch, one had to act much tougher than the stuff he knew to be in his bones. It helped to pick a fight occasionally and to put the boots to your adversary once you got him down. Fear and rage being first cousins, you could do it if you had to.

But I can't tell you what it's really like, day to day, being a Redneck: not in the cool language of one whom time has refurbished a bit or by analytical uses of whatever sensibilities may have been superimposed through the years. That approach can hint at it in a general way, knock the rough edges off. But it isn't raw enough to put you down in the pit: let you smell the blood, know the bone dread, the debts, the random confrontations, the pointless migrations, or purposeless days. I must speak to you from an earlier time, bring it up from the gut. Somehow fiction is more suited to that.

You may consider this next section, then, to be a fictional interlude . . . or near-fiction, maybe . . . voices from the past . . . essence of Redneck. Whatever. Anyway, it's something of what life was like for many West Texas people in the late 1940s or early 1950s; I suspect that even today it remains relatively true there and in other sparse grazing places of America's unhorsed riders: those who fight our dirtier wars, make us rich by the schlock and dreck they buy and the usurious interest rates they pay, those who suffer the invisible rule of deaf masters and stew in their own poor juices. Those white niggers who live on the fringes out near the very edge and hope, mostly, to accumulate enough survival techniques to skate by. What follows is, at once, a story that didn't really happen and one that has happened again and again.

II

Me and Bobby Jack and Red Turpin was feeling real good that day. We'd told this old fat fart bossing the gang to shove his pipeline up his ass sideways, and then we'd hitched a ride to Odessa and drawed our time. He was a sorry old bastard, that gang boss. He'd been laying around in such shade as he could find, hollering at us for about six weeks when we didn't pissant pipe fast enough to suit him. Hisself, he looked like he hadn't carried nothing heavier than a lunch bucket in twenty years.

What happened had happened in the morning, just before we would of broke for dinner. Red Turpin was down in the dumps because the finance company had found him and drove his old Chevy away. We tried to tell him not to sweat it, that it wasn't worth near half of what he owed on it, but that never wiped out the fact that he was left afoot.

The gang boss had been bitching and moaning more than usual that day. All at once Red spun around to him and said, "I'm gona git me a piece of yore ass, Mr. Poot, if you don't git offa mine." Well, the gang boss waved his arms and hollered that ol' Red was sacked, and Red said, "Fuck you, Mr. Poot. I was a-huntin' a job when I found this 'un."

Me and Bobby Jack was standing there with our mouths dropped open when the gang boss started yelling at us to git back to work and to show him nothing but assholes and elbows. He was jumping around all red in the face, acting like a stroke was on him. Bobby Jack said, "Shit on such shit as this. Lincoln's done freed the slaves," and about that time he dropped his end of that length of pipe and told that gang boss to shove it.

"Sideways, Mr. Poot," I hollered. And then I dropped *my* end in the dirt.

Mr. Poot squealed like a girl rabbit and grabbed a monkey wrench off the crew truck and warned us not to come no closer. Which would of been hard to do, fast as he was backing up. So we cussed him for seventeen kinds of a fool and pissed on the pipe we'd dropped and then left, feeling free as the blowing wind. I never been in jail long enough to have give thought to busting out, but I bet there'd be some of the same feeling in it.

Out on the Crane Highway we laughed and hooted about calling that old gang boss "Mr. Poot" to his face, which is what we'd been calling him behind his back on account of he just laid around in the shade by the water cans and farted all day. But finally, after four or five cars and several oil trucks passed us up, we kinda sagged. You could see down that flat old highway for about three days, and all there was was hot empty. Red got down in the mouth about his old lady raising hell soon as she learned how he'd cussed his way off the job. Bobby Jack said hell, just tell 'er he got laid off. "Shit," Red said. "She don't care if it's fared or laid off or carried off on a silk piller. All she knows is, it ain't no paycheck next week."

By the time we'd grunted answers to questions and signed papers and drawed our time at the Morrison Brothers Construction Company there in Odessa, and got a few cool 'uns down in a East Eighth Street beer joint, we was back on top. I swear, a certain amount of beer can make a man feel like he could beat cancer. We played the jukebox—Hank Williams, he'd just come out with one that reached out and grabbed you; seems to me like it was "Lovesick Blues," and there was plenty of Tubbs and Tillman and Frizzell—and shot a few games of shuffleboard at two bits a go. It was more fun than a regular day off because we was supposed to be working. I recollect Bobby Jack wallowing a swig of beer around in his mouth and saying, "You know what we doin'? We stealin' time." He looked real pleased.

Bobby Jack danced twice with a heavyset woman in red slacks from Conroe, who'd come out to Odessa on the Greyhound to find her twin sister that had been run off from by a driller. But all she'd found was a mad landlord that said the woman's sister had skipped out on a week's rent and had stole two venetian blinds besides. "I called that landlord a damn liar," the Conroe woman said. "My twin sister don't steal, and she wadn't raised to stealin'. We come from good stock and got a uncle that's been a deputy sheriff in Bossier City, Louisiana, for nearly twenty years."

Bobby Jack had enough nookie on the brain to buy her four or five beers, but all she done was flash a little brassiere strap and give him two different names and tell him about being a fan dancer at the Texas Centennial in 19-and-36. She babbled on about what all she'd been—a blues singer, a automobile dealer's wife, a registered nurse; everything but a lion tamer it seemed like—until Bobby Jack said, "Lissen, hon, I don't care what all you been. All I care about's what you are now and what *I* am. And I'm horny as a range bull with equipment hard as Christmas candy. How 'bout you?" She got in a mother huff and claimed it was the worst she'd ever been insulted. When Bobby Jack reached over and taken back the last beer he'd bought her, she moved over to a table by herself. I didn't care; she'd struck me as a high hat anyway.

A fleshy ol' boy wearing a Mead's Fine Bread uniform straddled a stool by us and said, "Man, I taken a leak that was better'n young love. I still say if they'd *give* the beer away and charge a dollar to piss, they'd make more money." We talked about how once you'd went to take a beer piss, you had to go ever five minutes, where you could hold a good gallon up until you'd went the first time.

Red Turpin got real quiet like he does when he's bothered bad. I whispered to Bobby Jack to keep an eye on the sumbitch because when Red quits being quiet, he usually gets real loud and rambunctious in a hurry. Then, along between sundown and dark, Bobby Jack got real blue. He went to mumbling about owing on his new bedroom set and how much money his wife spent on home permanents and started cussing the government for different things. Bobby Jack had always hated Harry Truman for some reason and blamed him ever time a barmaid drawed a hot beer or he dropped a dime in a crack. Now it seemed like he was working up to blaming Truman for losing him his job. I didn't much care about Harry Truman either way, but I'd liked President Roosevelt for ending hard times even though ol' Eleanor traipsed all over the world and run with too many niggers. My daddy's people come from Georgia before they settled over around Clarksville, and hadn't none of us ever been able to stomach niggers.

Bobby Jack kept getting bluer and bluer, and I commenced worrying about what he might do. He may be little; but he's wound tight, and I've seen him explode. Finally a flyboy from the Midland Air Base tapped his shoulder and asked if he had a match. Bobby Jack grinned that grin that don't have no fun in it and said, "Sure, airplane jockey. My ass and your face." The flyboy grinned kinda sickly. Before he could back off, Bobby Jack said, "Hey, Yankee boy, what you think about that shitass Harry Truman?" The flyboy mumbled about not being able to discuss his Commander in Chief on account of certain regulations. "I got your Commander in Chief swangin'," Bobby Jack said, cupping his privates in one hand. "Come 'ere and salute 'im." The flyboy set his beer down and took off like a nigger aviator, lurching this way and that.

Bobby Jack felt better for a little bit; I even got him and Red Turpin to grinning a little by imitating Mr. Poot when we'd cussed him. But it's hard to keep married men perked up very long. I married a girl in beautician's college in Abilene in '46, but we didn't live together but five months. She was a Hardshell Baptist and talked to God while she ironed and pestered me to get a job in a office and finish high school at night. She had a plan for me to go on to junior college and then make a tent preacher.

Red Turpin went to the pay phone back by the men's pisser to tell his wife to borrow her daddy's pickup and come get him. He had to wait a long spell for her to come to the neighbor's phone, because Red's had been cut off again, and I could tell right off she wasn't doing a great deal of rejoicing.

"Goddammit, Emma," Red said. "We'll thresh all that shit out later. Come git me and chew my ass out in person. It's cheaper than doin' it long distance." Red and Emma lived in Midland behind the Culligan Bottled Water place. "Lissen," Red said, "I can't do nothin' about it right now. I'll whup his ass when I can find him, but all I'm tryin' to do right now is git a ride home. ... What? ...Well, all right, goddammit *I* don't like hearing the little farknocker cry neither. Promise 'im we'll buy 'im another 'un." He listened for a minute, got real red in the face, and yelled, "Lissen, Emma, *just fuck you!* How many meals you missed since we been married? *Just fuck you!*" From the way he banged the phone down I couldn't tell for sure which one of 'em had hung up first. Red looked right through me, and his eyes was hard and glittery. "Some cocksucker stole my kid's trike," he said, and stumbled on back toward the bar.

Two old range cowboys come in about then, their faces like leather that had been left out in the sun, and the potbellied one was right tipsy. He was hollering *"Ahha, Santa Flush!"* and singing about how he was a plumb fool about "Ida Red," which was a song that had been made popular by Bob Wills and the Texas Playboys. He slammed me on the back in a good-natured way and said, "Howdy, stud. Gettin' any strange?"

He grinned when I said, "It's all strange to me," and went on in the pisser real happy. When Red followed the old cowhand in, I just naturally figured he'd went to take a leak. I moseyed over to the jukebox and played "Slippin' Around" by Floyd

Tillman, which, when I seen him play the Midland VFW Hall, he said he had wrote on a napkin late one night at a café in Dumas when all between him and starvation was forty-some cents and a bottle of Thunderbird wine.

In a little bit Red Turpin slid back on his stool and started drinking Pearl again, big as you please. About a half a beer later the second cowboy went to the pisser and come out like a cannon had shot him, yelling for a doctor and the po-leece. "They done killed ol' Dinger," he hollered. "I seen that big 'un go in right behind him. They's enough blood in there to float a log."

Four or five people run back toward the pisser; a general commotion started, and I said real quick, "Come on. Let's shuck outta here." But Bobby Jack was hopping around cussin' Red Turpin, asking what the hell he'd did. Red had a peculiar glaze in his eye; he just kept growling and slapping out at Bobby Jack like a bear swatting with his paw at a troublesome bee.

The barkeep run up and said, "You boys hold what you got." He yanked a sawed-off shotgun from under the bar and throwed down on us. "Skeeter," he hollered, "call the po-leece. And don't you damn bohunks move a hair." I wouldn't a-moved for big money.

The old cowboy had been helped out of the pisser and was sitting all addled at a back table, getting the blood wiped off his face. He groaned too loud to be good dead and kept asking, "What happened?" which was the same thing everybody was asking him. He seemed to think maybe a bronc had unhorsed him, and somebody laughed.

The barkeep relaxed his shotgun a smidgen. But when I leaned across the bar and offered him $12 to let us go on our way, he just shook his head and said, "It's gonna cost you a heap more'n that if I hafta blow you a twin asshole."

Two city cops come in, one fatter than the other; hog fat and jowly. They jangled with cuffs, sappers, and all kinds of hard-wear; them sumbitches got more gear than Sears and Roebuck. The biggest cop huffed and puffed like he'd run a hill and said, "What kinda new shit we got stirred up here, Frankie?"

The barkeep poked a thumb in our direction and said, "That big ol' red-haired booger yonder beat up a Scharbauer Ranch cowboy." I didn't like the sound of that, on account of the Scharbauers owned everything that didn't belong to God and had the rest of it under lease.

"What about it, big 'un?" the fattest cop asked Red.

"I never hit *him,*" Red said.

"Oh, I see," the big cop said. "That feller just musta had bad luck and slipped and fell on his ass in somebody else's blood." You could tell he was enjoying hisself, that he would of po-leeced for free.

"I never hit *him,*" Red said again. He commenced to cry, which I found disgusting. From the way Bobby Jack looked at me and shook his head I could tell it pissed him off, too.

"Yeah, he did," the barkeep said. "Near as I unnerstan' it, the boomer hit the cowboy without a word passin'. Far as the cowboy knows he might been knocked flat by a runaway dump truck."

"On your feet." The big cop jerked Red off of the barstool. He tightened his grip and lowered his voice and said, "You twitch just one of them fat ol' shitty muscles, big 'un, and I'll sap you a new hat size. And if 'at ain't enough, my partner'll shoot you where you real tender." Red kept on blubbering, whining something about somebody stealing his kid's trike, while the short cop fumbled the cuffs on him; me and Bobby Jack looked away and was careful not to say nothing. One time up in Snyder, I ask this constable what a buddy's fine would be when he was being hauled off for common public drunk, and the sumbitch taken me in, too. Next morning in court I found out the fine for common public drunk: $22 and costs.

The big cop went back and talked to the hurt cowboy awhile

and wrote down in a notebook. Now that his health was better the hurt cowboy wanted more beer. The barkeep give him one and said, "On the house, Hoss. Sorry about the trouble."

Then the big cop come walking back to me and Bobby Jack, giving us the hard-eyed. He said, "You two peckerwoods holdin' cards in this game?" We naw-sirred him. The barkeep nodded, which I thought it was nice of him not to have told I'd offered a $12 bribe. The big cop looked us over: "Where you boys work at?" We told him Morrison Brothers Construction. "Him, too?" He nodded toward Red, who was standing with his head down and studying his cuffed wrists.

"Well," I said, "I heard he quit lately."

The cop grunted and tapped Bobby Jack on the ass with his billy club and said, "Keep it down to a dull roar, little 'un. I'm tard, and done had six Maggie-and-Jiggs calls. Old ladies throwin' knives and pots at their husbands, or their husbands kickin' the crap out of 'em. I don't wanta come back in this sumbitch till my shift's over and I'm scenting beer."

They taken the old cowboy to the county hospital for stitches. When he passed by, being about half helt up, I seen his face had been laid open like a busted watermelon. I guess maybe Red's ring that he got in a gyp joint in that spick town acrost from Del Rio done it. Just seeing it made my belly swim and pitch. One time at Jal, New Mexico, I seen a driller gouge out a roughneck's eye with a corkscrew when they fell out over wages, and I got the same feeling then, only more so.

The Conroe woman in red slacks was sashaying around, telling everybody with a set of ears how we'd broke a record insulting her just before Red beat up the old cowboy, and you could tell she'd be good at stirring up a lynch mob and would of enjoyed the work. Everybody kept looking at us like they was trying to make up their minds about something. After we'd drank another beer and belched loud to show they wasn't spooking us, and dropped a quarter in the jukebox like nothing had happened, we eased on out the door.

I wanted to hit Danceland on East Second because a lot of loose hair pie hung out there. Or the Ace of Clubs, where they had a French Quarter stripper who could twirl her titty tassels two different directions at once and pick half dollars up off the bar top with her snatch. But Bobby Jack said naw, hell, he reckoned he'd go on home and face the music. I sure was glad I didn't have no wife waiting to chew on my ass and remind me that I owed too much money or had too many kids to go around acting free. I walked with Bobby Jack up to where he turned down the alley running between the Phillips 66 Station and Furr's Cafeteria, which was close to the trailer park where he lived. "Well," Bobby Jack said, "at least ol' Red won't have to worry 'bout gettin' a ride to Midland. He's got him a free bed in the crossbar hotel." We talked a little about checking on how much Red's bail had been set at, but didn't much come of it. To tell the truth, what he had did didn't make much sense and ruined the best part of the night. Without saying so, we kinda agreed he'd brought it on hisself.

I went over to the Club Café and ate me a chicken-fried steak with a bowl of chili beans on the side and listened to some ol' humpbacked waitresses talk about how much trouble their kids was. Next day I caught on with a drilling crew up in Gaines County, and it wasn't but about six weeks more that I joined the Army just in time to see sunny Korea, so I never did learn what all Red got charged with or how he come out.

2 ☆
Remembering the Hard Times

I don't know your reaction to all this woolly Depression talk—though I might if I knew your age—but here's one ol' boy it scares. Not mildly worries, mind you, or causes an occasional fretful tic, but simply disorders his brain and his innards. There are millions of us, in our mid-forties or over, who vividly recall the economic bust of Hoover's time. And a high percentage of us fear another depression more than we worry about heart attacks, cancer, hardened arteries, or like awards planned for us by the actuarial charts. Short of nature's most perverse inversion, that of burying one of my own children, I can't think of a more frightening nightmare.

Mounting Depression talk lately has influenced my daily conduct. I work more, feverishly hoping to gain a nest egg against whatever dread awaits, and have begun dogged small economies: turning off surplus lights; considering the cheaper cuts of meat; spending less on my twin indulgences—good books and good scotch—and I'm thinking of writing a letter of apology to an old friend, John Henry Faulk, who was a big-time network-radio star until blacklisted during the Joe McCarthy madness. I snickered on first hearing that John Henry had quit the city for a small Texas farm supplied with chickens and milk cows as a survival hedge against expected new privations. It doesn't seem so laughable anymore.

I am kicking myself, too, for having been such a spendthrift over the past ten years. Oh, yes, I have been a real butter-and-egg man, hitting all the whiskey and trombone towns, buying drinks for the crowd, and urging the good times to roll from New Orleans to Nantucket; it is a disease afflicting a certain stripe of man who once didn't have a pit to poss in, a reckless dispensation of resources almost as if one feared that the banks might fail again. In a manic spree about two years ago, I divested myself within three months of more than $12,000 on purely hedonistic pursuits—money above my true requirements or real obligations; funny money just burned and whooped away—and now, monitoring the gloomy economic forecasts, I think of how many chickens and moo cows it might have bought.

But where John Henry Faulk had the foresight to retreat to the earth's basic places and shelters, I did not. While deep in the Watergate dumps, I promised myself to move from Washington —that dreary ruin of marble monuments, rhinestone dreams, and brassy interlopers, where for years I had felt much the transient and grew no roots—to more commodious Manhattan quarters. Despite gathering misgivings and a plunging stock market heralding future economic turndowns, I accomplished the deed—just in time to witness the collapse of the Franklin National Bank, a branch of which reposed around the corner from my new digs. Although the Franklin's fall was played down in the press, publishers being businessmen first and sponsors of artists and prophets later, it represented the largest single bank failure in American history. Not the best possible welcome to the neighborhood.

I love it here—the apartment with its airy open view and light, the new gear and accouterments, those surging excitements of the Big Apple so long merely sampled by a visiting country boy hoping to throw his money away—but I am newly terrified at assuming the permanent cost of the place. My rent has doubled, and the taxicabs are metered. One encounters formerly prosperous ex-stockbrokers in the bars, searching the want ads and nursing their midday drinks. Construction men can't find work, in a city perpetually building and in constant need of rebuilding, and sit over their beers with haunted eyes and many damnations of their former hard-hat hero, Dick Nixon, on their lips. I think more on the $8,000 required to keep a teenaged son in boarding school, of older family members infirm or otherwise disadvantaged who increasingly require helpful attentions, of skyrocketing taxes (sales; property; city, state, and federal income taxes) and business expenses; and of my own loose excesses.

Most of all, I think of how unfriendly were the nation's Gothams to their hopeless millions in that earlier dark penniless time. I conjure up visions from old books and ancient newsreels of the special miseries of the cities: their breadlines, soup kitchens, corner apple salesmen, park-bench sleepers; grim gray men in endless ranks profitlessly seeking work, and their dismal Hooverville settlements of cardboard, fruit crates, tin, and rags. These had it rougher, I know, than those of us relatively fortunate enough to hunker down in the hinterlands, where we might grow a few vegetables and produce our own eggs, with a little creek fishing on the side; there are damn few squirrels or rabbits to be bagged for the family stew pot on the sidewalks of New York. So I sit here within spitting range of Park Avenue, luxury-spoiled and more prosperous than yesteryear might have believed, wondering what in God's good name I am doing taking for neighbors those Wall Street bastards my father railed and warned against in the long ago.

There are brave words from President Ford and his White House advisers that no new depression will be tolerated; apparently, Mr. Hard Times is to be run out of town like a ragged hobo and by a prosperous mob wearing WIN buttons. These jawbonings afford small comfort to one who remembers the optimistic rhetoric and arrogant explanations of the Great Depression. President Hoover: "Prosperity is just around the corner. . . . The worst will be over in sixty days. . . . Many people left their jobs for the more profitable one of selling apples [!!!]. . . ." Calvin Coolidge: "When more and more people are thrown out of work, unemployment results. . . ." J. P. Morgan: "The stock market will fluctuate." Jackson Reynolds, president of the First National Bank of New York: "Ninety-nine out of a hundred persons haven't good sense." John D. Rockefeller: "Believing that fundamental conditions are sound, my son and I have for some days been purchasing sound common stocks." Thomas W. Lamont of J. P. Morgan and Company: "It is the consensus of financiers that many of the quotations on the stock exchange do not fairly represent the situation."

Well, thanks a heap, old fellows; and thanks, too, to all publications from *Fortune* to *Reader's Digest* for their cheery reports of 1929–32 even as our belt buckles grew closer to our backbones and grass grew in the streets. And a special thanks to all you determined jawboners of the present moment who have succeeded to the pep squad. But, damn it, I *still* think I ought to be back home, trading cows with John Henry Faulk, and canning prickly pear preserves.

When I am required to write an autobiographical sketch, it invariably begins: "I was born on the first day of the first year of the Great Depression—1929." My subconscious imagines the Fates, wearing black capes and hideous grins, as they danced jigs and gleefully slapped their withered thighs in celebration of the tough surprises they had prepared for Baby King. My father then was a prospering blacksmith and had just built one of the finer houses in Putnam, Texas. I would mewl and gurgle in it little more than a year before the local oil boom would go bust and fly-by-night operators would escape, owing the village blacksmith more than 10,000 hard-money dollars. The Great Depression soon would show itself. My father lost everything; though he would live another forty years, he never recovered. The King family, like Steinbeck's wretched Joads, took to the road in search of that elusive prosperity President Hoover insisted was just around the corner.

My first memories are of living in a farmer's converted garage while my parents and older siblings went off to pick cotton each day. Sometimes they found somebody to stay with me, and sometimes they stationed me under a tree with an old collie dog to stand guard. The new Model T from Mr. Ford's new assembly lines, which my father had paid cash for just before the crash, was pulled by mules from cotton field to cotton field; gasoline was purchased only when it became necessary to find new work in distant places. We ultimately retreated to my father's old homeplace, where he had settled with his farming family in 1894; its fields had long lain fallow, so that older members of the family had to grub stumps and battle Johnson grass before being able to plant. There was a baking drought and a grasshopper plague. I don't know if you've ever seen thousands or millions of grasshoppers assault a cornfield, a grainfield, or a vegetable garden. First they chew down the main plants, not only stripping the blades or leaves but eating the stalk and then burrowing into the ground after the roots; when they're gone, it looks as if the field had been bombed or burned. Even when one had a bountiful harvest, prices were so depressed that little or no profit resulted.

By the time I was seven I, too, pulled a cotton sack or performed other agrarian tortures when not struggling with the mysteries of the rural Texas school. I cannot claim to have excessively enjoyed it. Indeed, my earliest private vow was to escape that farm and all the unrewarding toil it provided. I dreamed of running away from home but deduced that the road might not be a terribly profitable place after seeing streams of hoboes hop off freight trains on the Texas & Pacific Railroad to fan out in our rural community and beg back-door food handouts. My mother was terrified of them, especially when my father might be working in some distant field or pasture; he established an old iron bell on the veranda, and she was under instructions to ring it in times of peril. I recall my father's being ashamed to turn away hungry men, but my mother's fear overcame his humanitarian instincts. It was, simply, a time of fear.

I have since heard, or read, the Depression memories of others of my generation; almost uniformly, they claim not to have especially noticed their poverty because everyone was in the same boat. That knowledge did not comfort me: I knew we were dirt poor, knew it every waking hour, and I resented it and hated it as some deep personal affront. When my parents reminisced of the good times—in an effort, I suppose, to bolster themselves—I stewed and grew angry because I could not remember having shared them. When school adjourned each fall for crop gathering, I loathed being part of itinerant cotton-picking crews; we crowded like cattle into a series of failed old trucks, clattering from one cotton patch to another among exhausted parents and their crying kids; the hours were from daylight until dark, from "can to can't."

I hated going door to door with my mother in Cisco on Saturdays, trying to sell eggs or vegetables to people I imagined to be rich. I envied their radios, cars, telephones, and other superiorities. Bile sloshed in my innards when the high school football team played on Friday afternoons and found me short of the ten-cent admission price, and those of us without the wherewithal were herded into the tiny school library for guarding while our luckier companions skipped gaily off to the big game. "Pride goeth before a mighty fall," my mother quoted in an effort to make me accept the realities. But I became a quarrelsome kid, full of hates and aggressions, one likely to explode into fistfights or pointless rages. I could not have defined either a communist, socialist, revolutionary, or capitalist; my instincts and sympathies certainly were with all of those, save the capitalist, however. Alternately I despised what he represented and wanted to be cut in on what he had.

That we ate well, by raising our own hogs and chickens and cows and vegetables, did not satisfy the urge for coins to click. There simply was *no* money. I heard my worried parents talk at night, when they thought young ears were deaf in sleep, about the impossibility of new shoes or new clothes or a new plow. I eavesdropped while my father and his angry contemporaries in their faded blue-ducking overalls cursed the banks and threatened violence should mortgages be foreclosed or seed-crop loans be denied. Sometimes I would find my father standing on the porch or in the yard staring blankly into space, and the expression on his face frightened me. There were stretches when he might be gone for days, riding horseback through the countryside in search of stumps to grub or horses to shoe or any odd jobs that might contribute a dollar. As often as not, he returned with nothing to show; I began to dread his returns for the fresh despair they produced.

After such disappointments, my mother privately lectured me to make something of myself: to seek an education and some vague main chance; to get up and get out as soon as nature and circumstance permitted; to find some yellow-brick road. I had the notion that she somehow blamed my father, though I didn't think it quite fair. My father preached harsh sermons against the Goddamn Republicans; I learned, early on, that they were rich to the very last in number and didn't give a shit for the little man. To this day I feel obscurely guilty about once having voted for one.

I was too young to know of Franklin D. Roosevelt's election

in 1932; four years later, however, I knew that everyone save the Goddamn Republicans and inmates of insane asylums strongly backed him over Alf Landon. FDR had made it possible for my brother to obtain work in the Civilian Conservation Corps (he got bed, board, and $1 per day, $5 of which he kept at the end of the month, while a vital $25 came home to the family) and for my father to find occasional paydays improving country roads or bridges or building outdoor privies under the sponsorship of the Works Progress Administration. Obviously, FDR wanted us to have work and money; just as obviously, his opponents did not. *That* certain knowledge, combined with once seeing a weeping farm family's goods publicly sold at a sheriff's sale to satisfy creditors, would early make me a "yellow dog" Democrat—one who would vote for "a yellow dog" before crossing party lines to assist any living Republican.

Intellectually, I cannot now quarrel with contentions that for all of FDR's pump priming, America did not truly recover from its Great Depression blues until that full-employment boom provided by World War II. There was, yes, some economic marching up and down again. But you cannot convince me that all the midnight schemes of the brain trusters went for naught or that the paper shufflings of the New Deal's alphabet-soup agencies failed to make important improvements or contributions. In addition to the tangibles—jobs, new schools and other useful edifices, emergency food and clothing; even a slight relaxation in the skinflint loan policies of formerly heartless bankers—the New Deal brought hope where no hope had lived. And it brought the faint promise, at least, of a better tomorrow. When hope was all you had, it was worth much more than the dry and distant recapitulations of historians can make later generations understand.

When I learned at school that FDR would be making yet another of his fireside chats, it was my bounden duty to take the word home. After a hurried early supper, we walked a mile to a neighboring farm, there to listen with other families who had assembled for the latest radio word from the new messiah. Those were vital gatherings, the adults listening so intently that even the most high-spirited child knew not to require shushing. I clung to every word the man said; though I didn't understand much of it, I was comforted by the sound and roll.

Afterward—when Roosevelt's confident voice had wished us good night—while popcorn and parched peanuts were passed around, the old snuff-dipping farmers would wave their arms and say, "By gum, now, Clyde, that feller Rusavelt; he's got some good i-deers; why, I wouldn't be a-tall surprised if cotton went up! Yessir!" Then they would make their bitter jokes about Hoover steak (rabbits or squirrels) or Hoover cars (mule-drawn wagons) or Hoover cake (cornbread), and surely some old nester —his eyes glowing mischief—would say something like "I tole my ol' woman t'other day that I figger the Depression's purt near over cause I seen a jackrabbit runnin' down the road and they wasn't no more than three fellers chasin' it." They would explode in rough laughter, then, the sharper edges momentarily knocked off their fear. Uncle Tal Horn and Old Man Luther Parks might commence sawing on their fiddles—playing "Cotton-Eyed Joe" or "Buffalo Gals" or "Old Joe Clark"—while feet tapped, children squealed, and for a little while you could forget those new burdens soon to come up with the sun.

Remembering all that, I have aggressively caused severe social embarrassments over the years should some academic dandy or cretin ideologue look too smug and too well fed in contending that FDR was the opiate of the masses and delivered the masses not; some things, goddammit, you just can't put a price tag on, though the high-domed thinkers can't seem to get that through their noggins. I particularly recall going all spluttery and inarticulate in the home of John Kenneth Galbraith, Warburg Professor of Economics at Harvard, when some dinner guest said over the fine wine and cigars—in response to my Depression memories, issued while I was voluntarily straightening out everybody's economic misconceptions —"But why didn't your family move elsewhere, where opportunities might have been greater?" The sumbitch actually *said* that. He was a young professor, and so I suppose allowances perhaps should be made; but from that moment forward I have pretty well despaired of the Ivy League.

A woman named Caroline Bird wrote a fine book about the Depression and perfectly titled it *The Invisible Scar;* her theory ran that many of us shall go to our graves deeply wounded in our psyches by those have-not years. She's right as rain. My mother is in her late eighties now, living in that misty netherworld where yesteryear is more real than this living moment; I recently saw her cry anew in relating her deep hurt when my older brother went off to a CCC camp being established in distant Arizona: "We had two dollars and a dime. I tried to give Weldon a dollar, but he wouldn't take it. He struck off across the pasture, walkin' eight miles to Cisco to catch a government train, and it nearly killed me to see that boy go without a nickel in his pocket. I cried a long time after he was out of sight."

That brother is my senior by about fifteen years; though I worshiped him as a kid brother will, I grew extremely tired of hearing from others how he had dropped out of high school to wash dishes in a café so that I might be bought an infant's survival milk. No doubt it has colored our relationship through life; I was much older than I should have been before I could fully appreciate his sacrifice, simply because the guilt was too much. Indeed, I hardly had come of legal age when I provoked a fight with him in order to declare my independence. Not until I was nearing thirty did I forgive him for all he'd done for me.

As a young man in his earliest low-paying jobs I was torn between a natural instinct to instruct unreasonable, nit-picking bosses to go screw themselves and a deep, unspoken fear that should I lose *that* job, I might not find another. It was a thing I noted among many of my generation. They suffered dull mulework, performed overtime without compensation, and paled in the company of irascible supervisors; no matter that they then functioned in the post–World War II boom and had the added sweetener of a record local oil-based prosperity. Several old companions, I am certain, limited their career opportunities out of fear that should they fail in new adventures, they might find themselves on the streets. Sometimes, now, when they and the moon are high, they grouse in their cups of having been born in the wrong time. One old friend actually gave a party celebrating the tardy death of Herbert Hoover, who long had been past hurting him—if, indeed, he ever had—and though mildly appalled, I might have attended had I been in town.

It is good, I suppose, that each succeeding generation has difficulty transmitting its darker experiences to the next. Thus, fresh hope is not stillborn, people dare to dream, and the young are free to take those foolish risks and experimentations necessary to the full life. But whether attempting to replant their fears in a new generation or honestly hoping to help the young avoid their own mistakes, parents have a way of harping or preaching on their own private dreads; as these dreads are the product of their own histories, their children—of another time and place—cannot identify with them. It was maddening, when I chastised my own children for wasting food or time or opportunity, to comprehend ultimately that my Great Depression sermons were accepted as nothing more than the private preoccupations of an old fossil. They humored me along, sometimes exchanging quick, secret smiles, but I knew they could no more envision breadlines or failed banks or one-third of a nation ill-fed, ill-housed,and ill-clothed than I might understand the gibberings of some little green Martian. They are products of the affluent society and can imagine no other.

For all my occasional uses of the Depression in making the obligatory parental preachments, I did not truly think—for years—that it would be possible to have another. Indeed, as a young man working on Capitol Hill, I had the personal assurances of the late Speaker Sam Rayburn. One postwork afternoon in the late fifties, over whiskey in his hideaway office in the Capitol building, where the fortunate might be invited to attend what he called meetings of "the board of education," the old man said of bankers and businessmen who had the temerity to vote Republican, "Why, Roosevelt saved the bastards; he fixed it so things can't *ever* go bust again. He put in laws propping up the economy, and he saved those bastards, and now they don't appreciate it." I believed him, for had not Rayburn personally sponsored dozens of FDR's bills in Congress? Was not America booming again? It was a time when few Americans questioned the authority of Authority; a time when myths were for promoting and old bad dreams were for forgetting. Yes, we had coins to rattle and folding stuff in our pokes, and you could count on the future unless the Russians blew up Wall Street with the Bomb.

We were almost a decade away from the time when we might begin to suspect that many of our problems might be beyond quick solutions, that the answer did not always handily repose in the back of the book, that we paid for our factories and highways and shiny shopping centers in the coin of polluted streams, disfigured countrysides, new slums, and urban tangles. In Sam Rayburn's time, we could not have imagined that day when the oil-producing nations not only would cease snatching off their hats in Uncle Sam's presence—mighty, unconquerable Uncle Sam, who always won his wars and ruled supreme as the quintessential industrial and technological state—but would actually back him against the wall and then shake a finger in his face. The time had not yet come when Europe would suspect the dollar and puzzled American tourists would find themselves stranded in foreign ports because suddenly their money wasn't preferred. We gave little or no thought to the increasing problem of constant balance-of-trade deficits, and we really couldn't imagine that Americans in significant numbers would take to those cheap imitations of radios, cameras, and such that the Japanese shipped here in such astounding quantities.

For some time now we've lived with the uneasy notion that certain external events may be beyond the economic control of Washington or Wall Street; the cat's long been out of the bag where official infallibility is concerned. We don't like to ponder it, but maybe we've got to be willing to risk an uncontrollable and unconscionable war if we're to get all the oil or other scarce resources we require. Nobody's saying "war" out loud from public podiums in Washington, but there are mutterings; those who understand that wars are fought more for material gain than for those more ethereal reasons found in wartime rhetoric or brushed-up history books must have had the dark, unthinkable thought even before Washington began "warning" the oil-producing nations of the dangers inherent in their escalating profits; not for nothing, I suspect, does the Pentagon have a paper plan for seizing certain Mideastern oil fields should things become intolerable. These, of course, are just "war games" the Pentagon says, and they are plotted to cover any eventuality, however remote; so don't worry about it.

We are, face it, no longer a country or a society of unlimited resources. We never were, of course; but it *seemed* that we were, and we acted accordingly. The economic and political realities of the world are such that my older nightmares have come back into fashion. I fear that it *can* happen here again, and probably will. One of these days this nation of pyramiding credit, inflationary spirals, impossible taxes, suspect dollars, gross waste, bloated bureaucracies, union demands, cheating business ethics, and conflicting international complications may go down in such a heap that the dust and roar may not subside until we've scrapped the old ways and the old system. Morose thoughts, indeed, for one who knows that midtown Manhattan doesn't look like a good place to stake a cow and who knows, too, that fireside chats are unlikely to comfort as they did in that earlier time.

3 ☆

Most Likely to
Succeed

In the summer of '73 they paraded across our TV screens, squirming men with plastic faces, Bright Young Men gone wrong—Good Germans, yes, just following orders—men unable, even under the quasi-philosophical proddings of Senator Howard Baker or the scriptural lectures of Senator Sam Ervin, to explain their mindless felonies above their desires to be good team players. Which was, of course, a compounding of original sins, in that they failed to contact truth; lied, even, because what they could not bring themselves to say was that cancerous ambition ate on them in the night, that they were Success-haunted. Like Charles Colson, to a man, they would have walked on any number of aged grandmothers—to say nothing of the Constitution—to serve themselves and King Richard. But mainly, I think, to serve themselves, although their mischief had been done in the name of the flag.

I watched the parade and drank and fretted and felt uncomfortable in the extreme. For the Watergate gang seemed a near incarnation of an earlier, rawer self. Not that the grizzled middle-ager of the present identified with them in the specifics; horrors, no. But residual pieces of an earlier self shuddered at what might have been, given more big-league opportunities (a

38

decade ago, two decades ago) in Washington. I told my soul that
never could I have become a Jeb Magruder: no, the smooth
ass-kissing corporate water boy was not my style. But I might
have become a Bob Haldeman, yes, given enough rope. Several
times I saw him looking out of hard, cold eyes I once had observed in the shaving glass. So one thought on ambition, success,
drive: what they all meant, and where they properly should be
valued in the general scheme of things. One's mind went back
in time. . . .

Near the end of junior year in high school my class named
Kent Hardy as Most Likely to Succeed, a shocking miscarriage
of justice, boiling my runner-up juices in anger and shame. It
was not an election closely watched outside the participating
precinct; I now know that hundreds of merchants, working-
men, and housewives accomplished their small-town-Texas
drudgeries unaware of my ruin as voted—38 to 15—by the Class
of '46. At the time, however, I assumed the community's full
scorn and half its pity. The galling loss may have been a factor
in causing me to flee to the Army before my senior year.

I think my extreme reaction was more than the peevish huff
of a seventeen-year-old lad who perhaps secretly cherished
himself above the norm. Of ambition, it is true, I bore a burden-
some load. There was a better side of the tracks to attain; possibly a wider world called from somewhere east of Dallas or west
of El Paso. As Kent Hardy's great expectation was to become
the minister of our town's First Baptist Church, I judged him
unable even to define success. For I knew, in all the private
places, that the boy in that wind- and sun-blistered little village
most eager to claw and scratch his deliverance slept in my bed
each night.

Not that I failed privately to envy certain of Kent Hardy's
assets. He had his own car; he lived in a better house; he wore
superior clothes. I coveted his deep voice, easy laugh, smooth

social patter, constant cheer. Kent made people smile; I seemed to make them nervous.

We shared a common Boy Scout troop, football squad, and debate class. I liked Kent Hardy. Hell, everybody did. Had they voted him Most Popular Boy, why, then, surely I would have led the cheers. But in football drills, debating jousts, and the other direct ways the young have of judging their peers, I had observed that Kent lacked a certain thirst. While he aspired to lead West Texans to Christ, I wanted them—saints or sinners—to read of me in the New York *Times.* There was never any doubt in my mind that the Lady Success, had she any pride in her companions, would choose me over carloads of Kent Hardys.

Kent never got around to doing Jesus' good work. He entered a church college only after the U.S. Navy had taught him sin's better side. A year later he returned to the old hometown as a radio announcer. My own military service had been laid by; following an even briefer flirtation than Kent's with higher learning, I also had gone home again.

Still, the Class of '46 appeared to have made a proper choice. Kent, rumbling bass voice repeating news from the wires of the Associated Press or offering the bargains of local merchants, earned $67.50 per week as compared to my $55 reward as a cub newspaperman. Kent honked for me each morning (*he* still owned the car), and we sleepily shared bitter café coffee before straggling to our jobs; we drank stronger gargles together on weekends. Our respective marriages were accomplished within a short span; our firstborn shared playpens. We exchanged secrets and such memories as young men have. I don't remember that we talked much of Success or our futures, should you exclude my occasional beery midnight boasts: "Kent, goddamn if I know how or when or even *why.* But one day, ol' buddy, my goddamn ship's comin' in. One day, you hide and watch me, I'm gonna have boatloads of money and people gonna *hear* about me."

Kent would laugh—it seemed he was always laughing in response to my bitchings, complaints, and wild crazy dreams—and accommodatingly say, "You know, by God, I believe you will. And when you do, you'll have servants waiting on servants." The truth is I was sore afraid of failure and was pep-talking myself.

In 1954 I went away; Kent Hardy didn't. On visits from Washington, where as a congressional aide I studied at close range the magic and sideshows of Senate Majority Leader Lyndon B. Johnson, I briefly saw Kent. Or goosing my new mechanized horses down flat West Texas highways, I would hear his bass voice roll out of the car radio, offering bargains in golden-ripe bananas, banking services, back-to-school clothes. And I would often think: *Jesus, how long will Kent be content to read that shit?*

It was not a question one could ask him, however. Our brief reunions taught that Kent Hardy now believed me to be a socialist menace directed by international cartels: an agent of meddling bureaucracies conspiring to bring racial integration, impossible taxes, and maybe firing squads searching house to house for true patriots. One night, as he damned the Warren Court and speechified on the spotless virtues of Free Enterprise, I struck back in anger: "Kent, how goddamn much money you make?" Well, he said, in case it might be any of my business, what with commercials he taped outside his regular job, he was up to $8,000 or $9,000 or maybe a little better. I said, "If what I'm doing is socialism, then give me socialism. 'Cause I'm drawing down seventeen thousand dollars plus, ol' buddy, and that's just the beginning!" A gainer of mindless, mean, sweet revenge, I satisfactorily fantasized in my motel room of rejecting the written apology of the Class of '46.

Now it is 1973. Many in that class are dead, and others are wounded. Back in the old hometown to attend family complications, I have passed Sunday's slow dance in a motel room by discovering, via the telephone directory, that twenty-seven members of the forty-man 1945 high school football squad retain local addresses. This is astonishing, for despite periodic visits, I cannot recall the last time I encountered one of them. Several scotches later I dial Kent Hardy's number. "Goddamn, King, Bobbi Jo and I figured out the other night that we haven't seen you in eight years." I ask whatever happened to Jimmy Eagan, Dun Andrews, Hal Lindsey, Willard T. Young, Becky Anson, Peaches Simpson.

Jimmy's doing good as a lawyer in Lubbock. Dun runs a sporting goods store in Seminole or Brownfield. Nobody's heard of Hal since he went to Hollywood to become a movie star. Willard T. Young is a mid-level executive at the leading local bank, once was district governor of the Lions Club, and has the right eyes watching him. Becky married a rich rancher from Marfa and is reportedly heavier than any single beef-on-the-hoof her husband owns. Peaches Simpson, an oil company secretary, has known three marriages and divorces and is on the way to drunk each day by good sundown.

Waiting for the Hardys at the motel, I wondered why I had felt compelled to make contact. If I had not made boatloads of money, I had, by boyhood standards, got near to a small canoeful. I had published books, been nominated for prizes, and—yes! —and even been mentioned in the New York *Times*. I lived well: dined with U.S. senators in Georgetown; occasionally accompanied classy ladies; held membership in the family circle at Manhattan's literary watering hole, Elaine's. It wasn't exactly *bad,* you understand—hell, sometimes it was real good; I never once thought of trading it back for my youthful cotton-patch or oil-field sweat—but somehow it had failed to set me free or ring my bells as I'd once imagined. I had a certain tinny, minor fame, right; if my isolated village had produced and exported an ambassador to bigger courts, then probably I was it. But it seemed little enough to call on when nights grew long and dry and empty. And of course, some nights had: One wife had quit by divorce, and one by death; my children afforded what I thought to be a little more than the requisite unwelcome surprises; I drank too much and too long lay professionally fallow and often wandered at loose ends. It became a peculiar healing therapy occasionally to withdraw to the old hometown, scratching in memory's scattered dust for boyhood tracks, while wondering what vital component one had overlooked in earlier, clearer visions of the Good Life to come. On such a day late last summer I telephoned my former pal Kent Hardy.

It was difficult to find a reveling spot. My two suggestions proved long defunct. "We stay at home so much I've plumb lost track," Kent said as we searched the dark mini-city. "I get up at five o'clock, and that don't encourage much carousing."

Bobbi Jo, his wife, sat silently beside him. About the time the visiting pop sociologist mused that he might pay money for her private thoughts she said, "How you like this car?" Actually, she put a name to it: Mustang, Cougar, Barracuda, I don't know; something wild. I'm thrice ignorant about cars.

"Real fine," I lamely attested.

Bobbi Jo said, "We get a new one every two years."

I remembered Bobbi Jo from high school civics class: a silent, shy, sharp-nosed girl in cheap print dresses who always wore ink on her fingers so that she might have been a secret poet. She uttered not a word in class and made 97 on all exams. In the early 1960s she was enamored of the John Birch Society. A personal conquest of tuberculosis, children, and perhaps the Birch Society Blue Book had made her a woman of strong opinions. I now feared she might somehow tamper with whatever truths I sought from her husband. Bobbi Jo had long thought me generally polluted and crazed; I never knew when she'd be warily warm or next to hostile.

We entered a rambling dark beer joint. A local band hammered and sawed in inferior imitation of old country-western favorites. A tall, balding vocalist in a cowboy outfit tricked up with sequins sang of how candy kisses wrapped in paper meant more to you than any of mine. "Welcome to the nineteen-forties," I said.

Kent laughed: "Most of the bands around here are as old as us. They don't play anybody newer than Merle Haggard. Young kids are into country-rock or whatever they call that modern shit. I guess they have their hangouts, but damn if I know where they are."

A cocktail waitress, in a short skirt and tall hair, said, "Say, you sound familiar. Are you . . . Kent *Hardy?*"

My old friend grinned and attempted modesty: "Well, yeah, I was the last time I looked." She squealed, exclaimed, and fluttered her lashes and hands. *Son of a bitch. Foiled again. A prophet without honor in his own country . . .*

When Kent's fan twitched off to fetch beers, I said to Hardy, "Tell me about your life."

"Aw, you know. I get up, I go to work, I come home. And once in a while I prounce ol' Bobbi Jo."

She laughed. "We got us some real good this afternoon. For old folks."

"Course, we got us a problem." Kent chuckled. "We got careless and had a new baby about nine years ago. Surprised hell out of us. I wouldn't take for her, but it sure does discourage daytime prouncing. That poor little girl's been to more weekend movies than any kid in town. Every time *we* want a matinee, little Darlene gets one if she wants it or not."

"Now you're bragging," Bobbi Jo said, smiling.

Kent Hardy squeezed his wife's arm. "Yeah, lotta life left in this old girl. I've flat give up on her getting old."

In truth, the years have been good to Bobbi Jo. She is one of those late bloomers, ever so much more sensual in her middle years. The visitor felt stirrings of envy and lust.

"You remember Jack Kooch?" Bobbi Jo asked.

"Oh. Yeah. Quiet fellow. One grade behind us. Tried to dye his hair blond, and it turned out a shitty orange."

"Well, he's an artist in Austin or Houston or someplace," Bobbi Jo said. "The main thing, though, he turned out queer as a three-dollar bill."

"He don't show me much," Kent said. "They showed his paintings a few years back during Homecoming Weekend up at the high school. Buncha modern dabs and squiggly lines."

"I never would of picked him for a queer," Bobbi Jo said. "He played *guard* on the football team."

"Wasn't worth a shit, though," Kent judged. "I was damn near good as he was."

"Yeah, baby, but nobody in their right mind ever thought of *you* as queer. Though there was a time or two when I nearly wished it myself."

Kent ducked into his beer and surfaced to say, "Come on, now, Bobbi Jo, let's don't go digging up any dead cats."

In the strained silent beer gulpings perhaps we all capsuled the past. Fifteen years earlier Kent had enjoyed a semiserious extramarital fling with a loose-jointed, big-boned, ear-banging cowgirl who in high school had been much cherished as one of very few Christian bobby-soxers likely to put out. Goldie's peculiarity in her time was that she *liked* to diddle, which Good Girls simply didn't. Bobbi Jo, in her eighth year of marriage, had discovered the affair and temporarily thought she'd put it asunder by awarding the offending parties tongue-lashings. Later, discovering that this had not been totally effective, Bobbi Jo invaded the shop where the Other Woman worked as a beautician to indulge in enthusiastic hair pullings, jaw slappings, and profane screechings. Kent had been placed under virtual house arrest for some months; now, I realized, he continued to be taxed by occasional reminders of those days. Pioneer Woman lived!

Uncertain of whether the question might be propitious, I asked, "Kent, are you happy?"

"Happy?" One got the impression he had not lately taken that particular inventory.

"Yeah. Happy. In your work. Your life."

"Well. I guess. Bobbi Jo, we, you know, get along purty well. We fight and fuss like everybody else but nothin' serious. And the kids—that little nine-year-old girl's my sweetheart and joy. You know, I'm a better parent to her than I was to Ray. I think the difference is that I was about twenty-two or twenty-three when Ray was born—he's about that age now—and I was thirty-six when Darlene came along. And as you get older, you appreciate your kids more."

"What about Ray? I haven't seen him since he was—what?—a teenager?"

"Well, Ray, you know, he kinda got messed up in Vietnam." Wounded?

"Naw, well, yeah, he got a nick. But he got on dope. Nothing hard, just marijuana and speed. That's bad enough, I guess—I don't know; I've never puffed any marijuana even to experiment—but he hadn't got any monkey on his back. He's just restless. Young."

"Kent," Bobbi Jo scolded, "you know damn good and well Ray wouldn't have got on dope if he hadn't been wounded."

"Well, I know you *think* it. But that's not the way Ray talks to me man to man. We've, you know, spent some time drinking together. And it's just that everybody over there was doing dope, *officers* even, and Ray, he just joined the majority. Like I started drinkin' beer in the Navy 'cause everybody else did."

"Piss on that war," Bobbi Jo hissed. "It was the most useless fucking war that ever was." Her mouth tightened; she looked suddenly old and used. One wondered what damage her son's experiences had done to her Birch Society teachings.

Kent said, "Ray, now, he's not any bad boy. I got him in junior college right after he came back. For several weeks I thought he was doing real well: bought him a used car, and he'd drive off to college in the morning and come wagging his books home at night. One night I asked what he'd been studying, and real quiet—dropping his head like he did when he was little and I was chewing on him for screwing up some way—he said, 'Hell, Dad, I quit after three days.' He'd just been drivin' around, see, hanging out in bars. Trying to pick up girls. Well, you know, he's young. . . .'"

Stubbornly Bobbi Jo said, "All *I* know is it's been two years. And he either lays out all night or flops on his bed, gazing at the ceiling."

Kent spoke a bit sharply: "Well, dammit, now. *I* was at loose ends when I got out of the Navy."

The mother said, "Yeah, and in six weeks went off to college. And in a year had a pretty good job. And in eighteen months got married. And soon as we could, had a baby."

"Okay," Kent said. It was a dismissal. The band sawed through a wizened Bob Wills tune celebrating the rose of old San Antone. Draining his beer glass, Kent said, "Look, come over to the house awhile. We can talk better there." When the waitress brought the check, he kidded, "You want money, or will you settle for my autograph?" Confused, she blushed and said she guessed she'd better take the money. Kent Hardy merrily roared.

The Hardys live in a ranch-style rambler of red brick, at least a first cousin to others in their development on the outskirts of town; probably it is in the $30,000 range by 1973 prices and might be valued at twice that if located near a population center. The living room isn't all that lived in, harboring the look of a display case. We bypassed it, clattered down a hall, and entered a "family room" with a huge picture window looking onto a neat, lighted back lawn featuring a swing set. The family room was informal and comfortable; rows of records lined the walls, and a combination TV-radio-hi-fi set dominated. There were photos of the family on tables and a pair of bronzed baby shoes; on the walls were several plaques and scrolls lauding Kent Hardy for civic work. He mixed drinks from a wheel-about bar.

"You asked about my job," he said. "Well, except for going off to a Shreveport radio station about fifteen years ago—and I just stayed four months, the town was too big—I've been working for the same radio station since 1950. It's got its limitations; I realize I'm not gonna get rich. But, hell, I never had any true itch to get rich." His gesture took in the room. "I got a good house, drive a good car, got a good motorboat. I go fishing and camping on weekends five, six times a year. Don't owe any big money. Don't have any big problems. Got about two thousand dollars in the bank above current expenses. Got a few savings bonds. Got life insurance. Got hospitalization. Got Social Security when the time comes. Shit, you know, it ain't bad. Lots of folks would like to have it. I may not be on the *Today* show like you, but—"

"That's another thing, you bastard," Bobbi Jo joshed. "People told us they saw you on—was it *Today* or *Dick Cavett*?"

"Well, both," I said, much appreciating the question.

"Well, why in hell don't you send your friends telegrams so they can watch you?"

Kent laughed. "Oh, come on, Bobbi. He's got four hunnerd things to think about then. No reason he should think of us. Anyway, I know I'm a big duck in a little pond. I can go in some café or the barbershop, and some ol' boy'll say, 'Kent, next time you think about it, play a little of that "Everybody Has the Blues" by ol' Merle Haggard for me.' Or maybe he'll laugh about something I've said on the air. Or I'll get some little ol' deejay prize. And it's nice, you know, a little recognition. It's better than workin' in a factory or totin' a dinner bucket.

"You might remember back in the nineteen-fifties I started

training as an oil company draftsman. Thought I'd work radio part time, for kicks, but hook on with an oil company for the fringe benefits. Good retirement pay. Long paid vacations. Damn job nearly drove me nuts. Sit at that ol' drawing board all day choked by a tie and perched on a high stool that made my ass ache, making tiny lines that nearly put my eyes out. Shit, I felt like I was in a cage.

"Sure made me a bastard around home, no kidding. Bobbi Jo'll tell you. One night I was drunk and throwing things—just miserable—and Bobbi got to crying and said, 'Dammit, why don't you just *quit* the goddamn job?' Well, that sounded better than the five o'clock whistle. So I said, 'Honey, maybe we'll eat a lot of beans and hamburgers, but all I want to do is spin those records and talk to the folks and enjoy what I'm doing.' And we hugged and cried, and I swear I haven't had any regrets."

It was getting late, now, and drink flowed faster while the mind wildly raced. I said, "Kent, we've never talked about this. But how did you feel when they elected you Most Likely to Succeed?"

He laughed. "Surprised. I guess if I had a dream back then, it was being Most Popular, or maybe Most Handsome. I kinda saw myself as a campus politician, you know, and wanted everybody to like me. After I won that Success thing, Mother wanted me to apply to West Point. Without my knowing it, she sent a clipping about me winning to our congressman. Which surprised me, 'cause she'd always been so big in the Baptist Church that I'd assumed she wanted me to preach. Which I guess is why I thought about preaching. But I never felt any special kin to the Lord. And down there at college, I was restless and wanting to drink and screw more than I wanted to preach. So"—he laughed—"the world lost a Billy Graham." He shook his head and said, "God, weren't we *dumb* back then?" The motion carried without dissent.

I asked Kent Hardy what he thought of the Watergate mess.

He said, "Hell, you've been in politics. You know how many crooked deals go on. The Watergate folks just got caught." We argued, waving our arms; he refused to accept my contention that never in American political history, no matter past stains, had there been in high places such systematic looting and lying; hell, I said, such conduct had become *official policy;* it wasn't just a few greedy or paranoid nuts: The Nixon apple was rotten to the core.

"Talk about something else," Bobbi Jo interjected. "I'm sick of hearing Watergate, *Watergate,* WATERGATE. I'm one of those mad as hell because it interrupts my soap operas. You oughta hear us bitch to each other over the phone."

Well, I said, could we talk about whether Watergate had inspired them to think on Success or Ambition? On the soul tax they required?

"Naw, you know," Kent said, "I don't reflect all that much. Except for reading your first two books—I got 'em at the library —I don't think I've read a half dozen books since college. Music is what I think about"—and he gestured toward the hi-fi, pouring out country-western laments—"and my family and enjoying life. You know, we're not here long. Won't be but fifteen years till we're right on sixty, King, and I made the decision a long time ago to enjoy it a day at a time."

Bobbi Jo pinned me with a painted fingernail: *"You!* Are *you* happy?"

Taken by surprise, I issued several er-uh-ahs. Then: "Sometimes. Maybe. Not always. Well, who the fuck knows? Happiness may be indefinable. It's not a constant state. I can be in the clouds one minute and down in the dirt the next."

"Answer the question," Bobbi Jo said. She was pleased, I think, by my ambiguities.

Well, all right. I guessed I wasn't all that happy. But writers, maybe, had dark streaks that wouldn't permit them to be happy. Maybe if writers were happy, they wouldn't feel compelled to talk to themselves on typewriters all day. If writers belonged to a happy breed, would they lock themselves up and labor in solitude or feel guilty when they did not?

Bobbi Jo said, "Well, excuse me, but I don't think just because you write, it makes you any different. We all live in the same world."

No, I said, we don't. We live in very different worlds. There are many and varied worlds out there beyond this little town and these flat horizons. And if you wander them for years, those worlds become part of you. Their special problems, pressures, and pleasures become part of you. You react to them. They change your thinking, your feelings, your perspectives. Even your values.

Kent Hardy lurched for the portable bar; I lurched with him: two old soldiers fading away. He said, "Well, I don't know. You've been in those worlds. Maybe you know. Bobbi Jo and me, we've been to California once. Usually we stay in Texas or go to Oklahoma or New Mexico on vacation. But we're not fools. We see TV. We see newspapers. I think if you'd get back to the basics, you'd see our point of view."

Shit, I said, I had *invented* the basics. It was all I dealt in.

"No, now, that's not true. We've talked enough, and I know you well enough—hell, lemme say it real straight—that you've been running around looking for something you ain't found. Being up there in New York, writing books, traveling on expense accounts, chatting with Cavett and Hugh Downs on TV —*that* ain't *real*! What's real is down here. Family. Home. Friends. *That's* real. I gotta tell you, I wouldn't trade with you."

I said, "Conceding the bullshit quotient in my life-style, Kent, and all the frivolities . . . and useless lace . . . and rusty tinsel . . . well, I wouldn't trade from *my* end."

"I guess not," he said. "People just built different. We could talk till doomsday and not settle it."

Drunk, feverish, flailing my arms, feeling we had hit all around the target but had never come close to the bull's-eye, I shouted, "But dammit, Kent, don't you ever feel you *missed out* on some things? Don't you ever wake up and think that maybe you've never risked the full adventure of yourself? Don't you—and I'm gonna speak real plain, Kent—don't you ever get just fucking stone *bored* repeating all that fluff about how much gold-ripe bananas are going for over at the Piggly Wiggly store?"

We had wandered through a sliding glass door out into the backyard under the high Texas moon; Bobbi Jo, waving good night and calling something indistinguishable, weaved off to bed. We swayed under the sky, and Kent said, "Aw, I've had my doubts. You know, I'll see something on TV and maybe for a minute it'll make me wish I could visit Russia or get drunk with Barry Goldwater or something crazy like that. But the difference, see, is I never let that stuff bug me. It just don't seem real very long. Sure, I guess we wouldn't have had Darlene at our age if we didn't need a little more . . . excitement . . . something new . . . more than what we've got." He frowned and sloshed and swirled his whiskey.

"But," he said, "I always purty much knew what I wanted. Hell, I was a free agent, same as you. *I* could have roamed. Just nothing much nipped at my heels. And I'm glad. You, now, you been chasin' bubbles since the first day I saw you. And that's fine —for *you*! My own view is, I got it better than most people. Look, we started out close to even, way back yonder. How come —you remember Joe Bob Frady—how come he stole everything that wasn't nailed down and is doing life for habitual . . . uh . . . criminality? How come Bert Childress made all As and Bs and drives a goddamn truck? How come Morris Scroggins made a draftsman, or Ed Wooten carried the same city mail route for twenty years and dropped dead last summer at forty-three? I don't know, shit, you got me rambling on here like I'm crazy.

"We talk down here about cars and our kids and football. We cuss the politicians, and we laugh a lot. Hell, I don't know, you don't laugh all that much. Tomorrow—day or two, anyway—

you'll fly off on an airplane to some damn stinking crowded city. Maybe some nut'll blow it up with a bomb. Won't anybody ever know if it was a Jew or a A-rab or somebody tryin' to collect insurance. Or you'll be going to a New York drugstore and a damn nigger dope fiend you never saw before might walk up and stab your ass to death. Now, sure, I could start to work tomorrow and get killed in a car wreck on the Andrews Highway. But it would be *different.* I'd be somebody's fault, it'd be common, and folks would say, 'Well, shit, poor old Kent. Somebody run a stop sign.' It'd be something you could understand."

I was in a fog now, unsteady and red-eyed, trying to separate the men we had become from the boys we had been, boys who'd known such common roots and experiences that one might have presumed they never would have gone in such divergent directions. A risky assumption, of course, and—obviously—a patently false premise. Were our differences planted in the genes, so that our futures had been predestined and beyond our control, or did it amount to no more than that I had gone away while Kent Hardy had not? I looked on my old friend as a stranger; yet somewhere in all the confusions I still felt some stubborn hard core of love. And yet, and yet . . . I was impatient with him because he'd never risked the full adventure of himself. If he didn't owe it to the rest of us, had he not owed that risk to himself?

Kent inexplicably was shaking my hand, gripping it tight, in the manner of the fundamentalist evangelicals of my youth when they'd tried to coax young recalcitrants forward to accept Christ Jesus. "Come on home," he said. "Come on back down here, goddammit, and relax."

"Yeah," I said. "Well . . ."

There was just no way to tell him that I laughed less there, and relaxed less there, than any place on the map.

4 ☆

Playing Cowboy

When I was young, I didn't know that when you leave a place,
it may not be forever. The past, I thought, had served its full
uses and could bury its own dead; bridges were for burning;
"good-bye" meant exactly what it said. One never looked back
except to judge how far one had come.

Texas was the place I left behind. And not reluctantly. The
leave-taking was so random I trusted the United States Army to
relocate me satisfactorily. It did, in 1946, choosing to establish
in Queens (then but a five-cent subway ride from the clamorous
glamour of Manhattan) a seventeen-year-old former farm boy
and small-town sapling green enough to challenge chlorophyll.
The assignment would shape my life far more than I then suspected; over the years it would teach me to "play cowboy"—
to become, strangely, more "Texas" than I had been.

New York offered everything to make an ambitious kid dizzy;
I moved through its canyons in a hot walking dream. Looking
back, I see myself starring in a bad movie I then accepted as
high drama: the Kid, a.k.a. the Bumptious Innocent, discovering the theater, books, a bewildering variety of nightclubs and
bars; subways and skyscrapers and respectable wines. There
were glancing encounters with Famous Faces: Walter Win-

chell, the actor Paul Kelly, the ex-heavyweight champion Max Baer, bandleader Stan Kenton. It was easy; spotting them, I simply rushed up, stuck out my hand, sang out my name, and began asking personal questions.

Among my discoveries was that I dreaded returning to Texas; where were its excitements, celebrities, promises? As corny as it sounds, one remembers the final scene of that bad movie. Crossing the George Washington Bridge in a Greyhound bus in July 1949—Army discharge papers in my duffel bag—I looked back at Manhattan's spires and actually thought, *I'll be back, New York.* I did not know that scene had been played thousands of times by young men or young women from the provinces, nor did I know that New York cared not a whit whether we might honor the pledge. In time, I got back. On my recent forty-sixth birthday, it dawned that I had spent more than half my life—or twenty-four years—on the eastern seaboard. I guess there's no getting around the fact that this makes me an expatriate Texan.

"Expatriate" remains an exotic word. I think of it as linked to Paris or other European stations in the 1920s: of Sylvia Beach and her famous bookstore; of Hemingway, Fitzgerald, Dos Passos, Ezra Pound, and Gertrude Stein Stein Stein. There is wine in the Paris air, wine and cheese and sunshine, except on rainy days when starving young men in their attics write or paint in contempt of their gut rumbles. Spain. The brave bulls. Dublin's damp fog. Movable feasts. *That's* what "expatriate" means, so how can it apply to one middle-aged grandfather dodging Manhattan's muggers and dogshit pyramids while grunting a son through boarding school and knocking on the doors of magazine editors? True expatriates, I am certain, do not wait in dental offices, the Port Authority Bus Terminal, or limbo. Neither do they haunt their original root sources three or four times each year, while dreaming of accumulating enough money to return home in style as a gentlemanly rustic combining the best parts of J. Frank Dobie, Lyndon Johnson, Stanley Walker, and the Old Man of the Mountain. Yet that is my story, and that is my plan.

I miss the damned place. Texas is my mind's country, that place I most want to understand and record and preserve. Four generations of my people sleep in its soil; I have children there, and a grandson; the dead past and the living future tie me to it. Not that I always approve it or love it. It vexes and outrages and disappoints me—especially when I am there. It is now the third most urbanized state, behind New York and California, with all the tangles, stench, random violence, architectural rape, historical pillage, neon blight, pollution, and ecological imbalance the term implies. Money and mindless growth remain high on the list of official priorities, breeding a crass boosterism not entirely papered over by an infectious energy. The state legislature—though improving as slowly as an old man's mending bones—still harbors excessive, coon-ass, rural Tory Democrats who fail to understand that 79.7 percent of Texans have flocked to urban areas and may need fewer farm-to-market roads, hide-and-tick inspectors, or outraged orations almost comically declaiming against welfare loafers, creeping socialism, the meddling ol' feds, and sin in the aggregate.

Too much, now, the Texas landscape sings no native notes. The impersonal, standardized superhighways—bending around or by most small towns, and then blatting straightaway toward the urban sprawls—offer homogenized service stations, fast-food-chain outlets, and cluttered shopping centers one might find duplicated in Ohio, Maryland, Illinois, or Anywhere, U.S.A. Yes, there is much to make me protest, as did Mr. Faulkner's Quentin Compson, of the South—"I *don't* hate it. I don't hate it, I *don't.* . . . " For all its shrinkages of those country pleasures I once eschewed, and now covet and vainly wish might return, Texas remains in my mind's eye that place to which I shall eventually return to rake the dust for my formative tracks; that place where one hopes to grow introspective and wise as well as old. It is a romantic foolishness, of course; the opiate dream of a nostalgia junkie. When I go back to stay—and I fancy that I will—there doubtless will be opportunities to wonder at my plan's imperfections.

For already I have created in my mind, you see, an improbable corner of paradise: the rustic, rambling ranch house with the clear-singing creek nearby, the clumps of shade trees (under which, possibly, the Sons of the Pioneers will play perpetual string-band concerts), the big cozy library where I will work and read and cogitate between issuing to the Dallas *Times-Herald* or the Houston *Post* those public pronouncements befitting an Elder Statesman of Life and Letters. I will become a late-blooming naturalist and outdoorsman: hiking and camping, and piddling in cattle; never mind that to date I have preferred the sidewalks of New York, and my beef not on the hoof but tricked up with mushroom sauces.

All this will occur about one easy hour out of Austin—my favorite Texas city—and exactly six miles from a tiny, unnamed town looking remarkably like what Walt Disney would have built for a cheery, heart-tugging Texas-based story happening about 1940. The nearest neighbor will live 3.7 miles away, have absolutely no children or dogs, but will have one beautiful young wife, who adores me; it is she who will permit me, by her periodic attentions, otherwise to live the hermit's uncluttered life. Politicians will come to my door hats in hand, and fledging Poets and young Philosophers. Basically, they will want to know exactly what is Life's Purpose. Looking out across the gently blowing grasslands, past the grazing blooded cattle, toward a perfect sunset, with even the wind in my favor, and being the physical reincarnation of Hemingway with a dash of Twain in my mood, I shall—of course—be happy to tell them.

Well, we all know that vast gap between fantasy and reality when True Life begins playing the scenario. Likely I will pay twice to thrice the value for a run-down old "farmhouse" where the plumbing hasn't worked since Coolidge, and shall die of a heart attack while digging a cesspool. The nearest neighbor will live directly across the road; he will own seven rambunctious children, five mad dogs, and an ugly harridan with sharp elbows, a shrill voice, and a perverse hatred for dirty old writing men. The nearest town—less than a half mile away and growing by leaps, separated from my digs only by a subdivision of mock Bavarian castles and the new smeltering plant—will be made of plastics, paved parking lots, and puppy-dog tails. The trip to Austin will require three hours if one avoids rush-hour crushes; when I arrive—to preen in Scholz Garten or The Raw Deal or other watering holes where artists congregate—people will say, "Who's that old fart?" Unfortunately I may try to tell them. My books will long have been out of print; probably my secret yearning will be to write a column for the local weekly newspaper. Surrounded by strangers, memories, and galloping growth, I shall sit on my porch—rocking and cackling and talking gibberish to the wind—while watching them build yet another Kwik Stop Kwality Barbecue Pit on the west edge of my crowded acreage. Occasionally I will walk the two dozen yards to the interstate highway to throw stones at passing trucks; my ammunition will peter out long before traffic does. But when I die digging that cesspool, by God, I'll have died at home. That knowledge makes me realize where my heart is.

But the truth, dammit, is that I feel much more the Texan when in the East. New Yorkers, especially, encourage and expect one to perform a social drill I think of as "playing cowboy." Even as a young soldier I discovered a presumption among a high percentage of New Yorkers that my family owned shares in the King Ranch and that my natural equestrian talents were unlimited; all one needed to affirm such groundless suspicions were a drawl and a grin. To this day you may spot me in Manhattan wearing boots and denim jeans with a matching vest and western-cut hat—topped by a furry cattleman's coat straight out of Marlboro Country; if you've seen Dennis Weaver play McCloud, then you've seen me, without my beard.

Never mind that I *like* such garb, grew up wearing it, or that I find it natural, practical, and inexpensive; no, to a shameful degree, I dress for my role. When I learned that Princeton University would pay good money to a working writer for teaching his craft—putting insulated students in touch with the workaday salts and sours of the literary world—do you think I went down there wrapped in an ascot and puffing a briar pipe from Dunhill's? No, good neighbors, I donned my Cowboy Outfit to greet the selection committee and aw-shucksed and consarned 'em half to death; easterners just can't resist a John Wayne quoting Shakespeare; I've got to admit there's satisfaction in it for every good ol' boy who country-slicks the city dudes.

New Yorkers tend to think of Mississippians or Georgians or Virginians under the catchall category of "southerners," of Californians as foreigners, and of Texans as the legendary Texan. We are the only outlanders, I think, that they define within a specific state border and assign the burden of an obligatory— i.e., "cowboy"—culture. Perhaps we court such treatment; let it be admitted that Texans are a clannish people. We tend to think of ourselves as Texans no matter how long ago we strayed or how tenuous our home connections. When I enter a New York store and some clerk—alerted by my nasal twang—asks where I am from, I do not answer "East Thirty-second Street," but "Texas," yet my last permanent address there was surrendered when Eisenhower was freshly President and old George Blanda was little more than a rookie quarterback.

More than half my close friends—and maybe 20 percent of my overall eastern seaboard acquaintances—are expatriate Texans: writers, musicians, composers, editors, lawyers, athletes, showfolk, a few businessmen, and such would-be politicians or former politicians as Bill Moyers and Ramsey Clark.

Don Meredith, Liz Smith, Judy Buie, Dan Jenkins, you name 'em, and to one degree or another we play cowboy together. Many of us gather for chili suppers, tell stories with origins in Fort Worth or Odessa or Abilene; sometimes we even play dominoes or listen to country-western records.

There is, God help us, an organization called The New York Texans, and about 2,000 of us actually belong to it. We meet each March 2—Texas Independence Day—to drink beer, hoohaw at each other in the accents of home, and honor some myth that we can, at best, only ill define. We even have our own newspaper, published quarterly by a lady formerly of Spur, Texas, which largely specializes in stories bragging on how well we've done in the world of the Big Apple. Since people back home are too busy to remind us of our good luck and talents, we remind ourselves.

No matter where you go, other Texans discover you. Sometimes they are themselves expatriates, sometimes tourists, sometimes business-bent travelers. In any case, we whoop a mutual recognition, even though we're strangers or would be unlikely to attract each other if meeting within our native borders. Indeed, one of the puzzling curiosities is why the Dallas banker, or the George Wallace fanatic who owns the little dry-goods store in Beeville, and I may drop all prior plans in order to spend an evening together in Monterrey or Oshkosh when —back home—we would consider each other social lepers. Many times I have found myself buddy-buddying with people not all that likable or interesting, sharing Aggie jokes or straight tequila shots or other peculiarities of home.

If you think that sounds pretty dreadful, it often is. Though I am outraged when called a "professional Texan," or when I meet one, certainly I am not always purely innocent. Much of it is a big put-on, of course. We enjoy sharing put-ons against those who expect all Texans to eat with the wrong fork, offer coarse rebel yells, and get all vomity-drunk at the nearest football game. There is this regional defensiveness—LBJ would have known what I mean—leading us to order "a glass of clabber and a mess of chitlins" when faced by the haughty ministrations of the finest French restaurants. (My group does, anyway, though I don't know about the stripe of Texan epitomized, say, by Rex Reed; that bunch has got so smooth you can't see behind the sheen). I hear my Texas friends, expatriates and otherwise, as their accents thicken and their drawls slow down on approaching representatives of other cultures. I observe them as they attempt to come on more lordly and sophisticated than Dean Acheson or more country than Ma and Pa Kettle, depending on what they feel a need to prove.

That they (or I) need to prove anything is weird in itself. It tells you what they—yes, the omnipotent They—put in our young Texas heads. The state's history is required teaching in the public schools, and no student by law may escape the course. They teach Texas history very much fumigated—the Alamo's martyrs, the Indian-killing frontiersmen, the heroic Early Day Pioneers, the Rugged Plainsmen, the Builders and Doers; these had hearts pure where others were soiled—and they teach it and teach it and teach it. I came out of the public schools of Texas knowing naught of Disraeli, Darwin, or Darrow —though well versed in the lore of Sam Houston, Stephen F. Austin, Jim Bowie, the King Ranch, the Goodnight-Loving Trail over which thundered the last of the big herds. No school day was complete but that we sang "The Eyes of Texas," "Texas Our Texas," "Beautiful Texas." I mean, try substituting "Rhode Island" or "North Dakota," and it sounds about half-silly even to a Texan. We were taught again and again that Texas was the biggest state, one of the richest, possibly the toughest, surely the most envied. Most Americans, I guess, grow up convinced that their little corners of the universe are special; Texas, however, takes care to institutionalize the preachment.

To discover a wider world, then, where others fail to hold

those views—to learn that Texans are thought ignorant or rich or quite often both, though to the last in number capable of sitting a mean steed—is to begin at once a new education and feel sneaky compulsions toward promoting useless old legends. Long after I knew that the Texas of my youth dealt more with myth than reality, and long past that time when I knew that the vast majority of Texans lived in cities, I continued to play cowboy. This was a social and perhaps a professional advantage in the East; it marked one as unique, permitted one to pose as a son of yesterday, furnished a handy identity among the faceless millions. In time one has a way of becoming in one's head something of the role one has assumed. Often I have actually felt myself the reincarnation or the extension of the old range lords or bedroll cowpokes or buffalo hunters. Such playacting is harmless so long as one confines it to wearing costumes or to speech patterns—"I'm a-hankerin' for a beefsteak, y'all, and thank I'll mosey on over to P. J. Clarke's"—but becomes counterproductive unless regulated. Nobody has been able to coax me atop a horse since that day a dozen years ago when I proved to be the most comic equestrian ever to visit a given riding stable on Staten Island. Misled by my range garb, accent, and sunlamp tan, the stable manager assigned what surely must have been his most spirited steed. Unhorsed after much graceless grabbing and grappling, I heard my ride described by a laughing fellow with Brooklyn in his voice: "Cheez, at foist we thought youse was a trick rider. But just before youse fell, we seen youse wasn't nothing but a shoemaker."

Though I wear my Texas garb in Texas, I am more the New Yorker there; not so much in my own mind, perhaps, as in the minds of others. People hold me to account for criticisms I've written of Texas or accuse me of having gone "New York" in my thinking or attitudes. "Nobody's more parochial than a goddamn New Yorker," some of my friends snort—and often they are right. I, too, feel outraged at Manhattan cocktail parties when some clinch-jawed easterner makes it clear he thinks that everything on the wrong side of the George Washington Bridge is quaint, hasn't sense enough to come in from the rain, and maybe lacks toilet training. Yet my Texas friends have their own misconceptions of my adopted home and cause me to defend it. They warn of its violent crime, even though Houston annually vies with Detroit for the title of "Murder Capital of the World." They deride New York's slums and corruptions, even though in South El Paso (and many another Texas city) may be found shameful dirt poverty and felonious social neglect, and Texas erupts in its own political Watergates—banking, insurance, real estate scandals—at least once each decade. So I find myself in the peculiar defense of New York, waving my arms, and my voice growing hotter, saying things like "You goddamn Texans gotta learn that you're not so damned special. . . ." *You* goddamn Texans, now.

My friends charge that despite my frequent visits home and my summering on Texas beaches, my view of the place is hopelessly outdated. Fletcher Boone, an Austin artist and entrepreneur—now owner of The Raw Deal—was the latest to straighten out my thinking. "All you goddamn expatriates act like time froze somewhere in the nineteen-fifties or earlier," he said. "You'd think we hadn't discovered television down here, or skin flicks, or dope. Hell, we grew us a *President* down here. We've got tall buildings and long hairs and some of us know how to ski!" Mr. Boone had recently visited New York and now held me to account for its sins: "It's mental masturbation. You go to a party up there, and instead of people making real conversation, they stop the proceedings so somebody can sing opera or play the piano or do a tap dance. It's show biz, man—buncha egomaniacal people using a captive audience to stroke themselves. Whatta they talk about? 'I, I, I. Me, me, me. Mine, mine, mine.' " Well, no, I rebut; they also talk about books, politics, and even *ideas;* only the middle of these, I say, is likely to be remarked in Texas. Boone is offended; he counterattacks that easterners do not live life so much as they attempt to dissect it or, worse, dictate how others should live it by the manipulations of fashion, art, the media. We shout gross generalities, over-statements, "facts" without support. I become the Visiting Smart-ass New Yorker, losing a bit of my drawl.

Well, bless him, there may be something to Fletcher Boone's charge, I found recently when I returned as a quasi sociologist. It was my plan to discover some young, green blue-collar or white-collar, recently removed to the wicked city from upright rural upbringings, and record that unfortunate hick's slippages or shocks. Then I would return to the hick's small place of origin, comparing what he or she had traded for a mess of modern city pottage; family graybeards left behind would be probed for their surrogate shocks and would reveal their fears for their urbanized young. It would be a whiz of a story, having generational gaps and cultural shocks and more disappoint-ments or depletions than the Nixon White House. It would be at once nostalgic, pitiful, and brave; one last angry shout against modernity before Houston sinks beneath the waves, Lubbock dries up and blows away for lack of drinking water, and Dallas-Fort Worth grows together as firmly as Siamese twins. Yes, it would have everything but three tits and, perhaps, originality.

Telephone calls to old friends produced no such convenient study. Those recommended turned out to have traveled abroad, attended college in distant places, or otherwise been educated by an urban, mobile society. A young airline hostess in Houston talked mainly of San Francisco or Hawaii; a bank clerk in Dallas sniggered that even in high school days he had spent most of his weekends away from his native village—in city revelry—and thought my idea of "cultural shock" quaint; a petrochemical plant worker failed to qualify when he said, "Shit, life's not all that much different. I live here in Pasadena"

—an industrial morass with all the charms and odors of Gary, Indiana—"and I go to my job, watch TV, get drunk with my buddies. Hail, it's not no different from what it was back there in Monahans. Just more traffic and more people and a little less sand." I drove around the state for days, depressed by the urbanization of my former old outback even as I marveled at its energy, before returning to New York, where I might feel, once more, like a Texan: where I might play cowboy; dream again the ancient dreams.

It is somehow easier to conjure up the Texas I once knew from Manhattan. What an expatriate most remembers are not the hardscrabble times of the 1930s, or the narrow attitudes of a people not then a part of the American mainstream, but a way of life that was passing without one's then realizing it. Quite without knowing it, I witnessed the last of the region's horse culture. Schoolboys tied their mounts to mesquite trees west of the Putnam school and at noon fed them bundled roughage; the pickup truck and the tractor had not yet clearly won out over the horse, though within the decade they would. While the last of the great cattle herds had long ago disappeared up the Chisholm or the Goodnight-Loving Trail, I would see small herds rounded up on my Uncle Raymond's Bar-T-Bar Ranch and loaded from railside corrals for shipment to the stockyards of Fort Worth—or "Cowtown," as it was then called without provoking smiles. (The rough-planked saloons of the brawling North Side of "Cowtown," near the old stockyards, are gone now save for a small stretch lacquered and refurbished in a way so as to make tourists feel they've been where they ain't.) In Abilene, only thirty-two miles to the west, I would hear the chants of cattle auctioneers while smelling feedlot dung, tobacco, saddle leather, and the sweat of men living the outdoor life. Under the watchful eye of my father, I sometimes rode a gentle horse through the shinnery and scrub oaks of the old family farm, helping him bring in the five dehorned milk cows while pretending to be a bad-assed gunslinger herding long-horns on a rank and dangerous trail drive.

But it was all maya, illusion. Even a dreaming little tad knew the buffalo hunters were gone, along with the old frontier forts, the Butterfield stage, the first sodbusters whose barbed wire fenced in the open range and touched off wars continuing to serve Clint Eastwood or James Arness. This was painful knowledge for one succored on myths and legends, on real-life tales of his father's boyhood peregrinations in a covered wagon. Nothing of my original time and place, I felt, would be worth living through or writing about. What I did not then realize (and continue having trouble remembering) is that the past never was as good as it looks from a distance.

The expatriate, returning, thus places an unfair burden upon his native habitat: He demands it to have impossibly marked time, to have marched in place, during the decades he has absented himself. He expects it to have preserved itself as his mind recalls it; to furnish evidence that he did not memorize in vain its legends, folk and folklore, mountains and streams and villages. Never mind that he may have removed himself to other places because they offered rapid growth, new excitements, and cultural revolutions not then available at home.

We expatriate sons may sometimes be unfair: too critical; fail to give due credit; employ the double standard. Especially do those of us who write flay Texas in the name of our disappointments and melted snows. Perhaps it's good that we do this, the native press being so boosterish and critically timid; but there are times, I suspect, when our critical duty becomes something close to a perverse pleasure. Easterners I have known, visiting my homeplace, come away impressed by its dynamic qualities; they see a New Frontier growing in my native bogs, a continuing spirit of adventure, a bit of trombone and swashbuckle, something fresh and good. Ah, but they did not know Texas when she was young.

There is a poignant tale told by the writer John Graves of the last, tamed remnants of a formerly free and proud Indian tribe in Texas: how a small band of them approached an old rancher, begged a scrawny buffalo bull from him, and—spurring their thin ponies—clattered and whooped after it, running it ahead of them, and killed it in the old way—with lances and arrows. They were foolish, I guess, in trying to hold history still for one more hour; probably I'm foolish in the same sentimental way when I sneak off the freeways to snake across the Texas back roads in search of my own past. But there are a couple of familiar stretches making the ride worth it; I most remember one out in the lonely windblown ranch country, between San Angelo and Water Valley, with small rock-dotted hills ahead at the end of a long, flat stretch of road bordered by grasslands, random clumps of trees, wild flowers, grazing cattle, a single distant ranch house whence—one fancies—issues the perfume of baking bread, simmering beans, beef over the flames. There are no billboards, no traffic cloverleafs, no neon, no telephone poles, no Jiffy Tacos or Stuckey's stands, no oil wells, no Big Rich Bastards, no ship channels threatening to ignite because of chemical pollutions, no Howard Johnson flavors. Though old Charley Goodnight lives, Lee Harvey Oswald and Charles Whitman remain unborn.

Never have I rounded the turn leading into that peaceful valley, with the spiny ridge of hills beyond it, that I failed to feel new surges and exhilarations and hope. For a precious few moments I exist in a time warp: I'm back in Old Texas, under a high sky, where all things are again possible and the wind blows free. Invariably, I put the heavy spurs to my trusty Hertz or Avis steed: go flying lickety-split down that lonesome road, whooping a crazy yell and taking deep joyous breaths, sloshing Lone Star beer on my neglected dangling safety belt, and scattering roadside gravel like bursts of buckshot. Ride 'im, cowboy! *Ride* 'im. . . .

Part II ☆
Others

of outlaws, con men, whores,
and other artists

☆

Interlude

I like to write about the underside of our society.

In my early twenties I was a police reporter in Texas and New Mexico. There I saw, and wrote about, all manner of gore and small-bore corruptions: hot-blooded killings and cold-blooded ones, fatal accidents ranging from automobile crashes to lightning bolts, passionate trials, crooked cops, racist judges; thieves and thugs and con men.

One story got two deputies fired, and almost sent to prison, for physically abusing prostitutes; another series persuaded a grand jury to change a police verdict from death by suicide to a murder never solved. I once was threatened with jail for refusing to identify a certain news source to a highly irritated grand jury, because everything it did or said in secret kept appearing in print under my by-line; I *couldn't* reveal my source, he being the district attorney, without seeing him go to jail and possibly being disbarred. On the other hand, I didn't hanker to go to jail in his stead. So I simply lied to the grand jury, in itself a criminal offense, by claiming I'd received all these anonymous calls from a voice I'd never heard before and was unable to identify. Once I falsely impersonated an FBI agent (in order to get the goods on the deputies who'd abused the prostitutes); too often, I'm afraid, I took shortcuts that may have infringed on the civil liberties of others and certainly played havoc with due process. I don't believe I'd do much of that again. For one thing I'm more civilized; for another, I'm older and tamer. Back in those days I had both cops and robbers tell me to my face that they'd soon see me dead; I never for a moment believed any of them, putting it down to big talk by little men. Now I might pause to evaluate them more carefully. I loved those raw old days, God help me, more than was becoming. And to some extent I miss them.

It was my good fortune that my recreational habits helped me get stories and gain new insights into the people I wrote about. I frequented the beer joints of the Southwest—"fightin' and dancin' clubs"—because I loved (a) country music, (b) beer, and (c) the kinds of characters to be found in those crazy places—though not necessarily in that order. I met there and became friends with a man still doing life in Texas as a habitual criminal —he was a killer, armed robber, and safecracker—who, for years, each Christmas sent me a leather billfold he'd hand-tooled in the prison craft shop. I first learned from a commercial "working girl" in such a place of the physical abuse being heaped upon prostitutes by crooked deputies who also took their money for allowing them to work. A police informer in such a joint told me why a certain big-time gambler was permitted to operate in a posh section of town—drawing the community's best blood as regular customers—while two-bit games were busted in the town's black section; again, payoff money was involved as well as racism. In those scabby bars, and behind bars of quite a different kind, I met con men, dope traffickers, double-crossers, and not a few singing cowboys and cowgirls bursting with raw poetry trying to get out. Thanks for the memories, old pals, and for your hand in my laborious education.

For a time, in those formative writing years, my fellow reporters joshed me as "Friend of the Whore." I was always sympathetic to whores, and it was for more reasons than that they provided better services to mankind than do, say, most preachers or bankers. I think it was because I sensed something of the tough lives they lead and didn't believe they needed to be harassed beyond the bounds of the law. The law is hard enough on outcasts without other people winking when those in authority step beyond it. Never for a moment did I believe in the myth of "the whore with a heart of gold." Most whores are indescribably screwed up and abysmally ignorant: all the more reason to help them if you can. And it's nice when, years later, they inadvertently help you. . . .

There is some poetic justice in my biggest commercial success to date having been written about whores—though, I like to fancy, *The Best Little Whorehouse in Texas* is about more than that. It began as a magazine article in *Playboy* (pretty much as you'll find it in the upcoming section), and with the help of my collaborators—Peter Masterson and Carol Hall; plus the choreography and staging talents of Tommy Tune—it has become, in turn, an Off-Off-Broadway success at Lee Strasberg's Actors Studio; an Off-Broadway smash; and, ultimately, a Broadway hit. I am now writing a novel by the same title. And the motion-picture rights to *Whorehouse* have been bought by Universal. *Hooray* for whores, I say! God love 'em!

The other pieces in the upcoming section deal with people or things I'd secretly love to be: a country-western star, a cool big-time gambler, a smart trader, and a badass that everybody likes. I hope it won't take too much drama away to admit I've never had much luck being any of those.

5 ☆

Mr. Badass
Is Back in Town

There he is up on the stage under that outlandish foot-tall Montana Dick hat like Tom Mix wore (only his is black, where Mix paraded white to signify a Good Guy purity), spangled in rhinestones from crown to spur, hulking and profane in your basic badass black, sometimes wearing a Lone Ranger mask and *always* careful to get it on record how he's meaner than a junkyard dog. *Yes, sir, folks, step right up and tremble in the presence of David Allan Coe, a.k.a. the Mysterious Rhinestone Cowboy. See the baddest mutha on the country-music scene or perhaps this side of hell's rowdier slags.* If you are not willing to accept that view of David Allan Coe, he may threaten to ruin your chops. At the very least he will tell you—as he often confides to his fans from the podium—of having spent time on death row because of hitting a fellow inmate in an Ohio prison and having such bad luck that the inmate proved to be such a sissy he died.

Right now, though—on this funky-warm February evening at Gilly's Club in Pasadena, an industrial sore linked to South Houston by an invisible border and shared malodors—David Allan Coe is ranting against "them assholes from *Rolling Stone*" and promising to whup up on 'em if they don't quit a-slandering him. Then he dedicates to that magazine's writers and editors an original composition, "I'd Like to Kick the Shit Out of You." The crowd whoops and stomps as if chasing the devil with big sticks, howling along with the gut-jangling guitars, and you know that ol' badass has reached right out and touched their primitive parts as instinctively as Lester Maddox or Huey Long might. Coe struts and scowls, belting the song, and a tough-faced little blonde in blue jeans tight enough to strangle sausage jumps up and down and shouts, "That sumbitch got more balls than a truckloada elephants."

At the conclusion of the song (a spoof of hippie and redneck attitudes toward each other), he swaggers to the mike and says, "Them *Rolling Stone* motherfuckers better be glad the old Rhinestone Cowboy ain't lost his sense of humor, or I might hire me about three go-rillas to kick ass. Wouldn't soil my hands on 'em myself." He nods in appreciation of the laughter and says, "Y'all hear about ol' Willie Nelson passing out onstage in Dallas the other night? Somebody said Willie got his pillboxes mixed up and took downers when he meant to take uppers. Well, hell, I been to the drugstore a time or two myself." Now the bad boy boasts of having cussed on a live radio show a couple of nights earlier. "They ought to have known better than to tell me not to," the musical outlaw suggests. "If they hadn't planted the notion in my mind, I probably wouldn't have opened with 'Hello, all you pissant motherfuckers in radioland.'" Sometimes, though Coe obviously wants his music taken seriously, one gets the notion he sings so as to be able between numbers to tell tall tales on himself or attack his enemies.

David Allan Coe has the red eye at *Rolling Stone* because they started the rumor he never killed nobody. Imagine! Who'd *they* ever kill, huh? They sit around in an air-conditioned office, where there ain't a bit of heavy lifting, and tap their limp wrists on the keyboard, and out jumps pure character assassination: tales that try to ruin a bad man's reputation just because he can't produce a body these twelve or thirteen years later. Next thing you know, *Country Music* officially doubts Coe's guilt, and then a goddamn TV station down in Dallas, and before long— if you don't watch it—the music fans and groupies out there in radioland and albumland and nightclubland are gonna start having *their* doubts. And that, good buddy, can get real expensive in a hurry. Now's just not the time for all that loose-lipped talk, no, sir! Not with Coe just starting to hit the good money, just beginning to pack 'em into the beer joints and coffeehouses at cover charges up to seven and a half a head. Why, hell, other night at the Exit Inn in Nashville even *Johnny Cash* wandered in to catch the show. Now, just as Coe's on the Top Forty charts with his first hit single ("You Never Even Called Me By My Name"), and just when he's beginning to sniff big royalties as a writer after the success Tanya Tucker made of his "Would You Lay with Me in a Field of Stone," the media are threatening all that, and Coe and his camp followers are as disgruntled with 'em as Spiro Agnew ever was.

Prison's a big thing with country-western musicians, almost a badge of honor. Spade Cooley, the old king of western swing, made it by stabbing his wife; Merle Haggard made it by entering locked shops or strange automobiles; Johnny Cash made the El Paso jail for bringing a guitar full of energy pills across from Mexico, before June and Jesus straightened him out; Jerry Jeff Walker wrote "Mr. Bojangles" as a result of breaking into the New Orleans jail on charges of rowdy conduct; Willie Nelson has been caught driving his car while full of many mood modifiers; Johnny Paycheck did time in a Navy brig for having assaulted a superior officer. Just about every country-western performer lucky enough to make traffic court sings of his outlaw days at some personal profit and badgers the nation's wardens to permit him to cut his albums behind the walls. Each of them may be tempted to tough up his criminal record a bit; there was a time when Cash made his stay in the El Paso jail sound like five years in Yuma Prison on piss and punk, though a lawyer named Woodrow Wilson Bean sprung him so quickly Johnny just barely had time to drink a cup of jailhouse coffee.

Where Coe differs from your routine outlaw singing cowboy is in his public approach to his checkered past. Haggard, Cash, et al. come on about half-shamefaced, crediting, in voices vibrant with pious sincerity, this old granny or that old flame or maybe even the Good Lord Himself for having pointed them toward more righteous paths. They are repented sinners at the mourners' bench; black sheep now safely back in the fold. None of that redeemed-soul jazz for David Allan Coe, baby. From the podium, he remains defiant: still the incorrigible rebel; still society's victim; still ready to extract Old Testament vengeance.

It has not escaped Coe that his fans eat it up, that—much like the more cerebral disciples of Norman Mailer—they expect for their door prices to see Peck's bad boy give the world a stiff middle finger and howl at the moon. So Coe thrusts his pelvic regions toward the microphone in Pasadena and growls to the expectant crowd, "I got a new album that's about three weeks overdue. They say they ain't gonna release it till I quit my public cussin'. Well . . . mutha*fuck* that shit!" Those cheering his stubborn courage have no way of knowing that, only hours before, Coe learned the album's release date had been pushed back because of purely technical problems.

When David Allan Coe hit Nashville about eight years ago— straight out of the Ohio penitentiary, it's true—he met the usual beanery and flophouse disappointments of your average unknown dreamer. He first called attention to himself by inventing the dark Rhinestone Cowboy image. Next, he bought a secondhand hearse, painted his name all over it, and parked it near crumbling old Ryman Auditorium (then the home of the Grand Ole Opry), feeding parking meters all day in the hope that well-connected Music City folk might become curious about him and that one thing might lead to another. Nashville had witnessed too many desperate acts, however, to get excited over one more hungry schemer wearing trick britches and a big hat while wasting his nickels. Coe's brother, Jac, recalls: "David started going into Tootsie's Orchid Lounge and places where the big shots dropped in, and I mean he *intimidated* people into hearing his songs. Threatened to wipe the floor with 'em if they didn't. And he'd heard, you know, that old expression, 'getting a foot in the door.' Well, David improved on it. Several times he went to publishing companies on Record Row and actually started kicking the door down! Bet your ass that got their attention." Shelby Singleton, who brought out on his SSS International label Coe's original prison-song album (which even Coe now admits was awash with "self-pitying" bad lyrics), has said, "I always figured David's stories were about ninety-two percent bullshit. But it made for good promotion."

Well, now, Shelby, 92 percent may be a little high. Coe *did* get sent away to Boys Industrial School in Akron at age nine, "the unwanted product of a broken home." He *did* serve several terms in prison for various offenses; he *has* scrambled a few folks' faces; and he's done more hard jail time standing on one leg than other country-western outlaws have served sitting down. This record doesn't seem to satisfy his sense of drama, however, since he is forever improving on it. Like his claim of having gone up for armed robbery. Nope, sorry, folks, that was his brother, Jac. And it was his father, not ol' badass himself, who served seventeen years for murder. The Mysterious Rhinestone Cowboy himself seems to have been more a victim of luckless circumstances than a deliberate Clyde Barrow, a kid—friendless and paupered—who became the easy victim of an uncaring system. There is almost a Keystone Kop quality about his record, though there's nothing at all funny about being locked up.

"The first time David went to prison," Jac says, "it was just pitiful, a real railroad job. A friend of ours had shoplifted this overcoat, see. David was about eighteen, and he wanted to look good, so he borrowed it. And he's walking down the street, and the cops stop him. Inside the coat, now, they find some dirty pictures. Hell, you can buy lots worse in most drugstores today. But the heat puts it on David for possession of obscene materials and sends him up. I was at the trial, and even though I was just a fourteen-year-old kid, I saw he didn't stand a chance." Later, joyriding in an automobile to which he had no title, David Allan Coe was busted again. Next, he's in the company of a known burglar when he's arrested, and ultimately convicted, for possession of burglary tools. "A screwdriver," Jac Coe remembers, sipping a beer. "That's all, man. A simple-ass goddamn ordinary fucking screwdriver! But, you know, he had a record."

Beefy and weathered at thirty-six, David Allan Coe advertises that from age nine to age twenty-eight he never "breathed free air" for more than sixty days consecutively. "Seems like my business was always in bad shape." He scowls, sitting in his painted and sloganized road bus (which, he has claimed, fellow ex-con Jimmy Hoffa bought for him not long before presumably getting wrapped in a concrete overcoat). It is almost show time in Pasadena; members of the Tennessee Hat Band scramble for their instruments and coax their strings to proper pitch. Warm-eyed groupies parade their offerings outside the bus, giggling and yammering. "Anything special out there?" Coe asks.

"Naw," one of the sidemen says, "just your usual run of fat asses and pimples. Buncha Mamie Rottencrotches."

"Then close the goddamn door," the bossman barks. One of his several roadies—young drifters who drive for him, toting and fetching as needed and jumping when he wishes—rushes to obey. Coe leans back and grins as if to say, *It's good being a star.*

"I got three hundred and sixty-five tattoos on me," Coe suddenly volunteers. "One for every day of the goddamn year." Yeah, well . . . I mean, what do you *say* to that? Congratulations?

Drop your drawers? Apropos of nothing he says, "A sumbitch over here in Houston's suing me for a million bucks, man. He tried to break into my set to make me sing 'Happy Birthday' for his girl friend. I gave the dude a lotta room, man, but he kept pushing. Now he claims I broke him up pretty bad." Coe regards a visiting journalist through half-lidded eyes and says, "I've been thinkin' of kickin' ass every time a reporter shows up around here." The journalist, who has read the threatening line from other interviews, laughs at the suggestion—even if only halfheartedly—and soon ol' badass is laughing, too.

Though the Houston plantiff may find it difficult to believe, and Coe himself may want to slice the gizzard of anyone who says it, the Mysterious Rhinestone Cowboy often can be something of a pussycat. Offstage, or behind the scenes when he forgets to strike poses, he is a curiously soft-spoken man who avoids the company of problem drunks, refuses to tolerate pot smokers on his bus for fear of a bust, is always trying to pick up the check for those around him, and romps with his tiny daughter. A hard worker, he is up at dawn to get his show on the road twenty-odd days each month, scolding and clucking over his charges like an old mother hen; he is not above driving his own bus or poking among its coils to assist repairs. Indeed, when he is not surrounded by scraggly hard-eyed killer bikers, he sometimes seems to tolerate and maybe, sometimes, to half fear, Coe has a gentle sense of humor and alert, intelligent eyes in a strangely placid face.

He clouds up, and his features harden, however, when considering suggestions that he may not be a killer. "My manager tells me if I provide any details, then shit, man, I could find myself facing a murder rap. I mean, man, I'm not gonna make any statements that could be interpreted as a confession. I'd be a damn fool to do that, man. I'm not going back to prison. Hell, I've got used to pussy and different things." This does not prevent his continuing to refer from the stage, however, to the

lonely, scared days and nights he spent on death row awaiting
execution until the Supreme Court rode to the rescue by abol-
ishing capital punishment, save in narrow special circumstances.*

Several things in that particular story are slightly out of joint.
Coe allegedly killed his man about 1963 or 1964; not until eight
or nine years later—by which time the Mysterious Rhinestone
Cowboy was hustling 'em in Nashville—did the Supreme Court
render its blanket decision. Coe since has said he was removed
from death row after *Ohio* repealed the death penalty. But
Ohio never has done that. A second speck in the churn is that
no record exists of David Allan Coe's ever having been tried for
murder in Ohio—or even charged with it. And how do you
make death row without the constitutional niceties having been
at least marginally observed? A member of the Ohio Department of Rehabilitation and Corrections has said, "Don't you
know that if we'd put him on death row without a trial, then
every ACLU chapter in America would have us hanging from
meat hooks?"

Coe's answer is that not everything happening in prison, or
elsewhere, is on the public record: "Look at Watergate, man.
Shit, for a carton of cigarettes I can get anything put into a
prisoner's file or anything scrubbed out. It's common for prison
officials to break the law and cover up. See, you straight dudes
—you don't know how it is in there, man! You and me, we're
comin' from different places in our heads. This TV station down
in Dallas, Channel Thirteen, it got to poking around in this
thing when it was doing a special on me. And they got a letter
from the warden or somebody, admitting that I was on L Block
—which is one and the same as death row, and they damn well
know it. But they said it was for breakin' the mail rules! And that

*Or thought it did, until Florida started leading the way in the late seventies
toward a new enthusiasm for official killing.

was the first time I'd heard that in my life. They can say what
they want to, make up what they want to!"

He is impatient with a rumor that crowded prison conditions
caused him to be randomly and briefly detained on death row
because of a shortage of institutional accommodations: "More
bullshit!" Understandably, he's growing tired of the game:
"Write about my music, man. Music's what I do; I *am* my music,
and I don't want people writing this other stuff anymore. My
parents are old, and all this crap hurts 'em. I don't wanta have
to drag 'em into it, but if we have to go to court, we can. And
they'll bring letters I wrote 'em from death row." Amazing.
Here is a man threatening to sue because some people question
whether he's a killer!

In earlier times (before, in Coe's words, "my credibility was
challenged"), he told a grim yarn of how he was in the prison
shower when another inmate entered and said, "You gonna
suck my dick, baby." Coe quoted himself as saying, "You got the
wrong man." According to various press versions, Coe then
claimed to have fatally clobbered the would-be romantic with
either a mop wringer, a galvanized bucket, a ripped-out shower
head, or a ball peen hammer, all of which sounds as if maybe
Coe was taking a shower in a toolhouse or a hardware store. He
says, however, that irresponsible or careless reporting accounts
for the varied versions: "It was a mop wringer. I've always said
that."

Only after his credibility came to be questioned did Coe
confide that two other prisoners may have been involved; he
has been cagey, naming no names and being stingy with details.
One of his alleged killer pals is represented as later having been
stabbed to death; the second is rumored to have confessed and
"may still be in prison." Though Ohio authorities insist they
have no record of such an incident, Coe says, "Look, if they find
the guy that confessed and he implicates me, then they'll grab
my ass for murder. There ain't *nothin'* the police can't do! If

they exonerate me of any and all crimes like they did Nixon, maybe I'd tell about it." Then, in other moments, he has said, "Man, I ain't confessing to shit. They beat hell out of me, and I wouldn't confess. Why do it now?"

While Coe may or may not be guilty of murder, he swears he isn't guilty of hype: *He* didn't start the sensational story; *Midnight,* the tabloid, ran the first sensational story. Coe recalls that his father was given a copy by a fellow worker at the factory. "To this day I don't know how they got their information. Some chick named Christa Lee wrote it. I called 'em, and they wouldn't tell me shit. From that article alone, other people started writing about it. People would come and ask me, and I'd say, 'Yes, I was on death row.' Why? 'For beatin' a guy to death.' But I wasn't going around shouting it. At that point of my life, I never thought I'd be where I am today, never be this popular, or I wouldn't have talked about it. Because if I have to name names, it will ruin my career."

In fact, Coe's coveted badass image is no longer all that vital to his career. Perhaps it helped him get started—sorted him from others who didn't have a story as promotable—for no matter whether the original yarn was written by a chick named Lee or a chick named Little, David Allan Coe was quick to shout how the sky was falling down. He took the story and ran with it; he glossed it, polished it, and relished it. Now, however, he is an accomplished and smooth professional entertainer, capable of bringing talent to old-fashioned country music, to the newer progressive country—redneck rock—to blues and even to hard rock. The man's good; the man's versatile; he writes fine lyrics, has a stage presence you can't buy and only a few can learn. Even Brother Jac says, "I wish David would change his image. He's on the way now. All that outlaw stuff ain't needed. He's makin' it on merit. Hell, he can even imitate all the greats. Ernest Tubb. Willie Nelson. Waylon Jennings. Haggard. Cash. Hank Williams hisself. You can close your eyes, and you'd think they was right there in the room singing to you."

There is a wink in David Allan Coe's voice when he does the imitations. He is, in fact, one of the few country-western performers to poke fun at the genre, an irreverence to drive the old country straights—Tubb, Roy Acuff, Buck Owens—right up the wall. Coe and Steve Goodman got together to write "the perfect country song," which, they agreed, must have in its final verse something about "Mama and trains and prison and old trucks and being drunk." The result was "You Never Even Call Me By My Name." It was a smash hit.

David Allan Coe is a puzzle. He's a man who, by his mother's recollection, wore dresses until the age of seven and by the age of nine knew only the institutional mercies of Boys Industrial School. He's entitled to certain confusions as to what is real and what is not. I get the notion that whether or not Coe is a killer, he believes he is, believes it as strong as horseradish; that even if it's half hype and half fantasy, all smoke and mirrors, it represents something vital and deep in his craw—something he would *like* to have done—a necessary purge, striking back at all those buckled and badged bastards who've caged him and shoved him and crowded him for almost as long as he can remember. (Coe's private bedroom in his touring bus features, on a wall, mug shots of a younger self, complete with prison-inmate number; under the pictures, and obviously patched in, are the typewritten words "WANTED FOR MURDER!") He is not an insensitive soul—his better song lyrics are proof he's no emotionless potato head—and a boy like that, you take him early and shake him quick and let him brood in isolation behind locks for twenty years or whatever, and, well, he's naturally gonna come out a shade strange as the rest of us measure it, because we're working with very different yardsticks. Myself, there's a dark hunk of me that hopes he really *wasted* that cat.

Almost show time in Pasadena. Coe steps down from the bus into an unseasonably warm February night sponsoring the vanguard of summer's flying creatures and lunges toward Gilly's under a pluperfect Texas moon. "I got arrested twice in one day last week in Nashville," he blurts. "First they busted me because this club owner down there filed papers to repossess my goddamn bus, man. I don't no more than hit the ground until they grab me for this check I'd wrote to buy some horses down in Tennessee. There'd been some mixup about deposits clearing, some such shit. It'll all come out in the wash, but it's been all over the newspapers. You can sing or write the best song in the world, man, but it's that other shit that makes the papers."

He is off then, in a last burst toward the stage, roadies and groupies trailing in his wake. In the spotlight, all his brooding cares seem to drop away; he looks vibrant and full of fresh tonics. Macho. Sardonic. Tough. Almost the first thing he rumbles into the mike is: "An asshole down in Nashville the other day tried to take my bus away from me, and he didn't know who he was fuckin' with. . . ."

He grins a bandit's grin in response to the cheers and rebellious yells, struts in place, and then—singing it hard, coming down on it—he gets his hips going something like the early Elvis used to do, as if dry-humping the world. Yes, sir, folks, ol' badass is back in town. Lock up your women and your money, and don't walk in the shadows.

6 ☆

The Best Little
Whorehouse in Texas

It was as nice a little whorehouse as you ever saw. It sat in a green Texas glade, white-shuttered and tidy, surrounded by leafy oak trees and a few slim renegade pines and the kind of pure, clean air the menthol-cigarette people advertise.

If you had country values in you and happened to stumble upon it, likely you would nod approval and think, *Yes, yes, these folks keep their barn painted and their fences up, and probably they'd do to ride the river with.* There was a small vegetable garden and a watermelon patch, neither lacking care. A good stand of corn, mottled now by bruise-colored blotches and dried to parchment by hot, husky-whispering summer winds, had no one to hear its rustling secrets.

Way back yonder, during the Hoover Depression, they raised chickens out there. Money was hard to come by; every jackrabbit had three families chasing it with the stewpot in mind. Back then, in rural Texas, people said things like "You can hear everthang in these woods but meat afryin' and coins aclankin'." No matter where a boy itched and no matter how high his fevers, it wasn't easy to come up with $3, even in exchange for a girl's sweetest gift. And so the girls began accepting poultry in trade. That's how the place got its name, and if you grew up most anywhere in Texas, you knew at an early age what the Chicken Ranch sold other than pullets.

You might have originally thought it a honeymoon cottage. Except that as you came closer on the winding dirt road that skittered into the woods off the Austin to Houston highway on the southeastern outskirts of La Grange, near the BAD CURVE sign, you would have noticed that it was too sprawling and too jerry-built: running off on odd tangents, owning more sides and nooks and crannies than the Pentagon. It had been built piecemeal, a room added here and there as needed, as with a sod farmer watching his family grow. Then there were all those casement-window air conditioners—fifteen to twenty of 'em, Miss Edna wanting her girls to work in comfort.

Since the 1890s, at least, the Chicken Ranch had been one of the better pleasure palaces in all Texas. You didn't have to worry about clap, as when free-lancing on Postoffice Street in Galveston, or risk your hide in machismo-crazed whore bars on Fort Worth's Jacksboro Highway, where mean-eyed, juiced-up, brilliantined, honky-tonk cowboys presumed themselves a nightly quota of asses to whip. Miss Edna, like Miss Jessie before her, didn't cotton to hard-drinking rowdies. Should you come in bawling profanities or grabbing tits, Miss Edna would employ the telephone. And before you could say double-dip-blankety-blank obscenity, old Sheriff T. J. Flournoy—"Mr. Jim"—would materialize to suggest a choice between overnight lodgings in Fayette County's crossbar hotel and your rapid cooperative leave-taking. The wise or the prudent didn't pause to inquire whether the latter opportunity included a road map. You just did a quick Hank Snow. Yes, neighbors, it was as cozy and comfortable as a family reunion, though many times more profitable. Then, one sad day last summer, the professional meddlers and candy-assed politicians closed 'er down.

God and Moses, what a shock to the 3,092 residents of La Grange, Texas, to say nothing of Chicken Ranch alumni around the world! Imagine corned beef without cabbage, Newcastle without coal, Nixon without crises. The Chicken Ranch was an old and revered Texas institution, second only to the Alamo and maybe Darrell Royal. History lurked there. Some claimed that La Grange had offered love for sale since 1844, back when Texas was a republic, which would put the lie to the Dallas *Morning News'* claim of being Texas's "oldest business institution." For sure, the Chicken Ranch traced, by document, back about sixty years. In a more primitive time, when there were fewer squirming concerns with goddamned imagery, the winning squad of the Texas–Texas A&M football game got invited by joyous alumni to the Chicken Ranch on Thanksgiving night. Think how fiercely a team might fight to win the Pussy Bowl! Yeeeeaaaah, *team!* Anyhow, businessmen and state legislators were comforted during their carnal wanderings; the wise telephoned ahead for reservations. Indigenous hill-country Teutonics, Slavics, and rednecks of many faiths brought their sons in celebration of maturities that an older culture more gently signified by bar mitzvahs.

Man, listen: The Chicken Ranch was gooder than grass and better than rain. Registered with the county clerk as Edna's Ranch Boarding House, it paid double its weight in taxes and led the community in charitable gifts; you could go into the lobby of the gleaming new community hospital and see Miss Edna Milton's name winking at you from the engraved brass plaque honoring donors, the same as the name of the banker's or the preacher's lady. The Chicken Ranch plowed a goodly percentage of its earnings back into local shops to the glee of hairdressers, car dealers, and notions-counter attendants. It was a good citizen, protected and appreciated, its indiscretions winked at.

They say that some years ago a young district attorney, who had made his own sporting calls to the Chicken Ranch, sheepishly appeared at the front door as the reluctant head of a raiding party mobilized by crusading churchwomen. On spotting the young DA, Miss Edna is supposed to have sung out, "Not *now*, George, the law has me surrounded!" And during Prohibition, an old sheriff called on Miss Jessie to say sternly, "I don't like to say nothin', but this *drankin'*, now, has just plain got to stop!" When Miss Jessie died, her obituary identified her as "a local businesswoman." Yeah, they had 'em a real bird's nest on the ground out there. Then along came Marvin Zindler.

Marvin Zindler was a deputy sheriff in Houston, enforcing consumer-protection laws, until they fired him. Not for inefficiency or malfeasance—Lord, no! Marvin wore more guns, handcuffs, buckles, and badges than a troop of Texas Rangers; he brought more folks to court than did bankruptcy proceedings. Some folks said Marvin would jug you for jaywalking; it's of record that he once nabbed a drugstore merchant for failure to stock the kind and size of candy bar at the price the merchant had advertised.

Marvin got fired for being "controversial"—which meant that he couldn't, or wouldn't, make those fine distinctions required of successful politicians. After all, Marvin's boss was dependent on public favor. No, sir, the law was *the law* to Marvin. Soon Houston merchants were screaming of how they received fewer considerations than did common pickpockets or footpads. They howled when Marvin tipped off television stations where he would next put the collar on a Chamber of Commerce member accused of selling fewer soap flakes in a container than its label claimed, and they were outraged when—a time or two —Marvin lurked around the magazine rack while television cameras were established and *then* made his bust.

A lot of good people, long goosed and flummoxed by many avid practitioners of free enterprise, dearly loved and cheered Marvin. But fellow deputies judged him insufficiently bashful when it came to personal publicity, and his superiors soon got a gutful of bitching merchants. Perhaps, too, the more sensitive wearied of daily contact with Marvin's ego, which may be approximately two full sizes larger than Howard Cosell's. Marvin keeps scrapbooks. He dresses like a certified dandy in his 200 tailored suits and has bought himself two nose bobs; he does not permit his own family to view him unless he's wearing one of his many silver hairpieces. Anyhow, they fired Marvin. Who landed on his feet as a television newsman for Houston's Channel 13.

Marvin approached news gathering with the same zeal he'd brought to badge toting. Not for him Watergate values: *The law was the law.* So Marvin began telling the folks out in TVland how a whorehouse was running wide open down the road at La Grange, which was news to Yankee tourists and to all Texans taking their suppers in high chairs. Even though a lot of people yawned, Marvin stayed on the case; you might have thought murder was involved. Soon he repeatedly hinted at "organized crime" influences at the Chicken Ranch.

One day in late July, Marvin Zindler drove to La Grange and accosted Sheriff Flournoy with cameras, microphones, and embarrassing questions. The old sheriff made it perfectly clear he was not real proud to see Marvin. Later the sheriff—a very lean and mean seventy-year-old, indeed—would say he hadn't realized the microphone was live when he chewed on Marvin for meddling in Fayette County affairs; perhaps that explains why the old man peppered his lecture with so many hells and goddamns and shits. Marvin Zindler drove home and displayed the cussing sheriff on television.

Then Marvin called on State Attorney General John Hill and Governor Dolph Briscoe: "How come yawl have failed to close the La Grange sin shop down?" Those good politicians harrumphed and declared their official astonishment that Texas had a whorehouse in it. Marvin told them they'd have to do better than that. Governor Briscoe issued a solemn statement saying that organized crime was a terrible thing, against the

American grain, and since it might possibly be sprouting out at the Chicken Ranch, he would call on local authorities to shutter that sinful place. If they didn't comply, the governor said severely, then he personally would employ the might and majesty of the state to close it. *Me, too,* said Attorney General Hill. Veteran legislators, many of whom could have driven to the Chicken Ranch without headlights even in a midnight rainstorm, expressed concern that Texans might be openly permitted loveless fucks outside the home.

Old Sheriff Flournoy was incensed: "If the governor wants Miss Edna closed, all he's gotta do is make one phone call, and I'll do it." The sheriff may be old and country, but his shit detector tells him when grander men are pissing on his feet and telling him it's a rainstorm. The governor didn't have to bother with the telephone charade. Soon after the story hit the national news wires, Johnny Carson was cracking simpering jokes about it and every idle journalist with a pen was en route to La Grange. They found the Chicken Ranch locked and shuttered, a big CLOSED sign advertising a new purity. Miss Edna and her girls had fled to parts unknown, leaving behind a town full of riled people.

Sheriff Flournoy was extracting his long legs from the patrol car, with maybe nothing more on his mind than a plate of Cottonwood Inn barbecue, when this fat bearded journalist shoved a hand in his face and began singing his credentials. The old lawman recoiled as if he'd spotted a pink snake; for a moment it seemed he might tuck his legs back in and drive away.

But after a slight hesitation he came out, unwinding in full coil to about six feet five inches. Given the tall-crowned cowboy hat, he appeared to register nearer to seven feet three and some-odd. Flournoy is a former Texas Ranger who looks as if he might have posed for that bronze and granite Ranger statue guarding the old Dallas airport lobby. You sense that he knows

how to use that big thumb-busting revolver thumping against
his right leg as expertly as legend insists. The fat bearded journalist also sensed that the old sheriff may have done plumb et
his fill of outsiders asking picky questions; he suddenly remembered that the third wave is the most dangerous one when
beaches are assaulted, the first two waves having stirred things
up and put the locals on notice. So he was real real polite and
friendly, grinning until his jawbone ached, and careful to let all
the old native nasal notes ring, in saying he sure would admire
to talk a little bit about the Chicken Ranch situation, please, sir,
and would the old sheriff kindly give him a few minutes?

The old sheriff's face reddened alarmingly. He stared across
the hot, shimmery Texas landscape, as if searching for menaces
on the horizon, and he rapidly puffed a cigarette; the hand
holding it trembled as if palsied. Then he said, *"Naw!* I'm tard
a-talkin' to you sonsabitches!"

Well. Uh. Ah. Yes. Well, the journalist had come a fer piece;
he had a job to accomplish; he'd hoped the sheriff might—

"You hard a-hearin', boy?"

The journalist cupped one ear and said, "Beg your pardon?"
He didn't want to leave any doubt.

The old sheriff spat. He said, "My town's gettin' a black eye.
All the TVs and newspapers—hell, *all* the mediums—they've
flat lied. Been misquotin' our local people. Makin' 'em look
bad."

Had the sheriff himself been misquoted?

"You goddamned right!"

To what extent?

"About half of it was goddamn lies."

Well, Sheriff, which half ?

The sheriff put a hard eye on the visitor. Puffing the trem-
bling cigarette, he offered a long look at his face. The sight was
no comfort. You had time to concentrate on his mountainous
great beak, deciding: *If he ever gets in a wide-nose contest with*

Nixon, he'll fair threaten the blue ribbon. More terribly, however, the visiting journalist recognized bedrock character and righteous anger, knowing, instinctively, that T. J. Flournoy was the type of man described years ago by his father: *"Son, you got to learn that some folks won't do to fart with."*

Then the sheriff said, "It's pure horseshit what they say about that being a multimillion-dollar operation out yonder. Hell. Goddamn. *Shit!* Them people was just scratchin' out a living like everybody else. The mediums, now, you goddamn people reported Edna running sixteen girls. And in all my years, I never knew more than nine. And it was all lies about organized crime."

Had the sheriff . . . uh, you know . . . received any er—ah—*gratuities* for services to Miss Edna?

The sheriff put his hand on his gun butt—*oh, Jesus!*—and fired twin bursts of pure ol' mad out of his cold blue eyes. "Listen, boy, that place has been open since before I was borned and never hurt a soul. Them girls are clean, they got regular inspections, and we didn't allow no rough stuff. Now, after all this notoriety, this little town's gettin' a bad name it don't deserve. The mediums, the shitasses, they been printing all kinds of crap."

Had the sheriff talked to Governor Briscoe or to the attorney general?

"Naw. No reason to. The place is closed."

Would it stay closed?

"It's closed *now,* ain't it?"

Yes. Right. And, uh, what was the prevailing community sentiment about the future of the Chicken Ranch?

"I ain't answering no more questions," the old sheriff said, stomping his cigarette butt with a booted heel. Two or three hot August Texas centuries limped by, while the visiting journalist vainly sought a graceful exit line.

The sheriff said, "Just you remember we got other thangs

than Miss Edna's place. This is as clean a little ol' town as you'll find. Hardworkin' people. *Good* people. That fuckin' Marvin Zindler, if he'd start cleaning up Houston today, why, in about two hunnert years he might have him a town half as clean as La Grange. I'm a-gonna go eat my supper now."

The old man wheeled, lunging away, stiff-gaited and jerky. At the door to the restaurant, he turned and paused to stare his tormentor out of sight.

The fat bearded journalist opted to permit La Grange twenty-four hours of cooling time. In truth, the salty old sheriff had unnerved him. For years the crazed back part of the journalist's brain had whispered that he might one day be riddled by rural lawmen, as had happened to Bonnie and Clyde: a penalty his mind paid, perhaps, for growing up in rural Texas during the violent outlaw days of the thirties. There had been lynchings in his home county and backwoods feuds and tempers shorter than a deadbeat's memory; his paternal grandfather, in 1900, had died of an old indiscretion complicated by a shotgun blast.

They tell a story in La Grange of how, years ago, a bad nigger rejected a deputy who came to arrest him by throwing down on the deputy with a shotgun. When the cowed deputy reported failure, old Sheriff Flournoy first fired him and then drove out to face the same shotgun: "Flipped up his pistol, by God, it still in the holster, now, and drilled that mean nigger smack 'tween the eyes!" Well, who knows? There were no eyewitnesses; maybe it was just another case of Texas brags. The journalist was in no position to judge the yarn's veracity; one of his ambitions was never to be able to. Besides, the journalist had an unfortunate habit of trick driving late in the day; obviously, if he were even slightly demented behind the wheel, it would profit him little to encounter an aroused Sheriff Flournoy on the sheriff's back-roads domain.

So, safe in Austin's familiar comforting precincts, he rang up an old associate to enjoy what proved to be a fourteen-hour group lunch. There was Brett Haggard, the freewheeling lawyer, who had visited jail for purposes other than counseling of clients. And Egbert Shrum, successful novelist and screenwriter, who semiheavily dopes. Willowy Kasha, who had no visible means of support unless you counted the guys who always seemed willing to pick up the check. Babs, the visiting schoolmarm from New Orleans, with the great bone structure and the $99 smile, who, curse it, appeared content in the company of a scraggly-bearded advertising man named Bubba Pool. As events progressed, we would be joined by Egbert Shrum's tasty young wife, Darling, along with assorted actresses, musicians, free-lance writers, and dopers, a retired prostitute, and other social marginals. Originally, however, when they gave us a humorless ejection from the Driskill Hotel bar—something about breakage and noise levels—there were but six of us. We were at that stage where we felt momentarily unconquerable, to say nothing of how much we knew: Is there anything better or more beguiling than the whiskey smarts?

We repaired, hooting, to a dark motel lounge on the banks of the Colorado River. Egbert Shrum, crazed by oven temperatures, many young scotches, and periodic deep sniffs of his Methedrine inhaler, flopped out his dingus in requesting that Kasha give him head. As the cocktail waitress was then approaching, Egbert had much help in storing his dingus. When it came his turn to order, Egbert said, "Would you mind very much if I smoked a joint in here?" Well, *Jesus,* you haven't heard such general shushings since John Dean told 'em at the White House he had the truth on the tip of his tongue!

The cool young cocktail maiden said, "It's fine with me. But somebody else might come in."

Egbert said, with unimpeachable logic, "They might not, too. You ever think of that?" Then he fired three joints of the killer weed; everybody puffed mightily in hopes of reducing them to harmless ashes before the crazy bastard got us arrested. Texas courts take even *light* doping real seriously; better to steal a cow.

Somebody suggested an orgy. Sweet Babs and Bubba offered their two-bed motel room upstairs. Lawyer Brett Haggard said excuse him, please, but being more thirsty than horny, he preferred to drink; he wouldn't mind watching, however, should we guarantee bartender service. Darling Shrum dashed cold water on the idea, leaving Egbert room for a speech on the folly of marrying narrow-minded women who'll cost you too much strange. In the end, it amounted to no more than drunken gropings under the table, a few wet kisses and ear-blowings, and discombobulated dope babble. Lawyer Haggard laid his head on the tabletop and gently snored. Bubba Pool traded the cocktail waitress a joint for her phone number and a free pinch of ass, though she instructed him not to call until her boyfriend had left Thursday to go back to Baton Rouge.

Many hours past dark, the luncheon party moved to the Soap Creek Saloon, in Austin's rural hills. A folk-rock band crashed and banged, turning conversations into face-to-face shouting matches; the average customer appeared little older than a prep schooler: hairy young hippies and their braless ladies. Egbert Shrum passed around his Methedrine sniffer. On spotting a young mother breast-nursing her child, he was reminded of how one Christmastide he'd made hisself eggnog from a visiting mother's milk. Egbert claimed that her product shamed Carnation. Hours, dope, and whiskey passed.

Around midnight a dozen hot, crazed, half-deaf children of darkness milled about an unpaved parking lot, chased there by smoke and noise and hopes of new adventures. Egbert Shrum, having cornered a trio of edgy youngsters, railed at them that he was Governor Dolph Briscoe, by God, demanding they support his closing of godless whorehouses where red-blooded daughters of Texas, some of whose great-granddaddies had martyred themselves at the Alamo, were being held in white slavery by agents of the Kremlin and Marlon Brando. "The Godfather's in this up to his Eye-talian ass," he railed. In the background, while Babs assisted his gadget, Bubba took a big splashy piss into scrub-oak trees. Salli Ann, the ex-prostitute, professed how much more fun it was to give it away than to sell it; the difference had driven her into retirement.

The Byrds slammed out a high-decibel version of how they liked "The Christian Life" while the luncheon party moved by stereophonic Ford camper to a private home. A half dozen revelers gasped and pawed at one another from a mattress laid in the rear, nothing much satisfactory happening, though a lot of wine got spilled. Arriving, the party found lawyer Brett Haggard slumbering under a fine old tree and guarded by a mean-tempered, spitting, and humping cat. "Brett brought his own pussy," somebody laughed in the moonlight.

Inside, the air soon knew more Mexican boo-smoke pollution; pipes and home-rolled objects passed around the circle, along with Methedrine inhalers, amyl nitrite caps, and doses the fat bearded journalist was not yet chemist enough to identify. Prone on the soft, furry white rug, he discovered himself experiencing serious time lags. In the midst of Willie Nelson's singing from twin speakers about Los Angeles smog, it would become apparent that Kinky Friedman and the Texas Jewboys had somehow thrummed halfway through "Sold American." Or his brain would stubbornly fight to grasp that which Egbert Shrum was shouting into his face, and then he would blink and open his eyes to find that he was alone or talking to any number of other people about a like number of things. The room reeled; his brain crackled and burned; he was aware, dimly, of distant desperate merrymaking shouts.

At an unknown hour he was aroused from a nap he had not been aware of taking: Shrum had popped an amyl nitrite cap under his nose, causing him to greet consciousness with his earlobes on fire, his head expanding as if with a winter cold, and his throat full of senseless, humorless, drugged giggles; his heart pounded fit to burst through skin. Candles had burned down. Three or four indistinct inert figures lay like grain sacks in the gloom.

"They're having a small orgy in the back bedroom," Egbert Shrum said; he was on his hands and knees, crawling. Well, was it any good? "I don't remember if I joined in," the fractured novelist said. "I *meant* to, I assure you. But I think I forgot. No, wait: I ran into Darling; yeah, that's it. And she spoke evil of my participation." He rolled over from all fours, snuggled into the furry rug, and quickly went night-night.

The journalist stepped over him and muttered, "Sleep on, faithful husband. . . ."

Finding the kitchen, the fat bearded journalist gasped and wheezed in sousing his head under the water spigot. Everything in him hurt, sizzled, or jangled. He wished much to throw at a Nixon dart board on the wall but knew the motions would cost excessive pain. "You getting too old for this shit, podner," he told himself, and spat lightly on the dart board. He thought about Hemingway's final solution, wondering enough about whether ol' Hem had had the right answer that he was glad no firearms offered themselves. Kasha, sleepy and moody and tousled, materialized to drive him to his motel. She did ugly to him for a bit, he permitting her to do the main work, while he drifted toward sleep, at once begging her pardon and muttering thanks. . . .

La Grange, in the morning sun, appeared as pure as rainwater; the aching journalist closed out its splendors with dark glasses. You'd be surprised how painful light blues and greens can be, the sun striking sparks on trees and grass and turning the high sky into one giant reflecting mirror.

At noon, Buddy Zapalac, ordering another beer, recalled the Chicken Ranch of his youth. He is a gleeful fiftyish, of iron gray hair, a stubby heavyweight's torso, and a blue-ribbon grin. You see him and you like him.

"In the thirties," Buddy said, "they had a big parlor with a jukebox, see, that they used to break the ice. You could ask a girl to dance, or she'd ask you. And pretty soon, why, you could git a little business on. Three dollars' worth." He laughed in memory of those old days when Roosevelt nookie had been cheaper than Carter coffee is now.

"You couldn't get any exotic extras. Miss Jessie—she ran the ranch back then—she didn't believe in perversions. They had wall mirrors in the parlor, see, where the girls could sit in chairs and flash their wares. But if Miss Jessie caught 'em flashing a little more than she thought was ladylike, she'd raise nine kinds of hell.

"Miss Edna, who was thirty or forty years younger, was a little more modern. I've heard you could get anything you could pay for: ten bucks for straight; fifteen for half-and-half; twenty-five, I believe, for pure French. The girls wore smart sports clothes for day trade and cocktail dresses at night. They tell me each customer was urged to buy a Coke for himself and one for the girl, see, at fifty cents each. Miss Edna, counting the bottles, knew how much trade each girl had done. Or so I heard. I understand each girl kept half of her earnings and donated the rest to the house. And the house paid room and board."

Buddy Zapalac owns the biweekly La Grange *Journal*. When the Chicken Ranch got busted, he was widely quoted as saying he intended to lend editorial support to Miss Edna and her girls. Over Cottonwood Inn beer he admits: "I didn't do it. Lost too many of my supporters. Businessmen, even a couple of preachers, told me in private they'd back me up. But people in a little town can't stand much heat. As the publicity built up, see, people started calling up or slipping around to say they'd decided against going on record. I didn't even run a news story."

There had been media reports of outraged La Grange house-wives taking to the streets with petitions, howling that the governor should—or should not—close the Chicken Ranch. Some said the infighting between the pros and the antis had been fierce.

"Ain't we in a nutty business?" Zapalac chuckled. "Exaggerated. Nothing much to it. Oh, yeah, some people circulated a petition. At one time, I heard, they had over four hundred names to keep the place open. Then people had second thoughts and took their names off. They ended up with about a hundred and twenty-five names, tops, so they junked the petition. Too much heat, see."

From what sources?

The editor spread his hands, shrugged. "Everywhere. Nowhere. Anywhere. People tend to believe, see, what they read or hear or see on TV. Or, at least, to be influenced. So they ran. Yeah, sure, I'm for the Chicken Ranch. I grew up with it, and I never once felt corrupted. When we were kids—big ol' bunch of rough Czechs and Germans, natural rockheads—we had a lot of fistfights. But never at the Chicken Ranch. It was traditional to be on your good behavior out there. You honored unspoken rules. See, if a local man got sweet on one of the girls, they'd ship that girl out in a New York minute. *Boom!* Gone. They *never* hired a local girl. Most of 'em came from Austin, Houston. Everbody always took care to keep the townsfolk and the girls from mingling off the job.

"Those gals put a hundred thousand dollars or more into this little town's economy. Every year. Outside money, mainly. And I read in a Chamber of Commerce bulletin that each tourist dollar is really worth *seven* dollars, the way it circulates locally. By that formula, Marvin Zindler ran off about seven hundred thousand dollars' worth of business. Not many of us here feel like thanking him.

"People treated those girls good. Went out of their way to be friendly. Let 'em come to the beauty shop or any store, and they got the red carpet. Having 'em marry and mingle was one thing; being plain courteous was another."

Deep in his craw, would Buddy Zapalac personally miss the Chicken Ranch?

He laughed. "Hell, I haven't been out there in years. Except, you know, to take some visitor who had his curiosity up. But, yeah, I guess so. I guess I'll miss it. It's been there since my memory has; it's a landmark. Some people, you know, they're talking about getting the Texas Historical Society to put up a marker out there. And, yes, I'd be for that."

It was unspeakably hot and stuffy in the La Grange telephone booth; all the journalist accomplished was breaking into a rare honest sweat. No, said a testy minister, he had ab-*so*-lutely nothing to say about the Chicken Ranch and, if quoted, would surely sue. Samey-same, more or less, when one reached businessmen, the community's semiofficial historian, and a suspicious old justice of the peace. Well, screw research; fall back on perceptions. Besides, beer halls are more fun than telephone booths anyway. . . .

In the cool dark Longhorn Lounge, where Tom T. Hall warbled from the jukebox of old dogs and children and watermelon wine, the journalist discovered four beer-drinking middle-aged men in sports jackets and business suits and an older citizen in khakis.

"Hail," one said, "La Grange has lots to offer besides the Chicken Ranch. There's Monument Hill State Park, as purty a place as you'll see. You can see the river from there. Go up there! Accentuate the positive!"

The old nester in khakis belched and said, "That shitass from the Houston TV, he didn't say a goddamn thang about our boys winnin' the state baseball championship."

Winking, one of the locals said, "That place has been shut down before. Back in the sixties, when Will Wilson was attorney general and got it in his craw to be governor, he closed 'er down." Winks. Sips beer. Winks again. "Yeah, for about two weeks."

Over the laughter he said, "They put up a big ol' CLOSED sign out front. Newspaper people came and snapped pictures. But if a regular customer went out there, he knew what back road to park on, and the girls slipped him in the back door."

Yeah? Anybody slipping in the back door now?

"Naw, sir. No way. Been too much publicity. Edna and the girls, soon as the story got reported on national TV, they shucked on out."

Where were they?

"Well"—one grinned—"I doubt you'd locate 'em in a nunnery. Likely they went on the regular red-light circuit. Big towns. Houston. Dallas. San Antone."

The old nester said, *"Gal-*veston, too. Yeah, and Corpus. That Dallas, it's got more thugs and prostatoots than New Orleans. You recollect Jack Ruby?"

What of Miss Edna?

"Rumor is she's got an old man over in East Texas. Owns a farm. Some say she's hiding there till this blows over. Don't anybody know, for sure, unless maybe our sheriff does. But ol' T.J., that stubborn cuss, he wouldn't tell if you helt his feet to the fahr."

Well, come on, fellers, whose official palm did Miss Edna grease for the pleasure of operating?

Shouted disclaimers clued the journalist that he'd overplayed his hand. In some heat a silver-haired man in a natty sports coat, who may have sold for Farmer's Life and Casualty, said, "That wasn't necessary, understand? That place paid good taxes, friend. It was clean. The girls had good manners. The prices didn't hold you up. Friend, they never so much as gave a *hot check* out there! I had a buddy, he was overseas during the Hitler war, and one of the girls out there, she mailed him cookies. Regular."

"Only people around here ever tried to close Edna down," the old nester said, "I guess you could call 'em religious fanatics, *they* quit after people stopped talking to 'em and they woke up to find garbage and such like dumped on their lawn."

Well, now, what about *that?* Didn't it show some long-range, perhaps less-than-gentle influence of the Chicken Ranch on the community and its standards?

"No comment," the khaki-clad one snapped, as if he'd waited a lifetime for the opportunity; his companions nodded agreement and turned to give full attention to their beers, showing the meddling outlander eight shoulders suddenly gone very cold.

Lloyd Kolbe. Lean. Well barbered. On the rise. Mid-to-late thirties. Quick to smile even when his eyes retain calculations in judging the moment's worth or risk. The quintessential Young Businessman: no bullshit, now, what with children to educate and two cars to feed and status to climb.

The owner of radio station KVLG in La Grange, Kolbe is large in civic clubs; he rarely misses the weekly Lions Club fellowship luncheon, where, should you fail to call a fellow member Lion Smith or Lion Jones in addressing him, the club Tail Twister will fine you two bits while everyone whoops and hee-haws. On Kolbe's desk, yes, is a picture of about thirty men in drag: startling, until he explains that it depicts local civic leaders in the Rotary Club's Womanless Wedding, staged, like the annual Lions Club broom sale, purely for purposes of charity. Close, Lloyd. You boys better watch it.

"I'm a native," Kolbe said, drumming fingers on a polished desk top. "I grew up knowing the Chicken Ranch was out there —no, I don't remember how early, it seems I just *always* knew.

As kids we joked about it, though it didn't preoccupy us; didn't mark us, didn't make any grand impression. You noticed as you grew up that adults didn't joke about it. Local people, you actually didn't hear them mention it until the big bust."

Like—and no offense, Lloyd—but like, maybe, those good burghers who didn't know what went on at camps outside their hometowns of Auschwitz and Dachau? Knowing it was a grossly unfair comparison, though nagged by the worry that somehow it might be *relevant,* the journalist couldn't translate the thought to words.

Kolbe was saying, "Some people think the Chicken Ranch discouraged industry from moving here. I don't think it did. And *if* it did, was that truly bad? We're progressive, and all that, but why should we ruin our pure air and clean streams and pretty farms? Industrial rot and blight . . . do we want to trade for a paycheck? People all over America are looking for La Granges to raise their families in.

"My own two children, I've watched and listened to see what effect the Chicken Ranch might have on them. And I can't see that it's had any. They accept it, as I did—it's just *there;* it has nothing to do with them or their lives. We talked about it one night right after the bust.

"On the other hand, I can't believe the town's lost significant revenue. I doubt if those girls spent anything like a hundred thousand dollars a year here. And, hell, even if they did, that's no money. You take three or four little ol' mom-and-pop stores, they'll equal that. The economic factor has been greatly exaggerated. Probably not over six or eight merchants benefited from the Chicken Ranch. The thing I hate is that La Grange is now known nationwide as a whore town. And we're better people than that."

Soon after the bust, with the town in an uproar, Lloyd Kolbe had proposed that three each pro and anti Chicken Ranchers debate on his radio station. "But it fell flat. People who privately favored the Chicken Ranch simply refused to go public. We settled for two programs where people called in. They could identify themselves or not. Most didn't. And those who did, well, yeah, I've erased their names from the tapes. I don't want to take advantage of people."

He flipped a switch. The tape brought forth the quavery voice of an old woman: "I was borned and raised in La Grange, and I've always been proud. But when we traveled to other states, people would say, 'Oh, that's where that Chicken Ranch is at.' And it was embarrassing. You didn't have any answer. Yes, I pray the thing is shut and *stays* shut."

A high school girl: "It's been here for about a hundred years! And I doubt the Mafia's been in La Grange any hundred years, don't you? After Marvin Zindler cleans up Houston . . ."

A housewife: "I'm definitely for the Chicken Ranch. Those girls got regular examinations. You knew, if your husband went out there, why, at least he'd likely come home clean."

A dissenting housewife: "Talk about regular inspections, it was no more than weekly. How many times you think they might've been exposed to syphilis and gonorrhea *between* inspections?"

Another housewife: "It's been a disgrace. Our kids, when they went off to college, were ashamed to name their hometown."

The Englishman: "I'm relatively new, from England, and I've observed the hazards of street prostitution. It's bad. Young girls —sixteen, eighteen, twenty—live the most sordid lives. I think the Chicken Ranch was the best thing that ever happened, a true community asset. You've had no rapes, no murders, no dope. . . ."

Old woman: "I'm from over here in Schulenburg. We don't have rapes and murders over here, and we don't even have a Chicken Ranch. So I don't think you need it." (Lloyd Kolbe, chuckling, broke in: "You mean, ma'am, that nobody drives the whole fifteen miles from Schulenburg to visit the Chicken Ranch?")

Local businessman and civic honcho: "I think Edna ran a real nice clean place. . . . I've traveled more than anybody in La Grange. In places like Chattanooga or Georgia or Illinois, I was proud when people knew about the Chicken Ranch. They spoke well of it. In my business place here, a fine-looking lady walked in one day with her son to ask directions out there. Her son had been sent by a specialist doctor to the Chicken Ranch for his health—'cause that's what he needed! I say bless the place. It should receive a medallion as one of the best-known historical spots and recreational facilities in the United States."

Old nester with prime Texas twang: "I'm from [a neighboring town], and I never heard nobody was hurt by the Chicken Ranch. If I didn't have no more faith in my sheriff's department than some of you people, why, I'd just move on down to Houston with the gay fellers. . . ."

Many invoked the Bible. Others awarded brimstone to Marvin Zindler and Governor Briscoe. The majority cited the town's prosperity and cleanliness in objecting to publicity "recognizing us for just one thing." The topper was a salty-sounding young woman: "I'm one hundred percent for the Chicken Ranch. And I think we ought to have a studhouse for the women."

Lloyd Kolbe shut off the tape, laughing. "Boy, we sure nuff had some phone calls requesting *that* lady's name. . . ."

Journalists are predators and vultures; they will rut around in anything, including trash and garbage, seeking firmer understandings or, perhaps, nothing more than cheap titillations or a lucky spin of the wheel.

When the Chicken Ranch closed, to judge by its trash bin, Miss Edna and her girls shredded their personal papers in the manner of diplomats under siege in a disadvantaged embassy.

One surviving letter—stained and ink-smeared—addressed to April and signed by Gene, spoke first of the weather, laundry chores, onion planting, and other mundane matters before addressing the human condition:

> I had been toying with the idea of skipping our August get-together and planning a longer one for September. But, when I heard from you, I couldn't see not coming to see you next weekend.
>
> April, please let me know if there is any chance of your coming to New York with me for a weekend on my vacation. If it is just wishful thinking on my part, please let me know so that I can make plans. Please don't leave it hanging in the air, like seeing you at the beach, until the time is past. . . .
>
> I don't expect you to write every day. I realize you have problems in that respect. You asked me to be patient with you, and I sure will try. But I hope that you can be patient with me also. After all, remember when I gave up a weekend of girl watching in Wichita Falls to be with you? I will be happy to wait for you, but you have to let me know from time to time that you want me to wait.
>
> There has always been the possibility that your interest in me was purely professional. I haven't really felt that was the case, and if I ever do, I will probably become conspicuous by my absence. . . . You are a very wonderful person, and I am glad that I met you, April, and I hope to keep that feeling for a long, long time. . . .

There was a little row of purple *X*s, representing kisses, in the traditional code of lovers, directly below a carefully drawn solitary heart and a single flower.

Yeah, I know. Corny. You wouldn't dare put it in a screenplay. But it happened, and real people were involved, and I couldn't get it off my mind. One line kept humming in my head: *There has always been the possibility that your interest in me was purely professional. . . .*

Getting drunk that night in Austin, I thought of the wretched seeking bastard who, if he went to La Grange as planned, found April gone and his surrogate honeymoon cottage shuttered. An old friend—a lawyer who daily sees the seamy side in trade—shook his head at the random and capricious work of Fate. "I went over there back in my law school days, and it was so goddamned proper I felt out of place. It was just too damned *wholesome* for somebody with a hard pecker hunting raunchy sin and eager to whip up his old Baptist guilts! And right over here"—he jerked a thumb—"just a few blocks from the Capitol building, there's a place where fags in drag—transvestites, wearing cosmetics and false titties—will take you upstairs and do anything for money that you can get done in Tangier. And down around East Sixth and Seventh, there are bars you can make the same sick deal. And even with all the fine amateur stuff floating around—on Capitol Hill, at the university, all the hippie girls, divorcées, and horny wives—you can buy a woman, if you insist on paying, of any color or creed. You've just got to know the right little ol' crummy hotels or motels.

"Probably the girls who tour the Texas circuit *are* owned by some syndicate. Anybody capable of reading knows that organized crime profits down here, but I'll be goddamned if I can see any Godfather tracks around La Grange. A guy who knows Marvin Zindler tells me that Marvin *really believes* that organized crime horseshit about the Chicken Ranch—but, he says, Marvin's idea of organized crime is two nigger pimps hauling four or five gals from town to town between beating on 'em with coat hangers. And it looks as if our fearless governor has the same notion of it." (Well, if he does, the governor may pick up a recent issue of the *Texas Observer,* a liberal crusading biweekly, and learn that Carlos Marcello's gang is moving into Houston, that old buddies of Meyer Lansky are disputing the Dallas spoils with a senior gang having Chicago roots, that the Syndicate is prospering in Galveston and Corpus Christi, and that in Dallas, one newspaperman—writing on local heroin traffic—was shot, and a second newsman there has received death threats for his probes into organized crime.) Get 'em, Governor Dolph, you fearless, grinning old bastard. . . .

I woke up in my Austin motel room to Second Coming headlines: In Houston, an hour's swift drive down the pike from the Chicken Ranch, had been discovered three monsters who routinely forced young boys into homosexual acts, tortured and abused them until the mind refuses to think anymore of their probable final horrors, and then shot or strangled them to death. Twenty-seven bodies would be discovered; with each new find, people argued in bars over whether the total represented a new national mass-murder record.

The remainder of the newspaper told of Watergate thugs who resented being investigated, of illegal Cambodian bombings, of five Austin kids busted for pot, of shortages and inflation and many balloons gone pop. I gazed out the motel window, toward the Capitol dome taking the morning sun, and thought of such great Texans as Charles Whitman, Lee Harvey Oswald, Jack Ruby. But I could sleep well tonight, secure in the knowledge that probably I wouldn't be raped in my bed. The Chicken Ranch had been closed. Hooray for Law 'n' Order. Rah. Rah. Raw.

7 ☆

Shoot-out with
Amarillo Slim

The grapevine had it that thirty-four men, putting up $10,000 each, would convene in Benny Binion's Horseshoe Casino in Las Vegas to settle the world poker championship and thereby make the winner temporarily rich.

Among the high rollers would be Amarillo Slim Preston, who had the reputation of beating people at their own game. My game was dominoes. I began to fantasize about giving Amarillo Slim a chance to beat me. Never mind that he once had defeated a Ping-Pong ace while playing him with a Coke bottle or that he'd trimmed Minnesota Fats at pool while employing a broomstick as a cue. I could think of no such flashy tricks available to him in a domino game, unless he wished to play me blindfolded. In which case I would merrily tattoo him and take his money.

I first played dominoes on the kitchen table in my father's Texas farmhouse before reaching school age. By age nine or ten I could beat or hold my own against most adults and had graduated to contests staged in feedstores, icehouses, cotton gins, and crossroads domino parlors. My father delighted in introducing me to unsuspecting farmers, ranchers, or rural merchants and then observing their embarrassment as they got whipped by a fuzzless kid.

As a teenager I hustled domino games in pool halls and beer joints, rarely failing to relieve oil-field workers of their hard-earned cash. In the Army, while others sought their victims in crap games or at the poker table, I prospered from those who fancied themselves good domino players. In later life I had written articles on the art of dominoes and, indeed, had been asked to write a book about it. I recite all this so you will know that Amarillo Slim would not be getting his hooks into any innocent rookie should he accept my challenge.

A few words here about the game itself. It is played with twenty-eight rectangular blocks known as dominoes, or rocks. The face of each is divided in two, each half containing markings similar to a pair of dice—except that some are blank. The twenty-eight dominoes represent all possible combinations from double blank to double six.

In two-handed dominoes, the players draw for the right to start the game, known as the down. After the dominoes are reshuffled, each player draws seven; the remaining fourteen rocks go into the boneyard to await the unwary, unlucky, or inattentive player.

Any domino may be played on the down, but subsequent play is restricted: Players must follow suit by matching the pips, or spots, on the exposed ends of the dominoes. Rocks are placed end to end, except for doubles, which are set down at right angles to the main line of dominoes. The first double played becomes the spinner and may be developed in all four directions.

Players may score in three ways: (1) After each play, the number of spots on all open ends is added; if the sum is divisible by five, the player last playing scores the total; (2) when a player puts down his last rock with a triumphant "Domino!" he scores the value of the spots in his opponent's hand; (3) should the game be "blocked"—that is, if neither opponent can play—the one caught with the fewer points adds to his score the points his opponent has been stuck with, to the nearest complement of five.

The basic strategy is simple: Score, keep your opponent from scoring, block his plays and make him draw from the boneyard, and then domino on him. The first player to score 250 points is the winner.

Dominoes is an easy game to learn and a difficult one to master. Any kid can grasp its fundamentals. After that, progress is largely determined by the player's ability to recall what has been played and what is out, by his understanding of the mathematical probabilities, and by his being able to read what his opponent is trying to do. The luck of the draw plays a part in any given game, sure. But over the long haul, what might be called personality skills are more important than luck. These cannot be taught, but develop out of each player's inner core and chemistry. Either you got 'em or you ain't. My successful record as a domino player satisfied me that I had 'em, and I wondered if Amarillo Slim did. So I tracked the fabled gamesman down in Las Vegas to find out and to see if I could compete with the legendary gambler. In short, I wanted to know if I could play with the Big Boys.

"How many spots in a deck of dominoes?" Amarillo Slim asked.

"Er-rah," I said. "You mean total spots? In the whole deck?" Amarillo Slim pushed his considerable cowboy hat to the back of his head, further elongating his weathered and bony face, and nodded.

I took a swig of beer to cover my frantic mental arithmetic. It was a question that never had occurred to me.* Slim patiently

---

*It should have. It would be vital to rapid calculation if one wondered whether to "block" the game. Since the odds rarely would be that close, I'd never bothered.

waited while dozens of big-time gamblers, participants in or witnesses to the World Series of Poker, milled about in the flashy Horseshoe Casino. "Well," I ultimately said with great certainty, "I'm not exactly sure."

Amarillo Slim Preston shook his head, as if somebody had told him his favorite dog had died, and the sorrow was just too much to bear. His eyes said, *What is this poor fool doing challenging me to play dominoes for money when he don't know his elbow from Pike's Peak?*

Slim said, "I'm tied up in this big poker game right now, pal; but I ain't catchin' the cards, and my stake's so small it looks like a elephant stepped on it. Soon as I'm out of it, I'll be happy to accommodate you."

After he'd been eliminated from the high-stakes world championship tournament (which, on another occasion, he had won), we agreed to meet the following morning at eleven. We would play three games for $50 each, though Slim made it clear he probably would show more profit pitching pennies than in playing dominoes for such a paltry sum. "I'm a fair country domino player," he admitted, "but I'm not any world's expert. You wouldn't be hustlin' ol' Slim, would you?" I think I thought I told the truth when I denied it.

I had a few drinks to celebrate my opportunity and mentally calculated that a twenty-eight-piece set of dominoes contained exactly 172 spots. When I recalculated to corroborate this scientific fact, I got exactly 169. And then 166. Using pencil and paper and rechecking four times, I became convinced the correct answer was 165. Exactly. Yes. *Seven-and-eight are fifteen, carry the one. . . .*

Then I realized what I had been doing and said to myself: *Don't let Amarillo Slim psych you out. Why, he's trying to play the Coke-bottle-and-broomstick trick on you! It doesn't matter how many spots are in the deck. He's trying to get you to occupy your mind with extraneous matters. Forget it.* One hour after

I'd completely and totally forgotten it, I thought: *Hell, he probably doesn't know the answer. He didn't give it, did he?* Then I calculated the spots three more times: 165, yep. But it didn't make any difference. Couldn't possibly have any bearing on the game. . . .

I was in the Horseshoe Casino at the appointed hour. Amarillo Slim was not. I searched the poker pits, the blackjack tables, the roulette-wheel crowds; among the rows of clickety-clacking slot machines; in the bars and restaurants. No Slim. I inquired of his whereabouts among gamblers, dealers, security guards, and perplexed tourists. I telephoned Slim's room three times and had him paged twice in two other casinos. No Slim.

Sitting at the bar nearest the poker pits and reminding myself not to drink excessively, I pep-talked my soul: *You're good. You haven't been beaten in years. Remember to play your hand and not to worry about his. Don't listen to his jabber, because you know he's a talker. Concentrate.*

In the midst of my tenth or eleventh drink I spotted the big cowboy hat. Under it stood Amarillo Slim, more than six feet tall and exactly two hours late. *Shoot-out time!* "Slim!" I cheerfully cried. He gave me a vague wave and a who-are-you look and continued to talk with one of his cronies. Could he have *forgotten* so important a match?

"Oh, yeah, pal," he said when reminded. "You got a deck of dominoes with you?" When I said I did not, Slim looked incredulous. "You *don't!*" he exclaimed. You never would have suspected that the night before, he had assured me the house would provide a deck.

"Well, pal," Slim said a trifle sadly. "No matter how good you are, I kinda doubt you can beat me without a deck."

"I'll go get one," I volunteered, eagerly plunging out of the casino onto the sunny and garish sidewalks of Las Vegas, dodging among crowds of people who looked as if maybe God had run out of good clay when it came their turn and had made them from Silly Putty. As I visited my fourth novelty shop ("Naw, sir, we don't get many calls for dominoes no more"), it suddenly occurred to me that Amarillo Slim had his opponent running errands for him. Here I was rushing around, getting all sweaty and hot, while spending $10 besides, in order that Slim Preston might have an opportunity to take fifteen times that amount from me. *No, forget that! It's defeatist thinking! Keep your cool!*

When I returned to the Horseshoe, Slim was playing in a pickup poker game. I caught his eye and held up the domino deck. Amarillo Slim looked at me—no, *through* me—as if he'd never seen such a sight in his life and then raked in a pot of chips big enough to choke a longhorn steer. After I'd waved the dominoes four or five times, faint recognition dawned in his eyes. "Oh, yeah, pal," he called. "Just wait there for me."

I waited. And waited. And waited some more. By now I was doing a slow burn. *Okay for you, Slim, you shitass. When I finally corner your stalling ass, it belongs to the gypsies, pal!*

A lot of Walter Mitty stuff began roistering in my head. I would so crush Amarillo Slim that he would retire from gaming for all time, publicly apologizing for his ineptitude. Meanwhile, however, I had time to eat a bowl of chili, whomp up on a friend in a practice game—250 to 95—and count the number of spots in the deck again. No doubt about it: 165.

Fully four hours after the appointed time, Amarillo Slim approached his challenger. He was tucking away a large role of bills newly accepted from two amateur poker players, who, now wiser and lighter, began to sneak away as if guilty of large crimes. *Play him tough,* I instructed myself. *Don't give him anything. He's just another ol' Texas boy, like you. He's just a little skinnier, that's all.*

"You bring your photographer?" Slim asked.

"Uh, beg pardon?"

"I thought you said this was gonna be in *Sport* magazine," he said. "You mean you didn't bring a photographer?"

"I forgot," I said, before realizing I'd made absolutely no promise of a photographer.

Slim grunted and sat down at the table. So as to reestablish authority, I said, "Here are the ground rules. Fifty bucks per game. Two hundred fifty points wins a game. You play the seven dominoes you draw, no matter how many doubles." Slim gave me a who-don't-know-that look.

I poured the new deck onto the table. Slim bent over the dominoes and said, "Whut the *hail*?"

"Beg pardon?"

"Is this here a *deuce*?" he demanded of a rock he held before his eyes. Squinting like Mr. Magoo.

"Yeah. Sure."

"Damnedest-lookin' deuce *I* ever saw," Slim proclaimed. "All the deuces look like that, pal?" I decided not to answer. Though the deuces in this particular deck were a shade peculiar in appearance, they were not enough different from the norm to make a federal case. Which Amarillo Slim now was doing. "Pal," he said, "I'm in a whole heap of trouble. I can't tell these funny-lookin' deuces from the aces. Why, you can wet in this hat if I can tell 'em apart."

Slim's lament began to attract a sizable crowd of professional gamblers and the merely curious. Among those pressing close to the table was a huge, grinning fat man called Texas Dolly, Doyle Brunson, who had reason enough to grin, having the previous evening won $340,000 playing poker. *The winnah and new world champ-een!* I suddenly was very aware of where I was, and who Amarillo Slim was, and that he'd been winning big stakes around the globe while I had been taking lunch money away from oil-field grunts and Pfcs. *If you're not nervous*, whispered a small inner voice, *then why are your hands shaking?* It was something like being the rookie deep back waiting to receive the opening kickoff in the Super Bowl, I imagine. And Vince Lombardi was coaching the other side.

I had decided on a conservative strategy for the first few hands, much as a football team might carefully probe the opposition's defense with basic fundamentals rather than quickly go for the long bomb. I would take any count available to me, no matter how small, rather than scheme to send Slim to the boneyard. If you send a skilled opponent to the boneyard too early, and he gets enough dominoes, he has more options and more scoring rocks available. So I would wait until the major scoring rocks had been played before going for the jugular; would settle for the field goal on my first possession. Grunt gains.

I won the down—coin toss?—and played the double five, at once scoring 10 and establishing the spinner. Fine; I'd run the kickoff back to my own 47; I held three other fives and figured to prosper from that spinner. Sure enough, I scored 25 points before Slim got on the board. Slim countered with combinations of sixes and fours, all the time mumbling how he couldn't tell aces from deuces "and here we are playin' for the whole kit and kaboodle." *Don't listen to him. Play your hand.* Every time I played a deuce—and often when I didn't—Slim said, "Is that thang a deuce, pal?" At the end of the first hand I led him, 40–25. I'd kicked my field goal.

In the second go-round I again was blessed with fives. Slim, however, was equally blessed with blanks. We traded large counts; I was reminded of a baseball game in which neither side could get anybody out. I'd make 10 and Slim would make 15; then he would make 15 and I would make 20. We each scored 65 points, so that after two hands I was up 105 to 90; Slim, of course, chattered incessantly about the funny-lookin' deuces I'd rung in on him.

The third hand was tense and low-scoring, each of us waiting for the other fellow to make a major mistake. Nobody did. We

only made 15 points each; the game now stood 120 to 105; I
silently congratulated myself on having not yet fallen behind
for a single moment.

After the fourth hand I was certain that I had him. He pulled
within 5 points early; but then I turned treys on him, and he had
none. He went to the boneyard twice and got nothing that
helped him. I dominoed on him for 30 points and now led, 195
to 155. *Duck soup. I got him. How's it feel, pal?*

Now Slim was rattling and jabbering like monkeys climbing
chains. I resolved to shut him out. *Keep track of what's played
and what's out. You're playing good dominoes. But you'll blow
it if you permit him to break your concentration.*

Having discovered that I preferred to play rapid-fire dominoes, Amarillo Slim now began to slow the pace. Though surely
he had not read it, he was utilizing a technique I had recommended: "Should your opponent prefer to play quickly, slow
the game. Conversely, should *he* slow it, then you should give
a wham-bam-thankee-ma'am response. Once you rob your opponent of his preferred pace, you control the tempo—and he
who controls the tempo usually will control the game."

Slim edged up on me, nickeling and diming me to death; I
began to feel like a team that had tried to freeze the ball too
early and had lost its momentum, its . . . yes . . . *tempo!* My lead
had dwindled to 15 points when it suddenly became clear why
he'd made such a fuss about the funny-lookin' deuces. I'd
turned it all fours on him, and he had none. He was drawing
from the boneyard, hunting for a four, when he suddenly exposed a domino in his hand and, peering at it as if he might
qualify for aid to the blind, innocently asked, "Is that thang a
deuce, pal?" I was astonished; clearly, it was not. Nor were the
next three or four dominoes he deliberately exposed to my
view.

By now the gamblers were hoo-hawing and laughing. The
cardinal rule of dominoes, the very *first* rule—its being a game
dependent on the calculating of odds and based upon the mem-

ory of what's been played and what has not—is that you never, but *never*, reveal anything of your hand to your opponent. Amarillo Slim was, in effect, playing me with an open hand! It was an insult of the magnitude a street fighter offers when he slaps another rather than hits him with a clenched fist. Such gestures say, *I can take you whenever I want you. You probably got to squat to pee.*

With the gamblers' laughter crashing about my reddening ears, I offered a good-sport grin as false and empty as an old maid's dream. There was a reason my face felt frozen somewhere between a grimace and a death mask: I now hated the bastard.

"Hey, pal," Slim said, "I'll make you a side bet of five hundred dollars that I can name the three rocks remainin' in the boneyard."

"No side bets," I said. "Play the game."

"Give you two to one," he offered.

"No, no. Dammit, play dominoes!"

By now it was all the old gamblers could do not to dance, so they settled for snickering, tee-heeing, and nudging each other with happy elbows. Without having any idea, then or now, of how it happened, I suddenly was behind by 20 points. You might say Slim had broken my concentration.

Slim then played a deuce, did an exaggerated double take, and said, "Whoee, kiss me sweet, damn if that wasn't a *deuce* and I didn't know I had any! Hell, pal, you'd of won that five hundred dollar side bet 'cause I was *sure* there was a deuce in that boneyard. And here I was lookin' at it all the time!" The gamblers enjoyed new spasms of mirth while I wondered if Nevada imposed the death penalty for mass murder.

Going into what proved to be the first game's final hand, I led by 10 points—245 to 235. How, I don't know.

"All you need's a nickel," Slim said. "I'll give you two to one and bet on you to win."

"No," I said, "No, no. . . ."

I searched my hand and the board but could find no combination that would make the decisive 5 points. It just wasn't there. *Play it close to the vest. You don't have any fives and only one blank and, therefore, no repeater rocks should he make a nickel or a dime. Play small dominoes. Nothing that'll let him get 15. Try for a combination of twos and threes so you can make that goddamn 5 playing defense. Since you don't have any counting rocks, he must have a pisspot full. Stop the long bomb! Intercept!*

I played the six-three, the three-outward; there was a blank at the other end of the board.

Slim said, "Uh-oh. What you thought was cookin' ain't on the fire. Now, pal, I'll bet you three to two that *I* win."

"No," I said. "No, no. . . ."

While I tried to calculate what obvious blunder I'd made that so dramatically had changed the odds, Amarillo Slim played the blank six. Now there was a six at one end and a three at the other and—*oh, outhouse mouse! I didn't have another six!* So I couldn't cut the six off. I didn't have a four, so I couldn't play on the spinner, which was the double four. The only three I had was the double three. And if I played it—and I had no choice, the rules said I *had* to play it; it was the only play I had—there would be 12 points on the board. And should Slim have the four-three and play it on the spinner, he'd make 15 and win. I cursed the gods for having given me a handful of sorry aces and funny-lookin' deuces and little else, in a hand where I would have been the prohibitive favorite given even minimal fives or blanks.

I put down the double trey, as the rules required. Sure enough, Slim played his four-three on the spinner and made the 15 points that did me in. I sat there feeling like the guy who'd had a three-lap lead in the Indianapolis 500 and then, fifty yards from the finish line, burned out his motor and died. *Five lousy points!*

"Hail, I just got lucky," Slim said. "You know, pal, if you'd taken that two to one bet on yourself, I'd owe you money. And that game could have went either way. . . ."

Round two. One of Slim's big-time gambler buddies stepped close to him and said, "Okay, you've had your fun, but you cut it a little close. Now settle down and play dominoes." Slim winked at him.

Amarillo Slim played no more open hands, though he re-sorted to physical tricks: holding a half dozen rocks easily in his big left hand (*you* try it); shuffling his own dominoes while I tried to concentrate on my next play; dropping a domino and permitting it to bounce a shade too long before snatching it back to say, "You didn't see that one, did you, pal?" *Now why, I wondered, did he want me to see that one?*

While the second game was still nip-and-tuck, tied at 130, Slim so loudly and frequently dreaded my "slappin' me with that ace-five" that I feared a trap. Did he truly fear the ace-five or . . . *no!* He wanted me to play it! Sure! He was using double-think on me! I paused so long, looking for the trap, that Slim said, "Ain't it your play, pal?" I ignored him, continuing to look for the trap. *Just because you don't see it doesn't mean it isn't there.*

So, naturally, I did not play the ace-five. I would not have played it with a gun at my head. Instead, I played the ace-four. And no sooner had done so than I realized, sickeningly, that I'd made my biggest goof since agreeing to the match. Now I was left with the ace-five as the lone rock in my hand, while neither aces nor fives were available to be played on. I would be forced to visit the boneyard. Even worse, there *was* a four available on the board; had I played my ace-five and held onto my four—*the last available in the suit, which meant that Slim could not possibly have cut it off*—then I would have guaranteed myself a cinch "Domino" and would have caught Slim with about 50 points in his hand. *Oh, you jackass!* My perceptions were arriv-ing a flash late; it was like a victim flying through the air while realizing that if he'd taken one half step to the right, the truck wouldn't have hit him.

I had flat let Slim talk me out of playing that goddamned ace-five, had been conned and flummoxed and sent off on a wild-goose chase looking for a trap that didn't exist. This had blinded me to what *was* there. I had reacted as a rank amateur, making the kind of blunder I had always relied on my kitchen-table opponents to make.

Amarillo Slim flashed a private grin that said, *We know who's gonna win now, don't we, pal? You dropped more than you can pick up, and it's all over.* It very shortly was. Slim dominoed on me for a crushing 55-point profit, making my blunder one of more than 100 points, considering what I properly should have extracted from him, and handily accounting for more than the margin by which he ultimately won: 250 to 165.

By now my game was in shambles. I worried not about winning that third game, or even hanging tough, for my pride and poise had deserted me and sneaked off to hide. I was concerned, instead, with not additionally making an ass of myself through the use of more sophomoric blunders. I imagined that the onlooking gamblers were rolling their eyes and giggling and perhaps whispering that I should take up paper dolls. Consequently, I played the last game as if blind, airless, and in a hurry to catch a bus. Slim won, 250 to 190, to complete his sweep. Don't ask me how, if you're talking about the play by play.

I counted out seven $20 bills and a lone ten-spot to Amarillo Slim, who scooped them off the table with a practiced hand while offering the other in tardy fellowship. "Pal," he said, "I really and truly enjoyed it."

I showed him the teeth through which I was lying and said, "Me, too, pal." Then I leaned in and said softly, only for his ears, "Slim, there are a hundred sixty-five spots in a deck of dominoes." Slim grinned and winked.

As a friend and I tried to leave the gambling arena by an invisible path, one of the chuckling leather-lunged old gamblers called out, "What did you boys beat ol' Slim out of?"

"About thirty minutes," I said.

8 ☆
Gettin' Stung:
Horse Tradin'

Madisonville is in deep East Texas about ninety minutes down the freeway from Houston, right over yonder by Point Blank and North Zulch, just a hoot and holler from Cut-and-Shoot. It is a close neighbor to the Trinity River and the Big Thicket, which naturalists and ecologists credit with indigenous growths of flora to be found nowhere else and which the timber interests see only as a big field of lumber. Madisonville also is the hometown of folk humorist John Henry Faulk and his irrepressible running mate, Peavine Jefferies—the classic good ol' boy, a giant of a man, a carpenter who advised a local lady when she asked him to install a new lock on her bedroom door, "Hail, you don't need none; just leave the light on so people can see you."

The little town is situated in the middle of some of the purest horse and cattle country remaining in an urbanized America. On a good day at Bill Andrew's Cattle Auction Barn, amidst the cracking of bullwhips or electric prods and the bawled terrors of mother cows and the bewildered bleatings of their stiff-legged calves, auctioneers working from can-to-can't may chant over 3,000 head of stock.

Just off the lobby, in a small, barren café running to plate lunches, cornbread, and vile coffee, sit men with faces almost

as weathered as their boots, their drawls or twangs the envy of
Central Casting; throwbacks to an earlier time. Over the clanks
of cups on saucers—when they are not cussing the government
or taxes—likely they talk of horseflesh. "Now, I had me this ol'
mare, a paint, run about fourteen hands high, and when she
fox-trotted, she put her feet down so light you'd of thought she
was a borned sore-foot. . . ."

It strikes a visitor that most of the men are old, or getting
there. Precious few are younger than middle-aged. One gets
the feeling that he is witnessing something sadly close to the last
gathering of the old buffalo hunters. Their way of life is passing;
the things they care about don't matter in much of America
anymore. One wonders how much they know of this. Take away
the pollutions of television, their only daily contact with urban
America if they stay off the freeway, and they appear to live in
a time warp. Their natural surroundings, and their small mean-
derings, create the false impression that the world has not
changed dramatically within the past fifty years.

Now and again the yarn spinners rotate like losers in a perpetual domino tournament, newcomers claiming metal folding
chairs as others scrape back to wander off toward the auction
pens, but almost always the talk is of horses, horses, horses. The
old horse traders seem strangely to enjoy recalling those times
when they got skinned: ". . . and when I woke up and seen that
buncha canners and dawgs the next mornin', I kept half ex-
pectin' to find a hoss with no more than three laigs."

Whinnies of laughter explode; withering thighs are slapped.
Somebody says, "Lee Roy, you sure musta been drankin' some
good tradin' whiskey."

Lee Roy grins and says, "Well, one thang 'bout good tradin'
whiskey. You ain't careful, by Gawd, it can work both ways."

"Horse tradin', it's a lost art," Jeff Farris complains. "Hell, it's
all auction-barn stuff. Not much man-to-man left in it. Why, I

recollect when traders roamed from town to town and people traded horses whether they needed to or not. It was pure impolite to let a trader pass through without riskin' hisself. Nowadays, I dunno, people keep pleasure horses and want 'em gentle. I bet we got two hundred families here with just one or two horses, and hell's fire, you couldn't get 'em out of a trot if you dynamited 'em. Seems like people in the *toy horse* business, that's about all."

Farris, at seventy-nine, remembers when horses were big business. At the turn of the century the combined value of all horses and mules in the United States was greater than that of all cattle, sheep, goats, and hogs on the nation's farms or ranches. The horse was king, supplying power and transportation vital to the rapid expansion of an entire continent—roles soon to be preempted by impersonal machines with no distinguishing gaits. Most horses, back then, were to be found west of the Mississippi. Madison County, Texas—deep in the piney woods—was prime horse and mule country because of their key contributions to the cotton or timber or cattle business. "I was messin' with horses time I was seven-year-old," Jeff Farris says. "Tradin', time I was fourteen. 'Course, now, you not likely to be too good until you forty-year-old or past, 'cause you can only learn by doin'. You can't learn horse tradin' in books or in school."

Farris looks the part of the veteran horse trader in his western hat, scuffed boots, rumpled khakis, and with an outdoorsman's windburned face. Each day, by horseback when the weather's good and by pickup truck if not, he bounces across much of his 1,286 acres, fretting over salt licks, calving cows, or rotting fence posts. "Me and a black boy runs this whole place," he says with pride. "Only thang is, I got mainly Brahamer cattle. And they're purty salty. I used to could outrun 'em, but I don't figger I can do that anymore. I rigged me up a chute with a cuttin' gate so I hardly ever have to git off my horse until I've cut the calves away from the spooky mother cows. Then I git down and vaccinate or castrate or whatever needs doin'."

What does one look for in a good horse?

"Well, that strictly depends. Now, say you lookin' for a work horse—a draft horse—you want 'im to be big-boned and square-built. You want a good bottom and good-sized feet and power in the hind legs. A cow horse, on the other hand, you want him to be tough and quick. Cattle, they a heap quicker than the average horse. They can turn around on a nickel's worth of space. Horses just like people. It's not all physical. Some horses can be taught, and some can't. You take a good work horse—a log horse—and say you have your log a-layin' here straight. It won't take a smart horse long to learn to pull around and take a running start on it and get the right angle.

"Nothin's better for a cow horse than to let 'im run wild for about five years and then castrate 'im. He'll be tough and wise. A pet horse, now, is likely to turn out mean and stubborn. They get spoiled, just like children, and once they do, you'll never get 'em to ride or lead or anything else they don't want to do. They'll turn on you, a pet horse will, and if you don't know what you're doing, a horse can hurt you quick."

What about all the notorious tricks of horse traders?

The old man squatted on his haunches and cocked his head. "Why, now, son, I truly don't know what you mean."

Aw, come on, old-timer. How about doctored horses and so on; all the legendary tales of flummery?

Jeff Farris smiled. "Oh, I reckon if a man's a mind to, he can use a few tricks. But a good trader, somebody livin' off his reputation, he won't use 'em, on account of it's shortsighted. You can outwit a feller, and that's all right. The code says he'll just take his losses and try to sting somebody down the line. But you skin a feller by doping a horse or workin' its mouth over to make it look younger, and once the word gets around, then you just a dead duck. You can't get a deal even by pourin' the best tradin' whiskey down the other feller."

Like every horse trader who has ever lived, Farris will admit to having been victimized by dirty tricks but swears never to have indulged in one himself.

"One time there was this ol' mule," he said, "and it was a good-lookin' job. Dappled and grass-bellied and fat. Well, I just had to have it. I led it around, and it was gentle and looked like the best deal I ever saw. Well, sir, I paid for it and had it penned, and along 'bout midnight that mule commenced kickin' and like to tore the whole barn down. It was a plumb *outlaw*! Well, sir, turns out the feller that'd sold it to me, he'd poured chloroform on a cotton ball and stuck it up that mule's nose so that when I bought it, it was near 'bout out on its feet. When that chloroform wore off, its true nature come out." The old man laughed at the great joke on himself. "One thang, though, that mule wasn't likely to hurt you. You couldn't get close enough to it.

"It's right common to trim a horse's forelocks, give it a haircut, at tradin' time. Sure, you want it to look good! Damned whistling! Some people—I never did—but some people feed horses green coffee to make their hair shine, and they dye 'em where they been scalded or scarred. That won't fool nothin' but a tenderfoot, though, because a real trader will *feel* around a horse's head or neck, and dye won't won't hide a scar from your fingers. A horse too scarred up, you figure he's been snubbed up against a tree or a post a lot to break 'im, and he's a bad actor.

"It's real low-down, but I've heard of people that fed arsenic to horses. You can start givin' a horse just a touch of arsenic and increase his dose a little over a long period—a month, say—and you'll have a horse lookin' fat and sassy if the dose don't kill 'im. But say some other feller buys 'im. Why, in a matter of days that horse will be down and dead because he's got a drug habit and can't live without it. He'll lose weight right before your eyes, and he's a goner.

"Say a horse has the heaves—say he's a rattler you can hear

breathin' fifty yards off. Well, sir, they tell me if you feed such a horse a little wet bran and turpentine—and maybe spike his water with bluing, like the womenfolks used to use to get their clothes white before detergents come in—why, he'll breathe normal as long as you don't trot 'im or run 'im. But hell, son, any trader worth the salt that goes in his bread is just naturally gonna trot or run any horse he's dealin' for. Unless he's buyin' him for a killer or a canner—you know, to make dog food and glue and such.

"So all them tricks, they don't work near as often as people like to tell. You gotta remember"—and here the old man laughed quietly, a gentle little burble, and the corners of his clear blue eyes creased—"that it's just second nature for horse traders to improve on the truth. They nearly always remember a thang better than it was."

Frank Coldiron, sixty-eight, is a character out of Hogarth: scraggly, balding; round red moon face; short, powerful, stubby body; and a raffish gleam in his eye. Coldiron is wearing overalls and a blue denim jumper, his eyes shrewdly calculating as he sits before the fireplace in his barebones living room, furnished with gaudy ceramic ashtrays shaped like circus clowns but not a sign of a rug on the old wooden floor; the floor sags and creaks so that one's feet seem to play off-key music walking across it. There is a picture on the wall of a fiercely painted Indian about to skag a walleyed steer with a bow and arrow, and another of Jesus profusely bleeding on the cross.

Coldiron sits in a dilapidated chair, its sprung springs lowering his bulk close to the floor and threatening to spear him in three places. He shouts his words as if addressing a convention of the deaf, a sure tip that he requires reciprocal courtesies. His taciturn wife, a shapeless mass in a faded print dress and summer anklets, sits on a straight-backed cane-bottom chair and stares into the fireplace; she periodically looses tobacco-

brown streams onto the burning logs: *pfft . . . pfft . . . pfft.*
Coldiron does not bother to introduce her.

"Never was much in horse tradin' for me," Coldiron shouts
for the benefit of the people in Baltimore. "You git started at
it and keep a-goin', kinda like runnin' downhill. My daddy was
a trader back when it meant somethin', but seems like he had
a natural talent for tradin' down to broke. Don't guess I've did
much better.

"But tradin', mister, it gits in your blood. Sure does. During
that last world's war, I got me a job with Lone Star Steel over
in Texas City. But nearly ever' week I'd ride the bus over to
Madisonville on Friday nights, givin' up twenty-five dollars in
that good government overtime, just so's to horse trade on
weekends. And thunder, like as not I'd buy some old snide for
twenty-seven dollars and have to sell it for fourteen dollars after
feedin' it a week. I'da been better off diggin' postholes.

"I had a kid of a boy then—he's dead now, died up in New
Mexico, I never quite learned why—who could ride anythang
I'd brang home. He'd ride them green-broke horses into any
auction ring in this part of the country, him bein' a little ol' slip
of a kid, and people would bid 'em up 'cause it looked like them
green-brokes had been gentled out. Truth to tell, that boy of
mine was the only two-legged critter in East Texas could ride
half of 'em." He laughed at the memory. "But I didn't want
nobody gettin' hurt, so after somebody'd buy them green-
brokes, I'd go up and say, "Mister, you ain't bought no kid horse
there.""

Had Coldiron ever been stung badly in a trade?

"You bet. You can't trade horses or keep bees without gettin'
stung. One night some years ago I was over in Livingston and
got to drankin'. There's this much to be said for liquor: It'll
make you trade quicker ever' time. Well, I come home with the
biggest buncha culls that ever seen the sun rise on 'em.

"I jumped up on the only spirited one in the bunch, and he

throwed me against a old blacksmith's anvil, and you might say that's all she wrote. Them thangs ain't made outta butter. Well, the old woman come in from a church social to find me all bloody and cold-cocked. She throwed a bucket of water on me and hepped me to my feet, and the first thang I said was: 'Well, there's another 'un for sale.' " The old trader laughs and shouts, "Lost between eight hundred dollars and nine hundred dollars on that batch. Sold most of 'em for canners at six cents a pound.

"I got a brother, he don't know no more about horses than he does 'rithmetic. One time he bought a mare and colt from a shyster, and a-course, it turned out they wasn't a matched set. That mare, she'd kick that colt a-windin' when it tried to suck. You could see right off it wadn't her colt. Hail, mister, that mare hadn't even foaled! Her bag was dry! Well, that was a low trick.

"So a little bit later I had a lot full of mules, thirty-odd of 'em, and that same shyster come along and wanted to buy 'em off me. He never asked me how old they was, and I never troubled to tell 'im. He paid me fifty-three dollar a head for them mules.

"Well, he taken 'em over to a government sale—the Army was buying worlds of mules back then—but the Army wouldn't touch 'em because they didn't buy nothin' less than three-year-olds. And them mules I'd sold the shyster, they wadn't but two-year-olds. I knowed within reason he had that government sale in mind, so I followed 'im over there with his money in my pocket and bought 'em back for nineteen dollars a head. Sure did rile 'im, yes, sir! He rared back and said, 'What kinda deal you call this?' and I said, 'Purty much the same kinda deal you give my brother on that mismatched mare and colt.' Well, he bucked and snorted, but he was stuck. I said, 'Mister, there ain't no law that says a feller's got to answer a question that ain't been asked of him.' "

Old-timers said to look up a horse trader named Alvin Lancaster "over yonder in Dew." Dew, Texas, is difficult to find. The problem is that you can pass through town and not know it until you're miles down the road making new inquiries. There's only a crossroads general store, an old spiritless church house, and maybe five scattered dwellings that look to have suffered about all the wind and sand and sun abuse they can stand. With the aid of the Faulknerian crossroads storekeep—unshaven, in faded overalls and stiff-billed baseball cap, drinking parched peanuts floating inside a Coke bottle—one discovers the Lancaster place down a certain zigzag dirt road. Nothing moves on it for several miles but shifting sand and my lone car.

White-haired and tanned and lean, looking like the man in the Marlboro Country ads, Alvin Lancaster has the disconcerting habit of laughing each time he proclaims a disaster. He sees disaster all around: The horse business has got to hell in a handcart; Jerry Ford's got his head up his ass; the world's loonies and crazies somehow are in charge of mankind's asylum. It all comes pouring out with no encouragement, punctuated by the varied bursts of laughter, as if Alvin Lancaster had been sitting for days waiting to tell it and, at last, somebody finally happened down the dirt road. You give such a man his head.

"Cow horses, you can't get but seven hundred dollars to one thousand dollars for the very best of 'em, and work horses, hell, you can't give 'em away. I don't know why I bother to trade anymore." A machine-gun burst of mirth. "It's like smokin' cigarettes; you know it's killin' you, but you can't quit." Ha-ha-ha. "I'll swear on a stack of Bibles not to buy another dadgummed horse, and next thing you know, I'll have a pen full." Ho-ho-ho. "This year I got to buying killer horses—people eat 'em, you know, in Germany and France and such places; damn sure do—for an ol' boy from Fort Worth, and damn if I didn't have a whole pen full when he decided to quit the business, and I'm stuck with 'em." Hee-hee-hee. "Horses eat, you know. Damn tootin'. It'll cost eight dollars per one hundred pounds for horse and mule feed. It's expensive even if you feed 'em just enough to barely keep 'em alive." Chuckle chuckle chuckle.

"Auction barns and killer horses has just about put an end to horse tradin' as I knew it," Lancaster said. "Used to be more individual. Hell, folks don't even know how to run auction barns anymore or how to spend a dollar." Chortle chortle. "You take some fellers from over near Huntsville, they're moneymen, but they couldn't tell a good Ohio-bred Percheron from a ol' walleyed canner. Well, they opened up the slickest-lookin' auction barn in the United States. Thing was, they spent all their money *on the front end!* Had big plush offices, a fancy café, computers put in to handle the sales. Why, they were smack-dab gonna eat everbody up! But they didn't provide any *facilities,* now, *in back!* Wasn't room enough to unload stock or to park trailers and trucks. Didn't have enough holdin' pens, and the chutes were too narrow—just a big damn mess. They went busted. Nobody can do anything anymore!"

Lancaster is merrily cynical about present-day traders. "Lot of 'em get their fractions mixed," he said. "A quarter horse—they get their name from runnin' fast as hot grease for a quarter mile—there was a time you didn't have to worry about the papers on 'em. Now it seems like people get papers on quarter horses that don't look like they can move more than a quarter of a quarter. Either that, or they go the other way and breed to so many thoroughbreds that the so-called quarter horse—and a truly good one's a fine cow pony—is too finicky and skittish and don't have enough stamina. A cow horse, you want it a little blocky and good muscles up front. You want it tough, but you don't want it nervous.

"In horse tradin' you got to always be up to snazzy, or you won't get it done. Now I've known a *blind* man, yes, sir, that was a rootin'-tootin' trader. A ol' Nigra. Over there in Madisonville. This must have been thirty years ago, but that Nigra could judge a horse's age without seein' in the mouth. Yep, you can close your eyes and slide your hand down a horse's jaw, and accordin' to how *smooth* it is, you can purty well guesstimate how *old* it is. An old horse, you know, has knots on the jaw. You couldn't hardly beat that blind Nigra in a trade."

"Tell 'im about that other Nigra," Mrs. Lancaster says. She is wearing a hairnet over salt-and-pepper hair, greenish slacks, a shimmery orange blouse, and open-toed wedged shoes from which peek green toenails. It is her only comment of a long afternoon.

Ha-ha-ha! "Well, I disremember his name, but this ol' Nigra was a real hustlin' man. Had a cleanin' shop and sold old clothes and raised mules and was altogether right propertied. For a Nigra. Well, one time he bought some real bad mules. Dogs, I mean. Real doggy mules. They'd been wore out, and he didn't have that team of mules ten days before one upped and died on 'im. Well, *matched* mules—you break the set, you see, and the survivin' one's worth less than half of what he once was. And these was matched mules. Well, that Nigra tried to give the survivin' mule to some feller in trade for the feller haulin' off the *dead* mule. But he wound up havin' to give not only the survivin' mule but ten dollars in boot to get the dead one hauled off! And that ol' Nigra said, 'I'm gonna quit this here tradin' business. It's way too hard to multiply and way too easy to subtract.'" Very much satisfied laughter from the teller of the tale.

Lancaster stands on his front porch, looking off toward a distant pen holding perhaps a dozen horses, and says, "Naw, I haven't got anything down there I'd be proud to show you. Couple of kid horses, and the rest is those canners and killers I got stuck with." Ha-ha-ha. He generalizes on the rules of the game: "You can't let the other feller know when you're hurtin' to trade. It's kinda like a good woman, she won't let her beau know how bad she wants to get married. If she's a little bit reluctant, why, she's got a better chance to spring her trap. Same thing's true of a trading man.

"Another thing, most people believe that a horse you can ride bareback is a sign of a gentle horse—that he'll just naturally ride better with a saddle. But that's not always true, no, sir. Some horses will let you ride 'em bareback, but they'll turn wild if you throw a saddle on their backs. I've seen some buck like rodeo stock. I wouldn't buy any riding horse without giving it the saddle test. There's another type of horse, he may not be bad to buck—but he'll be the dickens to mount. Some horses, you have to ear 'em down. Twist 'em by the ear until they learn who's boss and go down to their knees and *then* you mount 'em."

The tall horseman walks among roistering yard dogs and chews on a dead cigar. "A rule I've always lived by is if I don't know the man I'm tradin' with—know him of my own account or by word of reputation—then I don't take a thing in the world for granted. No, sir. I'll look for scars, dye, chronic colickers. A colicker, let 'im eat a little grain, and he'll go to swellin' and slobberin'. It's not easy to spot 'em, because except for being a colicker, a horse might look like the finest horseflesh around.

"I used to think I could tell a honest man through a thick door. Depended on types, you see. I thought a soft-talkin' feller who looked you in the eye would deal fair, and I believed that a loudmouth would skin you like a pot rabbit. But"—ha-ha-ha—"life taught me it could just as easy be the other way around." He pauses, looks off across the grassland pasture, and says, "Years ago I bought me a *blind* horse. Soon as I discovered it —it was at a auction—I traded it to a feller for a canner that had one foot cut nearly off. It was a matter of pride, I reckon, to see if I could unload that blind critter.

"The old boy with the gimp horse, he was so damn eager to find a fool to unload her on that I got twenty-seven dollars and fifty cents in boot from him, and he didn't discover that horse was blind until he tried to drive it to load. I about half expected him to come out swingin' and cussin'—he was right smart of a loudmouth—but he just grinned sheepish and went on.

"Few days later I was at a sale over in Palestine, and I recognized that ol' blind horse. The feller I'd traded it to, he'd put a kid up on it and had the kid ride it all around the auction ring. Dogged if he didn't sell it for a sixty-dollar profit, and it looked so good it was all I could do not to bid on it myself!"

I left Alvin Lancaster standing under the big sky, whooping at his own folly, convinced that as long as the world stays crazy, he'll have a mighty good time.

One night at John Henry Faulk's home on the edge of Madisonville, over frog legs cooked in a thick gravy, old Jeff Farris said slyly, "Son, you reckon you've learned enough to trade horses and still get home with your britches?" I said I doubted it. "Well, if you git stung fair," the old man said, "you're supposed to enjoy the joke on yourself and go 'bout your business. That's the code.

"Worst I was ever stung, I was helpin' to build a dam over near Highway Twenty-one here, and I needed me a good pullin' horse. Saw a man ridin' around downtown on a big, fine-lookin' roan. It looked like a real red-blooded horse, and it was built more for work than for saddle. Which was what I was in the market for.

"Well, sir, son, I purt near begged the man to sell me that horse! Seemed like he was terrible set against it. I'd talk and talk and git right up against a trade, and he'd back off from it. I finally got the horse, but I paid a dear price for it. Rode that horse on home, so proud I hoped folks was peepin' out their windows at me. I do believe it was the finest-lookin' work horse I ever seen.

"But when I tried to hook it up for work, hook it to a wagon or plow, that ol' roan horse just laid down like a dog doin' tricks. Yes, sir! Just let it *hear* a trace chain rattlin', and that horse'd lay down! You couldn't git 'im on his feet if you whupped 'im scratch bald! Durned pet horse, you see. Spoilt. My daddy had always warned me against pet horses, and there I was stuck with the craziest one I'd ever seen. Ride real good, yeah, but it wouldn't do no more work than people on welfare."

The old man gnawed on a frog leg, licking gravy off his fingers, and said, "Well, sir, I rode that horse 'round town a few Saturdays, 'round the courthouse square and like that. And people would say, 'That sure looks like a fine horse, Jeff,' and I'd say, 'Oh, it's a gem-dandy. I wouldn't take for it.' Somebody said, 'Jeff, that looks like a mighty fine work horse. But bein' as you got cattle horses, how come you ride it so much?' I said, 'Boys, this here is such a fine horse I can't hardly stand not to be with it.'

"People talk, you know. Yew bet. Gossip's quicker than the telegraph. So, naturally, news got around that maybe Jeff Farris had the finest all-'round horse in Madison County. I didn't dispute such talk. In time a farmer from over at North Zulch come over and begged me all day one Sunday to sell 'im that horse. I sure was hard to trade with. You'da thought I was dickerin' about one of my children. Finally, though, I let that farmer take it off my hands at a profit to myself, and then I tried to avoid North Zulch for the next few years."

Jeff Farris is extraordinarily proud of his neat, well-kept home on his 1,286 acres; of his stock ponds and pens, and of assorted accumulations, including the 260-acre "old homeplace" where he was born almost eighty years ago. It is his proud boast that he owned the first milking machine in Madison County, that he "dopes and cures" his own cedar posts for his fences after having chopped them, and that "I'm the only young man who stayed here in Madisonville and made any money to amount to anything. The rest, they had to leave. J. R. Parten got rich, but he had to go off to New York and Houston to do it. I started out tradin' horses and then got in turkeys and hawgs and cattle, and it just kept a-growin'."

The visitor says, "So you can truly say that you made your seed money as a horse trader?"

"Yep. You can say that."

"And your success as a smart horse trader was the big factor in your accumulations, right?"

"Oh, yeah. Not any doubt about it." The old man swabs at frog-leg gravy with a crust of bread, pops it into his mouth, chews, nods, and says, " 'Course, now, it didn't hurt much when I leased my mineral rights to Silver Dollar West 'way back yonder, and he struck oil on it."

9 ☆

The Great Willie Nelson Outdoor Brain Fry and Trashing Ejacorama

People kept telling me the Austin scene was the only thing happening in Jerry Ford's America other than inflation and Tupperware parties. The Texas city was represented as the new Haight-Ashbury and the new Nashville, the only wide-open dope-and-music resort available now that students were studying again and Tom Hayden had taken to wearing neckties and kissing babies. So I was properly startled when Dub, an old Austin friend, telephoned New York to invite me to a picnic. It seemed a long way to travel unless he could throw in a quilting bee or a big night of bingo over at the Elks Lodge.

"This will not be your ordinary family picnic," Dub pledged. "There will be many thousands running around in assorted stages of undress and craziness. There will be nonstop music, screwing in the bushes, and nineteen-year-old good things to eat."

"There's a catch to it," I accused. "Congressmen and ex-communists are gonna make patriotic speeches from start to quit."

"Severely untrue," Dub said. "This will be an unfettered celebration of your basic freedoms. Free beer. Dope at reasonable prices. Bonfires. Fistfights. I predict that four or five people will be killed in interesting ways."

On that assurance, I was drawn to Willie Nelson's Third Annual Independence Day Outdoor Brain Fry, Ball Break, and Mixed Doubles Doping, Picking, and Trashing Ejacorama.

You can look around Austin and decide that the sixties cultural revolution arrived on the Texas & Pacific several thousand trains late. Perhaps this is because Sheriff LBJ effectively kept home fires doused even as Watts, Saigon, and Gene McCarthy burned. Maybe it's only that Texans are as backward as their Oklahoma cousins claim. Some credit, or blame, Willie Nelson. Music, after all, is the prime reason for Austin's special ambience. The idlers and bums and dreamers—the credit-card revolutionaries, cosmic cowboys, street urchins, fake rednecks and genuine shitkickers, crazy artists and writers—cannot get drunk or high unless guitars are thumping in their ears. One weary of the realities—grinning Jimmy, bankrupt cities, Solzhenitsyn's bullshit, the Watergate hangover—may get lost in the music and hazes of thirty-odd clubs offering live bands and costumed hustlers wearing everything from fey glitter to smelly brogans. There *is* a little something happening there, though it is neither Nashville nor Haight-Ashbury. Dodge City on acid, maybe. Alamo II. Despite trouble defining it, I'll take Austin and give you Grand Rapids, Plains, Marvin Gardens, and the Short Line Railroad.

That was my mind-set, at least, when I flew in for Willie Nelson's Brain Fry, so full of airline hospitalities that I'd captained a sing-along among recalcitrants in the first-class cabin. As with New York, I always approach Austin improbably convinced that adventures both spiritual and carnal shall seize me and shake me and make my lights shine.

Dub appeared in the airline terminal wearing an Indian blanket, a dreamer's smile, and an Abe Lincoln hat. Travelers competed to ignore him as he swayed in invisible breezes near the luggage counter. "We're gonna have us several tons of fun," he prophesied, "unless we sober up or happen to get shot."

Who, shot?

Dub told about last year's picnic, when Billy Cooper ran such Independence Day fevers that he taught Dr. Jay D. Milner to dance. Cooper is Willie Nelson's chauffeur, famed for being found asleep in the back seat while the boss was being busted for drunk driving; Dr. Milner is Nelson's publicist, a self-described fifty-year-old groupie. Dub said, "They got to fussing over fifteen cents or cats or dogs or something. Anyway, Billy pulled out what he calls his bidness—I think it was a twenty-five automatic—and placed a few warm-up shots in a spectacular pattern very near Jay's feet." Dr. Milner, a college professor at Southern Methodist before redneck rock beguiled him, remained intellectual enough to imitate Bojangles Robinson all the way to Fort Worth and was not seen again until the Moon of the Cold Winds.

Dub told about Gino McCoslin, the slick little promoter of Willie Nelson's Brain Fry, doing business for Crackerjack Productions. Gino is an habitual gun-toter who once operated such a rowdy club in Dallas that lawmen appeared nightly with police dogs and to photograph the customers. Gino considers his reaction to official harassments was in the best traditions of civic spirit. "I didn't want to shoot their dawgs," he says, reasonably, "so I closed up."

Willie Nelson himself had known experiences with firearms. "When Willie was living in Nashville," Dub said, "one of Ray Price's fighting cocks kept molesting Willie's laying hens. Ray Price was important to Willie, being a superstar who recorded a lot of Willie's original songs. Ray didn't pay much attention to Willie's complaints about the fighting cock, so one day Willie took a shotgun and wasted the booger. Well, Ray Price had a running fit and said he'd never again record one of Willie's songs. And he hasn't. Willie says he reckons that shooting Ray's 'mean rooster' didn't cost him but about sixty thousand dollars and change." Lately Willie had toted around a

.357 Magnum until a Dallas policeman talked him out of it. Dub said, "Then there's Jerry Jeff Walker. One time he—" I groaned. It was not necessary for Dub to inform me of Jerry Jeff Walker, a.k.a. Dr. Snowflake, a.k.a. Jacky Jack Doubletrouble, a.k.a. Scamp Walker. He is the man who got reasonably rich off writing "Mr. Bojangles," which Richard Nixon claims as his favorite song; this gives Tricky Dix and Old Scamp something in common besides their having been born natural outlaws. Once I was hosting this sedate cocktail party at Princeton, see, for delicate literary academicians and their proper wives, when Jerry Jeff Walker—who'd been playing a club in New York— appeared very much unannounced, dressed like a buffalo hunter, and looking like three months on field bivouac complicated by the blind staggers. Jacky Jack Doubletrouble proved that he was a natural showman by immediately imitating the walks and lisps of sherry-sipping academicians; he crashed about, stepping on long gowns, and howling for Lone Star beer. He asked a highly placed faculty wife her relative expertise in the blow job discipline and generally cleared staid old Maclean House as efficiently as a drunk spade with a switchblade. He left in a snowstorm, at supersonic speeds and in a rental car charged to my American Express card. The car was found abandoned in midtown Manhattan, long on traffic tickets and short on operable parts. Jerry Jeff 's explanation was that he couldn't remember being in a car that night. No, Dub need tell me but very little of ol' Scamp Walker.

But Dub was saying, "And after these rodeo cowboys beat Jacky Jack up—I mean stomped a *mudhole* in his ass—he lay in a buncha broken furniture and looked up through the blood and said, 'Y'all ain't so fuckin' tough. I been beat up worse than this by motorcycle gangs.' "

Delicious paranoid rumors shivered through the Austin underground. In beer joints and dope dens, where locals congregate to hear redneck rock, were many dire predictions of shit storms to come down. "They're gonna stop traffic for driver's license inspections as a way of holding down the crowd," one heard. "Then they'll use that as an excuse to search cars for dope." "They" were understood to be grim-jawed agents of Texas law enforcement units, reportedly half bonkers at the prospect of maybe 100,000 Independence Day outlaws invading Liberty Hill—a small community thirty miles north of Austin—for twenty-four hours of assorted outrages against the bucolic calm.

Liberty Hill's good burghers were said to be recalling Altamont's stabbings, Brando's town-trashing Wild Ones, all the hairy freaks and bare asses and general chaos of rock concerts or street theaters past. Willie Nelson's Outdoor Brain Fry would simply flout the law more than the law could allow, Austin already having known its nasty dope-war shootings and having a controversial sheriff who enraged the squares by refusing to hunt down anybody who occasionally sucked personal amounts of marijuana. Liberty Hill's county commissioner threatened a halting court injunction; a grand jury was rumored to have returned a sealed indictment against a musical biggie said to tote around astonishing heaps of cocaine in a brown-paper bag; farmers and ranchers near the concert site were reported to be erecting barricades they would reinforce with shotguns. Austin's underground soldiers, who live for kicks of any kind, could hardly wait to march into battle.

Then along came an outlander, full of enough chemicals and wet goods to see very small profits in diplomacy, who said, "Bullshit! None of that bad karma is likely to come down." Everybody glowered and sputtered as if it had been suggested they get haircuts and jobs. But the outlander persisted: "Too much money involved. Music's become a big economic factor here. And Willie Nelson is the *papasita*, the grand old man, the Hemingway and the Moses and the Chet Atkins. Hell, children, don't you read the goddamn papers? Willie's become a Texas folk hero second only to Darrell Royal! Coach Darrell and Willie play golf and pitch washers and scarf Mexican food together three times a week. Willie played in concert with the Dallas Symphony, and all the moneyed culture vultures flipped. The state legislature legitimized him by proclaiming Willie Nelson Day. Now, why, children? Why?"

They sulked over their pipes and bottles. "Why, children, because the big boys smell *money*. Ol' Willie, he's becoming a *business* asset to Texas. Packs 'em in at top prices whether beer joint, concert hall, outdoor picnic. Big on TV, records, in music publishing. Willie's a *success*, man, and when you're a success, the powerful want to be your friend; they want to welcome you into the club.

"These old thumb-bustin' sheriffs and highway patrolmen you've been worrying about, they may not quote much poetry or bore you with small talk about international finance, but by God, they've been bred to read the signs! You think a few snuff-dipping little ol' peckerwood badge wearers are gonna buck the power? Do you young semirevolutionaries *honestly* think the sheriff fucks with the Fords up in Detroit or the Johnsons over here in Johnson City? Why, hell, how you kids expect to overthrow anything if you don't recognize the nuances of elitism?" Whereupon, the civics lesson having concluded, the class got up and walked out on the professor, grumbling.

Not only is Willie Nelson now welcome in the better homes, but he has trouble getting arrested. When Texas lawmen discover him driving with his eyes unusually aglow, he hands 'em his latest album and a big country grin and goes on his way as free as Dred Scott. Probably he could beat on a tin lunch bucket with a rusty file, while calling up his hounds, and fawning music critics for *Rolling Stone, Picking Up the Tempo,* the *Village Voice,* and others would proclaim a new native art form awash in social significance. The fact that Willie *may* be the best thing since Bob Wills, Hank Williams, or the butter churn is slightly irrelevant. The point is, Willie holds Texas in the palm of his hand. People even talk about his running for governor: pretty good for a former door-to-door salesman of Bibles, vacuum cleaners, and kitchenware.

All of which is about half funny, Willie Nelson being reputed as a member of a group of music makers loosely known as the Nashville outlaws. These are talents who never got accepted by the Grand Ole Opry or Nashville's glad-handing Record Row executives, because they failed to shave, wore earrings, racially intermarried, smoked other than menthols, snorted rather than dipped, or wrote and sang of more than calico visions, sweet fading mothers, or honky-tonk angels. They were considered "political," people making statements in the discharge of their art and by their life-styles, all of which cut much against traditional country-western grains. Nasvhille had got rich on corn, thank you, and didn't care to switch to people raising cain. Willie got discouraged, returned to his native Texas, and saw something waiting to happen.

Eddie Wilson booked Willie into his Amardillo World Headquarters in Austin, where he gained quick acceptance among youthfuls who'd been raised on deafening doses of rock 'n' roll. As all intelligent adults know, your average rock-'n'-roll band is made up of hairy apes, greasy rapists, and transvestites, who, the moment they sing a single intelligible word or strike one pleasing chord, doom their careers. Rock was invented, and is promoted, by the hearing-aid cartel and serves no other use. Anyway. . . .

Author Edwin "Bud" Shrake, perhaps Austin's most persistent midnight cowboy, says, "I guess redneck rock or cowboy rock or progressive country—whatever you call it—got its start the night Willie Nelson blew everybody's mind at Amardillo about five years ago; it must have been in 'seventy-one. Anyway, traditional country music had been around here longer than the Baptists, but it was a stepchild or even a idiot child. It was strictly for 'necks and 'kickers. There was a shame to it, sort of like having the itch. And if you had long hair and walked into a beer joint to hear live country bands, then you took the same risks as hunting tigers with a slingshot. Willie melded the dopers and the ropers."

When Amardillo was founded, in 1970, it depended on imported rock groups until Willie Nelson opened the door with his mixture of traditional country and progressive country licks. Soon Jerry Jeff Walker drifted to Austin from Florida; Billy Joe Shaver came in for a while from Nashville; Michael Murphy arrived from North Texas State to put "cosmic cowboy" in the language; the son of an Austin professor unleashed himself as Kinky Friedman and the Texas Jewboys. Music began to hear of Austin-based people named B. W. Stevenson, Dough Sahm, Milton Carroll, Steven Fromholz, Dee Moeller.

Maybe in Nashville Willie Nelson was known only as a fine songwriter—"Hello Walls," "Crazy," "Night Life," dozens and dozens—who sometimes tangled the fingers of studio musicians because of his unusual phrasing and weird uses of meter. In Texas, however, up to 100,000 now were expected to pay $5.50 for advance tickets or $7.50 at the gate to suffer and sigh through his latest musical brain fry. We waited. And when you're in Austin, the way to wait is soak up a little warm-up music. . . .

Jerry Jeff Walker was onstage at the Alliance Wagon Yard, passionately misquoting the poet Dylan Thomas. Possibly he wanted to recall the lines "Do not go gentle into that good night. . . ./Rage, rage against the dying of the light." Walker's brain was not doing its best work, however, and he settled for repeating, "Rage . . . *rage* . . . RAGE against the goddamn dark." Several dozen times. People raged *from* the goddamn dark, urging Walker to permit the show to proceed; J.J., who was born with enough chips on his shoulder to make up a two-by-four, howled his own curses, along with demands for beer, nookie, and nose candy. "That boy always did know how to have a good time," my pal Dub said.

Dr. Snowflake was dressed in green shorts, a dingy T-shirt, and tennis shoes; one had the impression he'd left the house on Sunday morning to pick up a quart of milk and the newspapers and simply forgot to go back. Which is pretty much what pretty Susan Walker would claim when she tracked her husband down to remind him that he had an early flight to Nashville to oversee the mixing of his next album.

This was near the end of one of those perfect days when Jacky Jack had attacked assorted inanimate objects with swift kicks before tossing his color television set into the swimming pool. Characteristic of his mood, he greeted me: "Hey, you pussy, you don't know enough about country music to write it on my balls. Man, you don't have no fuckin' *notion* of what we're doing down here." I murmured that possibly I might help him with his Dylan Thomas. Dr. Snowflake selected from among random spectators a young woman, whom he shoved forward: "*She* ought to be writing the piece, not you. This gal's got answers where you don't even know any questions, you ignorant piece of pigshit." I began to suspect that perhaps I'd offended Jerry Jeff a night earlier, when he'd volunteered to be interviewed and I'd dismissed him on the grounds of not feeling like asking questions. "How the fuck's a asshole like you gonna write two paragraphs?" the good doctor now inquired. I said, well, I currently had it in mind to stomp the eternal pluperfect dogshit out of him, personally, and then write three pages about it. Dub and Bud Shrake moved in to lead Dr. Snowflake away before he could learn whether I fought any better than rodeo cowboys or motorcycle gangs.

Gino McCoslin, official promoter, was reported to be "proud

crazy"; this I interpreted as meaning he wouldn't do to mess with. He proved to be a bearded, wiry little fellow who looked bigger and bigger once one realized that the metal stick of "bidness" in his belt appeared to be no worse than a first cousin to your average cannon and that he was tossing off double vodkas at the bar as if Prohibition might be coming back on the next train. Gino explained that he needed the cannon to guard gate receipts and occasionally to negotiate with the unreasonable. When he learned that I'd once lived in Odessa, he offered a brilliant smile and the observation "Oh, yeah, I stabbed a cat from Odessa one time." This put me at ease, being very much better news than that he had stabbed the cat five or six times. Gino wished me a good show, and I backed away, bowing and scraping, as if departing the odor of royalty.

We left our fifth or sixth Austin club in time to see two strangers break another stranger's leg with what appeared to be iron bars. "I never seen the shitasses before," he gasped. (This was translated in the newspapers as "The attack was unprovoked.") I asked Eddie Wilson at Amardillo World Headquarters to explain such recurring outbreaks of violence.

"Oh," he said, "it's all a matter of manners. We're arbiters of manners down here."

Beg pardon?

"Aw, you know, some ol' boy will call another one a chickenshit cocksucking motherfucker, and the second fellow will think that's ill-mannered and break the other fellow's jaw."

The night before his big concert, Willie tossed a *Giant*-like bash for himself and friends at Austin's new Hilton Inn, which, in a classic case of ill timing, had opened its doors only a few days earlier; something is inherently sad about seeing brand-new doors splintered and carpets burned fresh out of their wrappers. Willie had meant to hold it down to a roaring 500 intimates; but tickets got forged, and security broke down. I doubt whether more than 2,200 persons crowded in; the fire marshal came with a summons but couldn't get within two blocks. The little sausages with the toothpicks in them, the chili con queso, and the booze lasted about eighteen minutes, though there was sweat and smoke enough for multitudes. Willie came out with his band and bravely shouted "Whiskey River," "Red Headed Stranger" and for a cab. A select 100 or so repaired to the Governor's Suite—though Willie was too smart to be among them—and conducted themselves so sedately until past dawn that chambermaids ultimately wept among the breakage. By midnight, though the brain fry-concert wouldn't begin until noon, there were reports of 20,000 disciples waiting near Liberty Hill in a huge pasture containing a stretch of the San Gabriel River and two lakes.

Though the concert lasted eighteen hours, I am critically disadvantaged in that I heard absolutely no music. This is partly because my day contained certain gaps and partly because The Press, and roughly 5,000 pretenders claiming to be The Press, were confined two or three fenced compounds away from the stage—and behind it—in what I came to think of as Andersonville Prison. Like its Civil War namesake, this new Andersonville exposed its residents to sunstroke, rain, dust, thirst, hunger, ticks, chiggers, and brutal keepers. But, then, I am getting ahead of my story. . . .

Willie and Dr. Jay D. Milner, his public relations genius, had provided The Press with individualized T-shirts bearing our powerful names and literary connections. These would permit us to roam at will, even breaking into song with Kris 'n' Rita or Willie himself if being onstage with them tempted our good judgments, and generally were advertised as guaranteeing everything but romance with the Pointer Sisters. "Willie don't want a lot of confusion backstage," Dr. Milner told The Press. "Accredited press people only will be admitted. You may visit with the stars at your leisure." *Rita! Hot damn! You in trouble, Kris!*

Dr. Milner depicted an oasis of trailer houses full of frigid air-conditioner breezes, warm-blooded hostesses, hot food, cold liquors, and maybe palm trees. When we ladies and gentlemen of The Press had gorged our souls on angel's music or celebrity contacts, we would be free to repair to this perfect oasis, where everything would be provided except house slippers; just don't forget to wear your Willie Nelson T-shirts. Ten minutes later Dr. Milner came back to say that, well, er, ah, our T-shirts might not mean all that much, since they'd apparently been copied and were going for $5 each all over Texas. Now we would have to make do with Press Passes; sorry about you having to stand in line to get 'em, but they'll do the job, yessir, don't you worry. My Press Pass was blue. Blue Press Passes were represented as passports to everything but heaven and Albania. These would eventually entitle the bearers, if otherwise qualified, to drive on public roads.

We inched toward Liberty Hill at speeds more indigenous to the tortoise than the hare. Signs only twelve miles from the concert site promised parking at $2; sign a mere two miles away proclaimed the same service for $8. People walked along burdened by beer coolers, tents, watermelons, crying kids, folding chairs, picnic hampers, and their hindsight judgments; walking cases of sunburn, drunkenness, and shell shock were noted. Cars overheated and were abandoned where they exploded; grim rustics, sure enough, guarded their private roads with barricades of pickup trucks, scowls, and shotguns. My car required less than three hours to conquer thirty miles, a statistic causing much envy. The last 100 yards included fording a swift stream. It would be the last water I would see until it rained on Andersonville Prison.

We swaggered to the special gate reserved for Lords of the Press, confident in our individualized T-shirts and flashing our blue Press Passes. These so impressed security guards that they turned their backs. We then had the good luck to be joined by Gino McCoslin, who proclaimed his importance as official promoter and vouched for us as his good friends of The Press. One of the security guards grinned, grabbed Gino's head, trapped it in a wire fence, and began to beat on it. Gino did not appear unduly surprised but reached into his belt and got us admitted at gunpoint. It didn't seem unusual at the time.

Turned out we'd broken into Andersonville Prison. It was heavily overpopulated. Security guards at gates leading to the next compound, nearer to the stage by 300 yards, had guns of their own and didn't seem to fear Gino's. Gino ran away and came back with a stamp machine, which he applied to our blue Press Passes, causing them to say PAYMENT APPROVED. He said this would permit us to go anyplace we wanted. He was full of shit.

Bud Shrake and I decided to break out of Andersonville; our escape gave us a view of a broiling mass then 70,000 strong. It was scary. Writhing human forms as far as the eye could see. Tents and banners and bonfires and scorched earth and burned asses. Garbage and litter. Fellini's version of hell. There were shanties reminiscent of Hoovervilles, where people hawked blue jeans, souvenir programs, and fireworks. People noting our official Willie Nelson T-shirts complained because beer wasn't available, their hair hurt, the temperature was 106 degrees Fahrenheit, and no big-name acts had appeared yet. Many appeared to be crazed, with or without artificial stimulants.

"They are going to rip our official T-shirts off and stuff 'em up our asses," Shrake whispered. We rapidly headed toward the relative safety of Andersonville Prison, smiling and waving like Nixon-Agnew going up to claim the nomination, making loud promises of all the shameful conditions we intended to improve. Now, however, Andersonville Prison was guarded by a 300-pound Samoan whose stick was big enough to please Teddy

Roosevelt. He whopped my shoulders and neck with it awhile. Shrake squatted in the shade of the big fellow's considerable shadow, watching him work and frequently chuckling. I broke and ran.

We found a friendlier gate. It was in the charge of Paul English, a member of Willie's band who is also the boss's alter ego. English is a double for Satan, except for being too skinny: Willie has written such songs about him as "Devil in a Sleepin' Bag." Paul waved us in while accusing a security guard of pocketing gate proceeds. The fellow denied it. When a bystander shouted that the guard had, indeed, pocketed his $7.50, Paul English threw the guard to the ground and ripped out his pockets. What looked like $300 fell out. Paul kicked him in the jaw with a cowboy boot, prompting the guard to resign on the grounds of guilt by association. While Paul was recovering the money, several dozen music lovers decided to crash the gate. English produced a "bidness" of about .22 caliber, with a long barrel, and had the scientific satisfaction of seeing a moving mass immediately reverse its direction.

Ah, at last! The oasis of trailer houses Dr. Milner had reserved for The Press! They were stoutly locked from the inside and under siege from about 3,000 howling Andersonville inmates. By now we spat cotton and knew enough to whine and beg. A tall blond hostess named Cookie admitted us. Probably she only wanted to share her misery; somebody had forgotten to connect the air conditioning and to order food and drink. Cookie offered a choice of pretzels or salt tablets, though she couldn't provide water in either case. We gasped and made sweat and occasionally fainted. I do not recall any palm trees.

A friendly musician produced white powders from twin vials. One assumed them to be varied grains of cocaine. One should not have. One should have presumed them to be Methedrine and THC, or, more accurately, a bastard variety of the latter used to tranquilize hogs. One soon began to feel peculiar. One remembers trying to turn over somebody's camper, somehow shorting an electrical circuit in the process—sizzle! flash!—rooting in the dirt and oinking and being begged by friends to sit in the shade.

The Press was shrieking and whining to Gino McCoslin of betrayals and brutality. Gino leaned against a tree he thought he was propping up, focused on Europe with a dazed smile, and said, "Wheah!" about every eight seconds. Had I been a narc, I'd have arrested him on the evidence of his eyes; they appeared to be made of red glazed tile.

Gino did his best to talk. We leaned in and cupped our ears as if taking a deathbed confession. Gino appeared to be talking in strange tongues. Shrake translated approximately as follows: "Fuck it, I paid the goddamn politicians twenty thousand dollars to ensure security, and all they done was provide a bunch of killer bikers ripping off gate receipts and stomping the customers. You spoiled and pampered Press shitasses might do well to avoid them mean bastards. Git away, I'm busy holding up this tree."

Somebody shouted, "Goddamn it, you promised commodious accommodations, and we're paying two dollars a warm can for bootleg beer." Gino mumbled that he'd take a six-pack hisself if somebody would fetch it.

There was elected a Committee of Unrest and Indignation. Its purpose was to locate Willie Nelson. Better it had gone looking for Judge Crater. Willie and the other big, bright stars had locked themselves in their private trailers and would not give out their addresses among the acres of cars, campers, and trucks. Somebody said he'd seen Willie come out and sniff what appeared to be baking soda but that he'd disappeared in a cow pony's lope when a giggling gang of groupies began ripping off his clothes. (Jerry Jeff would have stayed and fought, by God.) "Willie was grinning," the informant volunteered. Willie is always grinning. When you talk to him, he looks at you and grins and grins and nods and nods and appears to be the world's best listener, until you realize he is not listening at all.

We found Dr. Milner, wearing a false beard and pretending not to be himself. Unmasked, he cleverly touted us to his Press-trailer oasis, where—he proclaimed—refreshments had newly arrived. We broke in by main force amid much shouting and grappling. The lucky got one can of warm beer, two bell tomatoes, and leavings of potato chips. It was exactly 144 degrees in there. All the hostesses were crying and trying to garrote people with their WELCOME TO WILLIE'S banners. No more than 150 people milled, cursed, and shoved in a space God had made for 20.

I spotted a tray of delicate steak sandwiches, dug in my heels, used my huge, swollen body as a shield, and wolfed them down quickly enough to qualify for the *Guinness Book of World Records*. A frail fellow in fruit boots began to beat my broad back with his tiny little fists and screamed, "You son of a bitch, you just ate the Pointer Sisters' supper!" I said there hadn't been enough to sponsor a good burp, anyway, and why didn't he just send 'em some watermelon? "Oh, you reprehensible racist *poot*," he screeched. They led him off burbling about steak sandwiches' being required in the Pointer Sisters' contract.

We were herded back to the stifling open air of Andersonville Prison, whereupon it began to rain like a tall cow pissing on a flat rock. The baked and blistered thousands cheered. There was a sharp retort—unmistakably, gunfire—and the cheers increased. "My God," Shrake said, "somebody just got *shot,* and people are celebrating it." Crouching in the rain and goofy with hog chemicals, I fervently hoped it had been Willie Nelson and that he'd been blown away as effectively as Ray Price's mean rooster. Unfortunately it had only been Paul English firing into the tent roof above the stage to rid it of dangerous water accumulations.

The Pointer Sisters' road manager appeared to announce that his charges refused to go onstage. Wouldn't sing without their supper, huh? But it proved not to be a food strike, merely a matter of pure terror. "Listen, you blame 'em? I mean, thousands of crazed honkies out there and them the only *blacks*? And people shooting guns and shit!"

Scott Hale of the Willie Nelson group led the manager onstage to convince him of security. "See how nice it is?" Scott beamed. "Everything's fine."

The manager said, "Yeah? Then how come your leg is on fire?"

Scott looked down to see that a bottle rocket had come out of the crowd and lodged in his right boot, which was sending up enough smoke and flames to lift off a moon shot. He immediately began to stomp and thresh across the stage, making wild owl-hoot noises. Many cheered, thinking he was dancing a spectacular cowboy polka.

The Pointer Sisters agreed to come out only if a flying wedge of 100 reasonably unzonked honkies would lead them onstage and off. The security guard leading the flying wedge was so loaded on scotch and Quaaludes that he fell backward at the top of the stage steps, causing a domino reaction. The much-buffeted Pointer Sisters squealed and grabbed their wigs and probably wished for Detroit City.

Along about midnight, sufficiently baked and wet and beaten, I decided I'd had enough entertainment, even though I'd not heard any music, laid eyes on Willie Nelson, or had a chance to strike on Rita Coolidge. It took only two hours to bog through the sea of mud, past grungy bikers pissing in open fields and assorted wounded groaning from the bushes in passion or despair, to find that my rental car was missing. Just plain gone.

The fellow who gave me a lift toward civilization kindly consented to sell the remains of his bottle of scotch for $27; by the

time this good Samaritan dropped me at my hotel it required
two bellmen and a baggage cart to get me to my room.

Gino McCoslin later managed to make it sound as if the Willie
Nelson concert had been an artistic triumph and a financial
disaster.

How was that possible, with huge multitudes paying what
theoretically had to approach a half million dollars?

Gino seemed to say that while maybe 100,000 people had
heard the wonderful music, pitifully few had paid for the privilege. He spoke of gate crashers, counterfeit tickets; 8,000 or
12,000 or 17,000 tickets allegedly stolen; receipts pocketed by
security men; record high expenses.

Tell me about the expenses, I said.

Gino mumbled huge sums rapidly, sticking to generalities
and claiming he was not authorized to open the books for in-
spection.

How much had been spent on Press arrangements?

Gino said it was $15,000 or $25,000 or maybe $50,000; he
remembered it had a five in it. I said if he spent over $2.98,
other than for the goat fencing surrounding Andersonville
Prison, then he'd been ripped off. Gino expressed absolute astonishment in saying mine was the first complaint he'd received. "Ol' Willie's generous," he said. "Willie spent so much
money making sure his friends and fans would be comfortable
he probably lost his ass." It was suggested that Gino might be
rehearsing his speech to the IRS folks. "No shit, now," he said.
"It'll take days to tote it up, but I'd bet my ass we didn't no more
than break even."

I recalled Willie's comment after his second Independence
Day picnic, where he also allegedly only broke even, when
asked if he would hold another: "Hell, I guess so. I'd hate to
throw four thousand thieves out of work."

Gino now was painting Willie Nelson as a good-hearted

raggedy-ass, who might have to sell his horses or find his wife a part-time job, when two pistol-packing cowboys came in. They grunted under the burden of several sacks, which they dumped onto a table. One said, "This here's the forty thousand dollars from advance ticket sales in San Antonio." Gino had the grace to wince.

I wanted to see Willie, I said, to commiserate with him in his poverty and maybe to kick his ass for sponsoring such a confused show. "Willie?" Gino said, surprised. "Shit, man, *Willie* ain't here! Willie and his old lady went straight to the airport for two weeks in Hawaii."

Later, at my friend Dub's house, we drank beer and smoked with various youthfuls while listening to Willie Nelson sing to us of red-headed strangers wild in their sorrow, of how cold it is sleeping out on the ground, of life's rough and rocky traveling. People muttered, "Great, man," and, "Outtasight," and, "Pick up on this 'un, baby," all around the worshipful circle. I'd been a Willie Nelson fan for years, back when there had been so few of us we took pride in being a cult; his mournful, melancholy music never had failed to reach me. But now all I could think of was Willie picking up the telephone in the Waikiki Hilton to call room service, he and God grinning together at the irony of his poor-boy songs.

Part III ☆

Politicians

of winners and losers
and some you can't tell

☆

Interlude

Politicians, and the political processes, seldom have had difficulty gaining my interest. I am not so much fascinated by the fine print of legislative acts, or the ideological arguments, as by the inner workings of political institutions or what varied chemicals slosh in the heads and innards of the political man. Winners and losers each harbor their special attractions, though —somehow—losers always seem to provide the better material for stories. Perhaps this is for no grander reason than that life has touched them up a bit more. Show me a politician who's never been knocked to his knees, and I'll show you a piece of plastic and a ball of putty.

Sometimes it's hard to tell who wins or loses. That is the case, I believe, with the title subject of "The Trial of John Connally." Mr. Connally thirsts for the presidency in 1980 as much as any American capable of working up a slobber, but will people think of him as a loser because he was indicted, tried, and is remembered by many as reeking of Watergate taint? That may not be fair, but it *is* a condition with which John Connally must live. And what psychological devils cavort in the private country of Connally's mind as he, a smart man, thinks on that handicap? Aye, *there*'s the story! Unfortunately, it isn't available to write. Politicians being what they are—human—it probably never shall be.

Mo Udall, unflatteringly labeled "The Loser" in the section to follow, certainly took his career lumps and knew heartbreaking near misses against Jimmy Carter. As one who's long known him as a friend, I think Udall gained a better understanding of himself than if he'd won. If he hasn't, he never amounted to much anyway. In terms of what's since happened to him politically, he survived a recall election and then defeated a strong, well-financed candidate backed by Arizona conservatives— many of whom, whether Republican or Democrat, had always voted for Udall because of his reputation for honesty and integrity; his national campaign, however, alerted them that he was much more liberal than they could tolerate. To that extent Udall may have lost some political pizazz back home, but I think it's healthy that his constituents have attained a clearer reading. Udall has become chairman of the House Interior Committee and remains a factor with which President Carter must deal. For the first fifteen months of Carter's administration, the President remained cool and standoffish. Finally, he invited his vanquished rival to the White House for a private chat and vittles; since that time they've worked fairly well together.

Most of the pieces in this political section treat the Congress. I feel as if I have three homes: Texas, my place of roots; New York, where as a young soldier I began to grow up and where I would return to continue, in middle age, the growing-up processes; and Congress, where for a decade between the ages of twenty-five and thirty-five, I learned something of the refinements of politics while working for three Texas congressmen. I also had the opportunity sometimes to work with, or around, my home-state senior senator. You may already have figured out that his name was Lyndon B. Johnson. The things I saw him do and heard him say behind-the-door were not earthshaking, because we were not all that intimate, but those early impressions *do* contribute to the final portrait painted in this collection: "The Alamo Mind-Set: LBJ and Vietnam."

My father got me interested in politics early. As you'll recall from an earlier story, I grew up hearing him, and his contemporaries, blame one President and one party for the Great Depression and praise another President and *his* party for delivering us from evil. Early on, I deduced that it was vital to have a voice in who might rule us if we cared about our asses. Some of my earliest memories are of tagging along with my father to political "pie suppers"—rallies where rural candidates, before speaking, bid on the baked goodies of the community wives, and then shared the pie or cake with the family of the good lady who'd baked it. At age ten I was handing out campaign cards and making passionately empty speeches to bewildered or bemused farmers in behalf of a county commissioner candidate with the wonderful name of Arch Bent; he won. Later I would campaign for friends in Texas who ran for district attorney, county attorney, sheriff, and so on. When one of these, a state legislator named J. T. Rutherford, won a seat in Congress in 1954, I moved from Texas to Washington with him and for a decade remained a second-banana politician on Capitol Hill. It was there, in the House, that I saw for the first time the inner tickings of a political institution and had the opportunity to study politicians of all geographic, ideological, moral, and tactical varieties. I know nothing, I think, that more prepared me for writing.

I think the reader can always tell whose side I'm on. I simply don't believe that "objective" political reporting exists; people without political beliefs have no interest in writing about politics and don't do it. We all come to the page burdened by our own political wisdom and infallibility; it's impossible to lay anything that awesome aside. Some of my academic superiors did not approve when I taught my students to parade their prejudices and biases in their writing, but I thought it both more honest and more practical than to attempt to teach impossible concealments. The reader will sense it if the writer is trying to hide something. He or she will strike false chords; his or her work will be hurt. If, on the other hand, the writer is free to wave his political banner, then the reader can clearly see it and allow for windage. That's what I try to do when I look at a politician.

10 ☆

The Trial of
John Connally

It was in July 1974 that they threw him off the bandwagon and into the briar patch. He had just returned home, to Texas, from a thirty-six-state speaking tour, one that the suspicious equated with future presidential plans. And why not? Though they'd laughed when John B. Connally switched political parties so untimely as to become identified immediately with the Watergate gang ("The only known case of a rat swimming out to the sinking ship"), he seemed to be overcoming the secondhand taint. Big crowds. Headlines. Star billings. For all his partisan or ideological detractors, Connally carried no personal odor of wrongdoing; he was determinedly keeping a high profile; at the rate large Republican cookies were crumbling, it seemed that John Connally shortly might be the only unbroken one in the box.

And then the Watergate special prosecutors turned their attention to John Bowden Connally, Jr., fifty-seven, the only show hog in a Republican pigsty—that distinguished and glamorous study in silver and bronze; the poor boy who'd worked up to three terms as governor of Texas and head of one of the nation's larger law firms; the man who'd served three Presidents and had been shot at the side of one and had spoken the eulogy over

165

another. This man who'd walked among kings and pharaohs he'd sometimes lectured was, incredibly, indicted by a federal grand jury for the taking of a grubby $10,000 bribe and then lying in a conspiracy to conceal it.

Juror Number 13 (though he did not yet think of himself as such) was stunned when he heard the news, and not a little gleeful. Though his personal contacts with the man had been few and perfunctory, he had never been fond of John B. Connally. Often he had fumed at Connally's utterances and actions, judging him a public official with little compassion for the disadvantaged, seeing in the overall package, despite Connally's advertised charm, a man who could be arrogant, cold, impatient, ruthless. Connally cuddled up to the high and the mighty, had superhawk instincts, was apathetic or hostile toward minorities or civil liberties; his complaints against the better parts of LBJ's Great Society, despite Connally's background as LBJ's favorite pupil and creature, had once prompted Johnson to rumble, "John ain't been worth a damn since he started wearing three-hundred-dollar suits." John Connally had employed the harshest rhetoric against such a decent man as George McGovern in heading Democrats for Nixon. For these reasons, and because Connally had long epitomized those Tory Democrats who regularly crushed his own kamikaze Liberal Democrats in Texas, Juror Number 13 was quick to enjoy laughter when Connally signed on as cabin boy aboard the political *Titanic*—only to leave the Nixon White House, mumbling about "that goddamned mess over there," after a dozen frustrating weeks as a presidential adviser no longer able to influence, and rarely able to see, the increasingly reclusive President. Connally's indictment gave the Juror hope that another of the bastards might get exactly what was coming to him.

The indictment charged that John B. Connally, Jr., while Secretary of the Treasury in 1971, had accepted two illegal gratuities of $5,000 from one Jake Jacobsen, a lawyer-lobbyist for the Associated Milk Producers of America, Inc.—a dairy farmers' cooperative—in return for having influenced the Nixon administration to increase federal milk price supports. Then (Jacobsen had sworn), when the Watergate going got sticky in 1973, Connally had returned $10,000 in cash and had conspired with him to conceal the original bribes by concocting a cover story that the money had remained in Jacobsen's lockbox in an Austin bank, untouched, for more than two years.

John Connally, over a period of months before his indictment, had increasingly sounded troubled and disenchanted: Public men were willy-nilly hounded, slandered, used for handy scapegoats in the post-Watergate morality (he said again and again) until the day might be fast approaching when good men would refuse to sacrifice themselves, their reputations, their families, their privacy. What most people did not know was that Connally had become convinced, in the months following his appearance before a federal grand jury, of a dark plot by the omnipotent They. "They are out to assassinate me politically," he gloomed to friends and family.

He was resting at his ranch near his native Floresville, in South Texas—where in better days he had lavishly entertained the Richard Nixons and the Big Rich—when the government's bomb went off. Connally called in the media boys to deny the allegations and defy the allegator. "Nobody can buy me," Connally said, and went into seclusion.

"But the thing was in John's head twenty-four hours a day for over a year," an associate says. "He's prouder than a penful of peacocks, and he felt disgraced. We worried about him."

While John Connally was in limbo and preparing his defense —choosing as his lawyer the celebrated Edward Bennett Williams, who is not only president of the Washington Redskins, but treasurer of the Democratic National Committee, and was high on the Nixon enemies list—Juror Number 13 did not preoccupy himself with the matter; it is axiomatic that the troubles of others, while walking slowly through the heads of the afflicted, whiz through the minds of the uninvolved at race-car speeds. But as the trial approached, and John Connally suddenly bloomed forth again, granting interviews to select friendlies, speaking to standing ovations before the Houston Rotary Club, even meeting privately for forty-five minutes with Jerry Ford during the President's Texas visit in February, it became apparent that this strategy aimed at depicting Connally as a proud, strong, victimized defendant. Connally associates increasingly put the bad mouth on Jake Jacobsen and let it leak that some dark conspiracy existed: This rotten charge against John was the only way Democrats had of keeping him out of the White House. So there would be a bloody fight, one that Connally's friends saw as vital not only to his personal restoration but to his political resurrection. The Juror began to consider what he knew of the case and of the people in it.

Of Jake Jacobsen it must be said that the Juror held him, at best, in minimal high regard. Jacobsen he had known as the man who had raised money for Governor Price Daniel in Texas and otherwise was a Tory hatchet man. Jake had always been a shadowy figure, one who stood in the wings and manipulated the puppets. He had always seemed a bit . . . well, opportunistic. There was something of the political eunuch in him, sniffs of one capable of serving many masters. Indeed, Jake could in 1962 back Governor Daniel against the challenge of John Connally, and then—once Connally won—ingratiate himself with the new king; he could leap forward to serve President Johnson in the White House and later—with LBJ bitter and withering in retirement while having bad dreams of his own death—cheerfully join John Connally in his Democrats for Nixon subterfuge. You thought of Jake Jacobsen, and you thought of one who always knew where the bread was buttered and would be there to get his. And perhaps more than his.

The State of Texas had accused him of plundering savings-and-loan companies (in which he had an interest) in multiple conspiracies to divert funds for his own use. In a matter of months the bankrupt Jacobsen went from paper assets of $3 million to deficits of $8 million; where once he had been an official of a dozen banks, he now had trouble cashing checks.

By the time Texas got through with Jake Jacobsen at the grand jury level he had been indicted on charges capable of sending him to the slammer for forty years. Think about it: 14,600 days and nights. Jake was fifty-odd. Forty years. It was then he plea-bargained with the feds, agreeing to testify against John Connally *only* if allowed to plead guilty to bribing him . . . *and to nothing else.* All other charges, state and federal, must be dropped, and efforts made to prevent Jake's disbarment in Texas. He thus traded a potential forty years for what appeared to be a certain two years: not a bad day's work.

Juror Number 13 had seen many boys off Texas farms and out of Texas factories and from the Texas slums grow rich while becoming Great, or pretending to. He knew the habits of Texas politics, knew that powerful incumbents had a way of being adopted by wealthy patrons; they mingled socially and ruled the state in something close to partnership. Periodically, scandals would erupt, and people would go to jail or be driven from office—state representatives, a land commissioner, a former attorney general or two, a speaker of the House. Was John Connally capable of the usual shortcuts?

In the large sense, perhaps. The Juror never had been wholly satisfied with Connally's explanation, at hearings to confirm him as Secretary of the Treasury, that the $225,000 he'd accepted in executor's fees from the Sid Richardson estate during three years as governor had been deferred payments for work earlier performed and therefore represented no conflict of interest. Connally had not made his contention more credible by telling the Senate Finance Committee how he had sacrificed by waiv-

ing a portion of his executor's fee in order to accept appointment from President Kennedy as Secretary of the Navy: "I
don't go around, Senators, bragging about it. I never said to
anybody until this morning that I took four hundred thousand
dollars to five hundred thousand dollars less than I could have
taken to serve my country." Without belittling the patriotic
instincts, did this ring true from a man who'd several times quit
public service for the announced purpose of making more
money faster, and who obviously loved and accumulated the
finer things? Once, in the early 1960s, Connally had fled the
country until publicity had died down about large amounts of
political money he had raised for Senator Stuart Symington;
again, in the late 1950s, when lobbyists were throwing around
so much money to pass a bill freeing producers of natural gas
from federal controls at the wellhead that Senator Francis Case
reported he'd been offered an out-and-out $1,500 bribe for his
vote, John B. Connally almost got pie on his face; though he was
not connected with the bribe offer to Case, he *was* one of those
tirelessly lobbying for the gas bill, and he'd been working toward that end with the Texan who *had* allegedly done the
deed.

But in the narrow sense, no. Was Connally not too proud a
human unit to hold his hand out for a nickel here or a dime
there? Was he not too vain? Didn't he perhaps have a shade too
much *class,* yes, to creep around accommodating a procession
of small-time bagmen?

But hold on. There seemed a third possibility, one neither
fish nor fowl. Both Jake and John were old-pro pols who'd
shared common political geography and cultures; they knew
how elastic campaign financing laws had been and understood
the benefits of mutual back scratching. Could it be that with
little embarrassment on the part of either man—given old
friendships, common causes, and an unspoken understanding
of the sophisticated operating nuances—money had changed

hands in transactions that neither had troubled to weigh on any particular moral scale? Had their sensibilities been deadened by habit and custom? And later, once the Watergate pot heated up and new rules seemed to be proclaimed, had they panicked out of a sudden tardy suspicion that the old rules might be terribly difficult to explain? *Possible,* the Juror thought. *Very possible.*

The defendant emerged from a black limousine into the stammer of flashbulbs and the yammerings of nearby jackhammers, running the gauntlet of press people, cameramen, the morbidly curious. Earlier, leaving the Washington Mayflower for the U.S. courthouse in a relatively scabby part of town, he had grumbled of dreading this spectacle most of all; it would make him feel like something in a zoo. It must have seemed incredible, to one who'd always presented himself for public inspections while wearing the cloaks of power, that bystanders now thought of him as the Accused.

In the courtroom, after greeting a sparse committee of Texas friends and perfunctorily joking about a weight loss, John Connally appeared nervous and dry-mouthed; he rubbed his hands as if to warm them and sampled the room in quick random glances. And why not a little sweat on the brow, some flutters in the gut? He knew more than a little of power, had chased it and caught it, had learned to use it like a club. Now the power of the state could send him to prison for up to four years and assess fines of up to $20,000 upon conviction for bribery; later, should perjury and conspiracy counts be successfully brought, it could total penalties of nineteen years and $50,000. Perhaps he now felt something of Jake Jacobsen's earlier fear and desperation.

Little at the prosecutor's table could have given the defendant comfort: four young, grim men of such dogged intensity that before the week was out newsmen would dub them the

Undertakers and offer a bounty of $5 for the first sighting of a smile.

Of these the honcho was Frank M. Tuerkheimer, thirty-five, the son of a Bronx butcher, who'd won honors at Columbia and New York University Law School before becoming an assistant to Robert Morgenthau, the U.S. Attorney for the Southern District of New York. Stolid and dark, with a tumble of neglected black hair, he seemed near to shy: a closemouthed man who would prove indifferent to small talk. His chief assistant was Jon A. Sale, thirty-one, also a graduate of NYU Law and of Morgenthau's office. These were cautious men, whose advertised common attraction was "a passion for justice"; they were young men with causes; no need to whisper to John B. Connally of how dangerous such men might be.

Of Edward Bennett Williams, fifty-five, heading the Connally defense, it has been said—not entirely accurately—that he is a man of clients, not of causes. Senator Joe McCarthy. The Washington *Post*. Jimmy Hoffa. The Democratic National Committee. Bernard Goldfine. Congressman Adam Clayton Powell. Senator Thomas Dodd. *Playboy*'s Hugh Hefner. Bobby Baker. Folk singer Peter Yarrow. Tough Tony Boyle. Frank Costello. Robert Vesco. Almost every time he represented one of them, the crank mail or hate calls came in. Robert Kennedy privately remarked in anger that Williams should have been disbarred for permitting Hoffa to take the Fifth Amendment more than 100 times; Republicans had attacked him for so advising Bobby Baker; Dick Nixon is on tape as threatening to "fix" Williams. Williams had developed a standard response: "If the day ever comes when lawyers grow timid about taking unpopular causes, the whole criminal procedure under our Constitution is in pretty serious trouble."

Williams . . . how to describe him? A man of many parts and faces. Sometimes he looks like Art Carney. Sometimes like an Irish bartender or a respectable, possibly dull senator from one of the prairie states. Sometimes a beefy-shouldered gumshoe, a union organizer, an old single-wing blocking back gone slightly to suet. Almost always he appears a little glum, as if maybe his feet hurt, or he'd rather not keep his next appointment. His eyes are narrow in a broad face; his nose is a potato; his hair sweeps back from a high forehead as if for efficient storage and terminates high on the neck in tight ringlets.

Juror Number 13 had heard that in private Ed Williams is a great raconteur, a fine and affable entertainer, who, while relaxing with such chums as columnist Art Buchwald and Washington *Post* executive editor Ben Bradlee, is careful to consume his share of the whiskey. It was reported that in preparation for the Connally trial he'd not touched even a social drop in eight weeks. A man, therefore, capable of the tougher disciplines; a serious man when it counts. In control.

The gossip ran that E. B. Williams almost desperately coveted a big victory; while he had won a settlement for the Democratic National Committee from the Committee for the Re-election of the President (resulting from the Watergate break-in) and had successfully represented the Washington *Post* in its Pentagon Papers actions, his last three or four noted criminal clients had gone directly to jail.

On the bench sat Judge George L. Hart, Jr., of the United States district court: sixtyish, a frail man with a pinched face, arthritic hands, and a wispy island of black hair atop his bald dome. Almost wizened. Judge Hart, who'd been criticized for virtually apologizing to Richard Kleindienst while wrist-tapping the former Attorney General with a thirty-day suspended sentence, had been advertised as stern and churlish; through the trial of John Connally, however, he would appear affable and folksy. In a posttrial analysis in the *New Republic*, Fred Graham, himself a lawyer, would argue that Hart's *in camera* decisions had benefited Connally to the last in number.

The jury, that delicate democratic instrument always capable of the unexpected, in its final statistics comprised ten blacks and two whites; seven women and five men. It contained an art historian, a café worker, three clerks and a retired clerk, a receptionist-secretary, a retired printer, a cook, a maid, and two unemployed persons. It averaged 48.7 in years, only two of the members being under thirty-five and only one under thirty; three had passed sixty, and three more rapidly were gaining on it. Edward Bennett Williams appeared to have made his selections well: He wanted no hippies, no young black dudes, no revolutionaries; none who might enjoy seeing a rich, white Establishment figure marched off in chains. Indeed, much of the jury looked like what might be found in the choir on Sunday mornings at the Church-of-God-in-Jesus-Christ-on-Georgia-Avenue: aging or aged black ladies, given to decorous dress and fruit hats and random shouts of *A-men.* People who believed in the redemption of sin. Juror Number 13 jotted a prediction: "Williams will not hesitate to quote the Good Book."

Williams's good work, alas, was not immediately recognized by all Texans who'd come to see John Connally through his dark hour. For months the word had gone around Texas, in time taking on the weight of gospel, that Big John had no more chance of a fair trial in Washington, Dee-Cee, than the proverbial snowball had in hell. Only the roughnecks and rednecks said *nigger,* though nigger often was well implied. "I'd pick that jury by complexion," said a prominent Texas lawyer not noted for bigotry.

"We will demonstrate," said Jon Sale, in opening for the prosecution, "that in 1971, Mr. Jake Jacobsen—then representing American Milk Producers, Inc.—spent more time with John Connally, then Secretary of the Treasury, than any person *other* than government employees. . . ."

Less than a month after Connally became Secretary in February 1971, Sale noted, Jake told him that his 40,000-member organization raised political-action funds by a method similar to payroll checkoffs used by labor unions: "Mr. Jacobsen made it clear his organization had money and would spend it to get what it wanted." It then wanted government milk price supports raised from $4.66 per hundredweight, or 85 percent of parity.* The desired 5 percent difference would gain ten cents per quart for milk producers. "Mr. Connally agreed to try to be helpful."

But only eight days later, on March 12, Agriculture Secretary Clifford Hardin ruled that milk price supports would remain at the old level. "This was unhappy news, so Mr. Jacobsen went back to see his friend John Connally on March 15. Mr. Connally again agreed to be helpful. You shall hear on a tape in evidence —a tape recorded in the White House—just how helpful Mr. Connally was. President Nixon was there. Secretary Hardin was there. Mr. Ehrlichman was there.... Mr. Connally certainly was there. He *dominated* that meeting ... and only *two days later* Secretary Hardin . . . established milk price supports at 85 percent of parity."

On May 14, "John Connally accepted as a 'thank you' a gratuity for what he'd done. That act began this criminal case." On April 28, by Sale's version, Jacobsen had visited Connally's office and was told, "You know, I was of help on that milk producers thing and I understand they have some political money. You think you can get some of that money for me?" (Connally, at the defense table, reddens; shakes his head *no no no no no.*) Sale said Jacobsen then told an official of the dairy co-op, Bob A. Lilly, that he needed $10,000 for Secretary Connally. "Cash is generally hard to trace," Sale said, "but this time the cash left footprints—a trail running from Mr. Lilly to Mr. Connally." On

---

*Parity: a level for farm-product prices, maintained by government support and intended to give farmers the same purchasing power they had during a chosen base period.

May 4, Bob Lilly borrowed $10,000 from the Citizens National Bank of Austin, took the money in cash, and handed it over to Jacobsen.

The prosecution's story continues:

On May 13 Jacobsen took the money in a briefcase to Washington, where he kept it overnight in the Madison Hotel. The next morning he divided it into two $5,000 bundles. One he delivered to John Connally with the comment "There's more where that came from." He then rented a lockbox and stored the remaining $5,000: "We shall introduce documents showing the time he rented that lockbox; Mr. Connally's logs will affirm that Mr. Jacobsen earlier went to Mr. Connally's office on that morning of May 14—at the time he will tell you he did, and left when he will tell you he did."

Jake had thought "to get more credit" by twice bearing gifts: "The trail of the second five thousand dollars is as clear as the first." On September 23, again visiting Connally's office, Jake told him, "I've got some more of that money."

Connally responded, "Fine. Why don't you bring it over tomorrow morning?"

"The log will show that they met the next morning—September 24, 1971. Little more than an hour before meeting Mr. Connally, Mr. Jacobsen entered his deposit box at American Security and Trust. . . . A year and a half later, when that box was forced open by authorities, it was found empty." Bank records would show that Mr. Jacobsen had not entered it since September 24, 1971, the day at issue.

"Events developed which caused Mr. Connally to return the money." In August 1973, when the milk producers came under federal investigation, Jake Jacobsen learned that Bob Lilly might spill it all to the feds. Jake frets; hopes the problem will go away. But by October 24, 1973, Jake knows *he* soon must give an accounting. He telephones John Connally (whom he has not seen for more than a year and who has resigned from the

Nixon Cabinet) at his Houston law office in the firm of Vinson, Elkins. Connally says he's coming to Austin and asks Jake to meet him there at the Sheraton-Crest Motor Inn on Friday, October 26.* Over morning coffee in Connally's motel room, they agree that the cash surely will be traced to Jacobsen. They then concoct a story.

Jake will tell the grand jury he offered the money to Connally "to make political contributions with," but that Connally turned it down. Why? "Because as a Democrat in a Republican administration I don't want to give it to Democrats, and as a member of the Democratic party I can't give it to Republicans." (Juror Number 13 to himself: This careful observance of the partisan niceties from one who could head *Democrats* for Nixon, then rush to change his registration as soon as victory was in the bag?) Sale also says they agreed Jake would testify that a year later he offered the money to Democrats for Nixon —but that Connally refused on the grounds that (1) milk producers were being criticized for throwing cash around, and (2) he didn't want to accept large cash contributions as a matter of policy.**

Sale's narrative goes on:

Within hours of the Austin meeting, Jake is subpoenaed. He telephones Connally, who blurts, "Jake, we've got to get that money back in your hands right away." Connally instructs Jacobsen to charter an airplane from Austin and pick up $10,000 in Connally's law office on Monday morning, October 29, 1973. There Connally leaves his private chambers for ten minutes; Jake, waiting, looks at pictures on the walls. Connally returns with a cigar box holding $10,000 in small

---

*Records show Connally was registered there, and witnesses attested that they did, indeed, meet there.

**Under cross-examination, Connally will say he accepted up to $3,000 in individual cash contributions for Nixon, "and they were duly reported."

bills and "a rubber glove or rubber gloves"; he throws the glove or gloves into his wastebasket and comments, "All this money is old enough." Jake flies back to Austin, and at 2:00 P.M. places the money in a Citizens National Bank lockbox.

In late November 1973 Jacobsen tells the grand jury the cover story. Will he permit federal agents to look into his Austin lockbox to affirm the $10,000 is still there? "Yes," Jake tells the grand jury. He beats it back to Texas; soon he's called by George Christian, former press secretary to Connally and LBJ, who asks him to meet Connally at Christian's Austin home on Sunday, November 25.

They meet there. After small talk, Christian excuses himself. Connally then says, "Jake, there's a problem. Some of that money I gave you is too new to have been available in 1971. You couldn't possibly have had it in your lockbox then. I've brought another ten thousand dollars to replace the money with older bills." Now it's Jake's turn to sweat: "John, I told 'em in Washington I wouldn't touch that . . . box until the FBI inspects it. I'll have hell getting in."

Connally replies, "Well, Jake . . . You've simply *got* to get in that box without leaving a trace." The prosecution says Connally then took $10,000—"wrapped in a newspaper"—from his briefcase.

But Jake says, "Not in here. Wait 'til we leave." They call good-bye to George Christian, who does not reappear, and enter Connally's car, where Jake takes the newspaper-wrapped money.

The events that follow are uncontested.

The next morning Jake seeks out Joe Long, his Austin law partner—and, conveniently, an official of the Citizens National Bank. After the bank closes to customers and few employees remain, Long opens the appropriate vault. But a late-staying bank employee, Virginia Straughan, on seeing this irregularity, insists that the men sign cards showing their entry. Long signs;

Jakes does not, mumbling that he is merely *with* Long—though, by his later testimony, he'd already switched the money. The following morning FBI agents look into Jacobsen's lockbox and find $10,000. "I'm sure glad it's all there," Jake tells the G-men.

But hold your horses: *Forty-nine* bills bear the signature of Secretary of the Treasury George Shultz, who in mid-1972 had *succeeded* Connally . . . and who, obviously, could not have signed them in 1971 or earlier. They simply could not have been in Jake's lockbox as long as he'd sworn. Faced with this discrepancy, his financial empire crumbling, and now under multiple indictments in Texas, Jake arranges to plea-bargain with the feds.

Edward Bennett Williams begins with a story of an old mountaineer who said of his pancakes, "No matter how thin I mix 'em, there's always two sides."

Williams knows that even George McGovern soundly trounced Richard Nixon in the District of Columbia, and that Nixon since has gone nowhere but down in local esteem. "This is *not* a Watergate case. John Connally had left government *long before* Watergate"; he does not mention that Connally came back, however briefly, as a White House adviser to Nixon long after the time, we now know, when Nixon had been stonewalling it and covering up behind the scenes. He lays the *Democratic* butter on: Connally's service under Kennedy; old ties with LBJ; his client is described as "the first Democrat" in the Nixon Cabinet. No mention, you bet, of John's having changed his partisan registration. Not with all those Democrat types holding the jailhouse key in their hands, no-sir-ree.

Williams now talks of price supports, parity, cost-price ratios; he drones figures and percentages until the eyes glaze. The purpose of this windy harangue suddenly dawns on Juror Number 13. For now Williams has John B. Connally in hip boots and gallused overalls; you can almost see Big John shoveling the cow barns for the poor downtrodden dairy farmer, helping with the milking, driving the milk cans to market in a pickup truck. No, sir, farmers have no greater friend than this Texan who understands; he, too, is of and from the soil. Lived on a little hard-scrabble farm in his youth. *Of course,* he wanted to help the dairy farmers! He knew better than most what happened when the market's bottom dropped out, when drought came or black-leg hit the herd or feed prices went up. He knew that in 1971 dairy farmers were in such bad shape that many were selling their cows for beef and quitting milk production. So, *yes,* John Connally told President Nixon and Secretary Hardin and anybody who'd listen, *By golly, we gotta help those dairy farmers!* . . . But he didn't take a dime for it.

Who and what was this fella Jake Jacobsen, anyway? Well, Jake had been *twice* indicted by the feds for perjury. The truth wasn't in him. "Evidence will show he also was indicted, at the very time with which we are concerned, by a state grand jury in San Angelo, Texas, for fraud, crooked deals, and crooked loans." Warmed up like a good relief pitcher, Williams is now humming his high, hard one in the form of selective shouting. "*Seven* felonies! He could get up to five years for *each* of them! And five *more* from the federal government for perjury." Williams stands near the jury box, quaking in outrage. *Imagine such a badass as Jake,* his attitude says, *telling lies on decent people. Fibbing on the farmers' friend.*

We do not dispute, Williams said, that Jake Jacobsen got $10,000 from Bob Lilly and *represented it* as being for John Connally. Sure, Jake twice offered it to John, and John declined. Why, lookee, Jake had known John Connally for twenty-five years, and he *knew* he'd refuse any shady deal. He *knew* he wasn't talking to a thief. Jake was safe in his offer! He *knew* he could keep the money for himself, and nobody would be the wiser.

Then came Watergate's brush-fire investigations. A worried

Jake calls John Connally and asks to see him; they meet at the Sheraton-Crest two days later. There, Jake tells John over morning coffee, "I'm gonna have to testify before a grand jury and your name may come up because . . . Bob Lilly . . . may have given the impression I gave you ten thousand dollars. But if I mention your name . . . it may hurt you politically."

Connally responds, "No, Jake, tell it like it is. I've done nothing wrong. You go tell 'em the truth, and let the chips fall where they may."

Lawyer Williams notes that on five occasions Jacobsen—under oath—said he'd never given money to Connally. "Then, on February 6, 1974, a grand jury in Texas returns indictments against him . . . he was stealing money from his stockholders. And he also was indicted for perjury. *The . . . next . . . day* . . . Jacobsen tells two milk producers' lawyers, 'I never gave John Connally that money, and I'll return the money to AMPI when I get a clearance from my lawyer.'"

Williams glares at the prosecution, seemingly so mad he could stomp. "Two weeks went by. Jacobsen's now under several indictments. Now—*now*—begins his scheme to see how he might extricate himself. In March 1974, he began negotiations to get many charges dropped. . . . On May 21, 1974, Jacobsen entered into an arrangement that *all* pending Texas charges would be dropped. Perjury charges here in the District of Columbia would not be pressed. There is a letter . . . to Jake Jacobsen . . . *from the prosecution* making that sweet deal!"

Long stare. Much silence. Jury rapt. Softly: "All he had to do was deliver John Connally. . . ."

Scene: the hall outside the courtroom. Time: two minutes after the conclusion of Edward Bennett Williams's opening remarks.

FRED GRAHAM lawyer and CBS-TV correspondent: "What do you think?"

JUROR NUMBER 13: "Williams didn't touch the lockbox records, didn't explain away the chartered airplane, left it fuzzy about the purpose of all those meetings."

GRAHAM: "He'll let Connally testify to those details. Frankly, I don't think the government has much."

JUROR NUMBER 13: "Well . . . sounds like a lotta documentation."

GRAHAM: "Bullshit, there's no corroboration! I think the jury will demand more than Jake's testimony and a few slips of paper. It's all circumstantial."

JUROR NUMBER 13: "But they correlate! Twice Jake goes to the lockbox, then he goes to see Connally. And during the money *re*exchange he reverses it: Connally first, lockbox second. Again, it happens twice. Doesn't it bother you?"

GRAHAM: Well, you maybe wonder why."

That night Juror Number 13, full of whiskey wisdom, bets a bottle of good wine on conviction. John B. Connally is going to jail.

Moments before Jake Jacobsen will take the witness stand, brother Merrill Connally says, as he and the former governor do their business at adjoining urinals, "John, now, don't lose your composure when that man starts testifying."

Connally booms a harsh laugh short of mirth: "Don't worry. I've known so many lying sons of bitches that one more won't crater me."

Jake Jacobsen looks like an astonished lizard: sallow, lean, gray hair, sharply arching black eyebrows accounting for the startled look; he peers over the top of half-moon reading glasses at his inquisitors. Prosecutor Tuerkheimer leads Jake through his oft-told story. Press row consensus is that Jacobsen hasn't handled himself badly under friendly guidance. But now Edward Bennett Williams rises for cross-examination.

Williams brings out that Jake has many times gone over his testimony with the prosecutors. Yes, the prosecutors had pretended to be Williams and had cross-examined him. Yes, they pointed out inconsistencies and refreshed his memory with documents.

The lawyer fires a barrage of questions as rapid as a Muhammad Ali flurry: How long after you were indicted did you begin to plea-bargain? Who made the first contact? How many hours did you meet with the prosecution? Over how many days? How many weeks? When and where?

Jake sometimes is uncertain; thinks maybe; is not sure.

Another flurry: You had fifteen bank accounts, didn't you? How many lockboxes? Didn't you swear in 1967 that you were deeply in debt? But in 1971 you swore your net worth was $3 million?

Perhaps; not sure; don't recall that.

Williams provides transcripts to improve the witness's memory. Jake admits to indictment on seven felony counts, culminating in perjury; agrees it could total forty years. Judge Hart intervenes to instruct that Jacobsen "has never been tried for those charges, and to this point is assumed to be innocent of them."

Jake testifies that in all their dealings Connally never told him how much money he expected.

WILLIAMS: "And he didn't appear curious about how much he might be getting?"

JAKE: "No, sir."

Williams grins as if he's just heard that elephants fly. Jacobsen is drinking more and more water, licking his lips; on press row a colleague whispers that Jake looks beaten down, subservient, "like Uriah Heep." Worse than that, really. I thought he looked like a pickpocket.

WILLIAMS: "Did there come a time when Mr. Lilly said he gave you a *third* five thousand dollars?"

JAKE: "Yes, but—"

WILLIAMS: "And you remember there came a time when you

had no recollection of it? You said you had an annoying 'inkling' that it *might* have happened?"

JAKE: "That's correct."

WILLIAMS: "Did you say that due to this 'inkling' you *might* have given the third five thousand dollars to Mr. Connally? . . . On December 16, 1971?"

JAKE: "Yes, that's what I said. My records show I'd been in my Austin lockbox on December 14."

WILLIAMS: "Did you say that as a product of your 'inkling' you deduced you'd given it to him?"

JAKE: "Well, I said I had no firm recollection. But I must have given it to him, because I'd have only brought it here for that purpose."

WILLIAMS: "Oh. You get all that out of an 'inkling'?"

Objection.

Sustained.

Edward Bennett Williams now leads Jacobsen into a discussion of when he flew from Austin to Houston, allegedly to pick up the first $10,000 from Connally in the initial money swap.

WILLIAMS: "What changed your recollection from it being 'one glove' to 'gloves'?"

JAKE: "The logic of it."

WILLIAMS: "Was it because the prosecution suggested that nobody would count money with *one* rubber glove on *one* hand?"

JAKE: "Well, the fact is you couldn't hardly count money that way."

WILLIAMS: "That's right, you 'couldn't hardly' do that, could you?" There is an unbecoming sneer in the lawyer's voice; he's just doing his job, yes, and his job is to shake and rattle Jake. But somehow it seems mean that a fellow with Jacobsen's trouble is ridiculed for a slip in grammar. Williams, however, is giving no quarter; he barks, "Now, was it a fifty or twenty-five-cigar box?"

JAKE: "I don't know the difference."

WILLIAMS: "You carried it to Austin, but you can't describe it? Can't say how big it was?"

JAKE: "I won't guess."

Jake says the $10,000 he removed from his lockbox remained for four months in a bedside nightstand. When he denies having cautioned his wife that it was there, Williams permits his eyebrows a skeptical dance.

WILLIAMS: "Do you recall saying to Mr. Connally that there was no possible way to express your gratitude for all he's done for you? That you had *never* been treated so decently by any high public official and so on? Did you ever say that?"

JAKE: "I don't remember saying that. But I might have said it."

Williams hands Jacobsen a letter dated April 28, 1972; it says roughly what he has just summarized. Jake reads it, looks up, blinks.

WILLIAMS: "Did you write that letter to John Connally?"

JAKE: "Yes, I did."

WILLIAMS: "Did you send it?"

JAKE: "Yessir."

WILLIAMS: "Pass the witness. . . ."

Jacobsen attempts to flee the press by choosing a back elevator; poor bumbler, he selects one directly across the hall from press headquarters and is besieged. "How do you feel about all this?" someone shouts.

"I don't feel good about it," Jake mumbles, inspecting his shoes. "The man was a friend of mine."

When the government's case is in, it appears weak. There are, and will remain, the nagging questions of Jake's timely visits to lockboxes before and after meeting Connally. But Jacobsen's testimony has so often appeared vague and bumfuzzled that a guilty verdict demands more. The government has presented very little more: people to prove that Jake had lockboxes and entered them; the pilot who flew him to Houston; Bob Lilly; a dozen technical experts attempting to explain how and when money circulates once printed—using up a day, to the layman's eye, proving that money is green and has numbers on it; it all amounts to little more than convincing proof of the uncontested facts. Juror Number 13 is not unaware that eyewitnesses to bribery are rarer than the whooping crane; few conspirators, after all, trouble to call in Howard Cosell to telecast their best moves. Still . . .

Gasps and stirrings in the courtroom when Ed Williams opens the defense by presenting famous character witnesses. Robert McNamara. Lady Bird Johnson. Dean Rusk. James Rowe, the FDR brain truster. Robert Strauss, an old friend of Republican John Connally and now *Democratic* national chairman. Barbara Jordan, a black congresswoman from Houston, who is identified with liberal causes and whose measured imitation-Churchill rhetoric wowed 'em when the House took up impeachment proceedings against President Nixon. These say that Connally's reputation for reliability, honesty, and integrity is "perfect . . . excellent . . . among the highest . . . extremely high."

But the star of stars is Dr. William Franklin Graham, Jr.—yes, the fabled Baptist Billy. God's own. His silver hair appears so well sprayed it resembles a crash helmet; he is lean and tan and jutty of jaw; if he expects to keep looking like that on reaching heaven, they'd better have a health spa Up There. Asked his occupation, Dr. Graham says, "I'm an evangelist preaching the Gospel of Jesus Christ all over the world." He has known the defendant for twenty-one years: "I was in Texas reading the Bible to a friend [Sid Richardson, the late oil king], and he said, 'Wait a minute. I'd like to have my lawyer hear this.' And in walked John Connally." Laughter. Yes, he'd kept up an association with Mr. Connally: "He's spoken from the platform in two of my crusades, and has attended others. In Washington or

Texas we've sometimes played golf . . . and we always share a
little prayer together."

At a recess Juror Number 13 rails against the government's
not having exposed Dr. Graham as the official moralist of the
Nixon administration: "Why, goddammit, not six weeks ago
Billy Graham came away from San Clemente proclaiming
Dick Nixon to be a man of great faith!" A visiting Texas lawyer, Warren Burnett, and Lynn Coleman, head of the Connally firm's Washington branch, grin at this layman's naïveté.
Coleman says, "Well, about five or six women on that jury
have *got* to be Baptists—unless somebody's tampered with
their religion." Burnett says he, too, would have called the
famous preacher. This skeptic's acceptance further outrages
the Juror; he vows he now would vote to give Connally five
years, Billy Graham two, and Ed Williams no less than six
months in jail.

The defense puts on Beverie Ware and Cynthia McMann,
secretaries in John Connally's Houston office. Williams estab-
lishes that they could see anyone going in or out of Connally's
private office. They say they did not see Connally leave during
his meeting with Jacobsen, contrary to Jacobsen's claim that
Connally went out to get the cigar box full of money. The
prosecution does not cross-examine, apparently on the theory
it won't help to have them repeat it again.

George Christian, now in public relations in Austin, is a pudgy
man with thin hair and the earnest but friendly manner of a
football coach hoping to recruit your son. He testifies that John
Connally, distressed over stories he was being investigated in
Watergate matters, telephoned, asking that Christian get together Jake Jacobsen and Larry Temple, a former Connally
aide, to discuss whether Connally should demand a public
hearing before the Ervin committee or some other forum.

Temple is out of town; Jacobsen consents to the meeting.

CHRISTIAN: "I left them after a few minutes because my four-year-old child waked up. I went upstairs, dressed him, took him to the kitchen for a bowl of cereal, and then rejoined them. . . ."

WILLIAMS: "They did not call good-bye to you and leave the house alone?"

CHRISTIAN: "No, sir. . . . We all walked out to the porch. I shook hands with both of them. Mr. Connally got in his car, and Mr. Jacobsen got in his."

WILLIAMS: "At any time did you see Mr. Jacobsen get in Mr. Connally's car?"

CHRISTIAN: "No."

WILLIAMS: "Did you see Mr. Jacobsen carrying a package wrapped in newspapers, or anything else in his hands?"

CHRISTIAN: "Not that I recall."

WILLIAMS: "Was Mr. Jacobsen wearing any clothing under which he could have secreted a package?"

CHRISTIAN: "No, he had on a short-sleeved sport shirt and slacks."

Cross-examination by Jon Sale:

"Did Mr. Connally have a briefcase with him?"

"Yes."

"Did he open that briefcase in your presence?"

"No, sir."

All right, so George Christian had refuted Jake's recollections of packaged money, of a money exchange in Connally's car. But a vexing thought: *Why* had Connally taken a briefcase to George Christian's home? He had come from his daughter's home, only a few blocks away, and it was there he returned. Why, then, had he toted a briefcase into the house with him— one that Christian never saw him open, one that apparently had no purpose?

*   *   *

John Connally is on the stand, impeccable in a pinstripe suit, looking like a $2 million shipment of silver. Yes, he had advised President Nixon to raise milk price supports. "As I recall, it was a meeting that dealt primarily with politics. . . . Frankly, I was the only one there who knew much about the problem, and so I led the discussion." (The White House tape did not appear to have harmed Connally; jurors heard him pitch for higher milk support prices on the grounds that (1) several midwestern states might be lost to Senator McGovern if Nixon did not; (2) Congress was certain to do it by legislation even if the administration didn't; (3) the milk boys were in an economic bind; *ergo*, it should be promptly done and credit claimed.)

WILLIAMS: "You've heard testimony that in April 1971, you asked Mr. Jacobsen for some money. Did you do that?"

CONNALLY: *"I . . . did . . . not!* . . . No such conversation ever took place!" He is red, grim, grinding his teeth. Wherever Jake Jacobsen has disappeared to, Connally's hot thoughts must burn his ears.

WILLIAMS: "Did you ever *receive* any money from Mr. Jacobsen?"

CONNALLY: "I did not. No, sir."

Why, Williams asks, had Jacobsen come to Secretary Connally's office in Washington on September 24, 1971?

CONNALLY: "Well, he told me [on the twenty-third] that the Home Loan Bank Board wanted him out of the savings-and-loan business and was trying to force him to sell under an unfair formula. He asked me to raise the question with Chairman Thruston Morton. My records show that I made two calls to Mr. Morton that day, and I'm sure that's what we talked about. . . . I think Jake came by [on the twenty-fourth] to find out if I'd learned anything."

Williams asks why Connally had Jake fly to Houston on October 29, 1973.

CONNALLY: "One of my best clients—Gus Wortham, of Gen-

eral Insurance Company—had applied for a bank charter . . .
and he feared it wasn't being processed in an orderly manner,
that somebody might be holding it up. I told Jake I was leaving
for Europe . . . and asked him to fly to Houston. . . . He said he
might not be able to get a timely commercial flight, so I suggested he charter an airplane. When he arrived . . . I explained
the Gus Wortham problem . . . and asked him to determine
. . . what might be causing the delay."

WILLIAMS: "Did you leave your office at any time during that
meeting?"

CONNALLY: "No."

WILLIAMS: "Did you give Mr. Jacobsen any money?"

CONNALLY: "I did not."

WILLIAMS: "You've heard testimony that you took five thousand dollars from him on May 14, 1971?"

CONNALLY: "That is false. Absolutely false."

WILLIAMS: "And again on September 24?"

CONNALLY: "That's false. I did no such thing."

WILLIAMS: "And that you gave him ten thousand dollars on
October 29, 1973, and again on November 25, 1973?"

Connally's voice is flat, matter-of-fact: "That is absolutely
false."

Juror Number 13 wondered about a couple of things: not
matters of evidence, no, but behavioral questions that buzzed
in his own bonnet. Since he knew something of the habits of
power, and knew that John Connally had access to inside gossip
and information from the big worlds of high finance and politics, it seemed inconceivable Connally could have failed to
know that Jake's ass was on the way to the ash heap. And knowing that, would Connally *still* have asked the troubled Jacobsen
to look into processing a bank charter for a trusted client—or
have invited him to George Christian's home as an adviser on
Connally's political affairs and conduct? It was possible, of

course, that Connally would have and did. From what the Juror knew of how quickly most politicians dropped another, shying away from him at all costs when the other fellow became tainted, it seemed damned improbable. If John Connally had, indeed, stayed hitched to Jake even as rumors of Jake's demise circulated, then he had violated acceptable political behavior and habits. Why?

Nellie Connally squeezed her husband's hand just before his cross-examination; he appeared slightly agitated: toyed with his glasses; smoothed his hair; fussed with a microphone. Prosecutor Tuerkheimer, indulging in what Williams later would characterize as "nit-picking," faulted the witness for discrepancies between his direct testimony and testimony earlier given to various investigative units: "Why didn't you just say your memory was poor?"

CONNALLY: "Well, I was trying to respond as fully as I could . . . in retrospect, I should have said I didn't know or wasn't sure. Frankly, I didn't think this was gonna amount to a hill of beans. . . . I knew I hadn't done anything wrong, and I thought my appearance would be over in thirty minutes. . . . Never in my wildest dreams—in my wildest nightmares—could I have dreamed I'd be sitting here today."

Tuerkheimer asks whether Connally couldn't have talked to Jake on the telephone rather than have him charter a plane to Houston.

CONNALLY: "Well, the Gus Wortham matter was of considerable embarrassment to me. Mr. Wortham had mentioned his bank charter much earlier and had called me again on October 10, and frankly, I'd not done anything about it. The Vice President of the United States had just resigned"—here a small grin —"and I had a complete lack of memory on the Wortham thing for a while, because other things injected into my mental processes. Moreover, I'd heard that Mr. Jacobsen had been morose.

I was concerned with his mental attitude. He wouldn't see anybody. Wouldn't even go out to lunch. I wanted to be sure he wasn't so withdrawn he wouldn't perform."

(Juror Number 13 to himself: Connally had seen Jake only three days earlier at the Sheraton-Crest in Austin. Why had he not *then* perceived Jake's condition?)

TUERKHEIMER: "Did you give Mr. Jacobsen any files or folders in the Wortham matter?"

CONNALLY: "No, I only had a few notes jotted down. . . ."

TUERKHEIMER: "Did you pay for the charter flight?"

CONNALLY: "Yes, I gave Mr. Jacobsen two one-hundred dollar bills. . . ."

TUERKHEIMER: "At the meeting at Mr. Christian's home . . . did you have any discussion of [Mr. Jacobsen's] or of your grand jury testimony?"

CONNALLY: "No, I asked how he was feeling. We engaged in a little small talk."

TUERKHEIMER: "What did you say to him as you walked across Mr. Christian's lawn to leave?"

CONNALLY: "I asked him if he'd heard anything on the Gus Wortham matter. He gave me an indirect answer. I thought to myself that he hadn't done anything on it. So I gave him, perhaps, a little unwanted advice. I said, 'Jake, you're going around with a hangdog look; you won't see your friends; you go around looking like a sheep-killing dog. You've got to get ahold of yourself. It's no disgrace to go broke. Take your bankruptcy, and then go practice law. Other people have done it.' "

Juror Number 13 now agreed with the newsroom consensus: Acquittal seemed certain. The government had failed to shake —or even to touch—the refuting testimony of Connally's secretaries and George Christian. The defendant himself had appeared poised, confident, and coherent; he had held his head up, while Jacobsen had the look of someone caught in a large social embarrassment. The jury had to have made comparisons.

"I kept waiting for the government to turn up the person who drove Big John to get the cigar box full of money," Texas lawyer Warren Burnett said, "or a cleaning woman who'd found the rubber gloves in John's wastebasket. I mean, I just couldn't *believe* the government didn't have an ace up its sleeve. Some little *dab*, anyway, of corroboration."

Summing up, Frank Tuerkheimer sang of the lockbox records. After they'd met at George Christian's, why, the next day, had Jake and Joe Long sneaked into the Austin lockbox? "These are two very remarkable coincidences, aren't they? Mr. Connally and Mr. Jacobsen are together again, and at the *next possible* opportunity Mr. Jacobsen goes to the safety-deposit box. There he is! After hours! And the next morning, sure enough, FBI agents find ten thousand dollars there. . . .

"If Mr. Jacobsen made up a story, why did he tell you he broke the ten thousand dollars down into two five-thousand-dollar payments? It would only double his jeopardy. If the tale is contrived, why didn't he say he'd given it all at once so there'd be fewer details to remember? Why would he risk exposure by concocting a money exchange at Mr. Christian's home? And if he didn't get that ten thousand dollars from Mr. Connally, where did it come from? Mr. Jacobsen was in bankruptcy! *He* had no loose cash floating around. When Mr. Jacobsen came to the government prosecutors, he said, 'I made payments to Mr. Connally on dates that will be reflected by my safety-deposit box records.' The evidence is consistent with that claim. . . .

"Mr. Connally originally told a grand jury the meeting at the Sheraton-Crest in Austin *didn't happen.* He was asked if he'd seen Mr. Jacobsen within the last three or four weeks. . . . He said, 'Oh, gosh, I last saw Jake a long time ago. I don't remember when.' This was just *nineteen days* after he'd met him at the Sheraton-Crest in Austin. . . . This man who tells you of all the important people he meets, all the speeches he made and wrote, all the powerful offices he's held, said from this witness stand . . . that he had so answered the grand jury because he didn't understand the question! John Connally understands the English language better than anyone in this room! He's a very, very smart man. . . .

"Why did Mr. Jacobsen have to charter a plane and *go* to Houston? . . . Why couldn't they have talked about the Wortham bank charter by telephone? Mr. Connally gave him no files. By his own testimony he was 'busy as hell' and trying to leave for Europe. Oh, Mr. Connally says, he wanted to *look* at Mr. Jacobsen to see if he was okay. . . . This would indicate he hadn't seen him 'in a long, long time.' But we *know*, now, that he had seen him only three days earlier at the Sheraton-Crest. . . .

"And isn't it strange, when the two men met at Mr. Christian's house, they didn't discuss their respective grand jury testimony? They were still friends. Isn't it incredible they didn't compare notes? Mr. Connally says they met to discuss how he might handle 'bad publicity.' . . . But they didn't discuss what they'd *said* before the grand jury? . . ."

Jake Jacobsen's mother wouldn't have enjoyed what Edward Bennett Williams says of her son: "a fraud . . . a perjurer . . . a swindler . . . a witness who cut a cynical deal for himself to avoid the penalty of his misdeeds." He dithyrambs against perjury: "For a man to swear to God, with his hand on the Bible"—and Williams assumes the pose—"that he's gonna tell the truth, and then spew forth lies, *that* is so despicable as to be beyond description. . . .

"Why do you think Jake Jacobsen kept dipping in and out of those deposit boxes? *Why, to clean them out!* Almost every week he had a note coming due; on the very day he took ten thousand dollars from Bob Lilly—allegedly for John Connally—

he borrowed one hundred thousand dollars from a Dallas bank. On the same day he took that *third* five thousand dollars from Lilly, he paid five thousand dollars on an indebtedness to [a bank] in Fredericksburg, Texas. The bankruptcy referees were after him; his house was crumbling; his financial empire gone; the sheriff was practically *at the door* in 1971. . . . He was a desperate man, embattled and beleaguered. . . .

"There came a time when he feared charges of embezzling his client's funds, and so a case conceived in greed was born in lies! He went to the prosecution and cut a deal. . . .

"This morning Mr. Tuerkheimer called John Connally a 'very, very smart man.' Well, no one has ever suggested he's stupid! So, I ask you, would John Connally hand ten thousand dollars over to Jacobsen and say, 'It's old enough to have come from Bob Lilly'—when that money had been signed by his successor, George Shultz, who didn't take office until June 12, 1972? He might not have *thought* of the money's age. But would a 'very, very smart man' have claimed the money was 'old enough' under those circumstances? I say it beggars our intelligence. . . .

"Jacobsen tells you that when *he* had the money in *his* box in Austin, John Connally suddenly says 'Uh-oh' "—and here Williams smartly smacks his own forehead—" 'there are some Shultz bills in there.' Now, how in the name of reason would *John Connally* know that? Who had the money, and access to Jacobsen's box, and could make that discovery?"

Ed Williams now is prancing and preening before the jury, coming on like an old-time pulpit pounder or a Chautauqua show rider. Indeed, one thinks of another analogy: a football team getting up steam and momentum in the last quarter, driving for the winning touchdown after earlier fumblings and hard luck. "Jacobsen tells you he took ten thousand dollars away from George Christian's house. Wrapped in a newspaper. You heard Mr. Christian testify that he saw him carrying nothing.

You heard him say that Jacobsen wore a short-sleeved shirt and slacks. Where'd he hide the money so that people didn't see it?
... Every time we've had the opportunity *to prove* that what Jacobsen said was false, we have brought witnesses *who proved him false.*

"And what of John B. Connally? Is he some captain of crime? Some scoundrel to be caught? Don't you know that once we introduced character witnesses, the state then could bring out *anything it had* to show his past was stained?" Williams glares at the prosecutors. "Don't you know they examined every record and bank account he has, trying to find loose money? You didn't hear anything from them of John Connally having money stashed in safety-deposit boxes, did you? No. They found no irregularities! Did you hear the prosecution once ask, *'John Connally, did you take any money from Jake Jacobsen?'* No! The government has no case. Its case is in shambles. . . .

"For you, members of the jury, this case is three weeks old. For the defendant, it is more than a year old. A year of accusations, humiliations, anguish, assaults on his integrity. Three weeks from now, this case may have faded from your recollections. You'll have gone on to other things. The prosecution will go on to other matters. The court will go on to other cases. But what you do in that jury room will place an indelible mark on John B. Connally for the rest of his life. Nothing in a life of glory and tragedy will be as final as your verdict. . . ."

In the halls the betting is on instant acquittal: *"No way* they can convict after Judge Hart's instructions!" (He had instructed the jury that Jacobsen's testimony should be "received with suspicion and acted on with caution.") New speculation was of John Connally's political future: Would he make a comeback, even shoot for the presidency?

One hour passes. Two. The jury sends a note requesting documents.

The Connally family and friends, apparently relaxed in the early going, now seemed to pay more in strain for their cheerful stances; E. B. Williams prowled the halls, preoccupied, engaged by talk neither of his beloved Redskins nor of Democratic politics. Connally was seen reading a Bible; coast-to-coast reports soon had him thumbing the Good Book for comfort. In truth, he was looking up a biblical reference Williams had made in his closing arguments about "the first recorded cross-examination in history" being in the Book of Daniel.

Juror Number 13 wandered off to consult himself. *Okay, how do you vote?* Not guilty. Yes. *Not* guilty. Certain matters continued to vex and haunt: those damnable lockbox records dancing in concert with Jake-John meetings; why Connally took the briefcase to George Christian's home; why Connally required Jake to charter a plane so as to inspect his demeanor when he'd seen him only three days earlier; why the defendant had told a grand jury he couldn't recall when he'd last seen Jake, though he'd seen him nineteen days earlier; why, with Jacobsen in trouble and the grapevine saying he had his ass in a deep crack for sure, Connally continued to meet with him and seek him out —unless the reasons were close to what the prosecution alleged.

But the law stressed reasonable doubt. One need only have *reasonable* doubt to acquit. Juror Number 13 had it aplenty. The government had brought a poor case, timidly presented. Jake was about all it had, and Jake, poor soul, wasn't much stuffings. To err on the side of John Connally in this one would probably be to err on the side of the angels, such as they were.

The jury had gone out at 10:40 A.M.; it now was 4:00 P.M. and seemed later. At 4:30, the jury asked for all of Jake Jacobsen's testimony, cross-ex, and redirect. Groans. All the wise-asses who'd predicted a quick acquittal were now saying, "The longer it goes, the worse it usually is for the defendant." Juror Number 13, now that he'd privately voted not guilty, amazingly found himself *rooting* for his old political nemesis. He was nervous for him; he took pains to mumble comforting nothings to the Connally family.

At 5:22 P.M. Judge Hart told a packed courtroom, "I am informed we have a verdict." Gasps. Hart warns that any outbursts will constitute contempt of court. Juror Number 13 takes one look at the jury and thinks, *Oh, shit.* They are solemn, looking to neither the right nor the left; it is axiomatic that acquitting jurors usually sneak glances at the defendant and his family. One juror dabs at her swollen eyes with a hankie. The foreman—a thirty-three-year-old white man, the art historian—stands on request; he, too, is somber enough to supervise a lynching. Not a juror has shown a sign of cheer. *Oh, shit.*

". . . *Not* guilty. . . ."

". . . *Not* guilty. . . ."

John Connally does not move. Nobody moves. The judge thanks the jurors and dismisses them; they file out under the protection of federal marshals, who will spirit them away by bus. Only then does the handshaking start, the hugging, the whooping, the happy subdued crying. Connally, engulfed, is beaming; some intelligent television reporter shouts the penetrating question: "Governor, are you happy?" The former defendant shoots the TV newsman a look to see whether he has gone mad and then roisters up the aisle, clasping all hands, saying, "Thanks for being so good to us," and, "I appreciate it," and a bushel of Thank-yous.

As he passes the press row, Juror Number 13 sticks out his hand and says, "I'm happy for you." John B. Connally beams, and apparently thinks he holds the hand of a famous comedian. "Thank you, Alan," he says.

There is a victory celebration of family, friends, and lawyers in the Mayflower Hotel suite of Democratic National Chairman Robert Strauss; lo and behold—Dick Nixon calls! His conversation with Edward Bennett Williams is stilted; after all, the Ghost of San Clemente *has* called Williams a son of a bitch and a bad man and once threatened to "fix" him. But Nixon congratulates the lawyer on a good, professional job and chitchats briefly of their favorite football team. To John Connally, Nixon says something about sanity being restored to Washington, thinks maybe the post-Watergate hysteria is over; seems to hint of political comebacks for both Connally and himself. "I got the impression," says a lawyer who was present at the party, "that Nixon was euphoric."

Following the verdict, Connally himself had seemed euphoric in front of cameras and microphones. "I have seen the system work today," he began, and went on to pledge to work even harder to preserve it.

He laughed when someone called out, "That sounds like a political announcement."

Frank Reynolds burbles on ABC-TV, "We haven't seen the last of John Connally."

A few days later—by which time the government has dropped its perjury and conspiracy charges, and Connally is at his Texas ranch putting off reporters with pleas of exhaustion and the flu—President Ford is asked if he sees the possibility of a political future for Connally. The President grins and says sure, he's clean and he's got a paper to prove it.

Juror Number 13 eventually identified and contacted more than one "real" juror; they were closemouthed and reticent—unwilling to be identified or quoted—but here's what he pieced together: At least two jurors originally entertained thoughts of conviction; there were at least two, probably three, ballots and some few tears; though the situation was tense, it never was chaotic. The last doubter was convinced by a final review of Jake Jacobsen's testimony and cross-examination. On the next ballot, they acquitted.

* * *

11 ☆
The Loser

I

One did not like to think of him as the Loser. He was not only an old friend but a fine man full of decent impulses and democratic juices; it was painful to think of the nation's having lost his potential to use power for good at the highest possible station.

But lose he had, time and again, across the length and breadth of the land. There was no getting around it. Nine consecutive times, in states where he'd had the money to make a major effort, "Second-Place Mo"—his own wry designation— had finished the frustrated runner-up. Once, in Wisconsin, he'd claimed victory over Jimmy Carter on national television: "How sweet it is!" Hours later, he learned what he and his advisers had privately feared even as he'd spoken to the nation of the joys of victory: that a trickling of Carter votes from rural areas had turned him into a loser—again—by a freckle and a hair.

Near the end, long after it was apparent that Jimmy Carter all but had the Democratic nomination in a sack, Mo Udall got barely enough votes to count in Tennessee, Arkansas, and other states in Carter Country, where he probably never should have entered. He had, in fact, entered primaries in twenty-six states, no matter how token his candidacy in some, without once coming away the winner. Udall was sensitive and defensive about this. Looking back—and he looked back a great deal—he could offer many rationalizations, excuses, and hindsights. Normal enough. But it didn't change anything. He'd been had. Defeated. Edged here; stomped there. What he'd offered and promised the country, the country didn't want.

So the Loser—a.k.a. Morris King Udall, then and now a congressman from Arizona—was girding himself to go upstairs and offer his sword to the Winner. The war was too recently concluded, in late June 1976, for Udall to feel good about it. He made it clear to relatives and a few old pals that he wouldn't crawl to Jimmy Carter or beg to keep his mules for spring planting. His surrender would be conditional and full of pride.

Outside the New York Statler-Hilton, Udall could glimpse Madison Square Garden—where in twenty-eight days more Democrats would convene to bestow Jimmy Carter's prize officially—and for a bit he played the Loser's game of thinking of what might have been. If only he'd had more money. If only he'd been alert enough to concede Iowa and had spent those wasted eight days in New Hampshire—where, in retrospect, one could see, victory might have been his for the taking. And had he won in New Hampshire, then Mo Udall—not Jimmy Carter—would have become the front-runner and, as such, might have expected smoother sailing in many primaries to come. If only, dammit, he'd had a few hundred or a couple of thousand more votes in Wisconsin or Michigan or Connecticut. . . .

"But, hell," he said, "if frogs had wings, they wouldn't bump their asses when they jump."

"Are you nervous?" a fellow asked.

"Well," Udall said, "they're not real fond of me up there." He pointed in the vague direction of heaven, though everyone knew he meant to indicate the Carter suite, where they were conducting the happy business of winners and where you couldn't stir the news media folk with a stick. Outside Udall's suite, a corporal's guard of newsmen kept the watch just in case he fatally slipped on a banana peel.

There had been bad blood between the Udall and Carter camps, especially since Michigan, where the Loser had come from twenty pollster's points behind almost to win it with a hard-hitting campaign accusing Grinning Jimmy of waffling on the issues and maybe of having two faces. It had been a calculated risk: Udall knew that to arouse Carter's ire, and again lose, probably would disqualify him for consideration as a vice presidential candidate even though the southerner sorely needed a certified liberal. Sure enough, Jimmy had abandoned his good ol' boy grin to accuse Udall publicly of "negativism" and, privately, was reported to have snorted expletives not indigenous to the Southern Baptist Convention.

Udall, too, had something scratchy in his craw. His original scenario—to start earlier than all other liberals and quickly reduce the Democratic primaries to contests between himself and the party's rightmost candidates—had worked to perfection. Except for one peanut-picking thing: Jimmy Carter. As with the rest of us, Udall originally hadn't taken him seriously. Now two years and $3 million had gone to waste.

"He thinks I'm a sumbitch," Udall said. Unspoken was the notion that this might be reciprocal.

An aide entered to say that Jimmy Carter, running behind schedule, could permit only twenty minutes to accept Udall's sword, rather than the original hour Carter had requested "so we can get to know each other better." Udall grinned as if to say, *I told you so.*

Udall, wife Ella, daughter Bambi, and stepson Buster were

in the midst of munching BLT sandwiches when an aide burst in to announce the party was expected upstairs "in exactly three minutes." Everyone jumped as if Jimmy Carter had yelled "frog." Except Mo Udall. He took a few more careful bites and said, "I'm probably not gonna make him happy. I don't want to be known as an obstructionist, I know he's the nominee. But goddammit, I just couldn't see rushing in like Frank Church and George Wallace and everybody else tripping over themselves to surrender." Udall had been pleased, when his New York delegates, meeting in state convention, had asked him earlier in the day not to withdraw officially. "As an official candidate," he said, "I'll have access to the committees and the convention machinery. I can dicker about the platform; maybe I can hold a foot or two to the fire on issues. And frankly, I wouldn't think Carter would respect me if I crawled."

He left the room, herding his family down the hall, at 12:02 P.M. and was back at 12:43, strangely calm and low-key. Bambi Udall, twenty-one and slim and lovely, hugged her tall father and said, "Old Man, I'm proud of you."

After social chitchat upstairs with family and staffers, the two Democratic adversaries had closeted themselves for twenty minutes. "All right," Bambi said, "what happened behind the door?"

"He was amicable," Udall said. "We didn't hug and kiss; but I explained my position, and he was attentive. He's a damn good politician, you know. He can turn it on. At one point I assured him that I'll campaign for him this fall"— family groans, they'd had enough of the campaign trail; Udall held up a restraining hand—"and told him that the economy couldn't continue to be patchwork, that about every forty years radical change is required, that a little Teddy Roosevelt is needed. I reminded him that when Standard Oil had been broken up into thirty-three companies, it helped everybody: stockholders' shares went up; there was room for more executives; even the poor consumer benefited a little. And I said we couldn't keep giving the Pentagon fourteen billion dollars in new money every year while the cities rot. And I told him, politely, of course, he could jack around waiting to get his feet on the ground or he can strike before the congressional honeymoon's over—like in FDR's first hundred days or when Lyndon Johnson took office."

"How did he react?" Bambi asked.

"He nodded and looked thoughtful," Udall said. Everybody laughed.

"I told him I'd be a factor in the House," Udall went on, "and if he offered good programs, I'd be his friend and advocate. And *he* said"—Udall paused, as if maybe it might be just sinking in —" 'You can perform a valuable service there, and I'll consult you often.' "

There was a silence. Then a visitor said, "Good-bye, vice presidency."

Bambi said, "No mention even of the Cabinet?"

"Oh, no, Bams. Hell, he's been planning his campaign four years. His Cabinet was probably settled in his mind long ago."

It was time now for Udall to go down and speak to the assembled New York delegates those proper words about unity and bloodying up the goddamn Republicans, and he loyally did. On the way down in the elevator, however, an old chum said, "Mo, how do you read the bastard?"

"Cool and impersonal," he said. "Maybe a little cold."

Udall made his conditional surrender public and headed for La Guardia Airport and Washington. As the Loser left the hotel, he may not have noticed that from a nearby newsstand Jimmy Carter—on the covers of *Time* and *Newsweek*—beamed and grinned at his retreating back.

II

It was almost as if they were apologizing to him.

Everywhere that Congressman Mo Udall went during the early stages of the Democratic National Convention in Gotham they clapped and cheered for him and told each other what a grand fellow he was. This might have been terribly impressive had one not known that not one in a carload had voted for him when it counted.

Yet, somehow, it was more than that they were giving him a decent burial. The reception Udall hosted at the Roosevelt Hotel, which drew more than 2,000 delegates and campaign workers, cheered him so enthusiastically the political realist might have thought him a long time dead and safe in the grave from making further mischief, like Herbert Hoover. Never mind that Mo had paid for the whiskey; Nelson Rockefeller, several times celebrating his own national disappointments, had looked and acted and was treated like a loser in similar circumstances. In Udall's case, somehow, they acted as if he still had the potential to appoint postmasters or make war. The crowd chanted "Mo Mo Mo" and surged forward to shake his willing hand. The last loser so venerated was Adlai Stevenson.

When Udall that convention week strolled the streets or dropped into Elaine's posh East Side nightery for a postmidnight drink and dinner, bystanders and patrons broke into spontaneous applause. It took the Loser a while to become accustomed to this. He kept looking over his shoulder, as if fearing he'd blundered onto a path intended for somebody important and might be blocking the view.

But if Mo Udall was the clear sentimental favorite for many at the 1976 Demo Convention, it remains a fact that his party rejected him as its most viable liberal candidate even though it had twenty-six opportunities to choose him in as many primar-

ies. And the postprimary goodwill, extended to him by delegates and East Side swells alike, didn't help him much in his
own hotel room.

Udall was lunching there with a few old friends when he
made the mistake of attempting to sign a check for the room-
service food. The waiter immediately threw up his hands as if
being hijacked and began to shout, "*No charge, no charge!*
Cash! Money!"

Udall, looking puzzled, said, "Say what?"

"Cash," the waiter repeated. "Twenty-nine dollars. Or I take
the food back."

Udall grinned as if it might be as funny as being caught in the
bathroom studying a stroke book, and pawed through his wal-
let. "Christ," he said, forking over, "that leaves me two dollars."
He dispatched a staffer to the Roosevelt Hotel's front desk to
cash a $300 personal check. The aide shortly returned, shuffling
and mumbling, to hiss that the desk would accept no more than
a $50 check. "I wonder if Jimmy Carter's having any trouble."
Udall laughed; you could hear razor blades in it.

The aide marched to the telephone and asked Stan Kurz,
Udall's national finance chairman, please to come to the hotel
bearing 300 cash bucks. When Kurz arrived, an hour later, he
handed the money to Udall and accepted the Loser's personal
check.

"Is this any good?" Kurz teased.

"About as good as those goddamn checks you've been writing
on my campaign fund." Udall chuckled.

"Well, then," Kurz said, "I think I'll drop it on the floor and
see how high it will bounce." Everybody laughed more than
was called for. Kurz said, "Uh, why wouldn't they let you sign
a tab?"

"Christ," Udall said, "don't you read the papers?"

In truth, Udall had become a victim of his own house rule that
none of his staff people could sign for room-service food or drink

because his campaign had ended a good $200,000 in the red and the bills were still coming in. He'd been embarrassed, in mid-campaign, by news stories revealing that American Express had cut off his credit once their computers beeped that he currently owed $124,000 and was not slowing down. "That was during the time when federal matching campaign funds had been frozen because Jerry Ford wouldn't sign the bill releasing them," he'd explained. "It was either American Express or rob a bank."

The candidate's wife, Ella, had been very much upset by a newsman's witnessing her husband being unable to sign for a $29 lunch and said, "Dammit, now, don't print that! We're not quite as ragtag as all this seems." She immediately realized she'd just as well talk to a stone and shrugged. "Oh, well, what the hell!" she said. She is a good lady who had learned to accept the realities.

"I'm proud of Mo," she volunteered. "He's kept going when I wondered how he could. He'd go to bed at three A.M. after losing another primary and be up starting over three hours later. He's adjusted to what happened. He told me, 'Tiger, let's go to New York and hold our heads up and have some fun.'"

Room service aside, of course.

Jimmy Carter is proceeding at this convention as if Mo Udall does not exist. Not for a moment did he consider the vanquished for the vice presidency. Not once has he consulted him on matters of substance. The Winner's prerogative, yes. Still . . .

On the surface Udall is all sweetness and light, pledging to campaign for Carter "with all my energies and resources." He perhaps feels less resentment toward Carter than he does toward more liberal pols who refused to endorse him during the primaries or whose own stubborn candidacies may have cost him victory in several states where Jimmy Carter barely nudged him out and when the victor still may have been stoppable.

Sitting in the hotel room, his stockinged feet propped up, he said, rather matter-of-factly, that such liberal candidates as Senator George McGovern, Senator Frank Church, and former Senator Fred Harris "didn't lift a finger to help me, and at one time or another they each stuck a finger in my eye."

Frank Church, Udall felt, went back on a gentleman's agreement by entering the Ohio primary and therefore forfeited the last chance of derailing Carter. McGovern publicly fired two of his staff aides for participating in a "stop Carter" movement only hours before the South Dakota primary; Udall is convinced that this headline-grabbing action was interpreted as an oblique endorsement of Carter and cost Udall victory in McGovern's home state. It's possible; the South Dakota election was that close. Even had Udall won it, however, he likely would have come to the national convention 1–25 rather than 0–26; but he doesn't want to hear that, and nobody says it.

"No," Udall says, "I don't think there was any conspiracy or any 'get Udall' movement. I think that I, and other liberals, simply made the mistake of believing we'd have a brokered convention. That it would be up for grabs. While we scrambled for our respective personal advantages, Jimmy Carter was winning with pluralities and getting the momentum going for him. By the time we woke up it was too late. We'd fragmented the damn thing."

Udall rose and prowled the hotel room, which now showed the debris of a late-night party of friends and supporters, including actor Cliff Robertson and entertainer Mark Russell. "I don't buy the conventional wisdom that this is an antiliberal year," he said. It didn't seem the time or place to point out that Udall himself had avoided the liberal label, once he'd got the national drift, and instead had called himself a progressive.

"I thought my early showings would unite liberals behind me," he said, "but it wasn't long until I knew that wasn't gonna happen. I'd go to labor leaders and former McGovern and

McCarthy and Bobby Kennedy people, and they'd play coy. They wanted to keep their options open. Everybody kept thinking that Hubert Humphrey or Ted Kennedy would come in from the wings at the last minute, and that really hurt." He paused and watched a television report featuring film clips of a crowd collected in front of Jimmy Carter's convention hotel, the Americana, silent and somehow remote and detached as if it had nothing to do with him or his dead dreams.

A staff aide, fueled by the inexhaustible gases of youth, burst into the room and blurted—as if it mattered—"Mo, damn, you won't believe this, but down in the lobby people are talking about you more than they are *Carter*! It's been that way everywhere I go!"

Udall tiredly grinned at this news and said, "Great. Where were they when I needed them?"

III

In the end, Ella Udall just couldn't bring herself to attend Jimmy Carter's inauguration.

"There wasn't an ounce of malice in it," she said of her decision later in the day, after the thirty-ninth President had taken the oath and had jauntily walked along Pennsylvania Avenue during the traditional winner's move on the White House. "It was purely a personal thing, an emotional thing. I thought I'd put it all behind me. But the notion of standing there on the platform, beside Mo, watching Rosalynn and all . . ."

She trailed off and sampled a light scotch and water. There was a hint of mist in her eyes.

Well, why not? Maybe—*surely*—Ella Udall had permitted herself to dream of standing where Rosalynn Carter stood, holding the Bible while her husband took the oath, and though the dream had been long gone, she wasn't ready to see it enacted by someone else. She had traveled—what?—six jillion miles and stood on nine billion platforms grinning until her jaws ached and had suffered how many million old boring party hacks and how many hundreds or thousands of hecklers, and for what?

"You're entitled," somebody said.

Ella Udall didn't want to be misunderstood. She fluttered a hand and said, "No matter that I *like* Rosalynn. I'm sure she'll be a fine First Lady. It's just a very personal thing, something inside me. It hasn't got anything to do with anybody else."

Representative Morris Udall took his place among the battalion of hoo-hawing congressmen who gathered on the platform behind the incoming President, most of them jostling for advantageous positions so that their proximity to the great event might be glimpsed on the tube back in Odessa and Montgomery and Wichita. He gamely clapped in all the right places and kept in place the smile he'd worn all day, even if it didn't seem always to fit.

"I feel good about today," he earlier had assured supporters from around the country who'd gathered in his office suite in the Cannon Office Building. Well, if he did, something was wrong with him. But you had to give him high marks for trying. "It's a good day for America," he proclaimed, "and a good day for me. I've been elected chairman of the House Interior Committee. I can have an influence on ecology and energy and on strip-mining legislation, and those were all a part of the Udall presidential platform." People applauded with all the enthusiasm of virgins who'd just learned they'd passed their Wassermann tests. A few diehard supporters among the hundreds who'd flocked to Udall's mild inaugural bash wore "Go Mo" buttons, though they'd had to provide them themselves.

"We thought of issuing our surplus campaign buttons," staff aide John Gabusi said, "but we decided it might be in bad taste. I wanted to put up this nine-foot-tall poster of Mo, with his presidential goals printed on it, but he overruled me. Said it was

Jimmy Carter's day, and he didn't want to appear to detract from it."

The party originally had been for Udall campaign workers only, plus a few old friends from Arizona, but people popped up from all over after the inaugural committee mistakenly listed the gathering as open to the public.

"We even had a couple from Georgia in here," Udall said with a good-sport grin. "No, sorry, Carter wasn't their name."

When the beer and snack goodies rapidly disappeared, Udall's staffers made wry jokes: "Goddamn if this ain't the campaign all over again . . . shortage of resources."

The night before, on inaugural eve, as Washington celebrated Jimmy and Rosalynn while photographers, Secret Service men, and everybody including Ned's old dog dogged the Winner's every step, Mo and Ella Udall and a few close friends quietly dined at The Monocle on Capitol Hill.

"Yeah, there was a little of what-might-have-been in the air," staff aide Bob Neuman said. "I remember Mo speculating on what might have happened had we spent more time and energies and money here and not there. We lost New Hampshire by only four thousand votes, remember, and it was the first primary. If we'd broken on top in that one . . ."

But Jimmy Carter had broken on top in New Hampshire, and everybody remembers what happened after that.

"The mood was good last night," Ella said of her night out. "It really wasn't melancholy. Our favorite Secret Service agent from the campaign was there, and a few staff people who'd been through it all."

As the Udall party left The Monocle after dinner, people stood as they passed each table and delivered an ovation. Mo Udall, visibly moved, controlled his emotions with a gag typical of him. Maybe it was a little strained as he said—on reaching the sidewalk—"Hey, anybody wanta go back inside?"

It wasn't necessary, for when the Udalls reached a Capitol

Hill saloon called The Gandy Dancer, with a nightcap in mind, the standing ovation business started all over again.

"No," Mo said to a working newsman, "I'm not sorry I ran. I thought I had something to offer, and I thought I had a shot. I made a lot of friends, and I think I gained some prestige. Sure, you think a little about what might have been; about the price. But you don't let it dominate you."

When everybody was safely in the booze, someone asked whether Udall might seek the presidency another day. He answered with an Adlai Stevenson story, told in the same circumstance after Adlai's second defeat by Dwight D. Eisenhower in 1956. "There were these two baboons, the only living creatures on earth after a nuclear holocaust. The female baboon sought out the male baboon with a come-hither look, and he said, 'Oh, no, let's not start *that* again.' "

The Udalls were on Capitol Hill early on Inauguration Day. "I fully intended to attend," Ella Udall later said. "But then it hit me, and frankly it's been my worst day."

Her husband went off to the ceremonies, where he was one among the many. Ella sat down with intimates to watch the office television set, and for a bit she joined the general banter and joking. Soon, however, she quietly entered a small side office. She shut the door behind her just as Jimmy Carter completed the oath making him the thirty-ninth President of the United States.

12 ☆

Body Politics

I was lunching with politicians in Washington recently when somebody asked—apropos of the sensationalized "sex scandals" preoccupying the media, the governed, and certainly the quaking pro pols themselves—why only Democrats had been discovered in the exercise of carnal freedoms. While I attempted to frame a response touching on the ideological, the answer came: "Well, there's no fun in getting a little piece of elephant."

Amidst the laughter, someone told of a new "campaign button" being worn by particularly well-endowed congressional secretaries: "I type 74 words per minute." There was much joshing about firing well-turned young lovelies and hiring old crones in corrective shoes. Someone repeated the joke circulating in Capitol Hill cloakrooms: "When they caught Wayne Hays and John Young, they said I couldn't sleep with my secretary. Then they caught Allan Howe and Joe Waggonner and told me I couldn't sleep with prostitutes. That leaves only my wife—and *she's* always got a headache." More yuks and chortles as everyone ordered fresh drinks.

Well, now, I fancy to enjoy a joke as much as the next man. But under the cover of giggles more appropriate to errant schoolboys convened behind the barn, our statesmen—and oth-

214

ers—are begging serious questions having more to do with honesty and individual freedom and the workaday realities than with mere rolls in the hay or a knee-jerk morality.

We of the media, particularly, may be guilty of sins even larger than those who attempt to joke away the subject. We are springing to our microphones and typewriters to tell of hot tails —pun definitely intended—on the Potomac as though Antony and Cleopatra spent their time playing backgammon when Octavia and Ptolemy Dionysus happened not to be looking. We tell it so straight-faced you'd think our jaws were numbed by novocaine, even though our cheeks are so full of tongue we're in danger of strangling.

Politicians, including Republicans, have been running carnal fevers outside their home beds since the first hairy tribe elected a leader on about the 103rd ballot in some lightless, airless cave. So have members of the media, not to mention doctors, lawyers, plumbers, housewives, carpenters, feminists, and you name it. Even such a pious parson as Reverend Billy James Hargis, the Oklahoma pulpit pounder, had occasion a few months ago to plead that the devil made him do it. The sad thing is that poor ol' Billy James probably believes that, when all he was doing is what comes naturally.

The sex drive is among our more basic instincts, even ranking ahead of the need for Coca-Cola or peanut butter. If nature had not so willed, no species would survive. We simply would be too indifferent to procreate and would bumble around eating grass or drilling oil wells or joining the Jaycees. Sex feels so good because its primary function in nature's order is to perpetuate not only the beautiful but also the ugly, and that's why rattlesnakes and giant turtles and sand crabs and fat congressmen get that wonderful urge the same as peacocks and cuddly pussycats and beautiful blondes and handsome dudes like me.

Nature knew it must bribe us with an overwhelming instinct to make sexual music together so the earth would not remain a lifeless rock. Whether you believe that evolution brought light in its timeless and tireless work, or that God in His earliest effort said, "Let there be light," *something* brought light long before the Pedernales Electric Co-op or West Texas Utilities Company. With light came heat, without which no life might exist. In time the great hot lump of earth cooled, and the moisture in its atmosphere fell as rain, and water gathered and pooled, and the winds came and helped the water wear away the cold stone. This formed thin coatings of soil, which eventually toddled its way downhill into the water. There the sun kissed this new mixture toward the end of bringing forth original life: microscopic, tiny, jellylike floating cells. These linked together and multiplied themselves and grew the instinct to keep on doing it.

The surface waters began to get overcrowded, and just floating around like little bits of jelly became boring. So some of these cells went off and decided to become fishes and underwater plants. Then the pioneers of *those* bold groups got washed upon the shore and lay around in the sunshine and opted to turn into snakes and dinosaurs and weird-looking clumsy birds. Finally, those who got tired of living under rocks and such and who wanted to cuddle decided to turn into warm-blooded mammals. The minute *that* decision was made, it was inevitable that one day we'd have Miami Beach and massage parlors and that one day Wayne Hays could not keep his hands off Elizabeth Ray, even if it meant paying her out of tax funds.

Now, the point is that no matter what those original little cells decided to become, they fought against great odds. They had to overcome Ice Ages and Stone Ages and the big 'uns always trying to eat the little 'uns. They caught chills and fevers and everything but city buses. It rained on 'em and hailed on 'em, and things growled at 'em in the dark. They had to grow their own gills or wings or whatever. All this, now, with all manner of ugly species thrashing about making faces and otherwise threatening them. Yet, no matter how howling or hairy were the enemies in pursuit, and no matter if nature's creatures had to creep or crawl or fly away from danger, enough of each species paused to get it on sexually that just about everything but the dumbass dinosaur survived. Against such irrepressible instincts, what's a poor politician gonna do?

Things worked swimmingly well until man came along to superimpose "civilization" on nature's order. Until man decided to govern sexual conduct, a baboon or a turtle (within the confines of certain loose processes of natural selection) could pretty much kiss and cuddle who he wanted to, so long as a stronger baboon or a meaner turtle didn't object. Man, however, discovered early on that anything as good as sex needed to be rationed and made difficult or else people would have too much fun. They'd loll around in the shade, cooing and touching when they ought to be up killing whales or inventing the spinning wheel or taking Dale Carnegie courses. The kings and the pharaohs and other precinct bosses fretted that if people made love rather than war, then there would be no booty to claim and fewer excuses to levy taxes. So they devised laws, some of which they credited to God, to get everybody out of bed and up and doing. These laws said that people could make love only under such restricted conditions as pleased the state. The young or unmarried would not be permitted to do it at all, the married could do it only to each other, and *nobody* should do it except to make babies. If a boy wanted to cuddle a boy, or a girl wanted to cuddle a girl, they ran the risk of jail—to say nothing of the worst possible social contaminations. If you had some for sale, the fruit of your commerce was a trip to the pokey. There were even laws saying that under certain conditions you couldn't give sex away, or accept it, even in a fair swap. They finally hit on the notion that if you showed too much imagination and discovered especially exotic ways to do it, well, then, they'd reserve you a jail cell for that, too.

All these antilove laws haven't worked, of course. All they've done is make people sneak around and lie and cheat and go crazy and kill each other—or, like poor old Wayne Hays, take overdoses of sleeping pills. It sure was simpler when we were floating around on the water as itsy-bitsy cells and reproducing ourselves while the sun smiled on us.

We are considering here more than sex and no less than personal freedom. Most people do not really believe in personal freedom, even though they think they do. While almost any American is quick to claim it as a birthright, many fewer are willing to extend it to others. We may give love to a child or a spouse or a neighbor, but in the matter of their free choices we tend to become policemen of the spirit and censors of the soul. We tell them "don't" more than we tell them "do." It is no accident that we are so shaped and formed: The Ten Commandments, no matter their worth, are stated in the negative; more laws are written to prohibit people than to set people free.

Richard Nixon once told an interviewer that people were like children. That is the basic presumption of the state, whether its agents label themselves liberal or conservative or lay claim to any of the various ideological isms. The state and its agents and allied institutions are collectively almost certain to repress, even when attempting benign acts. Example: that welfare law which, under the guise of assisting needy families, threatens to withhold benefits from poor mothers and their dependent children should a nonworking man live in the house. "We will allow you the freedom to eat marginally"—the state says—"but don't let me catch you doing any *loving* around here."

Our politicians are quick to proclaim that we are the freest and richest people in the history of man. That is probably true, and we are surely freer than the Russians and the Cubans and richer than the Hottentots, but before we are smitten with paroxysms of pride, we would do well to remember just how far we have to go. This free society can put you in jail for smoking the wrong substance or for spitting on the sidewalk or for thousands of other reasons. This freest government in the recorded history of man is licensed to kill you, to take your money, to lock you up, to restrict your freedom of movement and your social preferences. Now you'd think with all *that* power the state wouldn't demand the right to dictate how you may make love, and with whom, and under what conditions. But it does, old buddy. It does.

Your government will even go so far as to *entrap* you should you be overpowered by sexual instincts outside the limited permissions it has granted. Congressman Howe of Utah and Congressman Waggoner of Louisiana are far from the first men to fall prey to the state's bogus nookie salespersons. And since the slimy idea first hatched in some lilliputian official brain, prostitutes have been enticed to sell themselves—and then have been hustled off to jail by the same undercover creeps who entrapped them.

If diddling is so all-fired evil that we must discourage it through law, then why in the name of reason would the authorities attempt to *encourage* men or women to break that law? In this time of record crime are the jails so empty that clients must be solicited to fill them? Why have we become so miserable in spirit that if all the repressive laws on the books will not suffice to land our neighbor in jail, then we must get him there with trickery? These are serious questions, and they cannot be erased by giggling at jokes about "sex in Washington."

I have been waiting for one thoughtful and honest and humane man to rise in Congress and say—without pious preambles invoking the flag or claiming improbably pure institutional instincts—"Enough of this crap." No one has. No one is likely to. This is because politicians know that Americans are two-faced about sex, that although a high percentage of hanky-panky goes on among all socioeconomic groupings, the society prefers to live a lie and force others to live their sex lives as lies. So our public men are intimidated and cowed and afraid to speak out.

When poor Congressman Howe was entrapped in Utah, the press skewered him without paying the slightest attention to his constitutional rights of due process or the presumption of innocence. His political colleagues and church colleagues instantly turned into sharks. They demanded his resignation and his head. It was a panic reaction, and panic there should have been; but the panic was for all the wrong reasons and was misdirected as to source.

There should have been panic because a presumably free citizen of the Republic (no matter whether he happened to be a congressman, oilman, or mechanic) could have his freedom and rights so lightly held that the state would: (1) grubbily attempt to entrap him; (2) release to the press, before he'd had his day in court, a transcript of what he'd supposedly said; and (3) tardily admit, after that the damage had been done, *that it had no transcript of actual worth but had concocted one on the basis of what its entrapping and self-serving agents claimed to have transpired.* Nixon lost the presidency for trying to hoke up tapes, but at least he *had* some. The Utah police didn't. I have not heard a politician or a churchman or *any* of Congressman Howe's critics express the slightest indignation over these police crimes—and that is what they are.

Howe's story, that he had been lured to the scene by an invitation to a party from unnamed constituents, originally sounded weaker than 3.2 beer. But if the authorities would go so far as to release a bogus transcript, then who's to say they may not have set him up? Did someone want to ruin him politically, or did the cops panic when they found they'd netted a congressman in their tawdry net—and *then* concoct their fake record to cover themselves? Either way, their guilt is the greater, for *their* crime was tracking mud across the Constitution—no matter that Congressman Howe was later convicted for trying to spend his $20 illegally.

District of Columbia police were guilty of equally shoddy practices in the case of Congressman Waggonner. First, they entrapped him with a bogus prostitute. When they discovered they'd bagged a congressman in a town run by congressmen— rather than some poor powerless government clerk—they let him go and then covered it up until somebody tipped off the press. You'd think that after Watergate, Washington police would be the last to attempt a cover-up. Not so. Joe Waggoner could have bought the services of every streetwalker in the city and still would have done less damage to freedom and justice than did the cops.

I'm no pal of any of these particular pols, and certainly not of Wayne Hays. I think he richly deserves his designation as "the meanest man in Congress." This, however, does not detract from his constitutional rights, nor should it make him fair game for crucifixion. Among the intimacies the press revealed was that Hays, while making it with Liz Ray, kept one eye on her bedroom digital clock. How Hays does it or at what speed is no business of yours or mine, even if you *think* we may have paid for his hurried fun from our tax monies—as Ms. Ray claims we did, and as Mr. Hays insists we did not. And even if we did, so what? Politicians have hired drones since time immemorial for reasons other than their typing speeds, most of the time to pay off political debts, and no one, not even the Washington *Post,* raises much of a stink about that. Yet such employees perform little useful work, and how is that really different from Elizabeth Ray?

The answer, of course, is not at all—though certain feminists would have you believe that the crucial difference is that the delicate Ms. Ray was exploited. No sooner had the story broken than some women writers started trumpeting their denunciations of the Washington scene under headlines such as the one in the *Village Voice:* WAYNE HAYS MUST GO. Well, maybe she was exploited, though personally I've always felt that any person—man, woman, or politician—had the option of refusing to whore.

Ms. Ray, who approached the Washington *Post* as a woman scorned (after her friend Wayne Hays advised she would be most unwelcome at his wedding reception), was suddenly so eager to attain justice that she continued to perform her debilitating special nightwork—while, with her consent, reporters skulked about to eavesdrop. When the story crashed onto the front pages, she just happened to have hot from the publishers her trashy book about Sex in Washington, and held press conferences as far away as London; within a week her book winked and blinked from stores all over America. It is a classic case of coincidence, I guess we are supposed to believe. If Ms. Ray was exploited as she claimed, then she's by now gained parity with Wayne Hays in the exploitation department. And among *her* victims, of course, are those women on Capitol Hill who've been giving us taxpayers our money's worth all along—a fact that should have been noted by the outraged women writers as they vented their wrath on Wayne Hays and his male colleagues.

Sure, they do some hanky-pankying in Washington, and the same applies to the Texas legislature. A beloved former governor, who has prayed many pious public prayers, periodically used to call a sorority house at the University of Texas to establish trysts with a lovely lady I much admire myself. And a former lieutenant governor or two notoriously got around. But all this is as true of the private sector as it is in government. Politicians—provided they finance their own romances—are no more and no less "guilty" than the rest of us.

The politician, however, is more vulnerable to the public mood. There are not enough of you out there to vote me out of my job as a free-lance writer even should I kiss a goat, but your congressman's scalp is there for the taking. Since the sex scandals exploded, a United States senator from Virginia has been accused of offering to help a female constituent in exchange for her sexual favors. The senator's name made the papers before the Washington *Post* investigated and found his accuser to be a demented lady with a troubled history of telling many improbable tales. Should someone else, however—looking to be a cover girl or the author of the next sexsational book —name almost any public figure, he'll be in hot water from his home bed to his hometown even if wholly innocent. Such people, as with the rest of us, are entitled to their full protections and rights and legal assumptions. They will not, of course, receive them because more people are less rational about sex than any other subject.

13 ☆

Long Hair and
Banditry

The House of Representatives has two problems. One of them it is foolishly trying to do something about. The other it is foolishly neglecting. Briefly put, the Lords of the House are paying too much attention to hair and not enough attention to ethics.

The hair thing involves class discrimination. If you work on a congressional committee or in a member's office—if, in other words, you belong to the white-collar elite on the Hill—nobody tells you whether you may grow a beard or a mustache or how long to wear your hair. If, on the other hand, you labor in the dank basements and lost caverns of the House, then you become subject to silly, picayune rules.

The House Folding Room is not the most pleasant place in which to work. There, in the bowels of the Longworth Building, men and women accomplish the kind of mulework unlikely to excite the soul. They fold, insert, seal, stack, tote, and mail the many newsletters and other publications spewing forth from congressional typewriters. There are no two-hour, four-martini lunches among Folding Room personnel. They punch time clocks and grab fast-food snacks. They sweat and grunt. It is not glamorous work, though it is honorable and it is convenient to the Lords of the House.

Thanks to an old rule enforced by the departed and unlamented despot Wayne Hays, Folding Room males must put up with their mustaches being measured. Literally. They are not permitted to grow beards. Hair is not allowed to touch the shoulders. This makes absolutely no sense. Even if one assumes long hair or beards to be absolutely unsightly, the Folding Room people rarely see anyone except each other. They are not on public parade. No congressman in memory has paid a call on them. Their sweatshop is difficult to find with a blueprint.

Hair may not be the most burning issue in Washington; that such a henhouse rule persists, however, speaks volumes of the House. It discriminates not only against class but against sex. This, occurring in a body which brags about being the congressional unit closest to the people, makes a mockery of the claim. Congressman Frank "Tompy" Thompson, who succeeded Wayne Hays as chairman of the House Administration Committee, need make only one phone call to bring a touch more of democracy to Capitol Hill.

A larger problem than measuring hair is the matter of a Code of Ethics among congressmen. Oh, they have one. Sure. But about all it asks a member not to do is rob banks. They even have an Ethics Committee, which never once has initiated an investigation of its own; it is pretty much content to add that the members of Congress *please* should not rob banks.

When a congressman robs a bank, it embarrasses his colleagues, you see, because then they are forced to pass public judgment on whether robbing the bank might somehow put his seniority in jeopardy. This thought makes congressmen so uncomfortable, calling the old ways into question as it does, that every time a congressman robs a bank his colleagues grumble about it behind their hands. "I wish ol' Buford would quit robbin' them banks," they say. "It looks bad on the rest of us and causes us to get mean mail."

Well, face it, some congressmen are gonna keep on robbing

banks. That being the case, wouldn't it make sense for the Congress to crack down on those who do? Erring members need not be shot, but at least the leadership could quit voting them amnesty.

Representative John Flynt of Georgia is chairman of the House Ethics Committee. Probably he objects to his colleagues stealing fireplugs, though the theory has not been fully tested. Flynt seems to sleep undisturbed, however, no matter what else his colleagues do. It was curious to see the official ethics keeper pleading to save a subcommittee chairmanship for Representative Bob Sikes of Florida, who earlier had been knuckle-rapped by the House for having personally profited from his official connections and position—not just once, but time and again. Land deals. The way Flynt carried on about his southern colleague's being put in double jeopardy—a dubious argument in itself—you'd have thought he was Edward Bennett Williams speaking for the defense. What's wrong here is that Flynt's role in the House more properly casts him as the prosecutor.

I hear a lot about unusual expenses congressmen suffer. I am not unware that they must keep homes both in Washington and in their districts; I know of their travel expenses, their requirements to entertain, and that they are the targets of many charities. I know they are victimized by inflation and learn like the rest of us that the first rule of money is that there's never quite enough to go around.

Ain't any congressman I know of going hungry, however. It costs more than $1 million per two-year term in tax funds to keep the average congressman in the style to which he or she has become accustomed. They are not badly paid, and they enjoy many perks: subsidized haircuts, subsidized meals in their official restaurants, unlimited franking privilege, flowers for their offices, generous staff hire, travel allowances, and so on. Though you hear griping from them of how much more money they'd be making out there working the mines of free enterprise, you almost have to chunk rocks at a congressman to get him to quit before qualifying for his handsome pension. I think a lot of 'em know, deep in their craws, that it may not be all that easy out in the competitive free enterprise system once you've lost your powerful connections.

People ought not to come to office in the hope of getting rich, though many have done it. Stricter controls than exist should be placed on outside earnings, the accepting of thinly disguised honorariums, the conversion of campaign money to private uses, and anything remotely smacking of conflict of interest.

If we are not going to permit longhairs in the House catacombs, then at least let us permit fewer bank robbers in its chambers.

* * *

Postscript: My young son, Brad, had one of those grunt-and-sweat jobs in the House Folding Room when the above article appeared. Its first result was that his white-collar superiors called him on the carpet to berate him for finking to me. By the next day, however, word came from somewhere on high that no House employee should thereafter be denied permission to grow hair or beards or mustaches. In the larger matter of congressional ethics—dealing with "the bank robbers"—all that happened was that a few congressmen wrote me, or the Washington *Star,* claiming that they, their colleagues, and the Institution itself had been defamed. Won a little 'un; lost a big 'un.

14 ☆
Choosing
A New King

I

In the end it turned on the flip of a single card.

Texas Congressman Charles Wilson, who'd earlier placed into nomination his Lone Star State colleague Jim Wright, was the man who drew to much more than an inside straight. In his own words, cleaned up a smidgen to accommodate readers of this family newspaper, Wilson said, "When I saw that last card come up 'Jim Wright,' I damn near soiled myself."

Wilson was one of sixteen congressmen—four representing each candidate for the House Majority Leader's post—who served as official tellers when the Democrats elected the man who probably will become Speaker to succeed Massachusetts's Tip O'Neill. The drama of Wright's unexpected victory so stole the show that poor old Tip O'Neill's cut-and-dried elevation may prove little more memorable than a midseason victory over the New Orleans Saints.

That Jim Wright even was a finalist came as surprise enough. The smart-money boys told it that California's Phil Burton was the odds-on choice, with Missouri's Dick Bolling predicted to place handsomely and handily. Texan Wright was seeded to show only ahead of second Californian John McFall, who alone accommodated reasonable expectations by stumbling at the starting gate.

It was not difficult early on to imagine the smell of death in the House chamber or to hear the crash and crunch of dashed dreams. Simple Dick-and-Jane mathematics guaranteed more losers than winners, which is the way life generally works no matter the care you take.

Wright appeared the most intense of the candidates, which seemed slightly out of character. He is a compulsive grinner, much like Jimmy Carter, a low-keyed one who normally gives the impression of not being willing to pay a nickel to see a good earthquake. On this day, however, he seemed to sense the earth might move for him. He chain-smoked and paced. Earlier his longtime aid Craig Raupe—who had claimed an improbable eighty-nine first-ballot votes for his man—uncharacteristically refused to visit the open Democratic caucus. "I've suddenly grown superstitious," Raupe said. "Sure as hell if I go over there, he won't get thirty votes."

Phil Burton, normally intense in the extreme—hell, he *jangles*—only mildly fidgeted while awaiting the first ballot. He had the look of a man who expected to sleep well after a long run, one who as he had sowed now expected to reap. Dick Bolling sat calmly as if lulled by Quaaludes, maybe awaiting the fitting of his crown. McFall made himself relatively inconspicuous, as if hoping his absence somehow might make Democratic hearts grow fonder. He was a beaten man, and he knew it.

What the nominating and seconding speeches had in common was a high degree of candy-assery, all hands claiming that should they search the wide world over, they'd never find a quartet so dear to their individual hearts, and indicating they'd rather hit a cripple than go against the three good men it was their reluctant duty to go against. Such rhetoric honored the institutional norm in a body where ambition, backbiting, and razor fights parade behind a façade of stiff good manners. Except for an occasional rare acerbic such as Wayne Hays or the late Bob Kerr, none in Congress would describe a colleague who happened to be Jack the Ripper as anything more than a distinguished and able surgeon.

Almost alone among official nominators, Texas Charlie Wilson spoke of issues. As his man Wright was thought to be the heart-throb only of House mossbacks, Wilson reminded them of his colleague's early pro-civil-rights record and his aid to the nation's bankrupt and decaying cities: "My most profound experience this year was in Troy, New York, when Ned Pattison [of that district] took me on a tour of the hopelessly suffering slums. I spent the ride back regretting that I had refused Jim Wright's plea to vote for aid to New York. I realized that I had been narrow and provincial, and I regretted it, and I won't do it again." This confession dovetailed nicely with Wright's efforts to convince urban congressmen that he, alone among the candidates, might as House leader deliver southern votes to their tortured municipalities and—not so incidentally—reminded listeners that candidate Bolling had recently, publicly, and imprudently labeled his colleagues as "provincials." You can bet that Bolling, lolling on the front row, felt a sudden hard poke of hostility.

When they announced the first vote—Burton 106, Bolling 81, Wright 77, McFall 31—only Bolling's face seemed to show he now felt a kick in the gonads. Came the second ballot, and Bolling's pain proved fatal, the rules calling on each ballot for the low man to drop out: Burton 107, Wright 95, Bolling 93.

One may only speculate what might have happened on that ballot had not Wright partisans not-so-gently awakened Texan Henry Gonzalez, found sound asleep in the Democratic cloakroom only thirty seconds before the voting closed, and somehow produced in the same instant a second Wright vote, Florida's aging Claude Pepper, who rushed down the aisle bug-eyed and waving his voting card as if attempting to flag down a Greyhound.

Then came the final ballot. Phil Burton suddenly was up and doing, twisting arms and punching chests with an eager forefinger, though Burton's minions felt confident enough in some cases to tell Wright partisans what a nice race Wright had conducted and that no reparations would be exacted. As it turned out, this was akin to Wilbur Mills's telling Fanne Foxe he wouldn't mind if she jumped in the lake.

The official tellers went off to an anteroom and sat at two tables, counting the votes from as many ballot boxes. Let Charlie Wilson tell it from there: "Near the end of counting my box, Burton was five votes ahead there, and just one card was left uncounted. Then I heard somebody at the other table say, 'Jim Wright wins this box by five votes.' I reached out like my hand was deadweight and turned up the last card. It was 'Jim Wright.' " That's when Wilson almost soiled himself.

Well, you think of the losers. Dick Bolling, sixty, who two decades ago was a favored protégé of Sam Rayburn and was considered a certainty to rise to Speaker once Wilbur Mills had et his fill—but who fell from favor by publicly agitating for House reforms long before the notion was even marginally popular and long before most people outside Congress knew of the crying need.

You think of John McFall, fifty-eight, next in line to be Majority Leader among those on "the leadership ladder," but who had the misfortune to accept $4,000 in office-expense funds from those shadowy South Koreans now being investigated and too often seeing their names in the papers. And of Phil Burton, a tough whiz kid and maybe the top parliamentary technician in the House, who came as close to the brass ring as one may come without grabbing it—after only a dozen years in Congress —but who may have been a bit abrasive and a shade cocky. "Phil can rub your fur the wrong way without even knowing it," a colleague had confided.

Bolling and McFall probably can forget their better dreams

for all time; Bolling has a losing earlier effort behind him—withdrawing against Carl Albert for the good reason that "I cannot win"—and McFall, well, old John's a mite tainted, and spoilt meat don't hardly ever repair. Burton may get a future shot, though it's difficult to imagine the target ever being quite as inviting. When you lose 148 to 147 to a dark horse, they may never think of you as a winner again.

Jim Wright?

Well, he knows about defeat in the worst way, even though today he wears the cloak of a winner. Not many people know it or remember it, but shortly after World War II, when Jim Wright was a flaming young liberal in the Texas legislature—during those terrible days when the Cold War and Joe McCarthy had people looking for communists under every bed —one of two right-wing opponents attempting to prevent Wright's reelection was blasted to death by a shotgun one midnight on answering a knock at his front door. Wright's surviving opponent encouraged speculation that maybe the communists or their friends in public office had dispatched the fellow. Jim Wright lost the election and lived under a cloud.

Later—after it came out that the fellow had been killed by underworld figures for welching on a gambling debt—Jim Wright was politically rehabilitated as mayor of the small town of Weatherford, Texas, and ultimately made it to Congress. It seems rather fitting, given that background, that when Charlie Wilson reached for that final voting card, it would turn up a great big ace.

II

Probably I am one of few people who, given their druthers, would elect to be a U.S. representative rather than a U.S. senator, though perhaps this is the viewpoint of a dreaming dramatist and not that of a practical politician.

The House is more lusty and brawling and unpredictable; it contains more of mysteries. The Senate takes great pride in its clubbiness; while the House, too, knows its insider instincts, it somehow is more of bone and less of broth than the other body.

Now, this is not to say that the House is always a fun place or that it's ever perfect. It observes arcane mannerisms, men and women who'd love to bludgeon each other and rip out an occasional tongue speaking in public of their hated rivals in language usually reserved for the rituals of courtship.

Some years ago, when crusty old former Speaker John McCormack permitted his Irish temper to get the better of his institutional habits, so that he assured a colleague he held him "in minimal high regard," the collective intake of breath was audible even to backbenchers.

One reared among the freer expressions indigenous to West Texas beer joints often finds such ritualized conduct harmful to the cause of efficiency and directness. Yet, out of official chambers, it has been "my personal pleasure and high privilege"— as the Speaker traditionally says in introducing the President of the United States—to hear representatives employ vile invectives against their in-House rivals normally reserved for ex-wives, tax agents, and the lying-meddling-goddamn-press. I love the House when its juices boil, when the passions of its members burst the bounds of propriety, because that's usually when raw democracy is being better served than not.

The unspoken dirty little secret of the House is that its members who rise to power generally share, behind the obligatory grins and backslappings, the very human trait of enjoying select vengeful extractions which might please the wrathful Old Testament God. Personally I bet the Lord felt better when He uttered, "Vengeance is mine," than when He said, "Let there be light." And man, they say, was made in God's image.

That is why so many politicians lie to each other when they are being solicited for votes to elevate their competing brethren to higher in-House stations; nobody wants his dangle dropped in the dirt because he happened to give his allegiance to a loser. Choose the wrong man in a power fight, and you can wind up serving on the Toilet Paper and Ice Water Committee or find yourself unable to get the Lord's Prayer passed as a simple resolution even if you've set it to music.

Congressman Mo Udall of Arizona, after he'd lost the House Majority Leader race to the late Hale Boggs of Louisiana some years ago, wrote a memo to himself: "If I ever get in one of these fights again, remember that anything less than an outright declaration of support is worthless. The problem with my private 'hard count' was that, in considering twenty members who labeled themselves as undecided, I figured to eventually get four or six or ten of them. The fact is, I got none of them, and that's what can be counted on among the so-called undecideds in the future. Any man who is a viable candidate should, in the end, be having to beat off his colleagues with a stick."

This hindsight came to Udall after he'd convinced himself of a first-ballot strength of 90 or more votes and then received but 69. Do not think, however, that Mo Udall was immoderately naïve: in the most recent House leadership battle, Phil Burton was thoroughly convinced going in that he had 117 votes, Dick Bolling's great expectation was about 100, and Jim Wright's was 89; they respectively got 106, 81, and 77.

If the secret ballot did not exist as the House selected its leaders, great would be the carnage when it came to settling old scores. As it is, a winning candidate may *think* that a given colleague did or did not vote for him, but—except for those few who make nominating or seconding speeches, or otherwise get out front as an open activist—there's really no way he can know. You'll always find a few members who privately pledge themselves to more than one candidate, and that's why the private calculations almost always turn out to have been fatally optimistic. Phil Burton tardily discovered the dangers of House arithmetic when he said to Jim Wright, moments after the Texan had upset him, "Jim, you can count better than I can."

Wright sneaked up on the pundits—as well as on Phil Burton —and now the pundits are saying he probably can't hack it or that his election set back the reform mood of the House and that Wright probably will prove to be little more than a caretaker. The pundits may prove to be correct; there *is* a strain in Wright running toward the glad-handing and the cautious and the comfortably institutional.

What the pundits may have missed is a certain steel Wright has been careful to conceal. He long ago learned the degree of reluctance with which his colleagues bestow power, its being a precious gift they would prefer to reserve to themselves. The sort of sleeve-worn ambition paraded by Phil Burton and Dick Bolling accounts in large measure for their having failed and Jim Wright's having won. Wright out good-old-boyed 'em, and he meant to do exactly that.

For months before announcing for Majority Leader, Wright took careful soundings. He became convinced that Burton and Bolling, while each had strong partisans, would have trouble adding second-ballot strength because of reservations about their personalities and a general wariness of them. Jim Wright sensed or knew or observed that his colleagues, having in recent years trimmed the sails of crusty old leaders and chairmen who for years had ruled like men on horseback, feared to create new despots and lose the slack they'd won. What the pundits forgot —and what Jim Wright didn't—was that the House in choosing its leaders always has had a strong instinct toward preserving itself by serving the conventional rather than the risky.

Nobody paid much attention while Jim Wright put together a bigger financial war chest than any of his rivals and forged the same sort of broad-based alliance that so long served his old hero FDR: big city bosses (Daley of Chicago among them), southerners, and some few blacks. He managed to do this somewhat on the sly, representing himself as one who'd been more or less "drafted" by colleagues less than satisfied with the other availables. While he was putting his troops together, Congressman Wright was careful to make modest claims. He'd shrug and say well, he thought he had as good a chance as anybody; he'd been around a long while and had done his homework, and he believed his colleagues knew it. Everybody shook his head and said that ol' Jim was a nice guy, but he was in deeper water than he could swim in. And all the while, ol' Jim was down there where they thought he was drowning, stealing everybody else's bait.

Beneath that placid exterior and the crinkly grins, Jim Wright is a man of pride and passions and is capable of throwing temper fits. I know this because, years ago, when I was Jim Wright's administrative assistant on Capitol Hill, we had a number of spirited discussions, cussing matches, and two near fistfights. This proves more than that I may be difficult to get along with; it's evidence that Jim Wright will bow his neck and fight.

Wright is not unaware that his detractors expect him to preside less than firmly; though by nature he probably would prefer to persuade rather than use the lash, he may be eager to show he's tougher than people think. In short, the varied chemicals sloshing inside the new Majority Leader almost guarantee surprises and mysteries and probably some moments of nobility as well as instances of disappointing jackassery. That was true when I knew him better, and I think it still is.

Come to think of it, that description might be applied in general to the House; it accounts for why I prefer it over the more staid and more predictable Senate. To put it in human terms, the Senate with its larger pomp and power might be the more advantageous associate, but I'd much rather get drunk with the House.

15 ☆
Talking
Congress-speak

Members of Congress simply do not talk to each other. Oh, they exchange pleasantries and wisecracks; they pound each other on the back as if reuniting after twenty years, when in truth they saw each other at lunch, but that's nothing more than a loveless mating dance; an instinctive performing of rituals. Congressmen make speeches to each other on the floor, it's true, and during committee hearings. But they don't do enough of the kind of honest, one-on-one cold-turkey talking that permits them to cut through the malarkey and effectively solve problems.

This first came into focus for me a few years ago when one of the more intelligent members of the House complained, during a dinner party, that Congress wasn't coming to grips with three or four important bills then begging attention. As the complaining congressman was a member of the majority party, and well respected, I asked whether he'd mentioned the hiatus to the Speaker.

He gave me a look of pure astonishment. "No," he said, "I haven't talked to him."

Then, pray God, why not?

Well, he said, the Speaker wasn't an easy man to talk to; he didn't know anybody who really could talk to the man.

Had some of them at least tried?

The congressman flinched at the jab, but he began to ruminate on the subject; one got the idea he had not previously dwelled on it.

"For some reason," he said, "you just don't do that. Oh, you might talk to the Speaker or a committee chairman about a bill you have some particular interest in. But when it comes to correcting the institution's deficiencies or criticizing the performance of the House, you just don't do that."

Why not?

"It just isn't *done*. There's a veneer of good manners over everything, a sort of courtly sign language. For me to go to the Speaker and criticize the House for dragging its feet, well, that would be construed as direct criticism of the Speaker himself. You drop a hint, maybe: 'I surely am concerned that the committee gets to H.R. Eleven Twenty,' or 'We're taking it on the chin from the press about the energy bill.' That's about as far as you dare go, and you don't want to be too often remembered for saying even *that* much."

I said Congress was too damned preoccupied with tender waltzes; with form rather than substance.

My friend said, "Well, people so jealously guard their prerogatives on the Hill that you've got to be careful not to offend. Even your junior colleagues, if offended, can stick it to you. You'll need their votes or goodwill many times in the future. If they think you're being critical of their performances, or sticking your nose in their business . . ." The congressman drew a finger across his Adam's apple in a slashing motion.

"We're a bunch of egomaniacs," he confessed. "Every congressman here wouldn't be here if he hadn't beat somebody. So he's likely to think of his way of doing things as being superior. You're dealing with a court of princes, and sometimes the issues are emotional, explosive. Each office is a private grand duchy, and each congressman rules it by his own code.

"I guess that's why we've devised this elaborate and arcane

manner of speech, of approaching each other with verbal roses. It's sort of a safety valve. Toward the end of harmony, I think it's a wise practice. But there's not any doubt it leaves a lot unsaid and unresolved."

Amen to that.

I'm of a type to hang around saloons; if you hang around 'em enough on Capitol Hill, you'll eventually run into congressmen grumbling over their grog of a colleague who's disappointed them or worse.

A southern congressman we'll call Mike Daniels recently came snorting into The Rotunda—the night spot, not the chamber under the Capitol dome—with harsh words on his lips about a member of the House leadership. "He promised to put me on a given committee, when soliciting my vote, but he didn't do it. And after slitting my wrists, he hasn't even had the decency to apologize or explain." Well—he said—it would be a cold day in hell when the fellow got his vote again; the ingrate bastard could go to hell in a handbasket, et cetera, and so forth.

Had the disgruntled congressman called on his leader to complain of the dirking?

No, of course not.

Would he be willing to talk about it with the other fella or one of the fella's chieftains?

Be delighted, though *they'd* have to make the first move.

Very well.

I telephoned my friend Karple in the leader's office. Karple knew nothing of the trouble, but certainly he'd look into it. Thanks for the intelligence report—Karple said—because we don't like these things to fester.

In a few hours Karple called me back. Was I sure the disgruntled congressman was, indeed, Mike Daniels?

No doubt about it. Why?

Well, Karple had told his boss of Mike Daniels's foul temper. His boss had said, "Hell, I'm not mad at old Mike, and I don't want him mad at me. There's been some massive misunderstanding. I'll call over and soothe him." Whereupon the leader had, indeed, telephoned Mike Daniels.

"Mike," he said, "I just want to call and thank you so very much for your support. You are a friend, indeed, and I shan't forget it. How do you think things are going?"

"Ray," Mike Daniels said, "things simply could not be going better. I'm so proud of you it's all I can do not to sing and dance. It was an honor to support you for your exalted position, and I was just saying the other day how you are a gut cinch to make the history books." Or words to that effect.

Karple and I laughed over this meaningless mating waltz, and I agreed to try to find out what in the name of John C. Calhoun might be going on. Mike Daniels does not answer my telephone calls; he obviously is embarrassed, as he should be, because he played the institutional game rather than go to the root of his problem. He was content to bank his fire and indulge in Congress-speak.

A few days later a second congressman—we'll call him Cullie Blanton—began to put the bad mouth on the same political leader. Cullie fancied himself insulted at a party. "All I said," Cullie reported, "was that while I'd worked and voted for him, I hadn't really thought he would win—that I'd figured he would fall about ten votes short. Well, he told me I was a dumb son of a bitch for having thought it and an even dumber son of a bitch for having told him." Congressman Blanton muttered how the leader would be needing him again, probably before he would need the leader, and he just might tell the leader to go pee on a stump.

I called my friend Karple to undertake the role of peacemaker again. He said, "Well, now, Ray just wouldn't talk like that to a colleague. I think there's much embellished rhetoric in Cullie's presentation. But obviously his feelings are hurt, and we'll look into it." The next day I encountered my friend Karple. "Are you making these complaints up?" he asked.

It seemed that the leader had personally sought Congressman Cullie Blanton out in the House chamber. He draped an arm around Cullie's collarbone and told him he was the greatest thing since the banana split, that he loved him like a brother, and that he'd go to his grave grateful for Cullie's unswerving loyalty and support.

Cullie had blushed and dug a toe in the carpet while admitting to being guilty of unswerving loyalty and support. He said his heart would break if the leader didn't live to be a thousand and walk on roses at every step. He said he loved the leader not only like a brother, but more than life itself or even the U.S. Marines. He said he thought so highly of the leader's abilities and character and integrity that it made him dizzy and threatened him with nose bleeds. All this, of course, in that eloquent and arcane language congressmen employ against each other's tender sensibilities.

The leader went back to Karple and said, "Tell your friend King that I never shall understand why somebody once hired him to teach political science, he not knowing his ass from third base."

A day or so later a third congressman tells me how the same leadership figure has offended him by cutting him short in front of witnesses. He himself is a committee chairman, the offended solon cries in a whiskey bellow, and there shall come a day when he will take great delight in carving on the leader's liver and maybe feeding it to the hogs.

I did not call Karple that time, for fear the chairman would wind up sending the leader roses. I do wish, however, those important fellows would learn how to talk turkey to each other. It might even be good for the Republic, and certainly it would be good for their souls.

16 ☆
Stealing
Away Unloved

'Tis the Yule season, yes, but 'tisn't the season to be jolly in Washington. In this town of Muscatel memories and Dubonnet dreams, the political losers are full of bah-humbuggeries as they fold their tents and sullenly steal away.

Lame-duck President Jerry Ford has reacted so typically to defeat you'd think he had consulted a computer. Old Bumblehead has become the nation's most public recluse, being seen or heard so infrequently that he might rob liquor stores without a mask and go unrecognized by witnesses. Probably he is in the mood to do it.

Defeat to the politician, you see, is much more than mere losing. Alone among us, politicians are publicly told on a given day they ain't up to snuff and to pack their dirty duds and go away. It's as if your mama and daddy called you in one morning and said, "Boy, we don't love you no more. We're gonna break your plate and sell your bed, and we'd 'preciate it if you wouldn't hang around the neighborhood no more, because we don't want you embarrassin' that nice new son who's takin' your place tomorrow. And don't forget to clean out your closets for him."

From the way politicians need to be hugged and kissed and

approved by the masses, you'd think they'd all grown up as orphans. Once rejected, they are incapable of sleep, lose weight, cry in the dark, and show other symptoms of cancer. A number treat their ills with whiskey and tend to lose track of time. Why not? They suddenly don't have schedules to keep or speeches to make or votes to cast. Many don't know how to do anything else.

There is a cliché, which also is a truism, that "They never go back to Pocatello." Statistics support this. Some 800 ex-congressmen and ex-senators are so afflicted with Potomac fever that they never have gone back to the Nineteenth District. They have formed a club which periodically meets for purposes of therapy. Everybody runs up and grins and grabs and sings out, "Hey there, I'm former Senator J. T. Wingwoah of North Dakota, Eighty-eighth through Ninety-second Congress." There were old ghosts there who looked to have ridden San Juan Hill, and a lot of nondescripts who reminded me of shoe salesmen. And there were successful lawyers and lobbyists, oozing high-class snake oil. I once attended such a function, yes; all in all, it was the most depressing visitation I've made, except once when I crashed a meeting of Alcoholics Anonymous, though very much a friend of whiskey, and had to listen to it being bad-mouthed. There was about it the frenetic sorrowful joy of an Irish wake; the impossible reaching back of a class reunion.

I once knew a congressman who was accused of stealing and lying about it and who was handily retired at the next plebiscite. He did not want to believe it was happening to him, of course, and during his fruitless reelection campaign convinced himself that when folks spat in his face, he just happened to be in the way of where they'd decided to spit. When they beat him like a runaway slave, he was honestly surprised.

In his lame-duckery he became addicted to his physical office on Capitol Hill, as he had not formerly been, and would leave it for neither meals nor showers nor weekends. Truly, he *lived* in the damned place! In his last days he ordered minions of the Architect of the Capitol to come over and measure his office and take photographs so that he might perfectly reconstruct it in the basement of his home. This pitiful insanity was surrendered only after they brought him the bottom-line cost figures. He then bought his official chair from the government at cost, the Congress kindly permitting its rejects that eccentricity by public law, in the interest of helping them rehabilitate themselves and achieve reentry. I am told that these many years later he still rocks and hums in it while reading the *Congressional Record.*

The frustrations of the *Lameducus americanus* was perfectly illustrated by Vice President Nelson Rockefeller when he gave that stiff middle finger to hecklers as he accomplished a career-ending speech. Though people joked that Rocky was merely signifying how many billions he had, in reality he was showing the world the anger and hurt of political rejection. You may recall that famous picture of Rocky flashing his vulgar ire. He had a mad grin on his face, one of sheer crazed joy, and I personally think it was his finest hour. See, I been there. When a congressman I once worked for got beaten, I ordered an obscene rubber stamp I intended thereafter to imprint on all incoming mail. Seriously. When my lame-duck boss vetoed my notion, I quit speaking to him.

Politicians are required to grin when they don't feel like it and to kiss behinds when they ain't up to the pucker. They do it, of course, because they must pay the taxes of their trade. But they are human, and they resent having to do it, and they store up much secret bile: against demanding voters; stubborn enemies; the Goddamned Press. The moment they are defeated, all that bile boils over. They begin to think of the eighteen-hour days they've put in, all the errands they've run and the favors they've done, all the mandatory smiling and backscratching and debilitating puckering, and when it all comes to naught—when they look down and see it in dust at their feet, worth about as much as what the scared fairy left under the hat—they feel very, very much betrayed. Murderous.

While they are winning, politicians are surrounded by cheers and paid staffers who open their doors and compete to light their cigars, telling them by words and actions that they are the best invention since the can opener. Organizations give 'em plaques and scrolls commemorating them. They come to believe in their Destiny and Greatness, which is not difficult, because only the naturally egomaniacal are attracted to politics: would-be messiahs; seers; delivering angels; prophets. Name me another job (except writing) in which you get paid for bragging on yourself and publicly cussing people or ideas you don't like. So politicians get to considering themselves lordly and godly and I've never known one yet that didn't have his eye on the top of the stairs. Then, suddenly, the rug's pulled out from under 'em, and they go crazy.

To lose an election not only dashes dreams but can make you —in the eyes of your peers—absolutely invisible. There is a shame attached to losing, much like being cuckolded, because politicians lose their gonads when they lose the public favor. The same thing happens to them that happened to Samson once Delilah got her hands on the scissors. They just can't get it up. Survivors do not want to be around those who've recently lost because it reminds them, at least subliminally, that beneath the skin *they* are mere mortals and subject to unusual risks. There-but-for-the-grace-of-God, and so on.

So the loser loses not only his office and his gonads but his membership in the Club. He becomes a nonperson among his former colleagues as surely as if he'd botched up being premier of the Soviet Union. Even his loyal staffers desert him, they who so long had been at his beck and call and laughed when he told jokes; he now sees them looking around for more viable connections and taking little interest in his packing. This is particularly odious, in that the lame duck likely has forgotten how to tote or fetch for himself or to dial his own calls. He cannot cope. Invitations he once might have routinely renounced no longer come his way. He has much to sit in the dark and ponder. His soul becomes as sour as slices of quince.

I was on Capitol Hill the other day and chanced by a poor office where they were packing up to leave. You could smell death there and such melancholy as is associated with funeral homes, except that not only was it still and quiet, it was sullen. The office walls were blotched and pocked like an old wino's face, the ghostly shapes of absent pictures burned onto them, and scarred by removing surgery performed on hanging nails or bracing bolts. Huge wooden trash bins in the middle of the barren office loomed like giant coffins. The whole place had a raped look. I started to go in and ask everybody how they felt, but the jackassery of that question dawned on me just in time. They felt as if they were in hell with their backs broke; that's how they felt.

That's why Ron Nessen isn't holding many press briefings these days, and why the President isn't any more visible than a flyspeck, and why when you call the White House switchboard, you don't get an answer until about the sixth ring.

Merry Christmas.

17 ☆

When the Spoils
Turn to Ashes

For months Quiggly had been anticipating his personal participation in the joyous crush of Jimmy Carter's inauguration.

Though Quiggly had been a Capitol Hill staff aide for a decade, the Democrat's coronation would provide his first opportunity to feel a part of the historic process. In 1969, and again in 1973, he had sat ogling his TV set and munching hamburgers while Republicans celebrated with glad cries of "Bring Us Together" and "Four More Years." Each cry stabbed Quiggly deep. Would he never come in from the cold?

Sometimes, here in the winter of his great content, caught in rush-hour traffic plodding along Route 50 while en route from his Falls Church home to the Hill, Quiggly would find fellow commuters looking at him funny and then realize he had been laughing out loud. Though Quiggly was laughing at the prospect of millions of goddamn Republicans sitting in solitary melancholy before their television machines, he always leaned forward to fiddle with the radio dial as if he'd been laughing at some witticism of the air. After all, Quiggly told himself, it is obligatory upon winners not to rub it in past a certain point.

Quiggly felt certain he would be justly rewarded for his services to Jimmy Carter. Not that he expected to be subpoenaed to lunch with the new President and leaders of Congress, no. As a longtime administrative assistant on the Hill—"A.A." in shorthand; Quiggly eschewed the term because he feared people might think he meant to indicate a bottle problem and, hell, he didn't drink all that much; not really—Quiggly knew the pecking order and fancied himself a realist. He knew that he could not claim to have walked with Jimmy through the snows of Iowa, back when Carter had been unknown outside Georgia. Still, he had jumped on the bandwagon by the time of the Wisconsin primary, and he knew nothing could possibly be on the record to indicate his secret preference for Scoop Jackson because he hadn't even told his wife.

Quiggly thought that the week he'd spent going door to door for Jimmy Carter in numerous Wisconsin hamlets probably had saved the state from the clutches of Mo Udall. After all, the race had been so close that two of three TV networks had called the state for Udall. Sometimes he fantasized Hamilton Jordan turning to Jody Powell, as they addressed inaugural invitations by hand on the sun porch down in Plains, and saying, "Don't forget that young fella Quiggly with Congressman Smertz. He saved Wisconsin for us."

Quiggly did not receive an invitation to sit on the inaugural platform with Jimmy. Or with Billy or Miss Lillian or Amy. He did not receive a bid to one of the several inaugural galas or balls. He did not receive even so much as one of those souvenir noninvitations, which invited you to Washington if you could get a day off but did not guarantee so much as passage across the Fourteenth Street Bridge.

Quiggly dodged the question when his wife asked whether their inaugural tickets had arrived, changing the subject or having coughing fits. His wife had bought new gowns and accessories in case network TV cameras selected her in panning the crowd, and had arranged for the Quiggly children to overnight with friends so as not to impede her grand debut. She had even arranged to write her first-person impressions of the festivities for the weekly *Kumquat County Bugle* back home. What she had spent on beauty-shop experiments would go a long way toward efficient mass-transit solutions.

Quiggly privately figured there'd been an oversight somewhere. In time, he was certain, the cool efficiency of the Carter Organization would win through. Somebody among the Biggies —Jody or Ham or Rafshoon or like that—would telephone to say, "Listen, ol' hoss, we're plumb mortified by the mixup; after the public part of this drill is over, we want you and your good lady to come to a secret midnight supper at Barbara Howar's." Quiggly fantasized sitting much above the salt, perhaps between Joe Kraft and Yoland Fox.

Other than closely quizzing the Longworth Building mailman who delivered to his floor, Quiggly kept a low profile with respect to his missing tickets. When the mailman began to snarl and curse and show signs of paranoia, it dawned on Quiggly that perhaps he should go to the source.

Quiggly then telephoned Jack Watson of the Transition Team. After eight days his twenty-third call was returned by a young lady functionary whose name escaped Quiggly. This, as it turned out, was only fair.

"Mr. Biggly," she said, "what is it you wish?"

"Quiggly," Quiggly said. And told of his missing tickets to the inauguration and subsequent events.

"Mr. Wiggly," she said, "that subject is beyond the purview of the Transition Team. Excuse me, another line's ringing." Quiggly next heard the cold growl of the dial tone in his ear.

Do not think that Quiggly despaired. He held the case ace. Congressman Smertz. Good Old Smertz, whose bidding he long had done and in whose vineyards he long had labored. Good Old Smertz now would reciprocate, and gladly, and probably feel fewer pressures in retiring a smidgen of his great personal debt to Quiggly.

Congressman Smertz kept dozing off during Quiggly's presentation of his grievance. When he realized that his faithful aide's voice box had ceased operating, he smiled and shook his hand and called him a Great American and then asked whether Quiggly had called the Folding Room to make certain his newsletter would get out on time.

Quiggly sucked it up and told his congressman that he required a few more assurances than that. He explained how his Democratic wife, who'd never been invited to so much as a bail-bond fund raiser during eight years of Republican rule, had her heart set on witnessing Jimmy Carter's coronation at close range. Congressman Smertz told Quiggly not to worry about it, and had he finished drafting the bill that would turn Donkey Mountain into Leonard B. Smertz National Park?

For the next two nights Quiggly slept on the office couch so as to avoid quizzings by his wife. He would go home, he told himself, the moment Smertz had cut through the red tape. On the morning of the third day, the congressman said the subject was becoming a sore one with him, and where in hell was that goddamn Donkey Mountain bill at?

Quiggly bowed his neck and inquired as to the general admission tickets given to each congressional office. By now he was resigned to standing in the snow, with cold winds blowing in his face, somewhere on the other side of the Supreme Court building in the company of Iowa pharmacists and seekers of small patronage. Even this, however, would marginally qualify Quiggly to brag to his grandchildren of having been on hand when President-elect Carter had raised his.

Congressman Smertz said well, sorry, but such ducats were more precious than diamonds; that he couldn't surrender even one of his limited few because they'd been promised to his financial chairman, to the president of the powerful Earache Club back home, and to the mother-in-law of his daughter's third-grade teacher—and, incidentally, the office staff should not count on a holiday during the inauguration festivities. They'd be needed to greet visiting constituents while he, Smertz, was off eating parched peanuts and watching the big parade with Jimmy and Rosalynn.

Quiggly repaired to the Democratic Club in what once had been the Congressional Hotel, but now with more poetry was formally designated as Auxiliary Federal House Office Building Number One. There Quiggly fell to such dedicated drinking that soon he began to snort and paw.

Six or seven hours later Quiggly made telephonic contact with his boss. He opened with what charitably might be called a string of double negatives, all of them having to do with the congressman's personal shortcomings. "I would guess," Quiggly carefully articulated, "that your hat size is on par with your IQ and that your ego is a thousandfold larger than either or both." Quiggly went on to proclaim himself weary of playing the nameless nitwit to constituents in order to protect Smertz when Smertz had botched yet another issue or case or moment. Quiggly said he was sick unto death of writing wonderful speeches which Smertz mangled at every public opportunity, and he was weary of sitting in the shadows while the congressman preened himself in spotlights and took credit for all the hard work Quiggly had accomplished. "As to when I began to really hate you," he said, "I think it was on first sight."

He confided to Congressman Smertz that Mrs. Smertz had long been cavorting outside the home with a rival on the powerful Typewriter Repair Subcommittee and that he—Quincy by-God Quiggly—often, and with great joy in his heart, had booked them into one or another hotel room for their midday mischief. He told Smertz that he, Quincy by-God Quiggly, now fully intended to change his partisan registration and run against him, Leonard Bastard Smertz, at the next election permitted by the Constitution.

Quiggly had never felt so rid of binding gases; he went back into the Democratic Club and began to sing ribald and vicious songs about Congressman Smertz to the tune of "Hinky Dinky Parlay Voo."

When Quiggly began to denounce Jimmy Carter in particular and Democrats in the aggregate, two lobbyists—with natural instincts to be well thought of in the new administration—telephoned Dev O'Neill, the majority photographer. Dev got some wonderful shots of Quiggly being ejected from the Democratic Club by lobbyists and junior congressmen wearing broad smiles on their faces. Dev soon began selling eight-by-ten glossy prints for $10 each, but the lobbyists undercut his business by giving them away. Autographed.

Quiggly's wife quit him and returned to East Gulch, filing papers accusing him of mental cruelty, incompatibility, and public humiliations upon herself. His desk in Congressman Smertz's office stands empty, and in the small apartment where he sleeps on a cot he spends a lot of time searching the classifieds and cooking cold-cut sandwiches. Quiggly still has hopes of seeing the Carter inaugural festivities, provided they have a television set down at the unemployment office.

The Alamo Mind-Set:
Lyndon B. Johnson
and Vietnam

He was an old-fashioned man by the purest definition. Forget
that he was enamored of twentieth-century artifacts—the telephone, television, supersonic airplanes, spacecraft—to which
he adapted with a child's wondering glee. His values were the
relics of an earlier time; he had been shaped by an America
both rawer and more confident than it later would become; his
generation may have been the last to believe that for every
problem there existed a workable solution; that the ultimate
answer, as in old-time mathematics texts, always reposed in the
back of the book.

He bought the prevailing American myths without closely
inspecting the merchandise for rips or snares. He often said that
Americans inherently were "can-do" people capable of accom-
plishing anything they willed. It was part of his creed that
Americans were God's chosen; why, otherwise, would they
have become the richest, the strongest, the freest people in the
history of man? His was a God, perhaps, who was a first cousin
to Darwin; Lyndon B. Johnson believed in survival of the fittest,
that the strong would conquer the weak, that almost always the
big 'uns ate the little 'uns.

There was a certain pragmatism in his beliefs, a touch of

fatalism, and often a goodly measure of common sense and true compassion. Yet, too, he could be wildly romantic or muddle-headed. Johnson truly believed that any boy could rise to become President, though only thirty-five had. Hadn't he—a shirt-tailed kid from the dusty hardscrabble of the Texas outback—walked with royalty and strong men, while reigning over what he called, without blushing, the Free World? In his last days, though bitter and withering in retirement at his rural Elba, he astonished and puzzled a young black teenager by waving his arms in windmill motions and telling the youngster, during a random encounter, "Well, maybe someday all of us will be visiting *your* house in Waco, because *you'll* be President and your home will be a national museum just as mine is. It'll take a while, but it'll happen, you'll see. . . ." Then he turned to the black teenager's startled mother: "Now, you better get that home of yours cleaned up spick-and-span. There'll be hundreds of thousands coming through it, you know, wanting to see the bedroom and the kitchen and the living room. Now, I hope you get that dust rag of yours out the minute you get home. . . ."

Doris Kearns, the Harvard professor and latter-day LBJ confidante, who witnessed the performance, thought it a mock show: "almost a vaudeville act." Dr. Johnson peddling the same old snake oil. Perhaps. Whatever his motives that day, Lyndon Johnson chose his sermon from the text he most fervently believed throughout a lifetime; his catechism spoke to the heart of American opportunity, American responsibility, American good intentions, American superiority, American destiny, American infallibility. *Why, hell, boy*—he was saying to the black teenager—*this country's so goddamn great even a nigger's gonna be President! And you and others like you got to be ready!*

Despite a sly personal cynicism—a suspicion of others who might pull their dirks on him; the keen, cold eye of a man determined not to be victimized at the gaming tables—he was, in his institutional instincts, something of a Pollyanna in that, I think, he somehow believed people in the abstract to be somewhat better than they are. He expected they would *do* more, and more things could be done *for* them, than probably is true. There *was* such a thing as a free lunch; there *was* a Santa Claus; there *was,* somewhere, a Good Fairy, and probably it was made of the component parts of Franklin Roosevelt, Saint Francis, and Uncle Sam.

There were certain thoroughly American traits—as LBJ saw them—which constituted the foundation stone upon which the Republic, and his own dream castle, had been built; he found it impossible to abandon them even as the sands shifted and bogged him in the quagmire of Vietnam. If America was so wonderful (and it *was;* he had the evidence of himself to prove it), then he had the obligation to export its goodness and greatness to the less fortunate. It would not do to limit this healing ministry merely to domestic unfortunates—to the tattered blacks of Mississippi or to the bombed and strafed disadvantaged of the South Bronx—because man, *everywhere,* deserved the right to be just like us! Yessir! This good he would accomplish at any cost; it was why we had no choice but "to nail the coonskin to the wall." For if Lyndon B. Johnson believed in God and America and its goodness and greatness, he also believed in guts and gunpowder.

All the history he had read, and all he had personally witnessed, convinced him that the United States of America—if determined enough, if productive enough, if patriotic enough —simply could not lose a war. We have evidence from his mother that as a boy his favorite stories were of the Minutemen at Lexington and Concord, of the heroic defenders of the Alamo, of rugged frontiersmen who'd at once tamed the wild land and marauding Indians. He had a special affinity for a schoolboy poem proclaiming that the most beautiful sight his eyes had beheld was "the flag of my country in a foreign land."

He so admired war heroes that he claimed to have been fired on "by a Japanese ace," though little evidence supported it; he invented an ancestor he carelessly claimed had been martyred at the Alamo; at the Democratic National Convention in 1956 he had cast his state's delegate votes for the vice presidential ambitions of young John F. Kennedy, "that fighting sailor who bears the scars of battle."

On a slow Saturday afternoon in the late 1950s, expansive and garrulous in his Capitol Hill office, Johnson discoursed to a half dozen young Texas staffers in the patois of their shared native place. Why—he said—you take that ragtag bunch at Valley Forge; who'd have given them a cut dog's chance? There they were, barefoot in the snow and their asses hanging out, nothing to eat but moss and dead leaves and snakes, not half enough bullets for their guns, and facing the soldiers of the most powerful king of his time. Yet they sucked it up, wouldn't quit, went on to fight and win. Or take the Civil War, now; it had been so exceptionally bloody because you had aroused Americans fighting on *both* sides; it had been something like rock against rock, or two mean ol' pit bulldogs going at each other and both of 'em thinking only of taking hunks out of the other. He again invoked the Alamo: a mere handful of freedom-loving men, knowing they faced certain death; but they'd carved their names in history for all time, and before they got through with ol' General Santa Anna, he thought he'd stumbled into a swarm of bumblebees.

Fifteen years later Johnson would show irritation when Clark Clifford suggested that victory in Vietnam might require a sustaining commitment of twenty to thirty years. No—LBJ said—no, no, the thing to do was get in and out quickly, pour everything you had into the fight, land the knockout blow; hell, the North Vietnamese *had* to see the futility of facing all that American muscle! If you really poured it on 'em, you could clean up that mess within six months. We had the troops, the firepower, the bombs, the sophisticated weaponry, the oil—everything we needed to win. Did we have the resolve? Well, the Texas Rangers had a saying that you couldn't stop a man who just kept on a-coming. And that's what we'd do in Vietnam, Clark, just keep on a-coming. . . .

Always he talked of the necessity to be strong; he invoked his father's standing up to the Ku Klux Klan in the 1920s, Teddy Roosevelt's carrying that big stick, FDR's mobilizing the country to beat Hitler and Tojo. He had liked ol' Harry Truman—tough little bastard and his own man—but, listen, Harry and Dean Acheson had lost control when they failed to prosecute the Korean War properly. They lost the public's respect, lost control of General MacArthur, lost the backing of Congress, lost the *war* or the next thing to it. Next thing you know, they got blamed for losing China, and then there was Joe McCarthy accusing them of being soft on communism and everybody believed it. Well, it wouldn't happen to him, no, sir. *He* hadn't started the Vietnam War—Jack Kennedy had made the first commitment of out-and-out combat troops in force, don't forget —but *he* wouldn't bug out no matter how much the Nervous Nellies brayed. Kennedy had proved during the Cuban missile crisis that if you stood firm, then the Reds would back down. They were bullies, and he didn't intend to be pushed around any more than Jack Kennedy had. When a bully ragged you, you didn't go whining to the teacher but gave him some of his own medicine.

Only later, in exile, when he spoke with unusual candor of his darker secretions, did it become clear how obsessed with failure Lyndon Johnson always had been. As a preschool youngster he walked a country lane to visit a grandfather, his head stuffed with answers he knew would be required ("How many head of cattle you got, Lyndon? How much do they eat? How many head can you graze to the acre?") and fearing he might forget them. If he forgot them, he got no bright-red apple but received, instead, a stern and disapproving gaze. LBJ's mother, who smothered him with affection and praise should he perform to her pleasure and expectations, refused to acknowledge his presence should he somehow displease or disappoint her. His father accused him of being a sleepyhead, a slow starter, and sometimes said every boy in town had a two-hour head start on him. Had we known those things from scratch, we might not have wondered why Lyndon Johnson seemed so blind for so long to the Asian realities. His personal history simply permitted him no retreats or failures in testings.

From childhood LBJ experienced bad dreams. As with much else, they would stay with him to the shadow of the grave. His nightmares were of being paralyzed and unable to act, of being chained inside a cage or to his desk, of being pursued by hostile forces. These and other disturbing dreams haunted his White House years; he could see himself stricken and ill on a cot, unable even to speak—like Woodrow Wilson—while, in an adjoining room, his trusted aides squabbled and quarreled in dividing his power. He translated the dreams to mean that should he for a moment show weakness, be indecisive, then history might judge him as the first American President who had failed to stand up and be counted. Johnson's was a benign translation; others might see a neurotic fear of losing power—*his* power— to subordinates he did not, at least subconsciously, trust.

These deep-rooted insecurities prompted Lyndon Johnson always to assert himself, to abuse staff members simply to prove that he held the upper hand; to test his power in small or mean ways. Sometimes, in sending Vice President Hubert Humphrey off on missions or errands with exhortations to "get going," he literally kicked him in the shins. "Hard," Humphrey later recalled, pulling up his trouser leg to exhibit the scars to columnist Robert Allen. Especially when drinking did he swagger and strut. Riding high as Senate Majority Leader, Johnson one night after a Texas State Society function, in the National Press Club in Washington—in the spring of 1958—repaired to a nearby bar with Texas Congressmen Homer Thornberry and Jack Brooks. "I'm a powerful sumbitch, you know that?" he repeatedly said. "You boys realize how goddamn *powerful* I am?"

Yes, Lyndon, his companions uneasily chorused. Johnson pounded the table as if attempting to crack stout oak. "Do you know Ike couldn't pass the Lord's Prayer without me? You understand that? Hah?" Yes, Lyndon. "Hah? Do you? Hah?" Sitting in an adjoining booth, with another Capitol Hill aide, James Boren, I thought I never had seen a man more desperate for affirmations of himself.

Lyndon Johnson always was an enthusiastic Cold Warrior. He was not made uncomfortable by John Foster Dulles's brinkmanship rhetoric about "rolling back" communism or "unleashing" Chiang Kai-shek to "free" the Chinese mainland—from which the generalissimo earlier had been routed by the Reds. LBJ was, indeed, one of the original soldiers of the Cold War, a volunteer rather than a draftee, just as he had been the first member of Congress to rush to the recruiting station following Japan's attack on Pearl Harbor. Immediately after World War II he so bedeviled Speaker Sam Rayburn about his fears of America's dismantling its military machine that Rayburn, in vexation, appointed him to the postwar Military Policy Committee and to the Joint Committee on Atomic Energy. Johnson early had a preference for military assignments in Congress; he successfully campaigned for a seat on the House Naval Affairs Committee in the 1930s and, a decade later, the Senate Armed Services Committee. He eventually chaired the Senate Preparedness Committee and the Senate Space Committee. Perhaps others saw the exploration of outer space in scientific or peaceful terms; Johnson, however, told Senate Democrats that outer space offered "the ultimate position from which total control of the earth may be exercised. Whoever gains that ultimate position gains control, total control, over the earth."

He was a nagger, a complainer, a man not always patient with those of lesser gifts or with those who somehow inconvenienced him. Sometimes he complained that the generals knew nothing but "spend and bomb"; almost always, however, he went along with bigger military spending and, in most cases, with more bombing or whatever tough military action the brass proposed. This was his consistent record in Congress, and he generally affirmed it as President. On November 12, 1951, Senator Johnson rattled his saber at the Russians:

> We are tired of fighting your stooges. We will no longer sacrifice our young men on the altar of your conspiracies. The next aggression will be the last. . . . We will strike back, not just at your satellites, but at you. We will strike back with all the dreaded might that is within our control and it will be a crushing blow.

Even allowing for those rhetorical excesses peculiar to senatorial oratory, those were not the words of a man preoccupied with the doctrine of peaceful coexistence. Nor were they inconsistent with Johnson's mind-set when he made a public demand —at the outbreak of the Korean War, in June 1950—that President Truman order an all-out mobilization of all military reserve troops, National Guard units, draftees, and even civilian manpower and industry. He told intimates that this Korean thing could be the opening shot of World War III, and we had to be ready for that stark eventuality. In a Senate debate shortly thereafter, Senator Johnson scolded colleagues questioning the Pentagon's request for new and supplementary emergency billions: "Is this the hour of our nation's twilight, the last fading hour of light before an endless night shall envelop us and all the Western world?"

His ties with Texas—with its indigenous xenophobic instincts and general proclivities toward a raw yahooism—haunted him and, in a sense, may have made him a prisoner of grim political realities during the witch-hunting McCarthy era. "I'm damned tired," he said, "of being called a Dixiecrat in Washington and a communist in Texas"; it perfectly summed up those schizophrenic divisions uneasily compartmentalizing his national political life and the more restrictive parochial role dictated by conditions back home. He lived daily with a damned-if-I-do-and-damned-if-I-don't situation. Texas was a particularly happy hunting ground for Senator Joe McCarthy, whose self-proclaimed anticommunist crusade brought him invitation after invitation to speak there; the Texas legislature, in the 1950s controlled beyond belief by vested interests and showing the ideological instincts of the early primates, whooped through a resolution demanding that Senator McCarthy address it despite the suggestion of State Representative Maury Maverick, Jr., that the resolution be expanded to invite Mickey Mouse also. Both Johnson's powerful rightist adversaries and many of his wealthy Texas benefactors were enthusiastic contributors to the McCarthy cause and coffers.

Privately, LBJ groused of McCarthy's reckless showboat tactics and, particularly, of the Texas-directed pressures they brought him. Why—he said—Joe McCarthy was just a damn drunk, a blowhard, an incompetent who couldn't tie his own shoelaces, probably the biggest joke in the Senate. But—LBJ reminded those counseling him to attack McCarthy—people *believed* him; they were so afraid of the communists they would believe anything. There would come a time when the hysteria died down, and then McCarthy would be vulnerable; such a fellow was certain to hang himself in time. But right now anybody openly challenging McCarthy would come away with dirty hands and with his heart broken. "Touch pitch," he paraphrased the Bible, "and you'll be defiled."

By temperament a man who coveted the limelight and never

was bashful about claiming credit for popular actions, Johnson uncharacteristically remained in the background when the U.S. Senate voted to censure McCarthy in late 1954. Though he was instrumental in selecting senators he believed would be effective and creditable members in leading the censure effort, Johnson's fine hand was visible only to insiders. A correspondent for Texas newspapers later would remember it as "the only time we had to hunt to find Johnson. He almost went into hiding."

Johnson believed, however—and probably more deeply than Joe McCarthy—in a worldwide, monolithic communist conspiracy. He believed it was directed from Moscow and that it was ready to blast America, or subvert it, at the drop of a fur hat. LBJ never surrendered that view. In retirement he suggested that the communists were everywhere, honeycombing the government, and he told astonished visitors that sometimes he hadn't known whether he could trust even his own staff; *that's* how widespread spying and subversion had become. The communists (it had been his first thought on hearing the gunshots in Dallas, and he never changed his mind) had killed Jack Kennedy; it had been their influence that turned people against the Vietnam War. One of LBJ's former aides, having been treated to that angry lecture, came away from the Texas ranch with the sad and reluctant conclusion that "the Old Man's absolutely paranoid on the communist thing."

In May 1961 President Kennedy dispatched his Vice President to Asia on a "fact-finding" diplomatic trip. Johnson, who believed it his duty to be a team player, to reinforce the prevailing wisdom, bought without qualification the optimistic briefings of military brass with their charts and slides "proving" the inevitable American victory. "I was sent out here to report on the *progress* of the war," he told an aide, as if daring anyone to bring him anything less than good news. Carried away, he publicly endowed South Vietnam's President Ngo Dinh Diem with the qualities of Winston Churchill, George Washington, Andrew Jackson, and FDR. Visiting refugee camps, he grew angry at communist aggressions "against decent people" and concluded: "There is no alternative to United States leadership in Southeast Asia. . . . We must decide whether to help to the best of our ability or throw in the towel [and] pull back our defenses to San Francisco and a 'Fortress America' concept." Yes, sir, the damned dirty Reds would chase us all the way to the Golden Gate! LBJ believed then—and always would believe —in the domino theory first stated by President Eisenhower. Even after announcing his abdication, he continued to sing the tired litany: If Vietnam fell, then the rest of Asia might go, and then Africa, and then the Philippines. . . .

When Lyndon Johnson suddenly ascended to the presidency, however, he did not enter the Oval Office eager to immediately take the measure of Ho Chi Minh. Although he told Ambassador Henry Cabot Lodge, "I am not going to be the President who saw Southeast Asia go the way China went," he wanted, for the moment, to keep the war—and, indeed, all foreign entanglements—at arm's length. His preoccupation was with his domestic program; here, he was confident, he knew what he was doing. He would emulate FDR in making people's lives a little brighter. To aides he talked eagerly of building schools and houses, of fighting poverty and attaining full employment, of heating the economy to record prosperity. The honeymoon with Congress—he said—couldn't last; he had seen Congress grow balky and obstinate, take its measure of many Presidents, and he had to assume it would happen again. Then he would lean forward, tapping a forefinger against someone's chest or squeezing a neighboring knee, and say, "I'm like a sweetheart to Congress right now. They love me because I'm new and courting 'em, and it's kinda exciting, like that first kiss. But after a while the new will wear off. Then Congress will complain that I don't bring enough roses or candy and will accuse me of seeing other girls." The need was to push forward quickly, pass the civil rights bill in the name of the martyred John F. Kennedy, then hit Capitol Hill with a blizzard of domestic proposals and dazzle it before sentiment and enthusiasms cooled. Foreign affairs could wait. Even war could walk at mark-time speed.

Lyndon B. Johnson at that point had little experience in foreign affairs. Except for his showcase missions accomplished as Vice President, he had not traveled outside the United States save for excursions to Mexico and his brief World War II peregrinations. He probably had little confidence in himself in foreign affairs; neither did he have an excessive interest in the field. "Foreigners are not like the folks I am used to," he sometimes said—and though it passed as a joke, there was the feeling he might be kidding on the level.

Ambassadors waiting to present their credentials to the new President were miffed by repeated delays—and then angrily astonished when LBJ received them in groups and clumps, seemingly paying only perfunctory attention, squirming in his chair, scowling or muttering during the traditional ceremonies. He appeared oblivious to their feelings, to their offended senses of dignity. "Why do I have to see them?" the President demanded. "They're Dean Rusk's clients, not mine."

Defense Secretary Robert McNamara was selected to focus on Vietnam while LBJ concocted his Great Society. McNamara should send South Vietnam equipment and money as needed, a few more men, issue the necessary pronouncements. But don't splash it all over the front pages; don't let it get out of hand; don't give Barry Goldwater Vietnam as an issue for the 1964 campaign. Barry, hell, he was a hip shooter; he'd fight Canada or Mexico—or give that impression anyhow—so the thing to do was sit tight, keep the lid on, keep all Asian options open. Above all, "Don't let it turn into a Bay of Pigs." Hunker down; don't gamble.

The trouble—Johnson said to advisers—was that foreign nations didn't understand Americans or the American way: They saw us as "fat and fifty, like the country-club set"; they didn't think we had the steel to act when the going got rough. Well, in time they'd find out differently. They'd learn that Lyndon Johnson was not about to abandon what other Presidents had started; he wouldn't permit history to write that he'd been the only American President to cut and run; he wouldn't sponsor any damn Munich. But for right now—cool it. Put Vietnam on the back burner, and let it simmer.

But the communists—he later would say—wouldn't permit him to cool it. There had been that Gulf of Tonkin attack on the United States destroyer *Maddox*, in August of 19-and-64, and if he hadn't convinced Congress to get on record as backing him up in Vietnam, why, then, the Reds would have interpreted it as a sign of weakness and Barry Goldwater would have cut his heart out. And in February of 19-and-65, don't forget, the Vietcong had made that attack on the American garrison at Pleiku, and how could he be expected to ignore that? There they came, thousands of 'em, barefoot and howling in their black pajamas and throwing homemade bombs; it had been a damned insult, a calculated show of contempt. LBJ told the National Security Council: "The worst thing we could do would be to let this [Pleiku] thing go by. It would be a big mistake. It would open the door to a major misunderstanding."

Twelve hours later, American aircraft—for the first time— bombed in North Vietnam; three weeks later, Lyndon Johnson ordered continuing bombing raids in the north to "force the North Vietnamese into negotiations"; only 120 days after Pleiku, American ground forces were involved in a full-scale war and seeking new ways to take the offensive. Eight Americans died at Pleiku. Eight. Eventually 50,000-plus Americans would die in Asia.

Pleiku was the second major testing of American will, within a few months, in LBJ's view. In the spring of 1965 rebels had attacked the ruling military junta in the Dominican Republic. Lives and property of U.S. citizens were endangered, as Johnson saw it, but—more—this might be a special tactic by the Reds, a dry run for bigger mischief later on in Vietnam. The world was watching to see how America would react. "It's just like the Alamo," he lectured the National Security Council. "Hell, it's like you were down at that gate, and you were surrounded, and you damn well needed somebody. Well, by God, I'm going to *go*—and I thank the Lord that I've got men who want to go with me, from McNamara right down to the littlest private who's carrying a gun."

Somewhat to his puzzlement, and certainly to his great vexation, Lyndon Johnson would learn that not everybody approved of his rushing the Marines into the Dominican Republic, and within days building up a 21,000-man force. Congress, editorials, and some formerly friendly foreign diplomats blasted him. Attempting to answer these critics, he would claim thousands of patriots "bleeding in the streets and with their heads cut off "; paint a false picture of the United States ambassador cringing under his desk "while bullets whizzed over his head"; speak of howling Red hordes descending on American citizens and American holdings; and, generally, open what later become known as the Credibility Gap.

By now he had given up on his original notion of walking easy in Vietnam until he could put across the Great Society. Even before the three major "testings" of Tonkin Gulf, the Dominican Republic, and Pleiku, he had said—almost idly—"Well, I guess we have to touch up those North Vietnamese a little bit." By December 1964 he had reversed earlier priorities: "We'll beat the communists first; then we can look around and maybe give something to the poor." Guns now ranked ahead of butter.

* * *

Not that he was happy about it. Though telling Congress, "This nation is mighty enough, its society is healthy enough, its people are strong enough, to pursue our goals in the rest of the world while still building a Great Society here at home," he knew, in his bones, that this was much too optimistic an outlook. He privately fretted that his domestic program would be victimized. He became touchy, irritable, impatient with those who even timorously questioned America's increasing commitment to the war. Why should *I* be blamed—he snapped—when the communists are the aggressors, when President Eisenhower committed us in Asia in 19-and-54, when Kennedy beefed up Ike's efforts? If he didn't prosecute the Vietnam War now, then later Congress would sour and want to hang him because he hadn't—and would gut his domestic programs in retaliation.

He claimed to have "pounded President Eisenhower's desk" in opposing Ike's sending 200 Air Force "technicians" to assist the French in Indochina (though those who were present in the Oval Office later recalled that only Senators Russell of Georgia and Stennis of Mississippi had raised major objections). Well, he'd been unable to stop Ike that time, though he *had* helped persuade him against dropping paratroopers into Dienbienphu to aid the doomed French garrison there. And after all *that,* everybody now called Vietnam "Lyndon Johnson's War"! It was unfair: "The only difference between the Kennedy assassination and mine is that I am alive and it is more torturous."

Very well, if it was his war in the public mind, then he would personally oversee its planning. "Never move up your artillery until you move up your ammunition," he told his generals—a thing he'd said as Senate Majority Leader when impatient liberals urged him to call for votes on issues he felt not yet ripe. Often he quizzed the military brass, sounding almost like a dove, in a way to resemble courtroom cross-examinations. He forced the admirals and generals to affirm and reaffirm their recommendations as vital to victory. Reading selected transcripts, one might make the judgment that Lyndon Johnson was a most reluctant warrior, one more cautious in Vietnam than not. The larger evidence of Johnson's deeds, however, suggests that he was being a crafty politician—making a record so that later he couldn't be made the sole scapegoat.

He trusted Robert McNamara's computers, perhaps more than he trusted men, and took satisfaction when their printouts predicted that X amount of bombing would be needed to damage the Vietcong by Y or that X number of troops would be required to capture Z. Planning was the key. You figured what you had to do, you did it, and eventually you'd nail the coonskin to the wall. Johnson devoutly believed that all problems had solutions; in his lifetime alone we'd beaten the Great Depression, won two world wars, hacked away at racial discrimination, made an industrial giant and world power of a former agrarian society, explored outer space. This belief in available solutions led him, time and again, to change tactics in Vietnam and discover fresh enthusiasm for each new move; he did not pause, apparently, to reflect on why given tactics, themselves once heralded as practical solutions, had failed and had been abandoned. If counterinsurgency failed, you bombed. If bombing wasn't wholly effective, then you tried the enclave theory. If *that* proved disappointing, you sent your ground troops on search-and-destroy missions. If, somehow, your troops couldn't find the phantom Vietcong in large numbers (and therefore couldn't destroy them), you began pacification programs in the areas you'd newly occupied. And if *this* bogged down, if the bastards still sneaked up to knife you in the night, you beefed up your firepower and sent in enough troops simply to outmuscle the rice-paddy ragtags: Napalm 'em, bomb 'em, shoot 'em; burn 'em out, and flush 'em out. Sure it would work! It always had! Yes, surely, the answer was there somewhere in the back of the book, if only you looked long enough. . . .

He sought, and found, assurances. Maybe he had only a "cow-college" education; perhaps he'd not attended West Point; he might not have excessive experience in foreign affairs. But he was surrounded by the good men David Halberstam later, and ironically, would label "the best and the brightest," and certainly these were unanimous in their supportive conclusions. "He would look around him," Tom Wicker later said, "and see in Bob McNamara that [the war] was technologically feasible, in McGeorge Bundy that it was intellectually respectable, and in Dean Rusk that it was historically necessary." It was especially easy to trust expertise when the experts in their calculations bolstered your own gut feelings—and when their computers and high-minded statements and mighty hardware all boiled down to reinforce your belief in American efficiency, American responsibility, American destiny. If so many good men agreed with him, then what might be wrong with those who didn't?

He considered the sources of dissatisfaction and dissent: the liberals—the "red-hots," he'd often sneeringly called them; the "pepper pots"—who were impractical dreamers, self-winding kamikazes intent on self-destruction. He often quoted an aphorism to put such people in perspective: "Any jackass can kick down a barn, but it takes a carpenter to build one." He fancied, however, that he knew all about those queer fellows. For years, down home, Ronnie Dugger and his *Texas Observer* crowd, in LBJ's opinion, had urged him to put his head in the noose by fighting impossible, profitless fights. They wanted him to take on Joe McCarthy, slap the oil powers down, kick Ike's tail, tell everybody who wasn't a red-hot to go to hell. Well, he'd learned a long time ago that just because you *told* a fellow to go to hell, he didn't necessarily have to go. The liberals just didn't understand the communists. Bill Fulbright and his bunch—the striped-pants boys over at the State Department; assorted outside red-hots, such as the goddamn Harvards—they thought you could *trust* the communists. They made the mistake of believing the Reds would deal with you honorably when—in truth—the communists didn't respect anything but force. You had to fight fire with fire; let them know who had the biggest guns and the toughest hide and heart.

Where once he had argued the injustice of Vietnam's being viewed as "his" war, Lyndon Johnson now brought to it a proprietary attitude. This should have been among the early warnings that LBJ would increasingly resist less than victory, no matter his periodic bombing halts or conciliatory statements inviting peace, because once he took a thing personally, his pride and vanity and ego knew no bounds. Always a man to put his brand on everything (he wore monogrammed shirts, boots, cuff links; flew his private LBJ flag when in residence at the LBJ Ranch; saw to it that the names of Lynda Bird Johnson and Luci Baines Johnson and Lady Bird Johnson—not Claudia, as she had been named—had the magic initials LBJ; he even named a dog Little Beagle Johnson), he now personalized and internalized the war. Troops became "my" boys; those were "my" helicopters; it was "my" pilots he prayed might return from their bombing missions as he paid nocturnal calls to the White House situation room to learn the latest news from the battlefields; Walt Rostow became "my" intellectual because he was hawkish on LBJ's war.

His machismo was mixed up in it now, his manhood. After a Cabinet meeting in 1967 several staff aides and at least one Cabinet member—Stewart Udall, Secretary of the Interior—remained behind for informal discussions. Soon LBJ was waving his arms and fulminating about his war. Who the hell was Ho Chi Minh, anyway, that he thought he could push America around? Then the President of the United States did an astonishing thing: He unzipped his trousers, dangled a given appendage, and asked his shocked associates, "Has Ho Chi Minh got anything like that?"

By mid-1966 he had cooled toward many of his experts: not

because they'd been wrong in their original optimistic calculations, no, so much as that some of them had recanted and now
rejected *his* war. This Lyndon Johnson could not forgive; they'd
cut and run on him. Nobody had deserted Roosevelt—he
gloomed—when FDR had been fighting Hitler. McGeorge
Bundy, deserting to head the Ford Foundation, was no longer
the brilliant statesman but merely "a smart kid, that's all." Bill
Moyers, quitting to become editor of *Newsday* and once almost
a surrogate son to the President, suddenly became "a little
puppy I rescued from sacking groceries"—a reference to a part-
time job Moyers held while a high school student in the long
ago. George Ball, too, was leaving? Well, George had always
been a chronic bellyacher. When Defense Secretary McNamara
doubted too openly (stories of his anguish leaked to the newspapers), he found it difficult to claim the President's time; ultimately he rudely was shuttled to the World Bank. Vice President Hubert Humphrey, privately having second thoughts, was
not welcomed back to high councils until he'd muffled his timid
dissent and shamelessly flattered LBJ. Even then, Johnson
didn't wholly accept his Vice President; Hubert, he said, wasn't
a real man, he cried as easily as a woman, he didn't have the
weight. When Lady Bird Johnson voiced doubts about the war,
her husband growled that *of course* she had doubts; it was *like*
a woman to be uncertain. *Has Ho Chi Minh got anything like
that?*

Shortly after the Tet offensive began—during which Americans would be shocked when the Vietcong temporarily captured a wing of the American Embassy in Saigon—the President, at his press conference of February 2, 1968, made such
patently false statements that even his most loyal friends and
supporters were troubled. The sudden Tet offensive had been
traumatic, convincing many Americans that our condition was
desperate, if not doomed. For years the official line ran that the

Vietcong could not hang on, would shrink by the attritions of battle and an ebbing of confidence in a hopeless cause. Stories were handed out that captured documents showed the enemy to be of low morale, underfed, ill-armed. The Vietcong could not survive superior American firepower; the kill ratio favored our side by 7 to 1, 8 to 1; more. These and other optimisms were repeated by the President, by General Westmoreland, by this ambassador and that fact-finding team. Now, however, it became apparent that the Vietcong had the capability to challenge even our main lair in Asia—and there to inflict serious damage as well as major embarrassments. It dawned on the nation that we were a long way from defanging those rice-paddy ragtags.

It was a time demanding utmost candor, and LBJ blew it. He took the ludicrous position that the Tet offensive—which would be felt for weeks or months to come—had abysmally failed. Why, we'd known about it all along—had, indeed, been in possession of Hanoi's order of battle. Incredible. To believe the President, one also had to believe that American authorities had simply failed to act on this vital intelligence, had wittingly and willingly invited disaster. The President was scoffed at and ridiculed; perhaps the thoughtful got goose bumps in realizing how far Lyndon Johnson now lived from reality. If there was a beginning of the end—of Lyndon Johnson, of hopes of anything remotely resembling victory, of a general public innocence of official razzmatazz—then Tet, and that Looney Tunes press conference, had to be it.

Even the stubborn President knew it. His presidency was shot, his party ruined and in tatters; his credibility was gone; he could speak only at military bases, where security guaranteed his safety against the possibility of mobs pursuing him through the streets as he had often dreamed. The old nightmares were real now. Street dissidents long had been chanting their cruel *"Hey Hey LBJ/How many kids did you kill today?";* Senator

Eugene McCarthy soon would capture almost half the vote in the New Hampshire primary against the unpopular President. There was nothing to do but what he'd always sworn he would not do: quit.

On March 31, 1968, at the end of a televised speech ordering the end of attacks on North Vietnam in the hope of getting the enemy to the negotiating table, Johnson startled the nation by announcing: "... I do not believe that I should devote an hour or a day of my time to any personal partisan causes or to any duties other than the awesome duties of this office—the presidency of your country. Accordingly, I shall not seek, and I will not accept, the nomination of my party for another term...."

"In the final months of his Presidency," a former White House aide, and Princeton professor, Eric Goldman, wrote, "Lyndon Johnson kept shifting in mood. At times he was bitter and petulant at his repudiation by the nation; at times philosophical, almost serene, confidently awaiting the verdict of the future." The serenity always was temporary; he grew angry with Hubert Humphrey for attempting to disengage himself from the Johnson war policy and, consequently, refused to make more than a token show of support for him. He saw Richard Nixon win on a pledge of having "a secret plan" to end the war—which, it developed, he did not have. LBJ never forgave George McGovern for opposing "his" war and let the world know it by a lukewarm endorsement of the South Dakota senator in 1972 which pointedly was announced only to LBJ's little hometown weekly newspaper.

In his final White House thrashings—and in retirement—Lyndon Johnson complained of unfinished business he had wanted to complete: Vietnam peace talks; free the crew of the *Pueblo;* begin talks with the Russians on halting the arms race; send a man to the moon. But the war, the goddamned war, had ruined all that. The people hadn't rallied around him as they had around FDR and Woodrow Wilson and other wartime

Presidents; he had been abandoned, by Congress, by Cabinet members, by old friends; no other President had tried so hard or suffered so much. He had a great capacity for self-pity and often indulged it, becoming reclusive and rarely issuing a public statement or making public appearances. Doris Kearns has said that she and others helping LBJ write his memoirs, *The Vantage Point*, would draft chapters and lay out the documentation— but even then Lyndon Johnson would say no, no, it wasn't like that; it was like *this*. And he would rattle on, waving his arms and attempting to justify himself, invoking the old absolutes, calling up memories of the Alamo, the Texas Rangers, the myths, and the legends. He never seemed to understand where or how he had gone wrong.